Anunnaki
Awakening
REVELATION

RAY DAVIS

Posidigm Press, LLC
Framingham, MA

First Edition — February 2015

This book is set in 12-point Garamond

Published by: Posidigm Press, LLC
http://www.AATrilogy.com

Printed in the United States of America

ISBN: 0692761551
ISBN-13: 978-0692761557

"What you seek you shall never find.

For when the Gods made man,

They kept immortality to themselves.

Fill your belly.

Day and night make merry.

Let Days be full of joy.

Love the child who holds your hand.

Let your wife delight in your embrace.

For these alone are the concerns of man."

The Epic of Gilgamesh

To my wife, April, for her undying support of my writing and to the those intrepid thinkers out there who understand our universe and our history is far more complex and interesting than our popular narratives about it.

Contents

(1)
Operation Original Sin

April 9, 2003 near Karbala, Iraq. 01:12 hours
Lieutenant Lucas M. Biggs, U.S. Army Special Forces, looked at his watch with agitation.

"Where are the damn GMVs?" he questioned aloud.

His six-man team was assembled and waiting for their ride. He had orders in hand and a mission to accomplish, but the GMVs were 12 minutes past due.

Operation Original Sin—what a strange name for an operation, he thought. The reason for the name eluded him. The approach of two vehicles brought him back to the moment.

"All right, mount up. Keep your COM connected. I'll share our orders once we're mobile. Stevens, Washington, you're with me. Taylor, Dragon, Williams you're in GMV 2."

The hefty vehicles moved cautiously down a dark and dusty road snaking its way towards Baghdad. The route's designation as a secured area belied the numerous perils. The retreating Iraqi Army had mined many of the roads leading to Baghdad to slow the allied advance. Roaming bands of the Republican Guard continued guerrilla operations against allied rear positions.

Once in Baghdad, the team faced a perilous drive across the city toward the target. Rumors of Saddam's imminent fall were rampant. The city remained checkered with pockets of Iraqi Army and Republican Guard resistance. Where the military presence had evaporated, street gangs, armed with abandoned military weapons, dominated and terrorized neighborhoods. Fires burned throughout the city; the result of fighting and people without power trying to stay warm. Looting was rampant.

Biggs lived for these missions. This is what he signed up for seven years ago. He told the recruiter he wanted adventure and to defend the freedom of the nation that had given him so much.

The team must have sensed the danger too, as they were strangely silent for the first 20 minutes of the ride. Each man looking into his soul, thinking about his training, and wondering what was to come. As the GMVs entered the outskirts of the capital city, Biggs knew it was time to share the mission with his team.

"Biggs to GMV 2. Do you read?"

"Loud and clear, Lieutenant."

"As you can probably tell, we're headed into the heart of Baghdad. Our target is The National Museum of Iraq. We are on an extraction mission. I was in Major Anderson's office when the orders came down. I can tell you they came directly from CENTCOM."

Biggs paused and then continued, "We are to proceed to the National Museum of Iraq. Our mission is to extract an alphabet agency operative named Cutler and any cargo he deems necessary. Cutler's status is unclear. At last report, his situation was precarious due to a large Republican Guard contingent near the museum."

"How many hostiles are we likely to encounter, Lieutenant?"

"Cutler reported 30-50 Republican Guard in the immediate area. Let's be stealthy and quick—get Cutler and his contraband and get out."

Biggs had a homing device to help the team locate Cutler once in the museum. He studied an electronic floor plan of the building's interior.

The GMVs turned off their headlights and rolled slowly up a side street adjacent to the museum. The map indicated a side entrance along this street.

"That's it," Biggs called to his driver, "Pull over right there." The vehicles squealed to a stop on the darkened street.

Teams in both vehicles donned their night vision goggles and checked the operation of their weapons and COM. They waited for what seemed like hours. Finally, Biggs gave the order to dismount. Dragon and Washington took the lead. The team climbed some stairs and entered the museum through the side door. Moving in two-man cover teams, they worked their way toward the beacon. Biggs directed the advance using hand signals.

The dimly lit museum seemed an anomaly, as power outages plagued most of Baghdad. Its massive structure was silent and strangely untouched by the ravages of the bombing and street-to-street fighting. Cutler's beacon indicated he was located in a large room two floors below the main level. The map showed a stairway half way up the main hall.

The team moved stealthily up the left side of the hall toward the location of the stairwell. These missions always had moments of uneasy anticipation. You simulated as much as you could in training, but there was no way to replicate that spring-loaded feeling you get when your life is on the line. One moment you had to be ready to exhibit calm, clear thinking and in the next unleash unspeakable violence. Biggs could feel a lump forming in his throat and his heart banging away in his ears. The breathing of his team was audible. Something didn't feel right. Suddenly, there was a loud crash and the echoed sounds of boots and shouting coming from the far end of the main hall. Biggs identified it as Iraqi Arabic. The commotion reverberated through the hall and seemed to be coming toward them.

"Geez! Go, go," Biggs called as he waved his team toward the stairwell door now visible just steps ahead. The team descended the stairs quickly and efficiently, Dragon covering their six. Down two floors and through another stairwell door, the team found themselves in a pitch-black corridor. Biggs ordered the team to switch on the flashlights attached to their M16 rifles. A series of reinforced vaults fronted by heavy steel doors lined the hallway.

Biggs studied his museum map. "There is no way out of here except back up that stairwell," he announced. "Taylor, Dragon you cover our six. We'll find Cutler." The two men set up and readied themselves to take out anyone coming through the door.

Biggs and the rest of the team worked their way down the hallway and around one corner and then another. Finally, they saw a faint light emanating from an open vault on the right. The team positioned themselves outside the half-opened door. Biggs signaled on three. He counted down with his fingers three, two, one. They pushed through the door and leveled their weapons at a line of crates near the back of the vault.

"Who's there? I'm armed," asserted a strong voice from behind the crates.

"Mr. Cutler?" Biggs questioned.

"Yes. I am Cutler. Who goes there?"

"Sir, I'm Lieutenant Lucas Biggs. We're here on orders from CENTCOM to extract you and your contraband from the museum. Sir, please step out in front of the crates and keep your hands visible."

Cutler stood slowly, holding his hands up in front of him. He was a shockingly tall stalky middle-aged man with almost over emphasized Nordic features. Even in the dim light, his eyes pierced everything he looked at. Biggs was surprised and a little unnerved by the man's size.

"Sir, do you have some ID?" asked Biggs.

"Do you, Lieutenant?" Cutler replied curtly.

Biggs stared at Cutler. Cutler stared back. "All right, Mr. Cutler," Biggs finally said, "We're here to get you and your contraband out of here. We believe there are 30-50 Republican Guard in and around the museum—"

"More like 500, Mr. Biggs," Cutler blurted. "It's going to take two of your men to carry the contraband," Cutler ordered, pointing to a large crate in front of others. "It weighs about 200 pounds and the contents are fragile. They will need to leave their weapons behind."

Biggs questioned, "What is the contraband, sir?"

"The contraband is none of your business, Lieutenant. Let's just say Saddam thought the contents of this crate could save his regime. It is far too important to the world to let him control it."

"Excuse me, sir. My men are risking their lives for that crate. There are only six of us. We may have to deal with an unknown number of hostiles. My men are not leaving their weapons—"

"Lieutenant, I'm not going to argue with you. What are your orders?" Cutler asked as he moved around to the front of the crates and used his size to his advantage.

"My orders are to extract you and your contraband, sir."

"Were there stipulations in your orders?"

"At all risk, sir."

"Then I suggest you follow your orders," Cutler commanded menacingly and took a step forward.

His size alone intimidated, but Biggs held his ground. Biggs' men leveled their weapons at Cutler and looked to their leader for an order, but a frantic message from Dragon cut the standoff short.

"Lieutenant, we have hostiles." Biggs heard the sounds of automatic weapons fire over his COM.

"Dragon, Dragon," Biggs shouted. There was a static-laden pause on Biggs' radio.

"Sir, two hostiles down," Dragon reported, "We're fine, but I'm sure they reported our position. We need to get out of here."

Biggs looked back to Cutler and made a snap decision. "Washington, help Mr. Cutler carry the crate."

"Biggs," Cutler started.

"Mr. Cutler, we have one way out of here and that window is closing. This is my best offer. Grab an end!" Biggs shouted— determined to stay in command of the situation.

"Dragon, do you read?"

"Here, Lieutenant."

"We're moving out. We have Cutler and the contraband. I want to move up one level rather than back up to the main level. There is a stairway near the main entrance. We'll take that stair-well. Radio the GMVs to meet us out front."

"Roger that, sir."

"I want you and Taylor to clear the way to the next level. We're 90 seconds behind you. Biggs out."

"Let's move, gentlemen."

Cutler glared at Biggs and then grabbed one end of the crate. They hurried back up the corridor. Biggs and Stevens led the way, followed by Cutler and Washington carrying the crate, and Williams bringing up the rear. They reached the stairwell.

"Dragon, Biggs. Are we clear to the next level?"

"Clear, sir."

The team arrived at the next doorway. Dragon and Taylor were waiting.

"Smoke the stairwell," ordered Biggs.

Dragon pulled an M-18 smoke grenade from his pack, pulled the pin, and rolled it into the stairwell. He confirmed it was work-ing and closed the door behind them. They hurried across the large gallery toward the front of the building. Out of nowhere, the team came under fire from the far side of the vacuous gallery. Only the darkness prevented them from being wiped out. Washington dropped his end of the crate and took cover with the rest of the team. Cutler dragged the crate to safety and took a bullet in the leg for his trouble. Biggs noticed Cutler's leg was not bleeding from the wound. Just then, the sound of a klaxon-like alarm began blaring through the hall.

Biggs scanned the far wall using his night vision. He could see gunfire coming from holes in the wall. The fire was heavy and continuous.

"There's a false wall," Biggs shouted. "They're firing from behind a false wall. We're about 50 feet from the stairwell. It comes out near the front door. Dragon, roll another M-18. Taylor, lay down covering fire along that wall. Give us 20 seconds and then make your way toward the stairs."

"Now, Dragon!" shouted Biggs.

Dragon rolled the smoke grenade across the floor. It popped and smoke began to fill the gallery. Taylor sprayed fire along the far wall. The rest of the team began moving along the wall toward the stairs. Cutler didn't mention his leg. He and Washington reached the stairs first with the crate. Stevens and Williams went into the stairwell ahead of them, but a hail of bullets coming from above and below turned them back.

As Dragon and Taylor retreated toward the door, more than a dozen Republican Guard raced across the gallery towards them, firing as they ran. First Dragon went down and then Taylor. More Iraqis emerged from behind the wall and began closing on the team near the doorway.

"Taylor, Dragon," Biggs screamed into his helmet microphone, but there was no response. Their escape cut off, Biggs was trying to come up with a brilliant plan.

A bullet struck Washington in the forehead and he fell forward. Bullets were now coming from the advancing Iraqis in the gallery and through the door at their back. They were about to be overrun. Biggs braced himself for the inevitable. A bullet struck his right shoulder and then the left knee. He felt himself hit the floor. The pain pulsed through his body. He could see Washington, Stevens, and Williams lying on the floor. The blur of Iraqi boots moving around him. This is not how he saw it ending when he signed up seven years ago.

He caught sight of Cutler sitting against the wall. He'd taken several more bullets, but he was awake and fiddling with a device on his wrist. Cutler pushed a button on the device and a pillar of bluish-white light engulfed him and the crate. Cutler and the contraband vanished. Then the light enveloped Biggs and he lost consciousness.

Biggs awoke strapped into his seat in the GMV. Stevens and Washington were asleep in the seats next to him. The driver was also asleep. He looked at his watch. 06:32.

"What the . . . ?"

He checked his GPS. Their location showed as 38 miles southwest of Baghdad. The night before suddenly came rushing back to him. He checked for his wounds but found not a scratch.

"How can that be?" Biggs asked aloud.

He woke the others in his vehicle and then radioed the other GMV. He instructed everyone to meet outside the vehicles. No one showed any signs of their injuries. The previous night lingered in the air like a violent, hideous hangover. Everyone remembered the events of the raid on the museum. Everyone remembered the firefight and trying to escape. Everyone remembered Cutler. Where was Cutler? How did they travel almost 40 miles to the middle of the desert without any memory of it? Who healed their wounds?

Biggs asked, "Did anyone else see the bluish beam of light?" Not one member of the team recalled the light.

Biggs felt a lump in his throat and struggled to choke back tears. "All of you were down. I was down. I was sure we were all dead. I saw Cutler activate a device on his wrist. A bluish light filled the museum. The Iraqis were frozen. I mean, they were not moving. I saw Cutler and the crate disappear. I lost consciousness and then I woke up here."

Dragon said, "Lieutenant, I've heard of shit like this happening. We can't report this. Man, they'll say we're whacked! They send you for counseling and you wind up wasting away in a psych ward at Walter Reed."

"How can we not report it, sir?" asked Washington. "How do we explain that we failed our mission?"

Biggs noticed a large cut on Washington's thumb. "Washington, where did you get that cut?"

"When we came under fire, I dropped my end of the crate and cut my hand."

"All the rest of our wounds were healed, but not your hand. I wonder why."

Biggs became aware of something round in his pocket. He reached in and pulled out a small polished stone with writing on it. It had strange writing all over it that looked like hieroglyphics.

"What's that, sir," asked Washington.

Biggs peered at the piece for a moment. "I don't know."

"Sir," Stevens said, "Three o'clock."

The team saw three military police Humvees racing across the desert towards them. Biggs stuffed the item in his boot. The vehicles pulled up alongside the GMVs. An MP Major emerged from the lead vehicle and approached the team.

"Lieutenant Lucas Biggs?" asked the major.

"Yes, sir," Biggs replied and saluted.

"You are under arrest for the theft of two GMVs and the equipment contained. You and your men will have to come with us."

"Sir, we are on a classified mission authorized by CENT-COM," Biggs protested.

"I'm sure you are, Lieutenant. Why don't you accompany us back to HQ and we'll get this all sorted out."

Biggs looked incredulously at his men and then back at the major. He was tired and baffled. His obedience kicked in. "Yes, sir."

(2)
Maria Love

Washington D.C. - May 3, 2024. 1:42 P.M.
"Mr. President, Mr. President," Maria Love arose and raised her hand in unison with the throng of other reporters near the back of the White House East Room. Maria was the Chief White House Correspondent for the America's Next Network (ANN). She anticipated President Ron Paxton's last syllable to perfection. The big network correspondents had asked their questions and now the free-for-all was on for everyone else to ask a coveted question.

ANN was an upstart alternative news network based in Austin, TX. It began in 2018 and quickly gained viewership in an era when the big networks were losing credibility with the American public. Yet, those inside the Beltway viewed ANN as an interloper. Maria had been called only once in 15 press conferences. The opportunity caught her unprepared. She'd managed only to ask President Paxton a question about what he planned to get Mrs. Paxton for Valentine's Day.

Ugh! Are you kidding me, she often thought? *I have a chance to ask the leader of the free world a question and I find out that he cannot comment on what he's getting his wife for Valentine's Day because it's a surprise. Duh!* Even now—thinking about it—brought a rush of frustration.

Maria vowed never to be that unprepared again. She had worked for the past week on devising just the right question for

President Paxton. She arrived at an ingeniously worded question asking the President to comment on the new era of cooperation between China and the United States.

Maria's attractive brown eyes made momentary contact with the President, but Paxton averted her gaze and called, "Jacques Vallette."

Le Monde? Seriously, Ron, Maria thought, forgetting protocol, at least in her mind.

"Merci, Mr. President. . . ."

Maria instinctively began jotting notes about the French reporter's question and the President's response. That's what they paid you to do, when you didn't get to ask your question. You were a glorified court reporter taking dictation of the event rather than participating. Paxton finished his response and the whole cycle began again.

"Mr. President, Mr. President" Maria rose again. This time slowed by her distracting reverie.

Paxton paused and recognized Sarah Ann Reynolds a reporter from PBS.

"Thank you, Mr. President . . ." Maria went right back into note-taking mode. She preferred writing notes to an audio recording. She always went back and watched the press conference and she preferred to capture her impressions during the answers.

Suddenly, Maria saw her favorite icon appear on her micro heads up display. It was her husband, Jack. Owning the amazing multitasker she was, Maria opened the message with a quick flinch of her eye.

Jack texted, "Hey, beautiful, have you asked your question yet?"

Moving into hyper-multitasking mode, Maria quietly spoke, "Message respond. Jack. Not yet. Still trying."

Paxton punctuated his comment. Maria arose, "Mr. Presi—"

"Max Stemple, Reuters," called out Paxton.

Jack's icon flashed again. "Hang in there, beautiful. Remember tomorrow is get-away day. Hawai'i. Our paradise. Love you."

Just then Maria heard White House Chief of Staff Joe Bieber utter the three worst words possible at a Presidential press conference when you have not asked your question, "Thank you, everyone."

Mayhem broke lose in the East Room, as everyone scrambled now to get a question out hoping, praying the president might stop and respond. A chorus of "Mr. Presidents" erupted among the press corps. The synthetic sound of ComTab cameras filled the air, along with enough flashes to make the Oscar red carpet blush. President Paxton was ushered quickly from the room by staff and Secret Service.

Maria joined the steady flow of reporters leaving the White House eager to secure a spot to file their reports. Maria quickly passed through security and out to meet her camera operator Randy Matson. He was waiting for her at the preselected location in front of the White House. A network page quickly checked Maria's hair and makeup and gave her a thumbs-up.

"Randy, be sure to get the White House in the shot over my shoulder," Maria instructed. Randy was way ahead of her. They had teamed together for four years and he knew what she wanted before she asked.

Maria's location director, Cathy Sebring, was on her ComTab back to ANN headquarters in Austin. "Yes . . . now? Got it," Cathy said. "Maria, change of plans. We're going live back to Austin in 20 seconds."

Maria quickly sorted through her notes, readying herself for the questions she expected from the studio. The team was a blur of action around her.

Cathy began calling out the time, "In four, three, two, we're live."

The light on Randy's camera came to life and Maria was speaking to Chip Benson back in the studio. Maria answered Chip's questions and did the analysis like the pro she was, but all she could think about was Jack and get away day tomorrow.

Finally, finally Chip said, "Our White House Correspondent, Maria Love. Thank you, Maria."

Cathy gave the cut sign. Randy's camera went dormant and Maria was already unhooking herself from the equipment.

"So tomorrow is get-away day?" asked Cathy.

"Finally! I need a break from D.C.," Maria answered.

"Have a great time, boss," Randy chimed. "Which island?"

"We love them all, but this year it's Oahu, the North Shore. We have a condo in Haleiwa. Ten days of boring bliss."

"You're my hero," Cathy confessed with envy. "I wish my husband liked to travel. He says golf's as good as travel."

"We call Hawai'i our paradise. It's where we can relax, be ourselves. The concerns of the world seem to melt away there," Maria confided with a bit of dreaminess in her eyes.

"Do some melting for me," Cathy smiled.

(3)
Richard Holcomb

"Another late night, Dr. Holcomb?" asked graduate assistant Tom Robinson, pushing his head through the door.

"Always when the government calls," Holcomb replied.

By all appearances, Richard Henry Holcomb was a typical college professor. He lived in a beautifully reconditioned 18th-century house in the University City area of Philadelphia— complete with a white picket fence. He had two passions in life (ancient cultures and soccer) sometimes in that order.

He met Anne—his soul mate—early in life. She sat down next to him in Biology class on the first day of 9th grade. Anne wasn't scientific and Holcomb made it his job to get her through that class. Anne was artistic and Holcomb always believed she balanced him. For many years, she ran a quilting business out of their house. She fashioned herself a modern-day Betsy Ross.

They spent 42 years side by side experiencing all life had to offer. One moment she was there and the next she was gone. He'd never recovered from the moment he heard about the accident. Her death stung him in ways he never believed possible for his detached, scientific mind. Six years had passed and that moment never left him. Work was his refuge and his salvation.

Yes, by all appearances, Richard Holcomb was typical, even boring. Appearances can be deceiving. Holcomb was the top government expert on the ancient Near East. For more than 25 years, he'd worked on top-secret government projects related to

Middle Eastern antiquities. He often lived in the limbo between the science and history that made it into the media and college textbooks, and the truths known by only a few insiders. He was not always comfortable with the "lack of transparency" or the outright deception it involved, but Richard Holcomb was an interesting mix of liberal academic and conservative patriot. He assumed the authorities, or PTBs as he called them, had their reasons for keeping secrets. Still, he always fought to make public as much information as possible on his projects. Normally, the PTBs were not into hiding information as much as conclusions. In fact, raw information often served their disinformation purposes by creating sides and debate to form around the information, further obscuring the truth.

"I wish I could help you. Your after-hours projects intrigue me," said Tom Robinson.

"You have no idea, Mr. Robinson. I'd tell you all about them, but then I'd have to kill you and you're far too promising an archaeologist to do that to the world," Holcomb joked.

"Well, I grabbed a sandwich and a drink for you from the sub shop. I'll leave them on the table out here."

"Thank you, Tom. I may need you to cover my Sumerian Seminar this week. I have a feeling I'll be here. I'm close to something. I know it!"

Robinson knew the breakthrough must be something astonishing. Holcomb loved nothing more than to capture the imagination of young undergrads with the wonders of Near Eastern culture and mythology.

"Of course, Dr. Holcomb. You know how much I enjoy teaching your blocks. Do you need anything else before I leave?"

"Nothing. Good night, Mr. Robinson. Please lock the door from the inside on the way out."

The precaution was unnecessary. Two plain-clothes agents

always secured the door outside the facility. He had no idea what alphabet agency employed them. He was only confident they would fire on their own mothers if they tried to access his top-secret lab without proper clearance. Even the president of the university didn't have access to this building.

Holcomb had taught Sumerian, Akkadian, and Hittite culture and history in the Department of Near Eastern Languages and Civilizations (NELC) at the University of Pennsylvania for more than 35 years. He'd pursued the career growth path and achieved Associate Department Chair by 37, but his first love was research. When the opportunity to do advanced field research for the Global Progenitor Trust arose, he stepped down, taught his required three hours per semester, and returned to research.

Holcomb was tall and lanky with a runner's build and an engaging smile. His fitness and youthful appearance belied his 62 years. At one time, he was *the* wunderkind in the NELC community, having developed exceptional abilities to interpret ancient texts—especially Sumerian. After the first Gulf War, he'd come to the attention of the several government agencies and foundations. His colleagues considered him the dean of Sumerian culture and linguistics experts. It intrigued him that so many in the establishment seemed to share his insatiable appetite for all things Sumerian. Holcomb didn't always know what their motives were, nor did he care. What he knew was that their money allowed him to do the work he loved and serve the interests of his country. That was enough.

That was except for The Original Sin Project. TOSP had challenged his impeccable professional reputation, his patience, his beliefs, and, at times, his sanity. It had come to dominate his professional life, indeed, his entire life.

TOSP had begun with a call in the wee hours of the morning in mid-April of 2003. The call came from a man Holcomb knew only as Cutler. Cutler had been his contact on several other government projects. Holcomb knew him as a rather stoic and cold man and not particularly remarkable except for his unusual height. On that night, he heard an urgency he'd never before heard in Cutler's voice. Cutler instructed, well commanded, Holcomb to meet him at 04:00 at the secure lab on the UPenn campus. Despite the 21 years that had passed, Holcomb remembered it like it was yesterday.

Cutler and two other men arrived with a crate filled with nearly 800 fragments of Sumerian cuneiform tablets. Earlier that day, Holcomb had watched in horror as Iraqis senselessly looted The National Museum of Iraq during the fall of Baghdad. Within hours, he had cobbled together a petition and a host of near eastern scholars, archaeologists, historians, and concerned citizens urging the Bush Administration to take all possible steps to secure what the petition called, "artifacts of the cradle of civilized humanity." In the wake of the looting, Cutler presented him with what appeared to be stolen artifacts.

"Where did you get these?" Holcomb remembered demanding of Cutler.

"Calm yourself, doctor," Cutler cautioned, "these artifacts are of critical national security importance. We need you to reconstruct them and decipher them."

"You stole them from the national museum, didn't you?" Holcomb pursued.

Cutler often used his stature and menacing stare to intimidate. He eyed Holcomb and then softened, "Iraq is an unsafe place. We brought them here to . . . to protect them from harm."

Holcomb recognized the claim as intelligence double-speak. Cutler was a master of it. He slipped on his glasses and perused the mess of broken clay artifacts. His expert eye identified many as museum or collection pieces. They were clean, but salt and

water damage indicated poor maintenance. Other pieces appeared recently unearthed and unprocessed. There were hundreds of broken pieces. The two large men accompanying Cutler
looked like they fit that description.

"I'll have to assemble a team, Mr. Cutler. We'll have to clean
and conserve the pieces before we can assemble and begin translation. What are they?" Holcomb knew better than to ask, but
his professional curiosity got the better of him. He could see
standard Sumerian characters, but there were other unrecognized characters and writing.

He was almost shocked when Cutler answered the question,
"Doctor, we don't know what they are. The people I work for
need you to tell them. They're Sumerian, we think."

Feeling bolder, Holcomb asked, "If you don't know what
they are, how do you know they're a matter of national security?"

"As our forces closed on Baghdad, we intercepted some rather strange orders apparently flowing directly from Saddam
Hussein. He repositioned a crack battalion of his Republican
Guard; I mean the best of the best, to defend an interesting target. They weren't positioned to defend him, his palaces
or any military target. They were deployed in and around The
National Museum."

"Even a man like Saddam Hussein understands the value of
humanity's relics. Like it or not, history had placed him in charge
of those relics, Mr. Cutler."

There had always been an uneasy, but unavoidable alliance
between the Iraqi dictator and scholars studying ancient Mesopotamia. On the one hand, Saddam was a huge patron of archaeology and research in the region. On the other, he had his own
agenda—to become a new Nebuchadnezzar and restore Babylonian power. Yet, Saddam's ends served the research commu

nity's ends. Many a western scholar had been accused of defending Saddam when all they were really defending was access to their work.

"Maybe, but Saddam is a survivor. He's survived two wars and numerous coup and assassination attempts. Despite the fall of his government, he's still loose right now. In the hour of his demise, he's worried about protecting a museum. Why?" Cutler questioned.

"What convinces you these tablets reveal such earth-shattering information?" Holcomb insisted, donning a pair of protective gloves and starting to finger the artifacts.

"In the final hours before his regime collapsed, intercepted messages became cryptic. Saddam seemed to believe these tablets contained information about a super weapon capable of preserving his rule. He referenced restoring Babylon to its rightful place in human history."

"Did U.S. intelligence ever consider these were the meanderings of a desperate and delusional despot? These tablets are ancient, Cutler. I've studied tablets like them since my undergrad days. How could they contain information like that?"

"We don't know. We do know this, doctor. The now-deposed President of Iraq believes they do. We learned Saddam hired one of the top ancient linguists in Iraq to decipher these—"

"Who was the linguist?" Holcomb interrupted.

"Dr. Hakim Jaffer."

"In one of the last confirmed messages from the presidential palace, Saddam ordered Jaffer to destroy the tablets and commit suicide. We could not allow that to happen. So—"

"So you stole them," Holcomb finished.

Cutler bristled slightly. "I led a team in to recover the tablets and the archaeologist. We could not allow this information to fall into unfriendly hands. Apparently, Dr. Jaffer was willing to follow Saddam's second order, but not the first. I discovered him dead in the vault that housed the tablets. They were loaded in this crate for transport."

"Hakim is dead?" Holcomb had worked with Hakim Jaffer on several digs and had high regard for him.

"Yes, doctor."

"And the looting? Were you responsible for that as well?"

"The necessities of war, doctor. We don't know who has information about these tablets. We needed to create an environment where their disappearance would not be questioned."

Now it was Holcomb's turn to hide his anger. "So you put some of the greatest treasures of human history at risk. Now you expect me to help you?"

"Your country expects you to help, Dr. Holcomb."

In the 21 years since, these tablets consumed Holcomb's career—indeed his life. He led a team of cross-disciplinary experts to decipher what eventually became 37 complete tablets and 139 partial tablets—none previously catalogued. It took nearly five years of full-time conservation work to piece the tablets together to the point where translation could begin.

Then, without warning, Cutler pulled the plug on the project. He said the orders had come from "the top" and that the "timing wasn't right."

It was 15 years before Holcomb saw or heard from Cutler again. The man just disappeared. In the five years of restoration, the tablets had fired Holcomb's imagination. He wanted to know how ancient tablets could contain information vital to the national security of the 21st century's greatest superpower.

Then a year ago, Cutler suddenly reappeared without explanation, except to say, "Now, the time is right."

When the project was a go again, Holcomb quickly assem-

bled a new team. His first order of business was to use Polyno-
mic Texture Mapping to analyze the artifacts. This cutting edge
technique involved photographing each tablet with lighting from
more than 50 angles. A computer could analyze the sharper digital images. Manipulating the light source revealed writing eroded
beyond recognition to the naked eye. This saved wear and tear
on the tablets and made it possible for the team to collaborate
remotely.

From the beginning, nothing about these tablets fit Holcomb's paradigm of Sumerian history and language or world history for that matter. They contained gaping linguistic inconsist-
encies and holes. There were descriptions of the day-to-day life
of the ancient Sumerians containing prolific references to "the
gods living among us." Holcomb loved ancient Sumerian myths,
but he believed, as did most of his colleagues, that they were
myths. He'd always relegated talk of the gods being real players
in the development of human civilization to speculative, non-
academic writers like Zecharia Sitchin. However, there were unmistakable references in these tablets to gods and humans living
together.

It soon became clear that he was not dealing with a purely
Sumerian text. About 40 percent of the tablets conformed to
known Sumerian cuneiform or proto-writing. Holcomb engaged
experts in other ancient languages to help interpret the rest.
Astoundingly, the tablets contained bits of writing drawn from
nearly 25 ancient languages including ancient Egyptian, Avestan,
Vedic Sanskrit, proto-Mayan, proto-Hellenic, and what Sino-Ti-
betan linguists believed was a previously unknown proto-Chi-
nese. These made up another 35 percent of the text. Another
mystery was the way multiple languages from various parts of the
world   seemed   mixed   and   matched   on   some   of
the tablets.

The final 25 percent of the text fit into no known language or language family. The mystery language had similarities to nearly all of the other languages on the tablets. Some of the team's comparative linguists theorized it might have come from a previously unknown mother language—a possible progenitor of all the others. That assessment was profound. A single mother language to that many ancient eastern and western languages would indicate a common source for most of the known languages on the planet today. This linguistic analysis alone would have been rewriting history and making headlines were it not for the top-secret nature of the project.

The linguistic analysis made the age of the tablets a burning issue. Holcomb ordered Carbon 14 dating of the artifacts. The results stunned the team. They indicated that the tablets were older than the 70,000-year window of accuracy for C-14. Surely, the analysis was mistaken. Holcomb sent fragments to another C-14 lab with the same result. Like a doctor desperately trying to diagnose his patient, he sent fragments for Potassium-Argon testing because P-A is able to measure far greater age than C-14. This time Holcomb received an actual number.

Based on our analysis, read the P-A report, we estimate the age of your fragments at between 375,000 and 400,000 years old.

Modern science held that Homo sapiens emerged from African savannas about 200,000-250,000 years ago and attained full human capabilities only 50,000 years ago. Certainly, they (we) were not capable of the kinds of language on these tablets for tens of thousands of years after that. The historians, archaeologists, and linguists on the team were now confronting evidence that, if confirmed, would make every one of them heretics in their fields beyond the walls of this top-secret lab. How could a single document, containing nearly 30 languages from all over the world, date to an age like that? With his team in intellectual and professional crisis, Holcomb ordered one further test to confirm the results. The thermoluminescence test confirmed the P-A test. The estimated age of these tablets was 400,000 years.

As scientists are prone to do, debate broke out about the linguistic and dating analysis. That is when Cutler appeared at a project meeting and put the fear of God into the team. He took the tablets for *safekeeping* over Holcomb's objection. No one on the team had seen the actual tablets in more than a year. They were now working from digital images of the tablets.

"Remember you're working for the U.S. Government. The age of the tablets is not the government's interest. The government wants to know what they say. That's it! This speculation isn't helping us to reach that goal. If anyone has a problem with that objective, I'll walk you out of here right now."

"Do you know, Mr. Cutler, how this information would turn our fields upside down? Not to mention genetics and biology," argued Professor Michael Gates.

"I'm not interested, professor. Our national security may be at stake because of the information on these tablets. That's my only mission."

"I could go public," Gates spouted.

"Well, professor, this is the United States of America. You're free to do whatever you like and I can make your funding and grants go away. I even have the authority to make you go away. I trust it won't come to that."

Cutler stared and Gates swallowed hard. Cutler was a man whose stature, let alone his icy gaze, was capable of projecting an absolute aura of menace. Everyone in the room could feel it. Holcomb could never quite put his finger on what it was, but there was something unusual about Cutler. In the 30 years he'd known the man, he hadn't aged a day.

Holcomb broke the uneasy silence, "Cutler, threatening us

won't achieve your ends. You can't expose a group of scientists to such paradigm-shifting information and not expect some excitement. We understand our responsibility here and we'll get it done."

"See that you do, doctor. See that you do," Cutler said, turning his glare to Holcomb.

If nothing else, Cutler's brash threats allowed Holcomb to herd his scientific cats and focus on deciphering the texts. For three years, the best minds in ancient linguistics had struggled to put together the pieces of their age-old puzzle. Known languages translated easily but contained rather mundane accounts of ancient life. The theorized mother language defied all efforts to decipher it. Then there were what Holcomb called "Repeaters." These tablets were written in known languages with simple words, but the words repeated in meaningless patterns. Their significance eluded Holcomb and his team.

Holcomb sat back in his chair, hands behind his head, peering at the massive high-definition touchscreen before him. He reviewed English translations of Tablets VIII and IX. These two Repeaters frustrated him. The words were simple, but the meaning enigmatic. Were they a prayer? Were they a child's spelling lesson?

In moments like this, doubt crept into Holcomb's mind. Was Saddam Hussein crazy for believing in the significance of these tablets? Was Cutler crazy for believing Saddam? Twenty years hence, the whole world agreed Hussein had been a delusional dictator. Holcomb wondered if he was wasting his career on a historic goose-chase.

"Damn you," he muttered at the words on the screen. He began reading again:

> Twin Snakes. Enki, day, night, Adamu, Tiamat. Enki-
> Adamu. Enki-Adamu-Lulu-Adamu. Enki-Adamu. Enki-

Adamu. Enki-Adamu. Enki-Adamu Enki-Adamu. Enki-
Adamu. Enki-Adamu. Enki-Adamu. Enki-Adamu.
Enki-Adamu. Enki-Adamu. Enki-Adamu. Enki-Adamu.
Enki-Adamu. Enki-Adamu. Enki-Adamu. Enki-Adamu.
Enki-Adamu. Enki-Adamu. Enki-Adamu Enki-Adamu.
Enki, day, night, Adamu, Tiamat. Twin Snakes.

The tablet began with two references to the Sumerian god
Enki who, according to Sumerian texts, created human beings.
First were the telltale, intertwined serpents representing Enki as
master of life and health. Secondly, the tablets mentioned Enki
before repeatedly pairing his name with a Sumerian word—
Adamu—the first man.

Tablet IX made even less sense. It simply repeated the
Sumerian word Lulu:

Twin. Snakes. Enki, Lulu, Adamu. Lulu-Lulu, Lulu-
Lulu-Lulu-Lulu, Lulu-Lulu, Lulu-Lulu. Lulu-Lulu. Lulu-
Lulu. Lulu-Lulu. Lulu-Lulu. Lulu-Lulu. Lulu-Lulu. Lulu-
Lulu. Lulu-Lulu. Lulu-Lulu. Lulu-Lulu. Lulu-Lulu. Lulu-
Lulu. Lulu-Lulu. Lulu-Lulu. Lulu-Lulu. Lulu-Lulu. Lulu-
Lulu. Lulu-Lulu. Lulu-Lulu. Enki, Adamu.

Holcomb noticed that Dr. Sanjay Singh had come online.
The team had a highly secure voice-activated instant messaging
system they used to collaborate. Singh was a young researcher
with expertise in ancient Indian languages. He was working on
translating parts of three tablets that contained high percentages
of Vedic Sanskrit. He was coming up against the same obstacle
as Holcomb - words he understood, but words that made no
sense. Holcomb had come to trust the young man's clear thinking.

"Good evening, Sanjay," Holcomb said.

"Good evening, Richard. What are you working on tonight?"
"I'm trying to make sense of Tablets VIII and IX." Holcomb shared his desktop with Singh so they could both see the tablets.

"Ah, yes, your favorites," chided Singh. "What is the relationship between Enki, Adamu, and Tiamat?"

"Enki was the Sumerian god who created human beings. Adamu was the first human in the Sumerian myths. Tiamat was the first human woman. Maybe the text relates to the creation of human beings or maybe the relationship between the god and humanity. The text is all nouns. There are no verbs to indicate action or interaction. Simply the names repeated over and over again in pairs."

"And Tablet IX?" asked Singh, "What is the significance of Lulu?"

"Lulu was the name the Sumerian gods gave to humans. It means worker or helper. I just don't understand the purpose of repeating a word over and over," said Holcomb.

Singh and Holcomb had talked many times about the tablets, but each focused on translating his own portion of the tablets and they had never really collaborated before.

"That's strange," Singh said in a moment of recognition. Tablet XLVIb has Sanskrit text that translates nearly identically."

Singh shared his desktop and pulled up the English transliteration of the Sanskrit text for Tablet XLVIb:

Twin Snakes. Vishnu, day, night, Manu, Satarupa.
Vishnu-Manu. Vishnu-Manu-Pazu-Manu. Vishnu-
Manu. Vishnu-Manu. Vishnu-Manu. Vishnu-Manu.
Vishnu-Manu. Vishnu-Manu Vishnu-Manu. Vishnu-
Manu. Vishnu-Manu. Vishnu-Manu. Vishnu-Manu.
Vishnu-Manu. Vishnu-Manu. Vishnu-Manu. Vishnu-
Manu. Vishnu-Manu. Vishnu-Manu. Vishnu-Manu.
Vishnu-Manu. Vishnu-Manu. Vishnu-Manu. Vishnu,

day, night, Manu, Satarupa. Twin Snakes.
Twin Snakes. Vishnu, Pazu, Manu. Pazu-Pazu. Pazu-
Pazu-Pazu-Pazu. Pazu-Pazu. Pazu-Pazu. Pazu-Pazu.
Pazu-Pazu. Pazu-Pazu. Pazu-Pazu. Pazu-Pazu. Pazu-
Pazu. Pazu-Pazu. Pazu-Pazu. Pazu-Pazu. Pazu-Pazu.
Pazu-Pazu. Pazu-Pazu. Pazu-Pazu. Pazu-Pazu. Pazu-
Pazu. Pazu-Pazu. Pazu-Pazu. Pazu-Pazu. Pazu-Pazu.
Vishnu, Manu.

"So, I know Vishnu is the god of creation in Hinduism. What do Manu, Satarupa, and Pazu mean?"

"Manu is the first human male—basically Adam. Satarupa was his wife. Pazu can be translated as animal, creature, or Earthling."

"They are precisely the same message in Sumerian and Sanskrit," Holcomb puzzled.

"Hmm, what if the meaning is not carried by the words?"

"What do you mean, Sanjay?"

"What if the message is contained in the pattern of the words?"

"Like a code of some sort?"

"Yes."

Holcomb stopped typing and looked with new eyes at the tablets displayed on his screen. For nearly three years, he'd been looking for the meaning in the words. Maybe Singh was on to something. Was it possible that the text could contain a 400,000-year-old code? It seemed implausible, but nothing about this project was plausible.

"What do you know about codes, Sanjay?"

"Not much, but I think it could involve the number of times the words are repeated. Maybe that total is a number of significance," replied Singh.

The men painstakingly counted the number pairs on each tablet. Tablet VIII contained 23 sequenced pairs after the introduction. Tablet IX contained 23 sequences of the word Lulu—all paired except for the second sequence. It was elongated because it contained two pairs. Tablet XLVIb contained 23 instances of Vishnu and Manu paired together. Below that were 23 pairs of the word Pazu, again with an elongated second sequence. The solution eluded them.

"Sanjay, I'm just not seeing the significance, but I think you're on to something. This can't be a coincidence."

"Richard, what do you think the significance is of twin snakes?"

"Twin snakes—like a double helix. Oh, my God!"

A rush of excitement ran through Holcomb as the scales fell from his eyes.

"And the sons of heaven found the daughters of Earth beautiful . . ."

"What are you talking about, Richard?"

"Genesis and genetics. Human beings have 23 pairs of genes. Do a search for primate genes, Sanjay. How many sets of genes do primates have?"

Singh quickly searched Google for an answer.

When the answer displayed, the blood ran from his face.

"Richard, primates have 24 sets of genes."

"We're so closely related to primates. Why do we have 23 pairs of genes and they have 24?"

Singh continued reading, "It says here that primate and human genes are almost identical except that genes two and three are fused together in humans, but separated in primates."

Holcomb looked back at the string of 23 pairs. It revealed just as he expected. In both strings of 400,000-year-old text, the second sequence seemed to combine two pairs.

"Sanjay, do you see what I see?"

"How can this be, Richard?"

"I don't know, but it looks like these ancient texts are discussing a merging of the gods with primates to make the first human being. And we have it from two separate sources within the tablets."

"But that's impossible, Richard. That would break every scientific and cultural paradigm."

"Yes. It would. It also explains why this information is so important and top secret. The question is how did Cutler know these tablets contained such earth-shattering information?"

"What now, Richard?"

"Sanjay don't mention this to the team yet. I must have a conversation with Mr. Cutler."

(4)
Dream on a Plane

Maria slipped her headphones over her ears and leaned back in the airplane seat. Breathing in and breathing out, she tried to release her frustration with the indignities of the airplane screening process.

Why do they always target reporters for special attention? She thought.

She looked over at Jack. He was the love of her life. From the moment they met, she knew he was the one. He stood out in a room of people like a shining diamond on a beach. It felt right. It felt destined. She'd always had a sixth sense about things like that. She had a way of seeing how the pieces fit together before other people. That had helped her create success in her career. Yet, success did not equate to happiness. She felt an increasing sense of yearning—a yearning to know if the gerbil wheel of her existence was really all the meaning life held.

By day, Maria was a busy network reporter immersed in the soap opera drama of the world's most important city. Lately, though, she had spent many evenings on her patio, glass of wine in hand, staring at the night sky—staring and wondering. In all that vastness, was humanity the apex? Were our wars, our famines, our need to control each other the best this Universe had to offer? Were our arguments over what we called God and who that God favored really matters of cosmic importance? Exactly what kind of a God would create such a ridiculously structured Universe?

Jack had already tuned into sitcom reruns on the plane's ITV. He caught her glance for a moment and then zoned back into the ITV show. He had been working hard and she was willing to grant him this diversion. Besides, she was tired and wanted to sleep.

Maria selected the Yanni playlist on her ComTab and settled back for the five-hour flight from LAX to Honolulu. She closed her eyes and began to flow with the music. Soon she found herself in a reflective state halfway between waking and dreaming. Is this all there is? The question kept reverberating through her mind like an echo in the mountains.

As she fell deeper into sleep, she had a vision. She stood on the precipice of a great dark abyss. White noise filled her ears. Terrifying thunder and lightning too close for comfort punctuated the gale force wind blowing her hair sideways across her face. Maria wanted to run, hide, or wake up. She definitely didn't want to go near enough to the edge and peer into the blackness.

"No! Please! Anything, but that," she shouted.

Suddenly, Maria sensed someone there with her—a fatherly figure, a comforting force. She felt a hand on her shoulder, but turning she found no one there. A voice gentle like the evening breeze, but powerful as the ocean said, "Soon, Maria, soon." She succumbed to sleep.

"Soon what?" Maria shouted to be heard above the noise.

"Soon you will know. Soon you will share what you know," the presence replied.

"What will I know?" Maria shouted as she looked up and behind her to find the source of the voice.

"Everything!"

"Everything?"

"Soon, Maria, soon."

"Soon?"

"Risk, Maria. You live in a universe where risk is the cost of reward. Let me show you," insisted the voice.

Some force took control of Maria's body. She was running as fast as she could towards the edge, screaming in terror as she ran. In a moment, she flung herself over the edge and into the blackness. She closed her eyes, waiting for the worst. Then, there was only peace and silence. She floated gently through the blackness. Feelings of love overcame her. She felt a massive pair of hands cupping her body and gently guiding her toward a bright light that was rapidly approaching. She had never felt such peace and calm in her life.

Maria met the light with a jolt and awakened to the sensation of the plane reversing engines to slow for landing in Honolulu. She had slept the flight away.

That should do wonders for the body clock, she thought.

She checked the clock on the ITV monitor: 2:33 P.M. Hawaiian Standard Time. That made it 7:33 back home. They'd been up 14 hours and now it was midafternoon. Despite the sleep, she was groggy. Ten years of coming to this paradise in the heart of the Pacific had taught her she would find a second wind.

The beautiful island of Oahu was now filling her window. The plane slowed more and went into a sharp right bank coming about nearly 180 degrees. The force pushed Maria hard against the window. For a few moments, she hung 3,000 feet above the Pacific. Below the timeless waves rushed toward the shore, confident of their destinations. If only she could be so confident.

Now the runway came into the view. The pilot righted the plane and it leveled out smoothly for final approach. The landing gear stirred beneath the cabin. Maria watched the monitor countdown the altitude 500 feet, 400 feet, 200 feet, and then touchdown. The plane made a soft impact, a few bumps, and then the engines of the Boeing 807 slammed into full reverse; slowing the plane to taxi.

A flight attendant spoke over the intercom with a pleasant voice. "On behalf of the crew, welcome to Honolulu. The local time is 2:42. The temperature is 83 degrees with light trade winds."

Jack squeezed her hand. "Welcome to our paradise, beautiful. THIS is what it's all about."

He seemed definite and confident that his statement was true. He always was so certain. Maria smiled and nodded. *Is this what it is all about,* she wondered? As if on cue, she heard the voice from her dream in her mind saying, "Soon, Maria, soon."

(5)
Voices in the Night

Heart pumping radio bumper music

"Good evening and welcome to America Overnight. I'm your host, Greg Wise. Tonight we delve into the topic of human origins with an old friend of the program, Dr. Jaypee Escudero. Jay, how are you, my friend?"

"Greg, I am doing well," replied Jaypee in Filipino-accented English.

"For those who have not heard you on the program before, tell us how you got involved with the study of human origins and UFOs. You're a doctor of neuroscience, correct?"

"That is correct, Greg. I am a professor of neuroscience at the University of the Philippines. My interest goes back to my days as an undergraduate. I was not as serious about my studies as I should have been. I made the mistake of allowing a colleague to choose the topic on a term research project. She chose to research the brain physiology of UFO abductees."

"Now, that's not your everyday college project," commented Wise in an ironic tone.

"No. It was not. I thought this girl, my colleague, was crazy. I was sure we would fail our project."

"What did you find?"

"We tested almost 200 self-reported alien abductees from throughout the Philippines. They came from every conceivable ethnic, geographic, and socio-economic group. We found a well-defined brain wave signature common to nearly 70% of these people. Close to 85% of them showed abnormally high activity in the amygdala. That's the brain's fear center."

"That's simply fascinating, Jay!"

"Yes, but that was not all, Greg. We found an exceptionally high correlation between the brain pattern and the number of abductions reported by the subject. Further, the signature was more pronounced in subjects with more recent abduction experiences."

"What happened when you presented your findings?"

"We were not allowed to present our paper in class. This was a 200-level brain physiology course. Our professor referred our paper to the Psychiatry Department Chair, who called us into a meeting with the dean and him. They told us the brain anomalies obviously caused the UFO abduction psychosis and not the reverse. They took our paper and we never saw it again."

"But you didn't give up."

"No. I knew our data and our conclusions were valid. It was impossible to talk to these abductees and see them as ill. These were productive, respected people in business and government. These were village elders and high school students. They had nothing in common except these remarkably common stories, experiences, and brain patterns."

"And you learned something interesting about yourself, didn't you?"

"Yes. I have never shared this publicly. When we ran the experiment, we tested ourselves too. I mentioned the correlation between the number of abductions and the brain pattern. We stack ranked everyone in the study and I had the third highest correlation to the ideal abductee brain pattern."

"Have you been abducted?"

"I have no memory of being abducted. I have not been conscious of ever losing time. However, the findings were valid across our study subjects. I suspect I have been abducted, perhaps often, and have no memory of it."

"That's terrifying, Jay. I'd almost rather remember it than not remember it. It makes you wonder why some people remember so much and others nothing."

"I wonder that every day."

"How did this lead to your interest in human origins? You became interested in the writings of Zecharia Sitchin, correct?"

"I did, Greg. I found Zecharia's work intriguing, but I'm a scientist. I believed brain size must be decisive, if the theory was provable. I did my Ph.D. dissertation on brain sizes from early hominids to modern humans."

"That's intriguing, Jay. And you found that modern human brains were much larger than protohumans?"

"No. That was my hypothesis. I had never studied primate or protohuman brain size. I assumed modern humans had larger brains and that would demonstrate the leap forward predicted by Sitchin. I discovered Neanderthal, generally thought to be very close to modern humans in evolutionary terms, had a significantly larger skull and brain than we do."

"Does brain size predict intelligence?"

"Until the early 2000s, most people who studied this question said no or believed that intelligence was more linked to the size of the neocortex. However, numerous studies now show a correlation in the animal kingdom between raw brain size and intelligence. It seems to be pretty consistent except when you include modern humans in the equation."

"If bigger brains lead to higher intelligence, are we not the smartest creature on the planet?"

"Although there are some who think dolphins or whales

might be smarter than humans, our predominance on the planet, our advanced use of language, and our ability to abstract seem to lean in our favor."

"How and why does the human brain buck this trend, Jay? How do we generate that extra brain power with a smaller brain than Neanderthals?"

"That's the mystery, Greg. I've spent the past 15 years working on that question. Human brains have superior engineering. We have greater intelligence in a relatively smaller brain compared to other animals and even Neanderthals."

"What could explain this anomaly?"

"In my mind, Greg, the only reasonable explanation is a trans-evolutionary intervention. Darwinian evolution simply cannot account for the suddenness or the leap in complexity exhibited by the modern human brain."

"And you believe that what Sitchin and others have found in our ancient myths—about God or the gods engineering us—is accurate?"

"I do, Greg. I'm a Catholic and I believe in God. But as I read the Old Testament and the Sumerian texts that informed the pre-Abrahamic parts of it, I'm forced to ask if the actions attributed to God are the actions one could expect of the creator of the Universe?"

"What do you mean, Jay?" Wise queried.

"There are many instances where God's lack of omniscience is on display. There is a clear pattern of God or the gods wanting human beings to remain in fear and ignorance. This element of what we call today tithing is interesting in that it points towards a kind of economic relationship between the gods and man. God demanded not just 10 percent, but also the first 10 percent. Why would the God of the Universe require compensation from his creation? Now, theologians have found clever ways to explain these things away, but as a scientist I must ask the hard questions."

"Jay, I agree with you. There are way too many pieces, when you study these things, that don't fit the established paradigm. We don't have a good explanation of who we are and how we got here."

"Again, I need the science. When I look at our DNA and compare it to other primates, there is a glaring difference. We have 23 pairs of chromosomes. All the other primates have 24. Our second and third chromosomes appear spliced together. Pure evolutionists believe this to be a genetic accident. I must question that assumption, when I consider that many geneticists are now linking Chromosome 2 to intelligence. Was it just an accident? It looks like we had some help. It looks like someone gave us a push."

"Jay, let's take some calls," said Wise. "Let's go to the Pacific Coast line and talk to Reggie. Reggie, are you there?"

"Has the doctor ever heard of a UFO case where people died and were resurrected without a scratch?"

"What do you mean died," asked Jaypee, "like you have a memory of dying?"

"No, brother, like killed in a firefight along with several other soldiers and then awakening somewhere else with their injuries healed!"

"Reggie," asked Wise, "do you know someone that experienced this?"

"Yeah, man. It happened to my unit and me in 2003 during Iraqi Freedom."

"Jay, have you ever heard anything like that?"

"Never," admitted Jaypee, "but I'd like to know more. Reggie, how did this happen? Did you see a UFO?"

"We didn't see a UFO. I was part of Special Forces team.

They sent us to a museum in Baghdad to retrieve a crate full of tablets and some intelligence dude. We got into a firefight with a Republican Guard unit. They overran us and we all died. In the morning, we woke up 40 miles from Baghdad. Everyone's injuries were healed except for a large cut on my hand. It's been more than 20 years. That cut never healed."

"It doesn't sound like any abduction scenario I've ever heard," confessed Escudero.

"Why do you think this might have involved alien abduction?" asked Wise.

"Well, my CO saw the intelligence guy and the crate disappear in a blue beam just like Star Trek. A few minutes after that, well actually about six hours after, we woke up like 40 miles away. A squad of MPs drove right to our remote location in the Iraqi desert and arrested us."

"Arrested you for what?" Wise asked.

"They said we stole the vehicles. They held us in detention for six months before they sent us stateside. They never charged us with anything. We all received a general discharge. Four of my buddies died within five years. Only the CO and me are still around. Last I heard he was in a Psych ward at Walter Reed."

"That's a fascinating story, Reggie, but I'm still not seeing the UFO connection," Wise asserted.

"Man, about ten years ago I started having nightmares about that mission. I went to see a psychologist who recommended I try regressive hypnosis. I started remembering stuff."

"What kind of stuff?"

"All of us were lying, bleeding on tables in some hospital like nothing I've ever seen. These . . . doctors . . . were working on us. They were huge. I heard one of them say leave the scar on his hand as evidence. That was on my hand and was the only mark on any of us when we woke up."

"Well, Reggie, thank you for your service. What a story!" enthused Wise. "What do you think, Jay?"

"I think I'd love to meet Reggie. That's the most incredible thing I've ever heard," said Jaypee.

"East Coast, Dan, you're up next."

"Greg, that last caller is why I love your show and why I love you. You play along with these crackpots and make listening fun."

"You don't believe Reggie, Dan?"

"Come on, Greg. I think that person smoked a little too much weed while he was in Iraq. Only God can resurrect someone from the dead," the caller charged.

"Do you have a question for Jay?"

"No, I just have a comment. Zecharia Sitchin is a proven fraud. I can't believe an academic would put stock in his writings."

"Well, Dan," countered Wise, "What about Jay's research?"

"Scientists find what they set out to find and—"

"Dan," interrupted Jaypee, "My work's credibility is everything to me. You should look at the evidence before you make such claims."

"All the evidence I need is in the Bible. It speaks of our creation and there is nothing about aliens or DNA. You can make all the assumptions—"

"Actually, Dan, if you read the Bible carefully, you find—"

"Don't feed me that crap about aliens in the Bible. You can make all the leaps in logic you want, it's just not true."

"Thanks, Dan," Wise said, disconnecting the caller.

"Let's go to New Mexico. Zane, are you there? What's on your mind tonight?"

"Hi Greg, I was a friend of Mac Brazel's."

"Well, you must be rather old," chuckled Wise.

"No. I was there when Brazel found the UFO near Roswell. I was 31 years old in 1947 and I am still 31 years old. They used an anti-aging device on me and I don't age."

[Heart pumping radio bumper music]

"That's intriguing, Zane. Call me again. I'd love to hear more about it. I've got to jump! Thank you, Jay. Be well, my friend. We will have you on again in the near future. Around the world and beyond, keep your eyes to the skies. I'm Greg Wise."

(6)
Asking the Question

Maria awoke to the sound of waves gently washing ashore and a dog barking on the beach. She rolled over and found the bed empty. She gathered herself and went into the living room of their North Shore condominium. After years of renting, Jack and Maria finally made the leap and purchased a condo in Haleiwa along a stretch of quiet beach. It gave them a place of their own to stay and provided a nice source of extra income the rest of the year to help them afford the D.C. suburbs.

Their unit was on the second floor of a condominium complex. Only a few palm trees obscured their perfect view of the ocean. Outside they were mere steps from the soft sand. Fifty weeks each year she coveted that soft sand and now here she was. She'd spend all her time here if she could. This was paradise, if there was one on this dull little planet.

In winter, Oahu's famously turbulent north shore is home to some of the world's biggest waves. Daredevil surfers from around the world converge to test their skill. Jack and Maria preferred the placid summer north shore. Low tide exposed reefs and tidal pools. That brought out the hunters—tourists searching for seashells and locals seeking an easy lunch. Beyond the shallows opened the northern Pacific—blue, vast and beautiful. Jack and Maria found refuge here. They enjoyed reading or dozing to the white noise and gentle rhythms of the surf. When they felt the urge, they snorkeled to their heart's content.

Beyond ready, Maria planned to soak up every moment. She glanced at the clock. It read 7:45. That made it, um, oh who cared what time at home. Jack lounged on the lanai watching the locals seek their treasures. He must have been up early. A Starbucks Iced Caramel Macchiato and toasted bagels lathered in cream cheese (Maria's favorites) awaited her.

"Good morning, beautiful," Jack said with a smile and a kiss on the hand. He always called her beautiful and she liked it. The idea that someone could find her beautiful amazed her. Many people called her beautiful, but Jack was the first person she believed. Maria was tall and athletic. She had all the best elements of her Irish and Mexican heritage in just the right amounts. She knew the world saw her as attractive, but her insecurities shouted, "ugly duckling."

"Sure, you have to say that because you're my husband," she smiled, eager for him to disagree.

"Oh, is that so?" Jack responded playfully.

"Yes."

"Well," he said rising, "What shall we do today?"

"I don't know. What do you feel like doing?"

"I'll tell you what," Jack said, "I'm going to go grab a shower. Let me think about it and I'll get back to you." He went inside. Jack took notoriously long showers.

"I'm going to head on down to the beach," Maria replied. "I'll see you down there."

Maria sat on the beach sipping her macchiato. She dutifully took her ComTab to the beach with her and glanced briefly at her work email. She was on the alert for anything and everything White House or involving world affairs. Ugh. She had 212 emails and she had only been gone 24 hours. She quickly scanned them.

The Vatican says a belief in aliens is compatible with being a good Catholic. "Hmm. Good to know," she commented sarcastically and under her breath. She closed the work email, reminding herself that she was on vacation. She returned to the ComTab's home page and tapped the Twitter application.

"Let's see who is tweeting this morning."

She began typing.

MariaLove_ANN:

> Good morning. Sitting on the beach in Hawai'i and playing on Twitter. I think I'm addicted.

MariaLove_ANN:

> What is the meaning of our lives here on Earth? Is this all there is?

LUVLUV:

> @MariaLove_ANN having one of those days, eh? It will get better.

MariaLove_ANN:

> @LUVLUV I'm serious. Don't you ever wonder?

LUVLUV:

> @MariaLove_ANN sure I wonder, but who has time to think about it? I have soccer games, dance lessons, and college sports every weekend.

HipHipHippie:

> @MariaLove_ANN I believe we're here to find our true purpose and attain oneness with that purpose.

MariaLove_ANN:

> @HipHipHippie Then what?

HipHipHippie:

> We lose our ego and give ourselves to the flow of the Universe.

MariaLove_ANN:

> @HipHipHippie Then what?

HipHipHippie:

@MariaLove_ANN I don't know, but I'll let you know
when I get there.

1LifeLived:

@MariaLove_ANN You're thinking too much. Soak up
those rays and enjoy!

Everydayjesus:

@MariaLove_ANN I'm here to live for Jesus 24x7.

Ancient_Nanna:

@MariaLove_ANN Do you really want to know? Are
you ready for the answer?

MariaLove_ANN:

@Ancient_Nanna That's why I'm asking. I'm ready…I
think.

Ancient_Nanna:

@MariaLove_ANN What if the answers you seek, shake
your paradigms to their core? Are you prepared?

MariaLove_ANN:

@Ancient_Nanna There must be more to life than
deadlines, bottom lines, and finish lines. My paradigms
can use a little shaking.

Ancient_Nanna:

@MariaLove_ANN But Jack doesn't believe that, does
he?

MariaLove_ANN:

@Ancient_Nanna You know Jack?

Ancient_Nanna:

@MariaLove_ANN Yes, but only because I know you.

MariaLove_ANN:

@Ancient_Nanna How do you know me? Are you a
cyber-stalker? I'm going to block you.

Ancient_Nanna:

@MariaLove_ANN I'm no stalker. Please don't block

me. I have your answers…all of them.

Ancient_Nanna:

@MariaLove_ANN Please follow me so I can send you a DM. An adventure and your answers await you.

MariaLove_ANN:

@Ancient_Nanna Yeah. I'm on vacation. Maybe I should just watch some waves.

Ancient_Nanna:

@MariaLove_ANN Do you think you'll find your answer in the waves? Or among the press corps or politicians back in D.C.?

Maria hesitated.

MariaLove_ANN:

@Ancient_Nanna No. I'm following you. I'm listening. Send me the DM.

Maria waited with a mix of anticipation and angst for the message from Nanna. *Who was she? What did she want? Did she really have the answers? "There I am sounding like a reporter,"* she thought.

A minute passed, then two. Finally, a new DM appeared in her Twitter. It was an invitation from @1LifeLived to connect on Facebook. Delete.

"C'mon, c'mon," she heard herself whispering aloud.

"What, beautiful?" asked Jack, rubbing her shoulders as he appeared stealthily behind her.

"Oh!" said a startled Maria. "Nothing honey, just checking my Twitter."

Finally, the message came from Nanna. "Meet me at the Moana Terrace Bar and Grill at the Marriott Resort on Waikiki. Two o'clock."

Maria sent a DM back. "You're in Hawai'i? How will I know you?"

"I am. I will know you," Nanna replied.

"What will we talk about?"

"You're the journalist, Maria. You have the questions. So ask your questions. I'll do my best to answer them. 2 o'clock."

"OK. See you there."

The whole thing seemed a little creepy to Maria, but the meeting spot was nice and public. As a journalist, she'd braved far more frightening meetings. She once met an informant in the Afghan countryside during the height of the Afghan Civil War. Besides, there was something strangely comforting about this woman's words. Was she even a woman? Who can tell on the Internet? She was an informant claiming to have information about Maria's questions.

"Beautiful, why don't you put the ComTab down and enjoy the sun," Jack reached playfully and tried to grab it from her.

Maria pulled away equally playfully. "I am. I am." Maria paused for a moment and then announced, "Jack, I have to go into Honolulu today."

"Honolulu? We just got here," Jack protested. "I thought we were trying to get away."

"I know, I know. I forgot that Pete wants me to go meet the new Honolulu bureau chief while I'm here."

"Pete? You're kidding, right? The President of the United States ordered me to take my wife and relax on the north shore of Oahu for two weeks." Pete Rogers was Maria's boss. He was co-founder of America's Next Network. Maria, Jack, and Pete had all attended the University of Texas together.

"Give me your ComTab. I'm going to call Pete and tell him you're on vacation," Jack said, partly kidding and partly not.

"Come on, Jack. You know Pete."

"Yes. I do know Pete and I have fraternity pictures that would sink his media empire. Give me your ComTab."

"Let me just get this over with so we can enjoy our vacation,

OK?"

"Fine, let's go get dressed I'll drive you down to Honolulu."

"Jack, it's just going to be journalist talk," Maria resisted, "You'll be bored. Besides, he might start doing an informal interview on the administration's China policy. That would probably ruin your vacation."

Jack considered it for a moment. He certainly didn't want to deal with those consequences. He also knew his wife could be incredibly stubborn.

"Just let me go. I'll be back before you know it. Soak up some sun. Do some boogie boarding. Besides, when else am I going to get to drive the Mustang this week?"

"I see. You're just trying to get away from me," Jack grabbed her arm. She pulled away with force and her chair flipped over in the sand. Jack purposely followed her down and landed on top of her. They kissed. The passion had been there between them from the beginning and had never waned.

"You know better than that, mister. Let me get this done. When I get back, we'll cook a romantic dinner, sit on the Lanai, and watch the sun sink into the Pacific. Then we'll go search for sea turtles on the beach after dark."

"You know harassing sea turtles violates several Hawaiian laws," Jack chided.

"And then . . ."

"And then what?"

"You'll see."

"OK. Get out of here. Tell Pete I'm doing this under protest, though."

Maria was excited to have an excuse to drive the Ford Mustang Solar SE convertible. The vehicle had powerful solar panels built into its body and, in a place like Hawai'i, could generate over 60% of the car's energy requirements from the sun. She spoke the hotel address into the GPS, put the top down, revved the engine, and pulled out of the condo. Soon she was headed south on the Kamehameha Highway toward Honolulu.

As she drove inland and climbed, the beautiful north shore became a distant vision in the rearview mirror. The day was warm and breezy. Maria's long, dark hair rode on the wind and the warm tropical sun comforted her weary soul. For a moment, she felt free. Free from all the *gottas* that ran her life back in D.C.

She approached the Dole Plantation and noticed workers in the field harvesting pineapples. She'd never seen a harvest in progress. Many people don't know it can take two years for pineapples to reach maturity. She was a repository of tour guide information about the islands from her many trips to Hawai'i. Jack and Maria had probably done every tour there was to do— twice. Her expectations rose that she might find a roadside pineapple stand to purchase her favorite tropical snack. No luck.

"Radio on. FM 100," she said to the Mustang's onboard computer.

The mix of Hawaiian and Reggae music put her in a tropical frame of mind. The familiar theme from the old X-Files TV show played, while an announcer shared the details of a UFO convention coming to Honolulu.

"Come and hear world-renowned UFO researcher Dr. Jaypee Escudero speak this Saturday in the Mid-Pacific Conference Center at Hilton Hawaiian Village on Waikiki. Tickets are just $30."

"Who believes in that nonsense?" Maria asked the radio, shaking her head. "That's a money scam!"

Maria was skeptical of anything spiritual or metaphysical. She was raised Catholic. The word God carried serious baggage for her. God represented father figure. The concept salted the wound left by a father she never knew.

Maria's English teacher mom fell in love with an immigrant worker. By the time Maria arrived nine months later, he was long gone. He left his name Gomez, a baby, and a mountain of medical bills for her mother to pay on a teacher's salary. Maria had no memory of him and she held God responsible.

To Maria, church symbolized the guilt her mother heaped upon herself and the cold, loveless judgment pronounced upon her. There was always someone there to tear her mother down or condemn her circumstance. They were always the target of whispers and abruptly ending conversations. They preached love but rarely practiced it. Maria swore no one would ever treat her that way.

Maria atoned for the emptiness inside by over-achieving. In high school, she was an honor roll student, an all-state cheerleader, and the lead in the school musicals. The world saw her as successful, but she always felt like she was chasing a standard just beyond her reach. When the University of Texas offered her a scholarship, she jumped at the chance to leave California and start over.

Everything changed at a freshman mixer her first week at UT. She saw Jack Love standing across the room. He was a beautiful man in every way. Her knees went weak and the heart fluttered, but Maria was no shrinking violet. She marched right up to him and asked him to dance. She interrupted him debating three other guys about the virtues of retirement plan privatization proposed by the Bush Administration.

"Excuse me," she remembered saying. "They play music at these bashes because they expect us to dance. I'm Maria."

In five minutes, she felt destiny's clock ticking and Jack had forgotten about the day's politics. They danced all night and that was that. Maria wanted to be in love. Jack provided an escape from that world of shame and guilt back in California.

Jack was Austin born and raised. He and his family seemed so stable, happy, and welcoming. Politically, they leaned a little right for her tastes, but they were wonderful people. Jack's two older sisters were both married with children.

For the Loves, every Sunday revolved around church. They were Baptist and Maria attended church with them every week for almost four years. Maria enjoyed the change in energy from the Catholic Church to the Baptist. Still, church was something she did, not something she felt. In her experience, feelings risked hurt. Maria avoided them whenever possible.

They were engaged junior year and married a month after graduation. Jack majored in political science. His uncle was a former U.S. Senator from New Jersey. Maria majored in journalism and minored in ancient near eastern cultures. She wanted to be a journalist because a journalist could change the world, or so she thought.

With Jack's connections and aspirations to be "in the game," Washington D.C. seemed like the perfect location for the young couple. Maria went to work for a D.C. television station as a political reporter. Jack quickly used his connections to land a job on Capitol Hill.

Jack's faith was rock solid. He relished church but attended only sporadically. Sunday was a workday in a Congressman's office. Maria only insisted that they attend Easter Mass. She didn't know why. She felt some strange Catholic obligation to do so. Jack was happy to comply with this simple request.

Maria arrived in Washington a wide-eyed idealist. She believed politics, not religion, could redress the world's ills. A brief time on the Washington inside, quickly dissuaded her from that conviction. She witnessed corruption and greed from Republicans who presented themselves as "of God" to please their constituents back home and hypocrisy from Democrats who positioned themselves as bastions of human ethics and compassion. Behind closed doors with lobbyist dollars flowing, few lived up to either ethos.

Maria's faith in humanity took another hit when she covered the Great Middle Eastern War for Reuters. She witnessed neighbor turn on neighbor like animals over bread scraps and water rations. She watched people do unspeakable things in the name of their God paradigms. Human beings, she concluded, have this need to be right, always, no matter the cost. Human beings fight to be right. They die to be right. Most of all human beings kill to be right.

Maria returned from the experience determined not to bring a child into this world. Jack and Maria often argued about having children. It was the only point of constant contention between them. Jack understood her feelings. He understood her reasons. He just could not accept her conclusion.

"The world has always been this way," he once said, "Humans will die out if we wait for the world to be perfect before we have children. We have to take it as it is—do the best we can."

Jack was always steady, strong, and sure. In most situations, Maria loved and respected him for it. When it came to children, those characteristics bothered her. Jack's parents wanted grandchildren. Jack wanted children. He believed God's primary reason for marriage was to create children. His sisters had children. More than that, Jack had political aspirations. He knew a happy family made all the difference in the minds of the electorate. Having no children handicapped him.

On their last trip to Austin, Maria's mother-in-law pulled her aside to have the "Your body clock is ticking" conversation.

"Maria, you're 39 years old. If you don't have children soon, Jack is going to miss being a dad. Jack would make a great dad, don't you think? I want him to have that experience. You're not so young anymore. You know this isn't all about you."

Even now, the comment hurt. She worried about failing Jack. The sense of failure pulled on old insecurities that made her feel less than. She longed to be a mother, but that was a selfish thought. What about the child? She had no right to bring it here and expose it to Wars on Terror, hypocritically polarized politics and religious zealotry.

What a species! Maria thought. *Forty thousand children a day starve to death on this planet, while billionaires live carefree lives of waste. Global banks make and break economies to profit from the collapse and the recovery. We call that an enlightened economic order?*

"God, I've become so cynical," she said aloud.

What is our purpose? What are we here to do? The questions reverberated through her as she drove down H-2 toward Honolulu. She wanted answers. She needed answers. She needed them badly enough to lie to Jack and drive 45 minutes while on a vacation to meet a stranger.

Who was this Nanna? What answers could she possibly have? She doesn't know it, but she is dealing with a world-class reporter. I'll find out what she thinks she knows, Maria thought confidently.

Maria changed lanes and exited to Waikiki.

(7)
Wild Theory

Richard Holcomb was sprawled on the couch he kept in his lab, watching an ITV football match between Italy and Brazil. He rarely found time to watch football—he hated the word soccer. His focus ebbed from distraction. Holcomb enjoyed a good puzzle. He couldn't figure Cutler's eagerness for him to meet with a geneticist and a reporter to discuss his findings. What findings? He had questions, not answers.

Cutler's response was atypical. He had always demanded absolute secrecy on their projects. Now he pushed Holcomb to explore this wild-hair interpretation of the tablets and make it public. Something didn't compute.

Knock. Knock. One of the guards entered. "Excuse me, Dr. Holcomb. There is a Dr. Sloane McKay from the Global Genome Project here to see you, sir."

"Show her in," Holcomb said, fixing his hair to greet the rare guest to his lab.

Sloane McKay entered. Her striking red hair and engaging blue eyes lit the room. Her aura exuded confidence and intelligence. Holcomb sensed a challenge.

McKay reached out assertively for Holcomb's hand. "Dr. Holcomb? It's a pleasure to meet you. It's not every day I'm asked to interpret ancient tablets."

"Thank you for coming, Dr. McKay." I see Mr. Cutler shared details about the project."

"He told me you have some exceptionally ancient tablets and you believe human chromosomes are depicted on them. It certainly is an intriguing prospect."

"Believe is a strong word, Dr. McKay. I'm . . . curious."

"Let's have a look," said McKay.

Holcomb displayed the English translations of the tablets on his monitor.

"Here you see precisely identical texts compiled from several tablets. The upper translation is from Sumerian and the lower from Sanskrit. Each sequence contains two sections. Note both sequences begin and end with the caduceus."

"How does the caduceus fit?" McKay asked. "That symbolizes the medical profession."

"Today, but its origins reach far back into history and appear in many cultures."

"It's reminiscent of the DNA double helix," McKay said.

Holcomb let the comment go. It predicted the questions he was coming to shortly.

"In each instance, the first human males from Sumerian and ancient Indian mythologies are paired 23 times with the creator god from that culture. The second section in each sequence depicts 24 pairings of earthling or ape-man—basically primate."

McKay followed with interest but remained clueless to Holcomb's point.

"Note the *second* pairing in both god-man sequences differs in both cases. It combines god-man-primate-man. A combination seems indicated."

"Hmm," McKay said nodding and still lost. "You have words pairing and repeating and a combined pair in each sequence. I'm afraid I don't see the significance."

Holcomb smiled. "Nor did we at first. Dr. McKay . . . I assume you're familiar with the genome of both humans and other primates?"

"Of course."

"Dr. McKay, what's the main difference between human chromosomes and primate chromosomes?"

"There are many subtle differences—"

"Be basic."

"At a basic level, primates have 24 pairs of chromosomes and we have 23," McKay answered with clear expertise.

"My colleague and I realized the same thing. We sought meaning in the words, but realized the number of repetitions and the pairings might be the answer. What's the difference between the two genomes?"

McKay puzzled for a moment, staring at the screen. Then she looked at Holcomb. "Because . . . the second and third chromosomes in primates are merged into a single second chromosome in humans."

"Let me summarize," offered Holcomb. "We have 22 combined pairs of god and human and one pair—the second—combining god, human and primate. Could this symbolize a rudimentary description of the human genome? We have 23 pairs of chromosomes with the second a combination of human and primate. We have 24 pairings of the word primate symbolizing the primate genome."

McKay continued. "And you have it written in two ancient languages on ancient tablets."

"What we have, Dr. McKay is a conundrum."

"How old are these tablets?"

"We've dated them to between 375,000 and 400,000 years."

"Standard theories of evolution declare those dates impossible. It predates modern humans by almost 200,000 years. Proto-humans of that era lacked speech, much less written language."

"Much less knowledge of human and primate genetics," Holcomb said. "Thus, you see our dilemma. The apparent representation of chromosomes on artifacts this age is . . . startling"

"Could there be an error in the dating?" asked McKay.

"We've used every viable dating method I know and we've consistently landed on similar dates. The language aspect of this is incredible to those in my field. These tablets were discovered in Iraq, but include languages and proto-languages from all over the world."

"Why do you believe the word for God is paired with the word for man, Dr. Holcomb?"

"It's a puzzle, Sloane, and please call me Richard. The implication is profound. If these tablets do indeed reference chromosomes, then someone was writing about a genetic combination between the gods and human beings in the remote past. They even seem to reference your merged Chromosome 2. What is the significance of that chromosome?"

"Richard," McKay formulated her reply, "Chromosome 2 is one of the largest chromosomes. It produces many proteins used throughout the body. However, it is believed to have a significant impact on intelligence, perhaps even brain size."

"So, the combined human Chromosome 2 could differentiate our brain size from primates?" asked Holcomb, seeking confirmation.

"Well, it's difficult to make broad statements about the overall influence of any one chromosome," McKay explained. "Remember that DNA is only one piece of the genetic puzzle."

"OK," said Holcomb turning the learner.

McKay grew animated now. "Think about humans and chimpanzees, Richard. Our DNA sequence is about 95 percent the same and 99 percent of the coding DNA—the DNA that really matters—is identical. Yet, we look nothing alike and there are vast intelligence and behavior differences."

"Right," Holcomb agreed.

"Many in my field are so locked up in the creation vs. evolution debate. They can't give ground, even to common sense. Obviously, there's far more at work here than simply raw genetics. The expression of the genetics matters most. I have some wild theories, though."

"Really, I'd love to hear them," said Holcomb.

"I'm not always in step with my colleagues in the genetics community. I believe that's why Cutler put you in contact with me."

"A rebel . . . I like it," laughed Holcomb.

"It's well-accepted that DNA is life's blueprint, but RNA is the instruction manual informing genes how to express in cells. About 15 years ago, we discovered miR-941 on Chromosome 20. It was the first of several micro RNAs discovered in the human genome that are not present, or at least not expressed, in the primate genome."

Holcomb leaned in to listen closely. He always enjoyed hearing another scientist sharing the goods on his or her field.

"All the unique micro RNAs we have discovered in the human genome are heavily expressed in the brain, especially in the neocortex. When you look at just the DNA, humans and other primates appear almost identical. I theorize we are going to discover many more of these microRNAs because they are turned on, account for our difference in intelligence and behavior."

"So, you don't see any significance, beyond the curiosity, to this ancient DNA representation?" Holcomb inquired.

"On the contrary, Richard," Sloane replied sincerely and with awe. "Most of my colleagues are staunch evolutionists. They believe Chromosome 2 along with these microRNAs are accidental evolutionary adaptations . . . that our separation from the apes was just an evolutionary roll of the dice."

"So, you side with the intelligent design crowd?" asked Holcomb.

"No, Richard. I don't buy into the either/or argument. I believe there must have been some kind of intervention."

"What kind of intervention are you speaking of? Extraterrestrials?" Holcomb asked with transparent sarcasm.

"Are you making fun, Dr. Holcomb?"

"Not at all, Dr. McKay, but we suffered charlatans in my field for years proffering these ancient alien theories. I haven't seen one shred of evidence the ancient gods were anything more than our ancestors' imaginative way of coping with their environment."

"Maybe these tablets are your *shred*, Richard," asserted McKay.

Holcomb shook his head.

"Do you have a better explanation?" asked McKay.

"Not yet," Holcomb responded, "but there is an alternative explanation and I will find it."

McKay was not someone who let opposition deter her. Her blue eyes sparkled and a smile flashed across her face. "At least let me give you my reasons, before you dismiss my ideas."

"Go right ahead." Holcomb prodded. "I did bring you here to listen to your ideas. How rude of me not to let you express them."

"The difference between our genome and that of the other primates is *too* selective. It's too focused on the brain—on language and reasoning centers. The odds that evolutionary forces are responsible for such specific and target advancements are inconceivable. Then there are core duplicons."

"Core duplicons?"

"Yes. These are the genes, targeted on brain development,

that seem to have pushed the human brain well beyond other primates. Humans have many of these genes. Primates have one set. Other mammals have none. This factor truly separates us from the animal kingdom."

"But evolution theorists possess voluminous evidence showing we evolved from earlier hominids."

"Intervention Theory doesn't discount evolution. It simply indicates someone accelerated the process for human beings. The kicker is these core duplicons appeared in our genome in a sudden burst. We don't know how they got there, how they spread, or why they ceased multiplying. It's almost like someone lit a fire in our DNA and then put it out."

Holcomb fell into that staunch evolutionist mold. He was a seasoned debater, but not expert enough to banter with McKay on the specifics.

"I'm sure that most of your more conventional colleagues have found ways to marry these facts with evolution, why haven't you?"

"These changes created a break in the genetic chain between humans and every other animal on this planet. The microRNAs, the core duplicons, and other changes in our genome are just too rapid and too targeted on intelligence to be an accident. I believe our DNA and the genes that inform it were tampered with for a specific purpose—to make us more intelligent and fast."

"That's a rather fantastic theory, but I—"

"You really don't understand what your own tablets are telling you, do you?" McKay asked with surprise.

"Where you see extraterrestrial intervention, I see mythological gods in cultures I've studied all my life. Every one of them fires my imagination, but they're only myths. That's what the scientific evidence supports. That's what every expert in my field will tell you."

"What if they're not myths, Richard? Why did you bring me here? You had a theory and you wanted to see if an expert in genetics would buy it, right?"

"Well . . ."

"Not only do I buy it, but I believe it provides concrete evidence for my contention that someone intervened in our genetics to create us. Have you heard of junk DNA?"

"I've heard the term."

"I believe my colleagues have it all wrong when they talk about junk DNA as a *desert* or as having some support role to protein-producing genes. I believe those vast stretches of DNA represent untapped potential."

"Potential?"

"We're literally children wearing the DNA of adults. We're not equipped to use all of it. It's similar to the idea that we use only ten percent of our brains. I'm telling you. Unlock that excess DNA, Richard, and human potential expands off the charts!"

"That's a fascinating hypothesis, Sloane," admitted Holcomb. "I just can't see how you make the leap from minor evolutionary differences to aliens engineered us. What about Occam's Razor?"

"Yes, Richard! You have 400,000-year-old tablets that appear to depict the mixing of god and human DNA, but every bit of common sense and scientific training in you tells you that doesn't fit any conceivable theory. Occam's Razor, indeed!"

Holcomb felt like every aging scientist who helped create the status quo in his field and now confronted evidence with the potential to shatter it. McKay was right. Every fiber in his being wanted to argue and deny what was right there in front of him. He knew science needed to follow the truth, wherever it led. He just wasn't ready to be led there.

"Richard, would you allow me access to the tablets? I'd like to analyze them further."

"I haven't seen them in years, Sloane. Cutler has them and I don't think he's giving them back. I do have hi-definition photos of them."

"Great! I'm going to study these in more detail and I'll get back to you. I suspect there's more here that we're missing," McKay enthused.

"Thank you for coming," said Holcomb. "Please understand. Your ideas are interesting. I'm not ready to accept such a conclusion just yet. I look forward to your analysis."

"Intervention, Richard! I know how it sounds, but I'm telling you the evidence points directly towards intervention."

(8)
First Meeting

Finding a parking spot on Waikiki is next to impossible in the middle of the day—any day. At least Nanna had picked a hotel with its own parking. Maria pulled into the parking garage and left the Mustang with the valet. She caught the elevator and pressed three. The door opened to reveal one of Waikiki's most beautiful casual dining experiences. The Moana Terrace Bar and Grill looked across the street to Waikiki Beach. A row of swaying palm trees danced to the rhythm of the gentle trade winds. Umbrellas shielded diners from the bright sunshine.

Jack and Maria had eaten here often. The lunch hour had passed. A few older couples and a young couple in love sat at the tables across the terrace. Several children splashed around in the pool. Maria didn't see anyone who fit Nanna's description. What description? Maria realized she knew nothing about Nanna—not even what she looked like. She asked the Maître D for a table near the rail overlooking the street. She ordered an iced tea and waited.

Her ComTab blared. "Listen, Do You Want to Know a Secret? Do you promise not to—"

It was Jack and Maria's song. She had forgotten to set the ComTab to stun. She fumbled to answer.

"Hello," Maria said in a hushed and embarrassed tone.

"Hey. Where are you?"

"I'm sitting at your favorite restaurant on Waikiki waiting for the bureau chief."

Maria felt a pair of hands on her shoulders and a butterscotch voice saying, "Hello, Maria." A strange, but reassuring, feeling came over Maria. She'd felt it a couple times before, but she couldn't remember when.

Maria stood and turned, and cricked her neck to see the face of the person standing before her. "Honey, I have to go. He just arrived. Yes. I'll see you when I get back. Love you . . . Nanna?"

"Yes, Maria, I am Nanna."

The woman was tall—Maria estimated at least seven feet. She wore unusually large sunglasses that obscured her eyes. Her outfit was also unusual, especially for Hawai'i. It appeared lightweight, but not sheer. It glittered in the sunlight and culminated with a large hood that loosely covered her head. Maria could make out long blonde hair pulled back and tucked into the back of the hood.

There was something intimidating about the woman—other than her height. Her mannerisms and voice were soft and nonthreatening. Yet, Maria felt a powerful sense of menace sweep through her body.

"It's a pleasure to meet you, I'm Maria . . ."

"Love. I know."

"Shall we sit?" Nanna suggested.

"Certainly," Maria replied, working to conceal the fear coursing through her.

Nanna sat, framed by palm trees behind her and the broad blue Pacific beyond. Maria studied the woman sitting across from her. Her features screamed Nordic. Even by that standard, Nanna's skin was pale. Oddly, Maria noted she could only remember Nanna's face when looking directly at it.

"I hope you will forgive the sunglasses. Bright light harms my eyes," Nanna said apologetically.

"Of course," managed Maria, uncharacteristically tongue-tied.

Nanna began, "What is the meaning of our life here on Earth? Is this all there is? Those are big questions, Maria Love. Do you really want to know?"

"I see all business," Maria said. "They're big questions. I drove 45 minutes risking stranger danger to get some answers. That speaks well for my desire to know."

"Understand. I do have answers to your questions, but I must gauge your seriousness in asking them. Why do you want to know?"

"Why do I want to know? Doesn't everyone?"

"Yes, Maria. Everyone claims to want answers to such questions. Few people have the stomach for the answers. Even fewer people are willing to question what they must question."

"And what must I question to know these answers?"

"Everything!"

"That sounds challenging and threatening—like a journey rather than a simple response. Must it be so complicated?"

"Of course it's a journey. Thus has it always been, Maria. It's threatening only to false paradigms proliferating in the world today and those who perpetuate them."

"What false paradigms are those?"

"They are the very false paradigms prompting your questions."

"Do I know what those are?"

"They live within you—just below the surface. You long to articulate them, but they're just out of reach."

"Can you give me a hint?"

"You've had many hints. Don't look to me to fill in the blanks for you. Humans are far too willing to seek easy answers to complex questions. You allow authority figures and experts to spoon-feed you those answers. You have granted them the power to think for you I've come prepared to help *you* fill in those blanks."

"Let's begin there. Who are you and where are you from? Why did you contact me?"

"I am Nanna. I am here now. You contacted me."

"I contacted you? Do you mean the tweet? I was just—"

"Maria, see beyond the obvious. Technology astonishes, but it is far from the only way to communicate in our universe. Your heart called me long ago and your thoughts too."

"Sounds a little *New Agey* to me."

"Of course it does. Why wouldn't it? You've been conditioned to believe the world is only what your five senses tell you."

"I shouldn't trust my senses?"

"You shouldn't *only* trust your senses."

"You're confusing me. Why shouldn't I *only* trust my senses? What else can I rely on?"

"Why do Jack and you come to Hawai'i every year?"

"We like it here. It's relaxing."

"Is that all? Where does the impulse originate? Do you receive a letter, a phone call, a tweet inviting you back every year?"

"No."

"When you're home and you think about Hawai'i, what's happening? Why do you want to come back?"

"We have a good time here."

"Go deeper, Maria. Why?"

"Hawai'i calls to me—I long to be here. It's an inexplicable attraction. The idea, the impulse, to return comes from deep within me."

"Exactly. Everything in this world is thus connected. Hawai'i calls you without technology. You have called me without technology. Your senses persuade you it's not possible and yet it is."

The logic of Nanna's statement threw Maria off balance. The explanation countered all her training as a journalist. The world was a place of facts—facts backed by evidence or better yet proof. Where was the proof for what Nanna was saying? Those feelings—Maria did feel them within her. She heard that calling all year, as she longed to be back in the islands. Yet, it was completely subjective. Where was the objective proof? Would she accept an answer like that during an interview with a politician?

"But there's no evidence or proof for what you're saying."

"What about those feelings within you? Are they not real? Here we sit in Hawai'i because Hawai'i calls you. Here we sit talking because you have called me."

"It's circumstantial. It's subjective," Maria protested.

"Yes. Isn't it?" Nanna beamed.

"It's impractical. How does the President of the United States or a CEO work according to that principle? They have to make fact-based decisions. Their decisions affect peoples' lives."

Nanna felt satisfied by Maria's spunk and tenacity. That can be a good thing when balanced. "Agreed, but leaders don't need facts. They need *all* the facts. I'm not denying the validity of your senses or encouraging you to deny them. I'm saying they're incomplete, limiting, and only part of the equation. Consider realities that transcend your senses."

"Do you mean, God?"

"God? Now, there is an interesting concept. Who is God to you, Maria?"

Nanna had touched a very raw nerve for Maria. "I don't know."

"When next we meet, we can discuss that further. Think about it. Who is God to you? Are you familiar with the mythologist Joseph Campbell?"

"I've heard of him." Maria was happy the discussion about God transitioned quickly. She wasn't ready to go there and certainly not with Nanna.

"Campbell wrote about what he called 'The Hero's Journey.' He posited that those we call heroes transcend the group consciousness enforced by the tribe. The hero must push through society's scarecrows and into the invisible, where waited the reward for both hero and tribe."

"What a romantic notion," Maria remarked.

"To reach transcendence, the hero sheds preconceptions and experiences the true essence of existence. Most won't risk the journey and so the tribe relies on the hero, while despising her for challenging their cherished consensus. Maria, are you a hero?"

Now Maria's emotions burst the veneer of professional skepticism and confidence. Was she a hero? She'd never thought in those terms.

"I'm a woman who's tired and stressed. I'm a human being looking for answers. The world I see, the world I've experienced makes no sense. Does that make me a hero?"

"You are a hero, Maria. Trust me. Tell me why existence makes no sense to you?" Nanna pushed.

"We come here and we die. In between, we suffer and we struggle. Where's the meaning in it?"

"What meaning do you seek, Maria? Must it make sense?"

"Yes. I mean, it would be nice if there was some purpose behind it."

"I'm sure your philosophies and sciences offer answers. Do they not?"

"Science claims we're an accidental collection of molecules appearing for a time and then dissipating without consequence or meaning. It asserts we live in a universe that's as accidental as we are. We're a species riding a wave of random mutation to who knows where—maybe the next accident."

"So, don't believe what science asserts. Other possibilities exist."

"Then there's religion. Many religious people believe this life is meaningless preparation to a promised life to come. All our human experiences are without significance in some divine plan."

I watch both of these thought systems at work in our world and I'm forced to ask why? How can it all be an accident? How can an all-powerful God put inferior beings through a gauntlet of suffering unfit for an enemy?"

I *am not* an accident and my life, this life, is not a meaningless preamble! How can I choose between these two worldviews? Why must I? Is there nothing more?"

Maria felt momentarily exposed by her rant, but strangely freed by its emotional release.

She continued, "They say a career and making big money fulfills you. They say becoming famous fulfills you. They say having children fulfills you. They say, they say, they say!"

Maria felt the flush of emotion permeating her face and tears begin to flow. *What the hell*, she thought. *Here I am talking to a complete stranger. I'm ranting and now I'm crying.* There was something motherly and accepting about Nanna that seemed to evoke feelings and emotions from deep within her.

Nanna looked intently at Maria for a moment. "Gilgamesh, Gilgamesh. What you seek you will not find. The gods have secured immortality only for themselves. Satisfy your belly. Cherish the child who holds your hand and make your wife happy with your embrace. This is the fate of man?" She ended the statement with the inflection of a question.

Maria minored in near eastern cultures at UT. She remembered the famous quote imploring Gilgamesh to give up his quest for immortality and accept his fate.

Maria wiped her face. "Gilgamesh? Nanna, are you suggesting I abandon my questions, fall in line, and accept the world the way it is?"

"Maria, I'm suggesting that to ask the questions you're asking is dangerous. To answer them, is even more dangerous. I must know, beyond doubt, you are committed to seeing the answers through to wherever they lead."

"I suppose."

"No supposing! Are you a hero or are you ready to slide back into the comforting despair of popular culture and forget this conversation?"

"I want answers. Not more challenges!"

"Why did you study journalism and near eastern ancient cultures in school?" Nanna demanded.

Maria was uncomfortable with how much Nanna seemed to know about her. "Who are you?"

"Why did you choose those areas of study? Do you know?"

"I don't know. I wanted to be a journalist to change the world. To make a difference."

"Why near eastern ancient cultures?"

"I don't know it sounded interesting. What does this have to do with my questions?"

"Nothing is an accident, Maria. Nothing. You have been attracting this path for years. You simply did not know it."

"I'm not sure I believe that."

"That's your comfort zone, Maria. You don't want to believe in anything. You don't want to believe in science. You don't want to believe in God. You don't want to believe in humanity."

"That's not fair! You don't know me."

"You want to sit in your comfort zone and demand answers. A comfort zone is a safe and blissful place, but nothing ever grows there. You cannot grow there."

"Who are you?" Maria shouted at a volume that attracted the momentary attention of the other diners.

"Who I am is not important until you know who you are."

"You're speaking in riddles. I'm serious . . ."

"So am I," Nanna said with a tinge of anger before regaining her composure.

"Maria, finding the answers to your questions will help you and many other people. I must be sure that you're ready for this journey—that you're the right one for this task. The perils of exposing the truth are many."

"Fine. Great. I'll play the game. Where do I begin?"

"This is not a game," Nanna warned.

"All right, Nanna, I want to know. I want to understand. I want to be a hero. Where do I begin?"

"The beginning."

"The beginning? That's a very guru-like thing to say," Maria snarked.

"Your questions involve who you are and why your life has taken this shape. You must start with your mother."

"What does my mother have to do with this?"

"Your mother has everything to do with it. Something happened during your mother's pregnancy. The experience traumatized her."

"What? Was she sick? Was I sick? I've never heard anything about a problem with the pregnancy."

"She shared it with no one, not even you. She remains in denial. She believes it was a dream."

"She believes what was a dream? How do you know about

this? Were you a nurse at the hospital or something? What do you want from me?"

"Maria, you must trust me. I want nothing from you and everything for you. This is your journey, but I offer to walk it with you. My stake in the outcome matches yours."

"Why don't you just tell me?"

"I could tell you what happened with your mother. That would be the easy way. Remember, this process is not about me solving puzzles for you. If I provided the information, you wouldn't believe me. Ask your mother what happened. Ask her for the truth about your father."

"What about my father?

"Trust, Maria, trust. What is uncovered through a conversation with your mother benefits her and you. It also helps me build the trust we need to help each other on the remainder of this journey."

"That's it? You drag me all the way to Honolulu to discuss the meaning of life and your answer is talk to my mother?"

"That is all for now. Talk to your mother and trust, Maria."

Maria wanted to debate more; to demand more answers from this stranger, but she felt overcome by an unexpected calm.

"Alright, I'll talk to my mother. I came here with questions and I'm leaving with more questions," Maria said ironically.

"Enjoy your vacation, Maria. Jack and you need this time to rejuvenate for what is ahead. When you return to the mainland, contact your mother, and choose to unlock this door."

"You are so beautiful," Nanna said as she rose to leave. "You are so much more than you know. All of you are."

"When will I see you again?"

"You will know when it is time for us to meet again. When you are ready, I will be there."

"I'll be calling?" Maria managed a smile.

"Count on it, Maria."

Nanna brushed her hand against Maria's cheek, as she passed. Maria's eyes involuntarily shuddered, as a profound feeling of love enveloped her. Maria turned to say goodbye, but Nanna was gone. Confused, Maria scanned the terrace, but Nanna had vanished. She turned to face the beach. She watched the palm trees sway. She looked to the sky and experienced the puffy whites floating overhead. The buzz of Waikiki and the sound of the waves across the street seemed more vibrant than before. For the second time in Maria's life, someone had called her beautiful and she believed it.

(9)
Maria's Mom

Maria took Nanna's advice and enjoyed the rest of her vacation. It had not been easy. She was distracted and disturbed by her conversation with Nanna. Jack was always perceptive and had noticed her strange mood.

"You OK, beautiful?" he'd asked a thousand times.

Jack's hovering annoyed Maria sometimes, but she appreciated the thousands of ways he showed his love and concern. No one else had cared for her that way. Well, that wasn't true. Others had tried, but Jack was the first Maria allowed that close.

Jack was a beautiful man—blonde, tall, and athletic. If he wasn't a rising star in the Republican Party, you might easily mistake him for an NFL Quarterback. Maria felt lucky to have him. Their politics often seemed mismatched and religion, well, Maria went along silently with him on that subject. Jack was a practical guy who didn't go for woo-woo or conspiracy theories. Still, he maintained a strong faith in God that Maria just couldn't grasp. It seemed inconsistent to her. In her mind, God represented the ultimate woo-woo. Their love for each other easily overcame their differences.

They kept no secrets. Maria ached for hiding the Nanna conversation from Jack. It felt dishonest, unnatural, but necessary.

"I'm fine," she'd replied every time.

Maria wasn't fine and she wasn't going to be fine until she talked to her mother. She picked up the phone to call her mother several times in Hawai'i. Only the gravity of Nanna's words stopped her. Her journalistic instincts told her she must uncover this mystery face-to-face.

Maria told Jack she needed to spend a few days with her mother. The plan was for him to catch his connecting flight at LAX and she would rent a car and drive down to San Diego. They embraced for a passionate goodbye kiss.

"Thank you for paradise. I love you," Maria said.

"I love you too, beautiful. Say hello to your mother for me."

Jack aimed toward his gate and Maria headed for the rental car desk. By synchronicity, President Paxton was coming to San Diego for a town hall meeting in three days. Maria convinced Pete Rogers that it made sense for her to meet the president in SoCal. She loaded her car - a red Ford Mustang Solar SE convertible. The drive in Hawai'i hooked her. In minutes, she was cruising down the Pacific Coast Highway, her long hair flying in the wind.

Maria and her mother had issues. It wasn't because they didn't love each other. They did. For the first 18 years of Maria's life, they only had each other. Then Maria left for college in Texas, married Jack, and wound up in Washington D.C. Irene Gomez felt her daughter abandoned her for a "big life as a star." She rarely missed a chance to lace Maria with that guilt in emails and conversations.

Running? Maria was not running from her mother, but from a sense of not belonging, of wanting something more. Maria chuckled as she recognized the pattern between her behavior more than 20 years earlier and her current quest. I always want something more, she thought. I can never be happy with what is.

Her mother had moved several times since Maria left home and she had never been to this house. The rental car's GPS guided Maria to her mother's house without a glitch. She pulled into the drive, turned off the engine, and sighed deeply. The porch light popped on and Irene Gomez, spry for her age, was in the driveway to meet her daughter before she made it halfway to the door.

"It's wonderful to see you, Maria," said Irene, as the two women paused and embraced.

"Hey, mom. It's good to—"

"I watched the president's last news conference. I thought I might see you asking a question. Were you there?"

"I was there. I was just—"

"I couldn't believe they let that French reporter ask a question rather than you."

"Yeah, well . . ."

"Well, don't just stand there. Come in, dear. You must be hungry. I made shrimp tempura."

"Sounds wonderful."

There I got to finish a sentence, Maria thought. It was two words, but a victory. She'd forgotten how much her mother's propensity for cutting her off mid-sentence annoyed her. Irene Gomez was one of those people who felt more comfortable talking than conversing. Yet, she never really seemed completely present during a conversation. She was always swinging from one topic to another like a monkey swinging through the trees. Somehow, Maria had to find a way to make her mother focus for the conversation they needed to have.

Maria entered the house and found the table set and candles burning, creating an intimate setting for their reunion meal. They made small talk for a few minutes. Maria, never one to shy from a confrontation, decided it was time to broach the subject.

"Mom, was there anything . . . unusual about my birth," asked Maria, trying to appear unassuming.

"You know there was, Maria."

"What?"

"You gave me a false alarm three nights in a row before you finally came."

"That's not what I meant, mom. Was there anything unusual during the pregnancy? Did you have any unusual experiences?"

Irene looked puzzled, but unusually focused as she eyed her daughter across the table. "Well, there was that dream," she said playing with the food on her plate. "I've told you about that dream before, haven't I?"

"No, you've never told me about the dream. What was the dream about?" Maria's interest perked up.

"Maria, it's been a long time ago. I don't like to think about those days. My guru tells me I need to let go and move on." Irene closed her eyes and breathed in and out deeply.

"Mom, this is important."

"Maria, why are you asking me about a dream from 40 years ago?"

"Who was my father?"

"Oh, so that's what this is about. You know who your father was."

"What happened to him?"

"Maria, we've covered this ground before. His name was Gomez and he left us."

"Were you married?"

"Of course, we were. Why do you think my last name is still Gomez?"

"If he left us, why have you kept his name all these years?"

"Maria, you're stressing me out." Irene closed her eyes again, breathed in, and breathed out.

"Tell me about the dream, mom. What was it about?"

"Why is this important now? We've moved on. You have your big fancy job in Washington and I'm just trying to live a quiet life."

"I have a right to know," shouted Maria, rising and leaning across the table. In all their years of arguments, she had never challenged her mother so directly. Her desperation to know the truth surprised even her.

"All right, Maria. I had a dream. . . . Crazy dream . . . ! They came for me."

"Came for you? Who did?"

"I don't know. It's confusing. Before I was pregnant, they took me to a laboratory or an examination room. I'm confused."

"Where was the laboratory?"

"I don't know. I woke up there. The people seemed tall as trees. They were examining me—all over. They were experimenting on me!"

"Mom," Maria asked grasping Irene's wrists, "What kind of experiment?"

"I'm not sure. They were... That can't be, Maria. I don't want to think about this." Irene began to shake visibly. Her voice was cracking and tears were welling in her eyes.

"Mom, I know it's hard. Tell me about the experiment."

"They're prodding me. No! Not there!" Irene shouted, tears streaming.

Maria's concern grew. "Mom! What are they doing?"

"I don't know," Irene cried. "I want them to stop. I want them to stop so badly. It hurts. It hurts." Irene looked past Maria, as though she was back in the experience. She was sobbing uncontrollably now.

"I'm afraid, Maria. I'm afraid!"

"Afraid of what?"

"I'm afraid they'll come back!"

"Who?"

"The doctors."

"The doctors in your dream?"

"It wasn't a dream! I made that story up. I'd forgotten I made it up. I convinced myself it was a dream."

"Are you saying this really happened to you?"

"I don't know. I mean, maybe."

"Mom, I know it's hard. Please focus. What kind of experiment are they doing?"

"They're taking one of my eggs. You have no right! No one has the right to do this to me. It's against God and nature. Oh! Oh!"

"Mom, what's happening?"

"There's a woman there. Her eyes are calming me. She's telling me I'm to be a mother. Necessary. She keeps telling me this is necessary. Her name. She's telling me her name."

"She's telling you her name?"

"Yes. It's Anna. No, Nanna."

Maria felt the blood drain from her face when she heard the name. She went cold and silent for a moment. "Are you sure it was Nanna?"

"Yes. I'm sure. They took my egg and they . . . they altered it."

"Altered it?"

"Genetically—they altered it genetically and then they put it back into me." Irene slid from the chair and onto her knees sobbing. "It hurts so badly. They're telling me it's necessary. Her eyes. They're putting me to sleep. I'm not dreaming! I'm not dreaming!"

Irene took a deep breath. She seemed totally immersed now.

"What's happening?" asked Maria.

"I'm back in your grandmother's house. She's there. She's sitting on the couch. It's the middle of the night. Why is she up? Why are all the lights on? It's the middle of the freaking night! We shouldn't be up!"

Irene's trembling became more intense.

"I'm yelling at her, but she's not responding. She's sitting there with her eyes open looking straight ahead. She's in a trance. Please, wake up!"

"What happened next?"

"I wake up in bed. It's morning. The sun is shining through the window. I hear birds outside singing. We're all in our own beds. We both have terrible headaches. We both took the day off from work."

"Did grandma remember anything?"

"I asked her if she was up at all during the night. She said she fell into a deep sleep and she didn't think she moved all night."

Irene was sobbing uncontrollably. Maria moved around the table, bent down, and cradled her mother. She sensed her absolute terror.

"It's all right, mom. Whatever it was, it happened a long time ago."

Irene paused and looked up at Maria. "Maria, you didn't have a father. Two weeks after the dream, I was pregnant."

"You weren't seeing anyone?"

"No. No one. I was a good Catholic girl. I didn't do that."

Irene was gaining back her composure and the two moved over to the couch in the living room.

"So, what did you do? Who did you tell?"

"I couldn't tell your grandmother. She would have never believed me. I went to see the parish priest, Father Garrity. I told him about what happened. He told me there was only one immaculate birth in the history of the world and my pregnancy wasn't it. He thought I was lying to protect the boy. He thought I should seek counseling. Fortunately, I was 23 and of age. I swore him to secrecy."

"What did you do?"

"There was a boy, a friend. His name was Hector Gomez. I was teaching English to immigrant workers and we worked together."

"So, he wasn't an immigrant?"

"No. He was an American citizen. I made up the immigrant story so that no one would try to track him down. Anyway, I told him my situation. He was very religious. He cared about me. We cared about each other. But we never . . . you know," Irene shared, her head down and with a bashful shame in her tone.

Maria leaned forward and nodded in understanding. Normally this would have been too much information, but she managed to maintain a detached nonchalance.

"He believed me. He said if Joseph could believe Mary in the Bible, he could believe me. He thought that God had a purpose for my baby. He was so kind."

"What happened to him?

"He acknowledged the baby, you, as his own. We finally told your grandmother we had messed around and not taken precautions. We told her that we were going to get married and we were. But . . . ," Irene paused and looked off into space.

"But?"

"There were more dreams during the pregnancy. Hector tried to understand, but it was too much for him. He thought I was being attacked by demons and suggested I consider an exorcism."

"Exorcism? That's a little over the top, isn't it?"

"I don't know. Maybe. Anyway, Hector left before you were born and I never heard from him again. Everyone already believed you were his child and since I didn't have another explanation, I've let everyone—even you—believe that all these years."

"Mom, who was my father?"

"Honey, I don't know who your father was, but I know how I got pregnant. It was in that God-forsaken laboratory. It was those doctors."

Maria fell backward in disbelief. *There must be a mistake*, she thought.

"I've felt so guilty about it, Maria, but what was I going to tell you? I spent years and much counseling trying to come to terms with it."

"Why did you take all the abuse from people, from the Church all those years?"

"I gave the Church a chance. They shunned me. I thought, maybe I deserved it. I was doing penance for some wrong— that it was God's will."

"You believed torment was God's will for you? How could you believe something like that?

"I did what I thought was best for us - for you. In the last experience before you were born, they told me something about you. They told me you were special, Maria. They told me you would accomplish something and look at you, You're White House correspondent for a news network. I'm so proud of you."

"I think they may have more than that in mind for me, mom."

"What do you mean?"

"While Jack and I were in Hawai'i, a woman named Nanna approached me. I met her on Twitter. She claimed to have answers for me about the meaning of life. She sent me here to have this conversation with you."

"What? Maria, no! You must not have any contact with them."

"Who are they, mom?"

"I don't know! Most of these years, I've tried to pretend this didn't happen. Do you remember that TV show *The X-Files?*"

"I was a child, but yeah, I remember it."

"I was drawn to that show. I can only believe that I was part of some secret government experiment."

"That's a little far-fetched, isn't it?"

"More far-fetched than having a baby as a virgin?"

"You're positive about that."

"You don't believe me either." Irene began to break down again.

"Mom, I didn't say that. I'm just trying to make some sense of what you're telling me."

"I wouldn't believe me either, if I were you."

"Mom, don't do that."

"Do what?"

"The whole poor me thing."

"Poor me?"

"You know, when you play the martyr to steal energy from others. I love you, but you constantly do that."

Irene reflected a moment. "You're right. I do that too much. I don't mean to."

"It's OK."

"Maria, stay away from Nanna and the doctors. They may want to do the same thing to you that they did to me. I love you, honey. I don't want anything to happen to you."

"I'm a big girl. I can take care of myself. I've had five karate classes."

"Maria, I'm serious. Be careful. This is bad news. They're dangerous."

"I'm in town for a couple of days until the president's town hall meeting. I can get a hotel."

"I won't stand for that. You're staying here."

"Thanks, mom. I'm going for a drive. I need to process all of this. Dinner was delicious. I'll be back later."

Maria gathered her purse and her keys, and left the house. She'd maintained control of her emotions to calm her mother down. Now a rush of emotion coursed through her, as she drove up the coast. Years of pent up wondering about her father's identity flowed in a waterfall of emotion. The anger followed right behind it. Someone had violated her mother. She relived the many insults her mother endured over the years. What had she done to deserve that? Nothing! Who was Nanna and for whom did she work? Maria's anger and hurt grew, as well as her confusion and fear.

(10)
It Begins

Maria drove along the coast for two hours. She stopped at Huntington Beach for some ocean and air. The stars dotted the darkening sky. A chilly wind blew in from the Pacific. She wrapped herself in a blanket and sat in the wet sand—her arms hugging her knees. The cold and the anger pulsing through her caused her to rock back and forth. Confusion clouded her mind.

Maria jumped and scrambled backward on all fours, startled by a voice and a breath in her ear. "Are you all right, Maria?"

She turned to find Nanna leaning over her. She seemed to have appeared on the beach out of nowhere.

"Where did you come from and what the hell do you want?" Maria fired from her defensive position on the ground.

"I thought you might need to talk or a shoulder," Nanna replied.

"From you? Are you following me around? You have some nerve!" Maria shouted, tears now running down her face.

Nanna stepped forward, kneeled, and wiped the tears from Maria's cheeks. "Get it all out, Maria. Did you talk to your mother?"

"What do you think? You know the answer to everything else."

"I understand you're angry."

"Oh, do you? That's great. Your understanding is exactly what I need."

"What did she tell you?"

"That you ruined her life!"

"Maria, you must believe I made it as easy for her as possible, under the circumstances. She had the option to process the experience differently."

"Easy? Damn you! Don't you care?"

"Maria there is much you don't—"

"She's broken and hurt and confused. So am I!"

"Now, Maria, listen to me . . ."

"What's your angle, Nanna? Do you get off on torturing people?

"That's enough!" Nanna's anger flared.

"Enough? My mother's a basket case. The man I always thought was my father was just a friend trying to help her in an impossible situation. He didn't stick around because he was a very religious man and could not handle the truth of what had happened to her."

"What truth?" Nanna asked, seeking confirmation that Maria had the whole story.

Maria responded with venom in her voice. "You know, you're pregnant and you've never been with a man. People tend to think you're crazy when you make claims like that."

"What else did she say?"

"She said her dream involved medical procedures performed on her. Six weeks later she found out she was pregnant with me."

"Is that all?"

"She remembered a woman named Nanna. Imagine my surprise. She told me she protested, but you told her you had a right to violate her."

"Violate? I was helping her and you and all of you."

"Thanks for confirming your self-justification. She told me you insisted you had the right and that you were doing it for her own good."

"I tried to comfort her. I wanted to comfort her."

"Who are you, Nanna? Do you work for the government? Am I the result of some black project experiment?"

"No. Not the government. Not exactly."

"What does that mean?"

"Maria, I have so much to share with you and time is of the essence. I must be sure you're prepared or everything could be compromised."

"What could be compromised? Stop speaking in riddles, Nanna. Why did you abduct my mother? You ruined her life and now you're meddling in mine!"

"I have my reasons. I have a right."

"What reasons? What right? What about the rights of American citizens not to be violated by their government?"

"There is much you don't know, Maria."

"Enlighten me, Nanna. Are my mother and me lab rats for your twisted pleasure?"

"I know it must seem that way to you—"

"Yes, it does seem that way. Who was my father? Who are you? What did you do to my mother?"

Nanna paused and reflected for a moment. "Perhaps, in my zeal to make things right, I was convinced my ends justified any means. Maria, I can only tell you that everything I have done here on Earth was to right a grievous wrong by my species against yours. I hold human beings in the highest regard. In fact, humanity and its future are why I contacted you."

"My species? What are you talking about?"

Nanna grabbed Maria to stop her hysterics and looked down into her eyes. "I need you to listen carefully to me, Maria. This is going to sound a bit *out there* to you. I'm from a planet called Nibiru. Some of your scholars refer to my race as the Anunnaki.

Our planet orbits your Sun's nearest neighbor. Your scientists call it Proxima Centauri. We call our star Kronos.

"What the hell are you talking about? I'm looking for serious answers and you're telling me UFO stories," Maria shouted to little effect against the sound of the wind and surf.

"We came to your planet for the first time about 2 million earth years ago."

"That's crazy! We would have known. You can't keep a secret like that."

"Your modern intelligence agencies have known for decades. Some of your secret societies have known for centuries; well, since the beginning of recorded history. Knowledge of us and our planet is so top-secret it makes the Manhattan Project look like it was conducted in broad daylight."

"Do you seriously expect me to believe this, Nanna?"

"No, Maria. There is no time for you to believe it. The time has come to show you."

Before Maria could object, a bluish beam of light caught her motionless. In an instant, she stood on a pad at the end of a brightly lit and scientifically sterile hallway. Gold lined the corridor and precious stones comprised the floor. Maria glanced over and saw Nanna standing beside her. She felt dizzy and Nanna caught her as she nearly fell.

"Where are we?" Maria asked in astonishment.

"Welcome aboard the Rakbu, Maria."

"What's a Rakbu?"

"Rakbu is the name of my ship. It's an ancient Sumerian word that means *messenger*."

"Your ship?"

"Yes. The interstellar craft I have used to visit and monitor your planet for the past several Earth centuries."

The transport experience left Maria confused and wobbly.

"Interstellar craft? You mean you're—"

"Yes, Maria. I'm . . . not of this world," Nanna affirmed.

"That's impossible," declared Maria. "You're part of some kind of super-secret government experiment. You drugged me and brought me here."

"You're so quick to evaluate and judge. Why is it impossible? You don't believe this vast cosmos is here only for the people of Earth, do you?"

Maria realized she'd never given it much thought. She saturated her awareness with the comings and goings of everyday life. She certainly never expected to stand face-to-face with someone claiming to be from another world.

"I don't know why the Universe exists. That doesn't mean you're an ET," Maria said.

"ET. That's such a cold, generic term, but easy to remember. A kind of branding we engaged in to soften our image and make renewed contact easier. Your ancestors referred to us by many names, but the most apt was Anunnaki: 'Those who from the heavens came to earth.'"

"The Anunnaki are a myth!" asserted Maria.

"Be careful who you call a myth," Nanna retorted.

"Renewed contact? How long have you been here?" Maria felt the cobwebs starting to clear and her journalistic instincts rising to the occasion.

"It's complicated. The history you know won't serve you well in understanding. I need you fresh for this conversation."

"I'm listening."

Nanna sighed deeply. "The connection between our two worlds is ancient and profound. The current relationship is toxic and one-sided. I'm here to transform and equalize it. Humanity's view of the universe has been greatly distorted and information critical to your emergence as a galactic species hidden."

Maria puzzled at Nanna's words. Nanna paused, as if to summon courage.

"That's why I abducted your mother and why I prepared you for this moment. It's why I created you, Maria."

"You created me? That's funny. You're here to facilitate humanity's emergence as a galactic civilization? That's even funnier."

"Absorb this slowly. We genetically altered you for the journey we now embark upon. We selected you. You look human, but you're special, Maria. We made you more . . . like us. Your DNA is 49 percent Anunnaki."

Maria shook her head, "This is crazy! You're crazy! Why have my medical scans never detected this?"

"We are able to mask the genetic alterations from your current level of medical technology."

Maria felt angry and violated, but she sensed authentic intentions from Nanna.

"Listen to me, Maria. This is a shock, I understand. Embrace this for the opportunity it represents. The fate of two worlds relies on our actions—yours and mine. Trust me . . . please."

"Trust you? I'm not there yet," said Maria.

"Well, at least no animosity . . . a beginning," replied Nanna. "There is much more to share, but it's late for you. You require sleep. I've arranged quarters for you."

"My mother is expecting—"

"Worry not, Maria. You will arrive back tomorrow with a satisfactory reason."

Nanna stared intently into Maria's eyes. "You look quite fatigued."

Maria experienced a flash, as if their minds touched. She felt instantly exhausted. Nanna's suggestion seemed to have created the fatigue.

Two tall uniformed men appeared behind Maria, ready to escort her. Maria could barely stand.

"Good night, Maria. Tomorrow is an important day. Bring your journalist's questions. You're going to interview an eyewitness to history—me."

(11)
Truth Shock

Maria awakened in a state of absolute peace and bliss. She could not remember when she had enjoyed such restful sleep. She reached for Jack, but the bed was empty. As she came around, she noticed some strange things about the room. There were electronic controls on the wall across the way—lit in multiple colors. She felt a slight vibration and a low-grade, but pervasive, hum.

It's not mom's house, she thought. She didn't remember checking into a hotel. Nanna's face flashed through her mind. She remembered the odd events of the night before and Nanna's preamble to some big discussion.

She rose from the bed and walked over to the window. At first, the view baffled her. She viewed a massive whitish light (no object) from high above. She noted an inky blackness encapsulating the object's rounded border. Small sparkling lights punctuated the blackness. In the distance, another object was coming into view. It was bluish-white in color and looked like a magnificent marble. A sense of awe filled Maria as she realized what she was watching.

A tone sounded above the door to the room. "Maria, it's Nanna. May I enter?"

"Yes," Maria responded, not removing her gaze from the astonishing sight in the window.

Nanna entered and joined Maria at the window. "Beautiful,

isn't it? I take it for granted, but how special to feel you experience it for the first time."

"That's the earth," Maria pointed in shock.

"Yes. We are currently orbiting your moon. We find it provides us with a good vantage point to keep an eye on things."

"Keep an eye on things?"

"We monitor what happens on and around the earth quite thoroughly. The moon provides an effective *blind* for observation."

"Is this part of a top-secret, black budget operation?"

"Maria, I told you who we are."

"Right. The Anunnaki. If it's not a U.S. project, is it a project initiated by the UN?"

"Maria, why is this so hard for you to believe? Believe your eyes. Could your government build a craft capable of orbiting the moon, of transporting you here, or creating a breathable atmosphere and artificial gravity?"

"I don't know. They always say the secret technology government has is decades beyond what we know."

"Trust me; your government is not capable of creating a vessel that even approaches the sophistication of the Rakbu."

"Belief in aliens is conspiracy theory territory, Nanna. People think you're crazy when you believe in this kind of thing."

"Does this ship and that view seem like a conspiracy theory to you? I can assure you, Maria. These are not conspiracy theories. It's time for your species to enter the real world. Believe your own eyes!"

Maria looked at Nanna. Nanna gazed back at her with warmth and love. Maria peered back out the window. The blue marble was now spinning more completely into view. "I just don't—"

A voice on the intercom interrupted Maria. "Mistress, we are tracking a Z vessel rising through the earth's atmosphere. Sensors indicate human DNA aboard—a single male human."

Nanna's face changed instantly. Maria read it as a mix of anger and determination.

"Come with me, Maria," commanded Nanna, as she made her way toward the door. "Bridge, move to intercept the Z vessel," ordered Nanna.

Maria tried to keep up with Nanna, but Nanna's height made her strides much longer. Maria was 5'9" but she now realized Nanna was easily seven feet tall. Maria jogged to keep up with Nanna's speed walking.

They entered an elevator at the end of the corridor. "Bridge," Nanna called out. The elevator moved at an amazing rate of speed. The ride was smooth and quiet. Maria saw lights in the elevator shaft passing rapidly through the translucent wall.

"Commander, Enka, where are they?" Nanna urgently inquired.

"They are about to achieve orbit," came the response, "but they will detect us, Mistress, before we arrive. They may try to run."

"Ready the towing beam. Ready the weapons. Raise our shields."

Now Maria was growing concerned. Nanna was clearly tense and ready to spring like a cat.

"What's going on, Nanna," Maria asked—unsure she wanted to know the answer.

"You wanted truth, Maria. You're about to get a large dose of it."

The elevator stopped, the doors opened, and the two women emerged onto the bridge of the Rakbu. A dozen or more officers operated various stations around the massive circular-shaped room. A large throne-like chair rose from the center of the bridge. It swiveled 360 degrees and was rich with electronic controls. Nanna made her way toward the chair.

"Keep Maria over here and out of the way," she ordered two uniformed guards. They were significantly taller and larger than Nanna. Maria estimated them to be over eight feet tall.

Nanna ascended the throne and placed a solar crown upon her head. Bright beams of light, like sunrays, emanated from the crown. She began studying panels and readouts coming to her command chair.

"Time," she shouted.

"One minute," came the reply from a large officer at one of the consoles. "They've spotted us. They're preparing to go to light speed."

"Give me a visual." The other vessel appeared on large video screens that circled the bridge.

"Towing beam?" queried Nanna.

"We're not in range, Mistress."

"Weapons?"

"Coming into range . . . right . . . now!"

"Target their engines and fire," commanded Nanna.

Two blue energy pulses appeared on the screen and raced toward the other ship. They struck its underside and the ship visibly shuddered.

"We damaged their shields," reported one officer, "Their engines are still intact. They are coming about and preparing to go to light speed, Mistress, and returning fire."

The Z weapons struck the Rakbu's shield grid. The impact jolted the ship, but no damage.

"Fire again," ordered a stone-faced Nanna.

This time the impact of the weapons spun the other ship around and it floated for a moment before regaining its attitude.

"Their light drive is down, Mistress. They are opening communications and sending a visual."

"Open visual communication," ordered Nanna.

A small gray being with large eyes right out of a UFO convention brochure appeared. "Anunnaki vessel, this is Captain Kotz of the Z Alliance. Your actions are an outrage—"

Nanna cut him off, "Captain, our sensors indicate you have a male human aboard your vessel. I order you to transport him aboard my ship immediately or we will resume our attack on your vessel."

"We have a treaty," shot back the Z captain. "We are engaged in lawful interstellar commerce."

"Yes. Well, commerce in interstellar human experimentation is closed today."

"I will protest to your government about this incident."

"You do that. Please tell my brother, the King of Nibiru, that Princess Inanna sends her regards. Now, are you going to transport the human, or shall we continue our battle?"

"We are a trading vessel. Our ship is no match for yours. We will comply, but there will be repercussions for—"

"Close the channel and transmit the transport coordinates," ordered Inanna. "Keep weapons locked on that ship until they comply. Inform them we will escort them out of Earth Space."

"Inanna," muttered Maria under her breath, "Of course, I should have known."

"Mistress, the exchange of fire has attracted a high-resolution scan of the area by ground-based tracking on Earth. They may be able to get a lock and a visual on us."

Inanna turned to one of her officers, "Commander Enka, project a scattering field to deflect human scans and confuse their readings. As soon as we have the human aboard, order the Z ship to make best possible speed. We will escort them to the edge of Earth Space."

"Yes, Mistress," replied Enka.

Inanna removed her crown, descended from the chair, and walked toward Maria. "Maria, you must be hungry. Let's get you some breakfast."

Inanna entered the elevator and Maria followed. The doors closed behind them.

"You're Inanna," exclaimed Maria. "Are you *the* Inanna?"

Inanna stopped and turned toward Maria. She looked down on the human woman. "Yes. I am Inanna. I am the goddess of ancient Sumerian lore—the Queen of Heaven and Earth."

"What the hell just happened back there?"

"One moment, Maria."

"Dr. Enti," Inanna spoke into the intercom system.

"Here, Mistress," came the reply.

When the human is on board follow the usual procedures and return him to his place of origin."

"Yes, Mistress."

Inanna turned back toward Maria. She hovered over her somewhat menacingly, "You wanted some truth. You just received some. The Z's abduct human beings every day. This is why they have such a prominent place in your UFO lore. They conduct experiments and even traffic humans throughout this part of the galaxy. Your species makes quite good servants. I've made it part of my personal mission to stop as many abductions as I can."

"So, our governments just allow this," asked Maria incredulously.

"Your governments have no choice. Some have made deals with the Z's and other races to prevent the mass harvesting of humans."

"And where do the Anunnaki stand on human harvesting?"

Maria asked with contempt.

"I do not permit it. My government has its own agendas and secrets, concerning Earth. We can discuss this later."

"What is the usual procedure?"

Inanna looked quizzically at Maria.

"You ordered your doctor to perform the usual procedure on the human."

"His short-term memory will be erased and he will awake in his bed at home with a bit of a headache and an interesting dream."

"He's a human being, not an animal. You can't drug him like a bear in the woods. Doesn't he have a right to know what happened to him?

"Collectively, yes, you all have a right to know. For one individual, it's better this way. It could cause him great harm to know."

"It sounds as though it is causing all of us great harm not to know."

"That's why you're here. It's why I am going to explain everything to you so that we can implement a plan to release the truth in a non-harmful way. His experience would only bring him ridicule from many. Irrefutable physical evidence exposing the truth is the only way. That is the plan my uncle, Enki, and I are working on."

"I want to meet the human . . . memory intact," protested Maria.

"Maria," Inanna said with exasperation.

"I want to meet him." Maria did her best to look intimidating, as she eyed the larger woman.

Inanna glared back and finally said, "Very well.

Come to my office this afternoon at 14:00. I will let you interview him. I will let you interview me. I am on an urgent mission to atone for the past. Get some breakfast, Maria. The morning's events have tired me. I need to refocus. Bring your questions this afternoon—all of them! The time for full disclosure is at hand!"

(12)
Inanna's Cause

Inanna entered the Royal Quarters. Her opulent penthouse comprised Rakbu's entire top deck. The massive suite featured a 180-degree window spanning the ship's forward view, a private dining room, a large bedchamber, and her Royal Ascension Room.

The battle and the morning banter with Maria fatigued Inanna. To complicate matters, she had neglected her medication. Using a medical beam infuser, she dispensed the precise dosage into her arm. She grimaced, as relief slowly flowed through her body. The medicine mitigated the symptoms, but no cure existed for her condition. Dr. Enti gave her five to thirty earth years and that added urgency to every action.

Inanna lay down on the bed, closed her eyes, and breathed deeply. Rachel's face passed through her mind. Her thoughts swept back to that night 13,000 earth years ago—the night that changed her life's path.

A beautiful full moon hung above the Sumerian desert. Inanna sat in the mouth of a cave keeping watch on the valley below. She loved Earth's moon. No object in the Nibiruan sky matched its grandeur. An intermittent breeze cooled her face, punctuating the stillness.

The caves served as refuge and hiding place for the growing cultured human community. Cultured humans were those tutored in the arts of civilization by Inanna and her Uncle Enki in

direct defiance of a royal decree forbidding it. The decree promised death to Anunnaki or human engaging in such activities. An
educated human, read the decree, is a dangerous human.

Led by Enki and Inanna, this community of several hundred
humans and a few dozen Anunnaki had lived safely and in peace
in these caves for nearly three years. The caves were far from
Enlil's cities and difficult to spot from the air.

Inanna felt a tug on her arm. "Nanna, Nanna, look what I did."

Rachel, a seven-year-old human girl, proudly displayed a picture painted on a flat stone. Inanna had been teaching a group
of human children to paint and Rachel was her prized pupil.

"That is lovely, my child," Inanna said. "I'm so proud of
you."

Rachel hugged Inanna's leg, "I love you, Nanna."

"I love you, child."

Inanna felt tears well in her eyes. She did love Rachel and the
other children too. She loved the humans. Why did her father,
Enlil, hate them so? Wasn't their sentience obvious to anyone
with eyes? Why did her grandfather, King Anu, deny them education and a connection to The Father Creator?

A rolling thunder echoed across the desert, growing louder.
A wall of dust rose and partially obscured the moon, tinting it
brownish red.

Enki appeared in the cave entrance. "Is it a storm, Inanna?"

"I'm not sure, uncle."

Enki studied the darkened horizon. The thunder grew closer
and louder. "My God!" he exclaimed. "Royal Hoverbots."

Rachel hugged Inanna's leg tighter. "What is it, Nanna?"

They were now close enough to swirl the dust a few hundred
yards in front of the caves.

"Run, Rachel," Inanna shouted. "Run to the back of the cave."

"Are they headed for us, uncle, or just passing over?" asked

Inanna.

"I don't know," replied Enki.

The answer came in the form of laser fire strafing the mountainside. Inanna and Enki retreated into the cave with the rest of their community. The caves shook. Women and children screamed.

Enki mustered their small self-defense force—about 50 human men and a few aging Anunnaki warriors—to counter Enlil's crack Royal Guard now beaming into the caves. They established a skirmishing line near the front of the cave complex. The battle lasted mere moments. Enlil's troops overran the defense force and raced to the back of the cave complex where Enki, Inanna, and the rest of the community huddled.

Inanna heard the sound of their boots marching through caves. Rachel clung to Inanna, shaking. Enki waited helplessly with the rest of the group. The Anunnaki warriors approached led by a smartly dressed, brash young officer.

"Your Royal Highnesses Enki and Inanna, I am Commander Ninn. By order of His Royal Highness Prince Enlil, Governor of Earth, I place you under arrest on charges of educating humans."

"This is an outrage, commander. My brother has no authority to arrest me. I will protest to my father."

"Prince Enlil has apprised King Anu of the situation. The king has placed you and Princess Inanna in Enlil's hands for punishment. You are to be delivered to him in Uruk."

"What of the rest of our community?" Inanna asked.

"My orders are to implement summary judgment against the rest of your group."

"Summary judgment?" questioned Enki.

"The terms of the Human Education Decree are clear, Lord Enki. The punishment for both Anunnaki and humans is death. An educated human is a dangerous human."

"That's an abomination!" shouted Inanna. "You cannot murder these people."

"These are not people, Mistress. They are traitors and humans and they will be dealt with according to the law."

"They are sentient beings," cried Enki. "Neither my father, my brother, nor you have the right—"

"This is not about rights, Lord Enki. This is about control. Carry out the sentence immediately. You will both watch before being transferred back to Uruk."

Ninn motioned to his troops to secure them. The warriors moved into the crowd and began forcibly removing people. One came for Rachel, still grasping Inanna's leg, and roughly picked her up.

Inanna pushed the solider. "Take your hands off of her."

A second soldier hit Inanna from behind, knocking her to the ground.

"Please don't make this unpleasant business any more difficult than it is, Princess," Ninn suggested.

Guards led the Anunnaki and humans outside, separating them into two lines. A Royal Guard armed with pulse pistols appeared.

Commander Ninn formally pronounced sentence on the Anunnaki and gave the command to fire. Set to maximum, the pulse pistols vaporized them. There was weeping and wailing among the humans. They were next. Ninn didn't bother to make any formal pronouncement regarding them. He ordered the detail to aim.

Rachel got loose and ran towards Inanna. "Nanna. Nanna."

Inanna broke free from her guard and ran to meet Rachel.

Ninn pulled out his weapon and ordered. "Stand down, Princess."

"You can't do this, Ninn!"

"Oh, but I can."

He turned his weapon on Rachel and fired. To Inanna, it happened in slow motion. The pulse struck Rachel and literally pulled the atoms of her body apart. Then she was gone. Inanna fell to the ground weeping. Ninn wasted no time. He commanded the detail to fire and all the humans were gone.

They transported Inanna and Enki to Eridu for an audience with Enlil. Prince Ea, Inanna's brother, stood at her father's side. Ea was Enlil's shadow. He shared his father's disregard for the humans and he glared at his sister as she approached.

"Lil," began Enki, "an atrocity has been committed in your name."

"Careful, my brother," warned Enlil. "Your head is on the block. Now is not the time to debate The Human Question. You would do well to focus on your defense."

"We need no defense, father," Inanna replied. "We are guilty of nothing more than educating sentient beings."

"My daughter," Enlil said. "You disappoint. The humans are not sentient. They are a commodity created by us for our purposes."

"Created by me," corrected Enki.

Enlil glared at his brother. There was no love lost between them. They had been at odds from the beginning of the earth expedition. Enlil was jealous of Enki's genetic skill in engineering the humans. Enki saw his brother as immoral in his treatment of humanity.

"Regardless of who created them, brother, they are not sentient." A fearful human is a productive human. An educated human is a dangerous human."

"You force them to worship you as a god, father," Inanna said. "You infuse their psyches with fear—both here and in the afterlife."

"A fearful human, my daughter, is a productive human. An educated human is a dangerous human," Enlil retorted.

"You may be the Governor of Earth, Inc., brother, but history will prove you wrong. Humans are sentient. We created them and it is our responsibility to tutor them into a contributing member of the galaxy."

"You were always an idealist, my brother, and that idealism has now placed your fate in my hands," Enlil said.

"An educated human is a free being capable of seeing through your tyranny, Enlil. He would not cower before you and nothing frightens you more," Enki replied.

"This discussion is over," Enlil warned. "By rights, I should put both of you to death. Inanna, you are my only daughter and your mother died giving birth to you. I take into account your relative youth and the influence of my brother. I hereby sentence you to exile on Nibiru. You are to retain all titles and privileges, but you are never again to interfere with Earth, Inc."

"My brother, Enki," Enlil continued. "Part of me wants to execute you for the trouble you cause me, but no member of the House of En has ever executed another."

"Go ahead, brother, make me a martyr," pleaded Enki. "If my blood brings justice for the humans, then so be it."

"I will not make a martyr of you, brother. I order you incarcerated on Nibiru for 1,000 earth years. Upon release, I hereby strip you of all titles, save your Senate seat. You are to be branded on the forehead with the mark of the serpent. It shall forever symbolize your treachery and serve as warning to others who would challenge the crown or help the humans."

Prince Ea stepped forward, "Thus has Enlil declared. Let it be done immediately."

Inanna opened her eyes and looked around her bedchamber.

That day created today, she thought. Helping human beings realize their potential formally became a crime. She closed her eyes again and considered the path that led her to this moment of rebellion.

Shortly after this, Enlil banished all other Anunnaki from Earth. Prior to their ouster, Anunnaki royals and nobles sponsored and ruled human tribes and later city-states. Each was the patron god of his or her tribe. Enlil demanded his people refer to him as, "The Living God." He sent them to war against neighboring tribes to consolidate his power. He dared the rival tribes to produce their gods in the flesh. When they could not, he chided them for believing in dead gods and powerless idols. He demanded obedience to the only living god.

By the end of Enki's thousand-year incarceration, Inanna's grandfather and her father had passed on to The Father Creator's Realm. Her brother Ea ascended to the throne. He trusted no Anunnaki to run the earth for fear of rebellion. He banned Earth visits for all Anunnaki. He left his father's hybrid controllers (The Cadre) in charge of the planet's day-to-day operation.

Inanna and Enki used their positions in the Nibiruan Senate to champion liberalization on The Human Question. Ea stymied them at every turn. He was his father's son in every way and saw the humans as an Anunnaki asset, not as sentient beings.

Too many powerful Anunnaki—and their friends in the known galaxy—profited from Earth, Inc. To them, humanity, its labor, and even its DNA were commodities, created by the Anunnaki for the benefit of the Anunnaki. King Ea, through his hybrid-human overseers, kept humanity misdirected, fearful, and productive. The Cadre, as Ea called them, guided human civilization down paths benefitting the Anunnaki elite, but enslaving the minds and persons of human beings.

The Cadre were entrenched and embedded in the very fabric

of human civilization. They controlled human commerce by starting and manipulating economic systems. They managed war, peace, and famine through competing political movements. They manipulated human consciousness, tastes, and trends through media. Most nefariously, they dominated human psychology by co-opting religious institutions, as the gatekeepers of death and the afterlife. Fear was their tool; profit and control their goal.

For millennia, the humans worked as slaves for Earth, Inc. Human sentience and freedom was denied. The Anunnaki knew this perverted the true order of the universe. They knew it violated the tenants set forth by The Father Creator, but it was expedient and profitable.

Inanna's dispute with King Ea came to a head the second time he used weather modification technology to flood the earth and cull the human numbers.

In a fit of rage, she burst into King Ea's court. Dispensing with normal courtesies and the ritual bow, Inanna shouted, "Does the King of Nibiru think he can get away with the murder of sentient beings?"

Ea continued his administrative work. Without looking up to acknowledge his sister, he replied, "Inanna, their numbers were getting too large again. When there are too many for The Cadre to manage, they represent a rebellion threat. I know you love the humans, but don't be so emotional. We salvaged enough to continue Earth, Inc."

"What was your excuse this time, Ea? Did they not grovel enough before images of you in the temples?"

Ea looked up and scowled at Inanna. "Be careful, sister. I expected your protest on this matter, but don't test my patience."

"You murdered 70 percent of them and you ask me for patience. Why did you do it?"

"They had a production quota to hit. They fell short and they missed the mark. What kind of god would I be if there were no consequences?"

"You're no god, brother!"

"Go to Earth, Inanna. They bow their heads and ask for my blessings upon their activities. They paint massive images of me and put them in their temples. They are children. They require a firm hand."

"If they are children, it's because you have treated them as children. They are speaking to The Father Creator, not to you!"

"Really? Whose images adorn their temples and their charms? Is it not my image and that of our Father Enlil? They know not whom they call god. I'm as good a god as any to them."

"What a noble god you are! You murder them over results on your bottom line."

"That's enough, Inanna. Guards!"

"The Father Creator will not allow you to continue this farce, Ea," Inanna shouted as guards escorted her from the king's chamber.

"The Father Creator," Ea snickered. "You're too old to believe in fairy tales, Inanna."

"The Father Creator is no fairy tale."

"Guards, halt," commanded the king. He descended the steps, walked up to his sister, and stood face to face with her.

"Humanity's fate," said Ea, "is firmly in my hands, as is yours. No one has had contact with The Father Creator in historic times. I think he's a myth. Are you to base the human fate and your own on a shadow?"

"I have been in contact with The Father Creator," said Inanna. "He will not allow your dominion over the humans to stand forever, Ea."

Ea broke a rare Anunnaki grin, "You're delusional, sister.

You cannot help them. You might as well accept that and retain your peace of mind."

"We shall see, brother, we shall see."

When Inanna learned of her illness, she realized time was of the essence. Her path, her mission, became clear. Waiting for the intractable forces on the home world to change was no longer an option. Inanna determined to take matters into her hands. She knew her course of defiance was a dangerous one, but what choice had she?

She ingested a quick dissolving sublingual chip. This medication calmed her nerves, enabling her to pray and meditate. Doctors gave her two to thirty earth years to live. Her advanced age expedited the disease raging through her body, but she'd beaten the lower end of the prediction.

"Dr. Enti, she called out."

"Yes, Mistress," replied Enti.

"Please keep the human in stasis, but hold on the procedure. Prepare him to be in my conference room at 14:00."

"Yes, Mistress."

Inanna entered the most sacred part of her quarters—her Room of Ascension. This soundproofed chamber isolated her from everything but emergency communications from the bridge. Here she prayed and meditated—to commune and communicate with The Father Creator.

The room's gold-plated floor measured precisely 33 feet by 33 feet—the divine dimension. The walls were also gold, inlaid with lapis lazuli images, depicting the stories of her people. The angles of the walls merged into a pyramid shape, coming to a point at the room's apex precisely 33 feet above the floor.

The Anunnaki built hundreds of these communication pyramids on the earth for priestly classes to communicate with their Anunnaki masters, but never in the divine dimensions, which limited their true capabilities.

The room was deceptively technological. The real technology was in the materials and the shape. Long ago, the Anunnaki learned that gold and a pyramid shape were amazing transmitters of energy. A semi-lucent crystal at the pyramid's apex focused the energy and sent it speeding out into the Universe. A highly trained mind like Inanna's could link thoughts to that energy. She could magnify their power to manifest physical objects or to communicate with dimensions beyond the fourth.

Inanna entered and, as was her custom, lit several candles and incense sticks. She sat down in the middle of the room. She pressed her hands together and bowed at the waist.

"Greetings, Father Creator. I call upon your wisdom to guide me in my endeavors. I call upon your strength to complete my tasks. Let your blessings rain upon all sentient beings, wherever they live in the cosmos. May my mind become one with your mind?"

She closed her eyes and entered a meditative state. Immediately, she could feel the pains and the stresses of her physical body falling far behind. She turned the power of her thoughts to the future—The Future Possible. She focused on Earth and on humankind. She focused on a future when the great Anunnaki lie was revealed and humanity was finding its way forward without the nightmares created by that lie. She developed a clear image of what that Earth looked like—every human being claiming the self-determination and self-realization that were the right of every sentient being in the cosmos. She envisioned an end to fearful visions of God and the psychological anguish that came with them. She focused her intentionality on its fulfillment.

"Let it be so, Father Creator," she whispered. "Let them know your love, without judgment and fear. Let their connection to you be direct and without intermediaries or mind-numbing dogmas. Let it be so."

Inanna could feel the palpable energy of her thoughts being magnified in the room and transmitted out into the Universe. She turned her focus to Maria, beautiful Maria.

"Father Creator, let my daughter, Maria, find the answers she seeks. Let her become the person she came here to be—the person I created her to be. Let her be a beacon to her people—an embodiment of the truth, hope, and The Future Possible."

The room now filled with visible light and energy pulsating up the walls and out into space. A loud buzzing sound permeated the room. Inanna's form lifted and hovered above the floor. Despite the commotion, she felt her consciousness reach the realm of silence beyond the five senses and into the thirty-third dimension—the highest known dimension in this Universe. Silence, light, and serenity surrounded and embraced her. She was beyond space, beyond time, and in the presence of The Father Creator.

"Father Creator," called Inanna, "be present to me."

"I am always and everywhere with you, my child," responded a voice projected directly into Inanna's mind. A blinding light always accompanied that voice.

"My time is short, Father. My time of reuniting with you is at hand. I am eager to be free from the bonds of my form. But," she paused.

"But . . . you believe you must make things right with the humans before your time."

"Yes, Father. I ask again, please allow me to intervene directly to make things right on Earth."

"Inanna," thundered the voice in her mind, "however the humans came to be, they are here now and they are sentient. Your further direct interference can only do them harm."

"Has not enough harm come to them already?"

"When your race created human beings, you took on a responsibility. You violated that responsibility and the tenets of my creation in every way. I granted my blessing for your activities with the express agreement that the humans must generate the change themselves. Were you to do it for them, how will they ever grow?"

"Yes, Father. I understand, but they are corrupt, violent, greedy, and have an overdeveloped need to be right.

"Not unlike the Anunnaki, Inanna."

Inanna had no response to that.

They change slowly. Suffering is rampant. They live in poverty. They live in fear of each other and the universe around them. Yet, my government and their Earth controllers refuse to permit change through normal channels."

"Continue with your process. But the change, if it is to come, must come from the humans themselves."

"Father, how can the change come while so many still consciously blind the humans to the truth for their own benefit? Is the change possible for them? Is a different future possible?"

"My creation is wide open, my child. All things are possible for those who think, those who act, and those who believe. As the humans are now, so have many races been. They have the disadvantages of Anunnaki lies and your genetic manipulation. It lessened them, but they are yet capable."

"Thank you, Father. I doubt some times. May I be permitted to see what the future holds for them?"

"Inanna, their future can take many roads, but it must be their choice."

"Of course."

"How is your work with the human woman going? I am eager for human beings to be my children, rather than my grand-children. I am eager to welcome them into the family of light."

"It is slow. She is resistant and rebellious at every turn. She doubts and she doesn't seem to grasp the big picture."

"Are you certain the modifications have taken effect?"

"Yes. Our scans confirm that her Anunnaki DNA is acti-vated and that she has the capability to open herself to the truth—to you, Father Creator."

"There is significant baggage about God in her. Her attempts to communicate with me are muddled and riddled with unpro-ductive images and paradigms."

"They are the baggage of the great lie, Father. Maria and all humans labor hard beneath that lie."

"Help her, Inanna. She must do this, but she needs your guidance and your wisdom."

"And I need yours, Father."

"Always, my child. Trust, Inanna. When the moment and the situation are right, she will see and she will know."

"Yes, Father."

"Be well, my child. It is time for you to break some para-digms. I look forward to the moment of Maria's breakthrough. I have seen it and it is beautiful. It will be a momentous day when humans, for the first time, are directly connected to their source. Finally, they will be connected to the races of light across my multi-dimensional creation. I leave you with a gift, Inanna."

As Inanna came out of trance, the room returned to normal and she gently came to rest on the floor. For a moment, The Future Possible flashed through her mind. She saw a triumphant Maria, a triumphant humanity . . . free at last. And in Maria's arms, she saw the child—a special child. The future was, indeed, possible.

Inanna smiled, with a knowing, "Thank you, Father Creator,

thank you."

In her mind, Inanna heard, "Expect help from unexpected sources. The humans have it within them to do this."

(13)
Paradigms Broken

After a morning touring Rakbu's wonders, Maria was ushered into a large conference room for her meeting with Inanna. A cool beverage reminiscent of wine awaited her. She sampled it and found it dry, but passable. Inanna appeared out of thin air in a bluish, buzzing beam, punctual as always.

"So, that's how you do that," Maria said in amazement. "It's like a Star Trek transporter."

Inanna smiled, "Yes. Many of your science fiction concepts had their genesis in visions, dreams, and moments of insight. Let's just say, not all of those visions were accidents."

"Have we done anything on our own or are we always pawns in your games?" queried Maria.

Inanna's face sobered, "There are a great many things humanity does not know about its origins and the nature of this Universe. You are like a proverbial babe in the woods. I help where I can. Children must grow up."

"Why do you think so little of us?"

"You're pointing your finger in the wrong direction, Maria. I'm here because I do believe in humanity. My people and, especially, my government have a much lower opinion of you."

"Why?"

"Because they know you were intentionally designed to deliver so little."

"You're speaking in riddles again, Inanna."

"I'm not certain you're ready for this information, Maria. I know most of humanity is not, but I no longer have the luxury of time."

"Then just say it."

"Let's have a dialogue, not a presentation. Did you come prepared with your questions?"

Maria leaned forward in her chair confidently, "First, I want to see the abducted human."

"Dr. Enti," Inanna said into the air.

"Yes, Mistress," came the reply.

"Transport the human patient to my conference room."

A bluish beam materialized near the doorway and a slightly dazed and confused human male materialized. He appeared to be of Asian or Pacific-island descent.

"Don't be frightened," assured Inanna.

The man eyed Inanna and then turned his stare to Maria. "You are human," he blurted in heavily accented English.

"Yes. My name's Maria Love. I'm an American journalist. They brought me here the same as you. What's your name?"

"I am Dr. Jaypee Escudero, ma'am."

"Doctor," Maria inquired, "a medical doctor?"

"No, ma'am. I am a college professor in neuroscience and a UFO researcher in the Philippines," Jaypee replied.

"UFO researcher?" puzzled Maria.

"Yes, ma'am."

"You're speaking at a convention in Hawai'i in a few weeks. I heard it on the radio in Honolulu," said Maria, recalling the radio she so casually dismissed ten days earlier.

"That is correct, if I find my way home from here."

"This is Inanna. No one is going to hurt you."

"Inanna," Escudero stepped back. "Inanna of the Anunnaki?"

"Do you know Inanna, Dr. Escudero?"

Escudero averted Inanna's stare and kept his head slightly bowed. "Call me Jay. I know of her. She was an ancient Anunnaki goddess."

Inanna interrupted in an attempt to take back control of the conversation, "This is a touching human reunion, but we have an interview to conduct, Maria. Perhaps, the two of you can talk more later."

"No," Maria stated firmly. "I want him to be here for the interview, if that's OK with you Jay?"

"Yes, ma'am, of course."

"Awesome! And you can call me Maria."

"Thank you, Maria."

"How do you know about Inanna?"

"I work with alien abductees throughout the Philippines. I have concluded, from my research, the Anunnaki are not a myth. They are a historical reality. They have interfered with human development for centuries."

"Interfered how?" Maria pursued.

Inanna remembered The Father Creator's parting words to her. The unfolding synchronicity intrigued her. If she guided this conversation effectively, Maria and Jay might be able to gain some self-realization on their own.

"Maria, do you believe in creation or evolution?" tested Escudero.

Maria sensed Escudero's keen mind. He was already leading her where she did not wish to go. "I don't know. I mean the evidence is rather limited for both ideas."

"Exactly!" exclaimed Escudero. "Neither fits the facts. I am a scientist. I like facts. Creationist ideologies claim God created the universe and intervened only on this one tiny planet. They claim God has some special interest in human beings and the fate of the universe focuses on our reconciliation with God.

Where's the evidence or the logic in it? Evolution tells us we are the outcome of a billion accidents."

"Um, right," managed Maria.

"Don't you see, Maria? 'God did it' has little evidence to support it. 'Accidents did it' has too many holes. Where is the link between apes and modern humans? How do you explain the Cambrian explosion?"

"I can't," Maria agreed, now totally lost.

The fire and the confidence were building in Escudero. He no longer resembled the frightened man from moments before. "No one can. It is in complete opposition to Darwin's theory. There must be a third option. I believe it was interventionism and the Anunnaki did it," he asserted pointing at Inanna.

"Interventionism, I don't understand, Jay."

"Human beings were not created—not in the sense you hear about in church. We are not the result of evolution, at least not completely. There is no missing link species. The missing link is in our genes. Their genes are in our genes."

"Whose genes are our genes," queried Maria?

"Theirs," said Jaypee, pointing at Inanna.

Maria stared at Jay, trying to get her mind enthusiastic about his assertions. She looked to Inanna for confirmation.

Inanna looked more uncomfortable than Maria had ever seen her. Clearly, Jaypee had touched on a sensitive topic.

"Well, Jay, I'm sure you are fatigued from your adventure. Perhaps, it's time for you to be back in Manila. At Maria's request, we are leaving your memories intact."

Maria and Jay started to object, but Inanna raised herself in her chair. She stared down at the humans, as she gave the order. "Bridge, do you have Dr. Escudero's original coordinates?"

"Affirmative, Mistress. We were able to locate his address from his biomarker chip."

"Excellent. Transport him there now."

Maria managed to blurt, "Contact me," before the bluish light appeared and Jaypee vanished.

"Well, serendipity has provided you a preview of my secret," said Inanna.

"What he said . . . is it true?"

"It's part of what I want to share today, but only a small part."

Maria sat silently for a moment. A thousand questions rushed to her mind. She experienced a profound sense of disconnection. All she thought she understood about who she was vanished in a moment. She mustered, "How? Why?"

"Maria, it was in the time of my parents—about 500,000 earth years ago. Nibiru had passed through a tumultuous civil war that stretched our natural resources and damaged our atmosphere. Nibiru is a tidally locked planet."

"Tidally locked?"

"Yes. The same side of Nibiru always faces our sun—Kronos. The same is true of your moon in relation to Earth. The dark side of our world, despite our atmosphere, is so frigid that it is virtually uninhabitable."

"So all Anunnaki live on one-half of Nibiru?"

"Yes. We have perpetual day, but it is not like day on Earth. Even though Nibiru is twice the diameter and three times the mass of Earth, Kronos is a red dwarf star. Its mass is less than fifteen percent that of your Sun's and hundreds of times fainter. Yet, it is prone to sudden bursts of light and radiation."

Maria heard a story coming and settled in to listen.

"Our healthy atmosphere deflected the dangerous elements of these blasts, while absorbing the much-needed heat. The atmospheric damage was catastrophic. Orbiting a star like your sun, planetary extinction would have followed within a year. Our red dwarf slowed the effects. Still, had we done nothing, the outcome was inevitable. Our people, our civilization seemed doomed to die a slow death," Inanna's voice broke up with emotion.

"I'm so sorry, Inanna. It sounds horrible. What did you do?"

"Our scientists were well aware of gold's unique energetic properties. Your science remains largely unaware or in denial of these properties. Gold's value goes far beyond its beauty or rarity. Our scientists hypothesized they could seal the atmospheric holes and deflect the bursts by suspending gold dust in our atmosphere. Gold, Maria, that's what started this," lamented Inanna. The emotion of a moment before dissolved into a blank stare.

"I understand you needed to suspend gold in your atmosphere. I don't see what that has to do with Earth or humans."

"Nibiru has no naturally occurring gold. Our planet is highly oxidized and naturally occurring metals are rare. All the gold we possessed came to Nibiru through trade with Earth civilizations. We gathered all the gold we had and dispersed it in the atmosphere. The effects of the radiation were slowed, but it was not nearly enough gold."

"Wait a minute. What do you mean Earth civilizations? There was no civilization on Earth half a million years ago."

"That's correct, Maria. However, before then, your planet spawned many advanced civilizations. My people knew them and traded with them across the stars."

"How is that possible? Where is the evidence of these civilizations?"

Inanna chuckled, "The evidence for the newest of these previous civilizations is all around you, but your science refuses to acknowledge it. Older evidence is below the sea. Your scientists have yet to uncover it. Evidence for the oldest civilizations on

Earth is forever lost—the victim of your planet's subduction."

"I'm confused. You're saying the evidence for some of these civilizations is all around us. Where?"

"Artifacts from these civilizations exist around your planet. Your media has highlighted them. Yet, the scientific establishment fails to recognize clues because they are trying to fit them into a preconceived version of Earth's history, rather than where the facts lead."

"But wouldn't there be buildings and bridges and—"

"But there are, Maria. This is an interesting side note, but not what I brought you here to discuss."

"Right, the gold."

"Yes. Maria. Do you think governments are always truthful with their people?"

"Is that a trick question?" Maria replied ironically.

"It's important for you to understand that our two worlds have that in common. We may be millions of earth years ahead of you technologically, but our politics is very much like your politics."

"So much for the evolutionary theory of civilization," Maria chagrined.

"The conditions on Earth are very harsh for my species. We do not adapt well to your day-night cycle. Your Sun is much brighter and hotter than Kronos. The high oxidation factors actually shorten our lives. It all plays havoc on our biology. Staying for too long is psychologically and physically draining for most of us."

"So, the gold, Inanna," urged Maria.

"The conditions made life on Earth extremely difficult for the soldiers we sent to mine the gold. They often became riotous and disobedient. We maintained a military base on Mars, which is much more hospitable for us. We tried to keep our troops rotated. After about 50,000 earth years, the cost and impacts to our troops forced us to seek other solutions."

"Tell me more about how your people are being misled."

Inanna inhaled and exhaled to gain her composure. "The original reason we mined the gold was to repair our atmosphere. That was the truth. However, after about 10,000 earth years, we had enough gold to repair our atmosphere. During that period, one of our top scientists discovered that a special kind of gold (monoatomic gold) possessed remarkable properties."

"What kinds of properties?"

"It magnified the function of biological cells. Benefits included amplified mental function, enhanced strength, and even super-longevity. Our elite kept this secret from the Anunnaki people."

"So, you had kept mining the gold after your atmosphere was fixed for the benefit of your upper classes?"

"Yes. To this day, our people believe healing our atmosphere is the reason for our continued involvement on Earth. The truth remains, in your terminology, 'top secret' information. Constant crisis was good for the power of the elite. Our leaders wanted the gold and needed an excuse to stay engaged on Earth."

"How have you kept that a secret from your scientists for all these thousands of years?"

"It's simple, really. Science is a prerogative of the Royal family on Nibiru. My family funds all science on Nibiru. If the Royal family wants to hide information, it remains hidden. The other elites benefit from this lie too and so they have supported the secrecy. Many of them also profit from the interstellar commerce that is focused on Earth."

"There is interstellar commerce on Earth? How does this go on without us knowing it?"

"Our leaders taught your leaders well, Maria. They know. They can't stop it and so, like the Anunnaki elite, they participate and profit from it. That little abduction attempt by the Z vessel is a very common occurrence."

"What would they have done to Jay?"

"It's hard to say. The Z often take humans for pure experimentation or to augment their DNA."

"They would take his DNA?"

"Their race had a legitimate ecological disaster and their DNA was damaged. They're very intelligent, but their physical form is devolving. They believe human DNA can save their race. They have a treaty with my government and an agreement with many of your governments. They are allowed to take humans in limited quantities to prevent an invasion and interstellar war."

"Do you expect me to believe that?" Maria demanded.

"Believe what?"

"That Earth governments permit these abductions."

"I speak not of your elected officials, but to those running your planet."

"That's a discussion for another day, Maria. Let's stay on track with today's revelations. The Z Alliance abducts far more humans than you can imagine. Sometimes they take them aboard ships, as you saw today. Other times, they take people to underground facilities on Earth."

Maria shook her head repetitively. "It's inconceivable. How could that be going on without us knowing about it?"

"Without who knowing about it? The 'Powers That Be' are aware of these activities."

"And our governments allow it?" Maria demanded.

"They turn a blind eye, Maria. What choice do they have?"

"They could defend their citizens!"

"Against a threat they deny exists? How would they explain

that, even if they wanted to?"

"Would the Z have returned Jay?"

"It's hard to know. They take millions of human beings without a trace. Many never return. Others, repeat abductees like Jay, are taken throughout their lives."

Maria dropped into a nearby chair, visibly shaken. "How can something so pervasive, so sinister occur right under our noses?"

"What are the missing person numbers on your planet, Maria?"

Maria looked at Inanna baffled.

"Let me help you. About 300,000 human beings go missing every year. The assumption is they all disappear by earthly causes because no other possibility is considered."

All my life, I've embraced knowing, Inanna. At this moment, I wish I didn't know."

"Not knowing is no protection, Maria. The *Book of Possibilities* states, 'Once the viper is spotted, denial becomes a failed strategy.' Humanity must release its denial."

"Maybe you're right, but knowing feels worse than not knowing. I feel so small and vulnerable and frightened."

"I warned you in Hawai'i. The truth is a dangerous thing. There's more."

"Let's hear it," Maria said stoically.

"Our leaders used fear of ecological catastrophe to convince the Anunnaki people to support the creation of Adamu—modern human beings. You were created to keep the gold flowing to Nibiru."

"How did you create us?" Maria asked.

"My father Enlil commanded the earth expedition. Uncle Enki managed the mines. The revolts by our soldiers created poor gold production. Their labor proved unreliable and the costs unsustainable. King Anu, my grandfather, considered abandoning the operation. Earth, Inc. meant everything to my father. He pressured Enki to find a solution."

"We were created as a source of cheap labor?"

"Essentially, genetics became the answer to an economic question."

Maria regained some of her fight. "That sounds unethical."

"There were great debates on Nibiru. Many believed genetically engineering a sentient race of slaves violated The Father Creator's Creed. Enki continued his work, while debates raged. When news reached home of his success, the debate was over."

"How exactly did Enki create Adamu?"

"Seven Anunnaki women volunteered to do their patriotic duty and mother the new race. Enki labored and experimented for 4320 days, seeking the right mix of Anunnaki DNA and Lulu DNA. There were numerous failures."

"What is Lulu?"

"Lulu was the dominant species of hominids present on Earth in those days. The name meant Earthling. After the demise of the Lemurians, Lulu was the most advanced species on the planet. Enki studied them in the wild and found them to be intelligent and sociable. They had fire, performed simple rituals, and buried their dead. The latter indicated a spiritual dimension."

"What do you mean by spiritual dimension?"

"There was a great debate as to whether Lulu had attained spiritual sentience. To do the proposed experiments on a creature having those characteristics was unthinkable. Enki convinced King Anu and the legislature that Lulu lacked spiritual sentience. He has regretted that deception ever since."

"And so he created human beings by mixing 50 percent Anunnaki DNA and 50 percent Lulu DNA?"

"It was not that simple. The desired outcome was a creature meeting very narrow parameters. The creature must be able to survive and multiply. Mastering those two characteristics alone took many rounds of trial and error. Secondly, the creature must be smart enough to mine gold and meet his own daily needs. Third, he must always feel inferior and less than the Anunnaki."

"You created a slave race!"

"And so we did, Maria. And so we did. We designed you to keep your head down and work all the days of your life. We created you obedient to us. We built you angry and afraid."

"We are still angry and afraid, Inanna. We are still conditioned little workers. Are we capable of no more?" asked Maria.

"We failed, Maria. We utterly failed. You are capable of so much more. In fact, the elite on Nibiru came to see human beings as a threat. Your potential, if ever realized, may exceed ours. They refuse to allow it. We denied you your connection to the divine, cutting you off from connection to The Father Creator and installing ourselves as your imperfect, angry, jealous gods. We re-engineered your DNA to shorten your original lifespan. We created you imperfect and dubbed you sinners because you missed the mark in every way."

"What a small and selfish people you are," condemned Maria.

"Maria, I—"

"No! Don't try to explain. How can you live with what you have done? How do you sleep at night knowing you are responsible for doing this and for perpetuating it?" asked Maria with disdain in her eyes.

"Oh, Maria. I can no longer. That's why I'm here. That's why I involved myself in your mother's pregnancy. That's why I designed you to be a person who would question and who would want to put a stop to this, once and for all."

"You want me to stop it?"

"I cannot intervene directly. You must do it yourselves, but

I can help you," said Inanna.

"What a comfortable chair that must be for you? You create this mess by your intervention and then absolve yourself of taking action to put it right?"

Inanna's Anunnaki blood began to boil a bit and she had to regain her composure. "You're right, Maria, but that's the way it is. That's the way it must be. Intervention placed humanity in this bind. More intervention can only do more harm."

"Yet, you intervened in my life. You did something . . . I don't even know what to think. You've brought me here and told me this fantastic story and left me wondering if there is any hope for my race."

Inanna knew she—and the Anunnaki—deserved every angry word Maria spewed. Though a human talking to her in that tone violated her very being, she held her temper and took it.

"I need this to be a human-led effort. The elite on my world are not going to change their ways until there is disclosure. Those humans who work for our elite and have maintained and profited from this secret are just as bad."

"And how do you propose that we expose it?"

"Maria. You are the White House correspondent for a major network. You are going to ask the president about this on national TV."

"That's your plan!" exclaimed an exasperated Maria.

"My Uncle Enki and I have worked on earth for decades to put all the right pieces in place to prepare for this moment. You're a White House correspondent. That's no accident. I need you to speak with some witnesses and build a case that you can take to the president."

"Inanna, I've asked only one question ever at a presidential press conference. You're saying I'm going to get to ask a question and that my question is going to be about . . . UFOs . . . alien abductions?"

"Maria, I have the evidence. I even have an eyewitness to history, if it comes to that point. The world perceives The President of the United States as the most powerful person on your planet. Ducking and denying the question is impossible on live ITV. This can work."

"Are you saying that President Paxton knows about this?"

"I'm not sure how much President Paxton knows. What he knows or doesn't know is irrelevant. Asking the question in such a high profile manner will garner public attention. One courageous moment could open the door on a new future for humanity. Maria, I believe in The Future Possible. I need you to believe in it too."

Maria eyed Inanna for a moment. "Your plan is risky. He could duck the question or he might not know anything."

"Maria, it is a chance we must take. Your species lives in a darkness it calls light. Knowing what you now know, can you allow the deception to continue?"

"Wouldn't it be easier if you just landed the Rakbu on the White House lawn?"

"Easier, perhaps, but the powers that be on both our worlds could twist direct contact into a war. We need irrefutable evidence. We need proof and we need it public."

"Whom do I talk to? How would I get this information?"

"My Uncle Enki has a contact deep inside U.S. Intelligence. His name is Cutler. He will direct you to the people holding the pieces of this puzzle. You will have to put those pieces together. When is your next presidential press conference?"

The blood suddenly drained from Maria's face. The president! She was supposed to meet him in San Diego. "What day is it, Inanna?"

"23 Earth hours have passed since you came aboard Rakbu."

"I need to get back to San Diego. My mother is going to—"

"Your mother will not realize how long you've been gone."

"How do you do that?"

"Let's just say that human memory is flexible and we can easily bend it when necessary."

"You don't miss anything, do you?"

"Well, I almost missed the president," Inanna smiled. "We will transport you to the hotel where we have booked your room."

"The next news conference is in Washington D.C. three weeks from tomorrow. We need Pete Rogers on board, if we're going to do this thing. He has to reassign me and buy off on asking the president about UFOs. He's going to be skeptical."

"As were you," reminded Inanna. "And now?"

"Now, I understand what you're telling me, but I feel like a tornado swept through and uprooted everything I thought I knew. It's exciting and terrifying all at once. What about Jack?"

"What about Jack?"

"Should I tell him? Can I tell him?"

"You have free will, Maria. You don't have to ask my permission. How is he going to react?"

"I don't know. He's religious and very dogmatic about it. This could upset him more than it upsets me. Maybe I shouldn't tell him yet?"

"That's up to you, Maria. Set up a meeting with Pete when you are finished in San Diego. Let's work together to persuade him. Maybe he'd like to tour Rakbu."

Maria smiled as she contemplated the expected confrontation with Pete.

"Maria, I would also like to have you back aboard the ship before we begin this . . . project. There is another layer to this—equally important—that I need you to understand."

"OK. Can you give me a hint?"

"God, Maria. God."

Maria went a bit cold again. Her face gave away her angst about God.

"I know it's a tough subject for you, but that's because you don't understand. I will explain. Transport up after Paxton's speech. Perhaps, you can join me for dinner. Six o'clock sharp Pacific Time."

Inanna had Maria hooked, but she maintained her poker face. "All right, Inanna. Dinner sounds wonderful."

"Splendid! Well, you must be off. Bridge," said Inanna into the air, "please transport Maria to room 317 at the San Diego Marriott. I . . . I love you, Maria."

The words shocked Maria, but she could feel Inanna's genuine affection for her. "Goodbye, Inanna. Thank you."

The bluish beam encapsulated Maria. This time the experience was more comfortable and she remained conscious through it. She materialized in her hotel room in San Diego.

What an exhausting 24 hours, she thought. *Love? Inanna loved her?*

Maria wasn't sure how she felt about Inanna, but love was not the word she would choose.

(14)
Maria's Doubt

Maria materialized in her San Diego hotel room. A mix of feelings rushed through her. She felt guilty for not telling Jack. She felt nervous about telling Pete. Asking these questions of the President of the United States terrified her. Still, the possibilities of the journey ahead excited her. For the first time in a long time, she felt like her life could make a real difference.

She weeded through the messages on her ComTab, locating three important text messages and a video message from Jack. Her mother wished her a great time at the journalism conference in La Jolla. She appreciated the note and expressed her sorrow that they missed each other this morning. Inanna came through with a cover story for her mother, as promised. The second text message came from a man named Cutler. Inanna alerted Maria to expect contact from him. He was her Uncle Enki's "deep throat" in U.S. intelligence and her contact for the eyewitness interviews. Inanna was quite efficient.

She tapped play on Jack's video message.

"Hey there, beautiful. Hope you had a great visit with your mom. I miss you so much. I'm not sure what was going on with you in Hawai'i. You know I know you too well not to notice. Whatever it is, let's talk about it when you get home. Good luck tomorrow and safe travels, my love."

He finished the video with a blown kiss. Tears came to Maria's eyes, as she blew a kiss back. Keeping secrets from Jack was the hardest part.

The third text message came from Cathy Sebring. She thanked Maria for convincing the boss to let them come to San Diego and proposed breakfast. Sebring was Maria's location director. During their five years working together, she became the closest friend and confidante Maria had at work. Cathy was a bit "out there"—always attending a séance or participating in a global meditation event. Maria planned to be cautious about sharing her experience, but Cathy was more likely than most to understand. Cathy's husband lacked ambition, preferring to live as a dull homebody. Maria believed Cathy pursued unusual topics as a way to spice up her life.

The clock read 8:03 PM. Maria decided to run a bath and try to unwind. The adventure of the past 24 hours left her craving normalcy. Normalcy felt like a warm blanket. When adversity came knocking, Maria wrapped herself tightly in it.

"Let's have some mood music. ComTab play music. John Boswell. Skye Boat Song."

Maria closed her eyes and melted into the warm bath water. The inky blackness of space engulfed her. The beautiful blue and white marble spun into view. Earth's continents and oceans passed in a constant blur of motion. Hours became days. Days became weeks. Weeks became millennia.

What a miracle, she thought. *Everything I've ever known or conceived happened on that tiny illuminated sphere in the midst of this eternal darkness.*

She experienced a profound connectedness to every person, every creature, and every inanimate object on the planet.

Our problems are so small and our differences even smaller. We make them so big—convert them into life and death. It's crazy.

Her vision shifted. Her sense of immensity waned and an overwhelming sense of helplessness consumed her. She stood face-to-face with the world's massive challenges and they towered above her. Doubt and fear seized her.

Who am I to ask these questions, much less demand these answers? Maybe I should be content with my career and the embrace of my wonderful husband. Assuming Inanna was everything she claimed to be, it offered no guarantee life on Earth would change. If Inanna could make a difference, why does she need me?

Maria felt panic move through her and, despite the warm water, a chill settled into her being. Her lips quivered, partly from the chill and partly from an uncertain trepidation. Sensing her weakness, the inner critic opened fire. Better people, smarter people, have tried to change this world before and failed. Many of them wound up ridiculed or dead. Is that what you want? Why risk it? Play it safe. Do your job. Love your husband. Enjoy your two weeks in Hawai'i every year. That is all there is!

For a moment, Maria considered listening to the voice and sliding neatly back into the herd. She could forget Inanna and this silly quest. She could go back to pretending all that mattered happened on this tiny blue marble. A foreign call chiming in on her ComTab interrupted the symphony of self-doubt and retreat.

She got out of the tub, slipped into her robe, and called out, "Music off. Phone answer."

A heavily accented voice greeted her. "Hello, Ma'am. Is this Ms. Maria Love?"

The voice sounded familiar, but Maria could not immediately place it.

"Yes, this is Maria," she replied curiously.

"Ms. Love, this is Jay Escudero. We met yesterday aboard the alien spacecraft."

"Yes! Jay. How are you? Please call me Maria."

"I am well, Maria, thanks to you," Escudero replied. "For the first time in my life, I'm not left with vague memories and feelings of post-abduction depression. This morning I remembered every moment. I owe you a thank you for that."

"Well, we humans have to stick together, don't we?" said Maria embarrassed by the corniness as it left her lips.

"Indeed! I am calling you because I have a proposition for you."

"OK."

"Are you familiar with the show America Overnight?"

"I've heard of it," Maria cautiously admitted.

Cathy Sebring talked about the show almost every morning, but Maria had never listened. The show perpetuated a counterculture of conspiracy. Scientists, politicians, and journalists like Maria were always hiding something in this world. These people had alternative explanations for everything from the pyramids to swine flu. "Normal people" (people like Maria Love) didn't have time for such nonsense. Considering the past 24 hours, could she now count herself among the crazy?

"Well, I am a regular guest on the show," confided Escudero.

Maria only managed, "Oh."

"I am a regular guest on the program. I have talked about my research on UFO abductions and ancient aliens many times. As soon as I woke up this morning, I contacted the show's producers. They asked me to come on the show later tonight, 12 P.M. U.S. time, to discuss my abduction. Would you join me to share your experiences too?"

Maria felt out of her depth. How did she go from respected White House correspondent to a sought after guest on shows about UFOs? "Jay, that is very kind of you, but—"

"It was your first time, wasn't it?" Jaypee stopped her.

"Ah . . . yes," admitted Maria.

"I thought so. I understand, Maria."

"How did you know that?"

"Even as you sat at the conference table with Inanna, your face expressed disbelief. I have worked with many abductees. I have seen that look many times. People knowing they had an experience, but thinking they were crazy for believing it. It never gets easier, but the first time leaves you in denial. Even I feel it a little bit today, remembering my abduction for the first time."

"It's not that. It's just that . . . well . . . I have a very prestigious job and—"

"I know. I Googled you. You are a White House correspondent for America's Next Network."

"I'm impressed."

"Maria, do you know how many executives, celebrities, and other famous people have these experiences: and keep them from the world?

"I'm not really that famous—"

"They are worried about how it will look to others. Does that worry you, Maria?"

"Maybe . . ."

"I believe famous people have a special responsibility to speak out on this topic. We live in a world where fame is a currency, Maria. You must use it to spread the word."

"Jay, I hear what you're saying—"

"If the cowards did not come in the night and erase our memories, more people would know about this from firsthand experience. Instead, they hide in the shadows and we sweep it beneath a rug. Don't you think every human being has a right to know?"

"Of course I do, Jay. I'm taking this one step at a time."

"Maria, your abduction was special. It wasn't like other abductions."

"Why do you say that?"

"I've worked with over 1,000 abductees. No human being, in my experience, sits on the same side of the table with the alien and calls the shots."

Maria chuckled. "No one calls the shots for Inanna. I felt compelled to stand up for you. Inanna seems to need me. I simply leveraged my advantage."

"Join me, Maria. You must. *Maging ang pagbabago na gusto mong makita sa mundo.*"

"That's beautiful, Jay. What does it mean?"

"Do you know the Gandhi philosophy? He told us to be the change we want to see in the world? You must be that change, Maria!"

Now Maria felt like a coward. She wanted to be the difference, but she felt the glare of society's gaze. Despite her experience, she felt glued to convention. "I'm just not ready to go public with this . . . yet."

Escudero changed the subject. "OK. OK. Forget about the program right now. You might find this exciting. This morning I received a call from a very wealthy Japanese businessperson. He's offered to become an angel investor in my work. He's not interested in ROI. He wants the truth."

"That's exciting, Jay! What's his angle?"

"He has been abducted at least three times. He is willing to fund travel, research, whatever it takes to get answers. Will you partner with me?"

"That's so generous, Jay. Why are you so sure I'm a good partner?"

"*Ito ay sa mga mata.* It is in the eyes. And, because you were sitting on the other side of the table calling the shots," Escudero replied.

Being a novice in the topic, Maria saw nothing unique about her abduction. In fact, she struggled with the word abduction.

Inanna invited her aboard Rakbu for a private conversation—nothing more. Abduction seemed an overstatement.

Maria liked Escudero. She didn't want him to offend him.

"How can we partner?" Maria asked.

"We can exchange information and expertise. I know this topic *pasulong at paatras* (forward and backward). I have financial backing and you have connections. Together, we can make a difference on this topic."

Maria agreed. If nothing else, she gained a friend she could speak openly with about the topic. They spent another 20 minutes exchanging information.

Maria shared the plan to interview witnesses with information that could prompt "Disclosure."

"Jay," Maria confessed, "I don't even know what "Disclosure" means."

Escudero chuckled, "Disclosure is the global attempt to force governments to admit their knowledge of extraterrestrial visitation of the earth. It's *basura* (garbage)! Sure, it would make all of this much easier, but we do not need to wait for the government. The evidence is all around us. We simply need the courage to look."

"I admire your passion, your courage, Jay."

"Courage is easy when it is you they have been taking in the night," Jay replied.

Maria elected not to share the plan to question President Paxton. Jay shared his background and some ideas on how to proceed with their partnership. He also proposed a meeting in the near future. He promised his investor would fund the travel.

The call ended with Jay thanking Maria again. "Those Z beings seemed dangerous. I do not know if they have abducted me before. It was very lucky that Inanna and you came along. Salamat!"

"You're welcome."

"I look forward to our partnership, Maria. Mabuhay!" Jay said zestfully.

"Thank you, my friend," Maria answered.

Jay's enthusiasm invigorated and inspired Maria. His call was a synchronicity landing in the middle of her doubts and dispelling them. Inanna warned of this journey's perils. Maria now felt ready and 100 percent committed to seeing this through to the end.

(15)
Radio Regression

Maria tossed and turned in bed. Thoughts raced through her mind about Inanna, Jay, Jack, her mother, and this whole crazy business. Normally, her mind fixated the night before a presidential event. Tonight the president seemed small compared to the past 24 hours. Sleep eluded her.

She called out from bed, "ComTab. Internet Radio. America Overnight."

[Heart pumping radio bumper music]

"Good evening and welcome to America Overnight. I'm your host, Greg Wise. Tonight our good friend, Dr. Jaypee Escudero, returns to the program. Since his last visit, Jay experienced an abduction that he partially remembers. We are going to talk to Jay about his experience and do a first-ever radio regression to help him remember the rest."

"Jay, my friend, how have you been?"

"Greg, I am doing well and I am excited to make history tonight."

"Are you in Manila?"

"No, actually, I'm in Honolulu for the MUFON convention happening here this week."

"We'll get to the regression in a moment, but tell me about your abduction experience."

"It was amazing, Greg! I do not remember the actual abduction. I hope tonight's regression will help me remember. What I do remember is waking up aboard an Anunnaki ship commanded by Inanna."

"That's incredible, Jay. Do you believe you actually met the Sumerian goddess Inanna?

"Yes, I believe I did."

In many years of doing this show, I've spoken to many people about the Anunnaki. I've never spoken to someone who has been aboard one of their ships."

"The story gets better, Greg. I met a well-known American reporter aboard Inanna's ship. They abducted her too. She interviewed me along with Inanna. In fact, she said my memory was being kept intact at her request."

"Can you tell us who the reporter is?" asked an excited Wise.

"I would really like to, Greg, but I promised her confidentiality."

As Maria lay in bed listening, she could not believe that she was a part of this story. How crazy was it for her to tell a seven-foot tall woman in command of a ship that could probably level cities what to do?

"You say she is well-known?" pursued Wise. "Are we talking a nationally known reporter?"

"I'm sorry, Greg, I just can't say any more to reveal her identity."

"I understand. How fascinating, though! What else *can* you share?"

"I told the reporter the Anunnaki had genetically engineered us."

"What did Inanna do?" Wise queried.

"She stood there, looking down on me. She was very tall—seven feet or more. When I started sharing what I knew with the reporter, she had me beamed back to my bed in Manila."

"So, help me understand, Jay. You were on the Anunnaki

ship, but they didn't abduct you?"

"That is what they told me. They said the Z abducted me, but Inanna's ship forced them to release me. I am hopeful the regression will tell us the rest of the story."

"Do you have a hypnotherapist there with you? Are you ready to begin?" asked Wise.

"We are ready," replied Jaypee.

The hypnotherapist put Jaypee under with a series of relaxation techniques and some backward counting. When the hypnotherapist believed Jaypee had reached a relaxed state, she began asking questions. Millions in the America Overnight audience listened.

"Jay, I want you to go back to the evening of May 20. Do you remember that evening?"

"Yes."

"Tell me about it."

"I taught a full afternoon of classes. Afterwards, I met with one of my abductee clients and we discussed one of her recent experiences."

"Very good. Now let's go later into that evening. You're now at home. What do you remember?"

"I'm eating dinner. It's getting dark outside. It's dark very early tonight. I think I will go to bed."

"Do you remember going to bed?"

"Yes. I am laying there thinking about the day and . . . ," he paused.

"Jay, what is it?"

"*Aking Diyos! Aking Diyos!*"

"Jay, can you tell me in English?"

"They are here!" he shouted.

"Who is here, Jay?"

"Them! Aking Diyos!" Jay sobbed.

"Jay, I'm going to count backward from five to one. When I reach one, you will be able to calmly tell me what is going on. OK?" Five, four, three, two, one. I have counted one, Jay. You are completely safe. Please tell me what you see."

"They are all around my bed. They have come for me," he sobbed.

"Who, Jay?"

"The soulless ones."

"Can you describe them?"

"They are short and gray and they have large eyes. *Tulungan akong!* They're in my mind!"

"Jay, have you seen them before?"

"Yes. Oh, ang aking Diyos! Mangyaring, tulungan ako!"

"Ito ay ang OK, Jay. You're OK, Jay. What is happening?"

"We are floating . . . upwards . . . like a leaf falling from a tree, but upwards. Oh! We're on their ship."

"Can you describe where you are?"

"I am on my back. I can't . . . move. There are bright lights in my eyes and forms moving around over me. It is them. *Oh tae! Oh tae!* They are probing me! *Oh tae!* It hurts!"

"Stay with me, Jay. Where are they probing you?"

"My abodomen. *Masakit kaya masama!*"

"Jay, I know it hurts. What's happening now?"

"They are in my mind. They are telling me we will all die."

"Who will die, Jay?"

"All of us. They plan to kill all of us! They want me to be afraid."

"Are you afraid, Jay?"

"Yes. They will do it. They are going to kill me!"

"Jay, you are OK."

"No! I am not OK! Wait . . . something is happening. I feel a warm tingling sensation. I'm not on their ship anymore."

"Where are you?"

"I don't know. There is a very large humanoid standing over me. He seems friendly . . ."

Jay suddenly jumped out of trance. He was shaking and sweating, but he had no memory of the regression.

"Did it work?" he asked.

"Jay, my friend. This is Greg Wise. Are you OK? That was the most incredible thing I have ever heard?"

Maria was laying in bed absolutely wrapped up in Jay's experience. She felt his pain and angst. *This is real, she thought. I. . . we cannot pretend it's not.* She felt so sorry for Jay, but felt proud Inanna rescued him.

Greg Wise, clearly worried about his friend, said, "Let's take a break and talk when we come back." (Heart pounding bumper music).

Maria ignored the commercials. She felt an absolute connection to Jay. Who were these Z and why were they doing this to human beings? Inanna said her government allowed it and our government too. What a sick and twisted system. And our entire species living in the dark and in denial about the whole thing!

"This cannot continue," she said aloud.

Maria was interrupted by the bumper music—Van Halen's "Love Walks In."

"We are back," Wise said over the bumper music. "Before the break we did a first-ever live regression of our friend Jaypee Escudero. Jay, are you there?"

"I am here, Greg."

"I know you haven't had a chance to listen to the recording yet, but how was that for you?"

"Very stressful. I have a much better understanding of some of my subjects now."

"Do you remember anything?"

"I just remember being terrified and seeing images of everyone on Earth dying."

"What did you see?"

"The images were disjointed. I did not understand them. I just had a complete sense of dread. It was like judgment day."

"And then you seemed to be transported aboard the Anunnaki ship towards the end?"

"I'm not sure. I think so."

"Jay, we have always heard the Anunnaki can be rather unfriendly towards humans. Why do you think they helped you?"

"I do not know, Greg. I hope to have a conversation with my reporter friend soon. Maybe she can help me understand."

Maria felt a strong need to follow up with Jaypee and share more with him now. She suddenly realized not sharing and not participating was not an option. We were all in this together.

"Greg, I would love to be on again soon to discuss this, but I hope you understand I need to rest."

"Of course, Jay. Thank you so much for your willingness to conduct a live regression. It was riveting radio, but I know someone out there having these experiences was inspired by your courage."

Maria rolled over, her mind going here and then there. No more! This can't go on. If Inanna is giving me the opportunity to make a difference, I must do it! She faded off to sleep with a determination to change the course of human history, if that was her destiny.

(16)
Cathy Sebring

Maria awoke, drained of the previous night's bold determination. She again felt weak, vulnerable, and doubtful about her supposed pivotal role in history. *From superhuman to human in six hours,* she thought.

Preparation for the president's San Diego appearance provided a minor distraction. What did it matter? She was not going to get a question anyway.

How negative, Maria caught herself. *According to Inanna, something is going to change in the next few weeks and I'm going to be asking some of the most dramatic questions anyone ever asked a president.*

For today, though, she figured to maintain her obscurity.

Maria agreed to meet location director, Cathy Sebring, for breakfast. Sebring had a reputation for being . . . well . . . out there. They had worked together for several years and Maria knew she held some crazy beliefs. After the past three weeks, Maria's definition of crazy was narrowing.

"Good morning, Cathy," Maria smiled as she approached the table.

"Good morning, sunshine," responded Cathy, returning the smile.

"How did you sleep?" asked Maria.

"I never sleep well on the road. Besides, America Overnight captured me and never released me. You should have heard. They conducted a live hypnotic regression on a Filipino UFO abductee. It was wild! Did you hear it?"

Maria reflected on how many times she had avoided these conversations with Sebring. "As a matter of fact, I did."

"Did you hear the part about meeting a reporter on the ship? That's . . . out there. He said she was a well-known female reporter. Who do you think? Maybe Katie Couric?"

"It's hard to imagine a well-known reporter being on an alien space ship," Maria played along. "Do you believe his story, Cathy?"

"Why would someone lie about a thing like that?" asked Cathy with complete innocence.

"Well, I don't know. I just mean—"

"Can you imagine it, Maria . . . actually being on a space ship and talking to aliens? What would you ask them?"

Maria smiled uncomfortably. "I guess you would never know unless it happened to you."

"I know. I'd want to understand everything they know about the universe and why we're here."

"How do you know they have those answers?" asked Maria.

"Oh, they do!" Sebring assured. "Next I'd want to know how long they've been visiting Earth and how they can help our species escape its adolescence."

"You've obviously given this a lot of thought," Maria credited.

"Absolutely. Haven't you?"

"No . . . not really. I mean, it's interesting and all, but—"

"Maria, it's a big universe out there. Don't tell me you believe it's all here just for us?"

"Well . . . so . . . so, you believe in UFOs and aliens and abductions?"

"Absolutely. People focus on the abductions. They have other ways to communicate with us."

"Really?"

"Oh, yes! I belong to this group back in D.C. There's a woman who channels an alien named Zegatron. Zegatron's race is genderless."

"That's certainly different."

"They're a highly advanced civilization in the Pleiades system—probably a Type III or Type IV civilization," Sebring enthused.

"Type III or Type IV?" Maria questioned.

"You mean you've never heard of the Kardashev Scale for measuring the relative advancement of civilizations?"

"Um . . . I guess I missed that," Maria replied, feeling out of step.

"Nikolai Kardashev was a Soviet astronomer. He devised his scale in 1964, as a way to categorize alien civilizations. He suggested using a civilization's mastery of energy as a measure. There are actually astronomers searching for evidence of civilizations that might be harnessing the power of an entire galaxy."

Maria sat and stared, perplexed and mesmerized by Sebring's excited description.

"Zegatron's race builds no spaceships. They commune with sentient species throughout the universe, using only the power of thought. They connect with us when our minds are in a relaxed state—like in meditation. A civilization like that has to be Type IV or above."

Maria felt relieved that Sebring was still a little further on the fringe than her. "So, what do you know about the Anunnaki?"

"The Anunnaki were the ancient council of 12 gods found in nearly every ancient culture in the near east and the Mediterranean. Supposedly, they come from a planet called Nibiru," Sebring explained.

"Were they real beings or just myths?"

"Most experts think they were just myths, but I think that's crazy. How can so many cultures know about the same beings and it be just a myth?"

"I don't know. Maybe one group conquered another group and—"

"C'mon, Maria, be realistic," Sebring interrupted. "Obviously, these were real beings."

"What happened to them? Are they still here?"

"It's a mystery. No one knows. There were two brothers Enki and Enlil. They came to Earth searching for natural resources—especially gold. Enki created human beings and tried to educate and civilize us." Enlil demanded we worship him as a god. He destroyed humans more than once. When that failed to keep us down, he confused our languages to prevent us from working together to challenge him."

"Wow. What a nice guy," Maria mused. "And you believe all this actually happened?"

"Of course. There's too much evidence to deny it."

"What about Enki?" asked Maria nonchalantly, hoping to learn more about Inanna's uncle.

"Enki is really interesting and very controversial," said Sebring.

"How so?"

"Well, some believe Enlil had Enki depicted as the devil in the ancient stories, as punishment for trying to share knowledge with the humans," Sebring said.

She leaned in and whispered, "Some people even think the story of Eve in Genesis is a story about Enki trying to help humans attain knowledge. The story was later twisted by Enlil's supporters to personify Enki as the devil."

"Why would he do that to his brother?"

"Enlil was a megalomaniac. He craved worship and demanded to be humanity's only god. He felt threatened by his brother and other Anunnaki. He discredited them at every opportunity."

"That's fascinating, Cathy. You know so much."

"I've read and studied this information for years."

Maria changed the subject, satisfied she wasn't crazy. "Well, it's not Enki or Enlil we have to worry about today. It's President Paxton. Let's get prepped."

(17)
Evening in New Delhi

"Please pass the *biryani*," Sanjay Singh asked his eldest brother.

His mother's *biryani* embodied home cooking for him. As an esteemed professor in ancient language and culture at Delhi University, Sanjay could afford the progressive nuclear family lifestyle preferred by many middle class Indians. Instead, he maintained a traditional living arrangement—sharing a house with parents, siblings, in-laws, nieces, and nephews.

His family was a well-known banking and business family in New Delhi, but Singh chose the academic route. They practiced Hinduism devoutly. Sanjay attended services and observed holidays with his family, but he faked it more than he believed. He was a scientist and an academic. Both often cast him in the role of family black sheep. Sanjay's father (Manish) lived to discuss philosophy at the dinner table.

"Sanjay," began Manish, "You have been silent lately about your work. Do you find it unfulfilling?"

"No, baba. I am engaged in a most puzzling project—deciphering ancient tablets for the U.S. government."

"The U.S. government?" his father quizzed.

"Yes. The work fascinates, but our results to date defy logic. The project is classified. I can share no more."

"And everything must be logical, Sanjay?" asked his father, not waiting for the answer. "That is the trouble with the western mind. It deludes itself by dividing things until they make no sense. Here is spirituality. There is logic. Here is science. There is God. The Hindu mind finds the unity in it all."

"Baba, this is an old argument and I do not wish to renew it now," answered Sanjay.

"Simply stated, if you would pursue spiritual practice with as much vigor as you pursue science, answers might come to you," badgered Manish.

"I must be careful what I share, but we are analyzing tablets that seem to predate human civilization. Yet, they contain references to advanced scientific and technical concepts. It's baffling."

"There is your western thinking again, Sanjay. Your science is in conflict, not with the facts, but with the facts your science says are true. What of our ancient texts?"

"What of them, baba?" Sanjay replied with frustration.

"They plainly state civilizations date back much further than the few thousand years your science believes. The writings vividly detail technologically advanced beings in those times. How do you account for that?"

"Baba, please. I am a scientist. I research these subjects with a scientist's eye. Clearly, these texts are mythological and not based in fact."

"You need proof? You doubt the wisdom of our sacred texts unless you can weigh and measure it. You cannot weigh wisdom. Lord Vishnu manifests the proof everywhere you look, Sanjay."

"Perhaps, for you, baba. I want to believe, but subjective interpretations of reality are not scientifically valid. I do need proof."

"What would you accept as proof, putra? Must Shiva fly in the sky above you? Must he destroy a city?"

The rest of the family was becoming uncomfortable. Sanjay's mother asked him if he would like some more dalcha, hoping to change the subject.

"Thank you, but no, ma. Is it so wrong, baba, to demand proof? Is it so wrong not to believe even if a hundred generations have? Science nobly pursues truth through investigation and observation."

"Observation, Sanjay! Truth cannot be observed. The truth is experienced here and now through the ancient texts and our feeling of connection to Lord Vishnu."

Sanjay concealed the emotions welling within him. "I want to believe, baba, but I need to see to believe."

"You have been corrupted by the western mind," Manish threw his hands in the air. "There is no hope for you."

"Manish," began Sanjay's mother.

"Chandra, do not defend him. There is no defense. He chooses a mind of division over a mind that finds union with God."

"And what union with God is there in these arguments, Manish?" Chandra replied. "You find your union in the Temple. Sanjay finds his in science. Is one superior to the other?"

"He will find no union with God so long as he continues to study the world by dividing it. He must realize that God is within him and he is within God," argued Manish.

"There are many paths to that realization, baba," Sanjay replied. "My mind is such that I must see. I hope, one day, that I will see. Until that day, I will continue to search."

"God stares you in the face and still you search?"

"My mind cannot accept God as merely a concept. I must know who he is and I must know why he deserves my reverence."

"Fool," Manish shouted and left the table.

Sanjay's youngest nephew began crying. Sanjay excused himself from the table. Why did he allow his father to drag him into these debates? He always felt dirty after their fights. He grabbed his ComTab, left the house, and walked down to the end of his block.

He texted his friend, Rohan. Dr. Rohan Anand was a Professor of Astronomy at the university and friend since childhood. "Where are you? I need to be out of the house tonight."

"Café Coffee Today," replied Anand. "Join me."

Sanjay turned right at the bus stop and walked three blocks to the neighborhood coffee shop. He found Rohan seated in a back corner, ComTab open and studying star charts on an app.

"Sanjay," Rohan stood and embraced his friend, "how are you?"

"I'm well. I just experienced another culture clash with my father. I needed some distance from him."

"I ordered a coffee for you. Come sit down. What was the argument about?"

"The same old debate. I have abandoned our traditional ways in favor of western science."

"He sees the old India. You see the new. The nation moves forward with science and reason, not on superstition."

"I wonder," Sanjay began pensively, "is there not room for both the scientific and the spiritual? What would you do if Shiva appeared in the sky and destroyed a city?"

Anand laughed heartily. "I would take cover and then I would use science to determine what happened. I certainly would not fall back into superstition."

"What about when evidence contradicts established facts?"

"Sanjay, we are friends since we were small boys. I know when something troubles you. What is it?"

"I am working on a U.S. government project classified Top Secret. I cannot share the details, but we have uncovered tablets firmly dated hundreds of thousands of years before modern humans existed, at least according to current science."

Anand stared seriously at Sanjay. "So, the dating is wrong?"

"No. We have confirmed and reconfirmed with the latest dating techniques. The ages are valid."

"Then it must be a hoax?"

"These are the genuine articles. Besides, the tablet text describes advanced knowledge—genetics, astronomy, and other sciences," Sanjay said.

"The facts are puzzling," replied Rohan, "but science will find the answer. You don't need to invoke Shiva. Your father would invoke Shiva and so he remains trapped in the dark ages."

Sanjay proceeded gingerly. "What are your thoughts on Intervention Theory?"

"I am unfamiliar with that theory."

"The theory does not necessarily discount Darwinian evolution or deny intelligent design. It states human genetics were accelerated by an outside force."

"Outside force?" questioned Anand, his eyebrow raised.

"Our project leader hired a consultant to help us solve the conundrum. She believes someone or something genetically modified evolving proto-humans accelerating our evolution. She believes the tablets are evidence of it."

"Ridiculous! He should reject her theory as pseudo-science. From where could such intervention have come?"

With almost embarrassment, Sanjay looked to the sky and back at Anand.

"Sanjay," implored Anand, "I don't need to detail the reasons that conclusion is impossible, do I?"

Sanjay recited what he'd heard his friend declare many times. "No physical object can travel faster than the speed of light. The fuel needed to approach the speed of light is more than a spacecraft could carry. The distances are too great and physical hazards from dark matter make interstellar travel far too dangerous. Any advanced species would have understood this and given up long ago."

"Well stated, professor," Anand complimented with sarcasm.

"I've heard you express it many times, my friend. The logic seems irrefutable and so I have accepted it as fact."

"It is more than a statement of logic. It is a statement of the fundamental limits of the universe."

"How can we be sure, Rohan?"

"Mathematics, observation, common sense. Saying extraterrestrials did it, is as backward as saying Shiva did it. There is another explanation—a scientific explanation. You must continue searching for it."

"You don't believe extraterrestrials exist out there?"

"Whether they exist out there or not is irrelevant. They could not come here. I guarantee it. Your results are obviously troubling you and you're allowing your father to affect your reasoning. Keep following the science."

"And if Shiva suddenly appears in the sky?" laughed Sanjay.

"If Shiva suddenly appears in the sky," laughed Anand, "I will renounce astronomy and join an ashram."

(18)
Sloane McKay

Sloane McKay entered her dark 23rd floor Manhattan apartment and called, "Lights. Rossini. The Barber of Seville Overture."

The room brightened and Rossini's famous score energized the apartment. Sloane slipped into silk pajamas and returned to the living room. She poured herself a glass of Sauvignon Blanc and settled on the couch to review Holcomb's tablet images. There were more images than she anticipated—hundreds of them.

"ComTab, slow scan images," Sloane commanded.

The images slid past one at a time. "ComTab, reduce scan speed by ten percent."

Many images displayed symbols and writing incomprehensible to her. She scanned the images and sipped her wine.

"ComTab, freeze on image 63 and zoom," Sloane said, sitting straight up. "What the . . . ?"

She scrutinized an image displaying multiple double helixes represented by entwined snakes. Embedded in each double helix was a six-sided polygon with lines protruding from it. The lines connected to a smaller block containing the characters ME. Each double helix had a different number of ME symbols attached to it. The symbol might appear meaningless to the untrained eye. To Sloane McKay, they unmistakably referenced DNA methylation.

Studying that tablet and the next several, she arrived at a

startling conclusion. Genes, in her experience, were either expressed or repressed—turned on or turned off. Methylation typically locks genes in the off position. These images appeared to depict methylation being applied to dial genes up or down. That shouldn't be possible.

"ComTab," she said. "Access Global Genome Project database. Authorization SMKY98C. Enable."

"Authorization confirmed," replied the interface.

"Search. Can methylation control the degree of gene expression rather than just repressing it?"

"Searching database. All established evidence indicates the methylation always blocks gene expression," replied the database interface.

"Search theoretical."

"All current peer-reviewed data indicates that methylation silences gene expression. Three studies are currently underway around the world to study your question. Would you like to see peer-reviewed papers?"

"No. Scan all data, peer-reviewed or not. Is there any evidence for proportional genetic expression in methylated genes?"

"Working. One current paper indicates this may be possible. However, no mechanism to explain it or demonstrate it has been found."

"Speculate, based on all data. If this were possible, what might cause it?"

"All naturally known methylated genes are silent. Some genes become unmethylated in certain circumstances and return to a methylated state. Even in this case, the gene is either methylated or it is not. Therefore, the only possible explanation for partial methylation is genetic tampering."

Sloane was flush with excitement. "Hypothesize. Could we achieve this with current technology?"

"Negative. It would require advanced knowledge of the precise mechanisms at play between the gene, the methyl, and RNA. It would also require surgical techniques beyond current capabilities."

"Query . . . has the human genome been scanned for partial methylation of genes?"

"Negative."

"Are you able to scan the database and identify partial methylation?"

"Affirmative."

"Do it!"

"Working. There is evidence of partial methylation throughout the genome. It is focused in DNA residing in desert areas on certain chromosomes."

"The desert areas," Sloane said to herself. "Based on all current knowledge of chromosomal influence on individual attributes, what attributes would be most affected by the chromosomes where you detected partial methylation?"

"Working. Physical appearance. Physical size. Intelligence. Brain size. Skin pigmentation. Aging. Mental attributes: fear, loyalty, the need to fit into a social structure, need for structure."

"Hypothesize. Describe an individual with all of these DNA attributes unmethylated and switched on."

"Working. Such an individual would be 120 to 150 percent taller than the average human being, extremely pale-skinned, double the raw intelligence of the average human being, and with a self-actualized need to be in control. The individual would have an extremely extended lifespan."

Sloane sat back in her chair and slowly exhaled through her mouth.

"Take the activated DNA species as a baseline and compare

it to average human DNA. What epigenetic factors could potentially be inherited into the human genome from the base species?" queried Sloane.

"Working. Violent tendencies. Jealousy. Greed. Self-centeredness. The base species is self-righteous and highly judgmental. Its spiritual capacity and ability to love and demonstrate compassion are deficient compared to humans."

"Hypothesize. Based on current theories of environmental influence on genetic and epigenetic gene expression, define the environment of the base species."

"Data is limited. The margin of error is high."

"Fine. Continue."

"The base species exists in an environment that compares with Earth in the following ways. More gravity. Less light. Less radiation. Less oxidation."

"Excellent. Logout."

Sloane McKay was a rebel. She believed in intervention in the human past. She believed the gods were not gods at all, but fallible beings just like us. Now she believed she had a description of the suspect.

(19)
Dinner and God

Despite the excitement and revelations in recent days, Maria's stomach knotted at the thought of discussing God. Why did that word shake her so? She verged on conceding alien intervention in human origins, but the word God triggered defense mechanisms within her.

Despite her misgivings about the topic, Maria eagerly anticipated her reunion with Inanna. She started angry with Inanna and now their connection was . . . palpable. Maria felt their bond even standing in her hotel room. Her big questions remained partially answered, but Inanna had shifted the conversation in extraordinary directions. *I must remain objective*, she thought.

As always, Inanna was punctual. Maria felt the tickle of the bluish light seize her precisely as her ComTab turned 6:00. She materialized in an extravagant, yet intimate, dining room aboard the Rakbu. She sat facing Inanna, as a servant finished placing their meals in front of them.

"Good evening, Maria. Welcome to my private dining quarters."

"Very nice," affirmed Maria.

Maria scanned the room. The wall behind Inanna featured a large royal-looking seal, depicting Inanna's queenship over heaven and earth. Gold inlaid images laced the marble walls. They reminded Maria of Sumerian depictions of the gods from her undergrad days.

"I hope you enjoy seafood. I had Chilean Sea Bass transported aboard fresh this afternoon. It is a particular favorite of mine."

"I love seafood. Thank you, Inanna."

"Would you like a metabolism pill?" Inanna asked.

"A metabolism pill?"

"Yes. Your bodies are quite inefficient at metabolizing food. The pill helps."

"Your body is more efficient?"

"We absorb virtually all we consume. There is little waste and we need not eat as often as human beings."

"If we share your DNA, why the difference?"

"Maria, you must understand you were consciously made inferior to Anunnaki. Your bodies are less efficient and your brains less developed. You require more sleep, more food, and your lifespans are greatly reduced."

"How often do you eat and sleep?"

"A healthy Anunnaki eats about one meal every three days. We sleep a few hours each week. The drawback is we don't dream. Dreaming was an accidental benefit of your increased need for sleep."

"You don't dream at all?"

"No. How's your fish?" Inanna changed the subject.

"Fishing from space must be an interesting experience," Maria smiled.

"It's actually easier for us than for a human fisherman. Our scanners are equipped with the DNA signature of virtually every creature on Earth. We simply input the fish species. The scanners locate options in a few seconds and we transport the fish right out of the ocean and into our holding tank," explained Inanna.

"And all without a fishing permit," chuckled Maria.

"A fishing permit?" queried a confused Inanna.

"It's a joke."

"Ah. I have come to enjoy the human sense of humor, but I have never mastered it," said Inanna.

"I've seen you smile, but you never laugh, Inanna. Do the Anunnaki not have a sense of humor?"

"We are a very stoic people, Maria. Even common Anunnaki are that way. We royals, well, most of the fun has been bred right out of us."

"I think having fun is an important part of life," shared Maria.

"You have to understand, Maria. Our civilization developed against the odds on a world far less hospitable than the earth and orbiting a star far less energetic than your sun. Life on Nibiru was much harder in our ancient times than on Earth. It's a miracle we survived to become a technological civilization. Our civilization had little time for fun."

"That's sad, Inanna. I feel sorry for you. How far back does your civilization reach?"

"We have written records stretching back 11.5 million earth years. That goes back to a time similar to earth's stone age."

"And how long have you been traveling around in ships like this one?"

"It is recorded that we began interplanetary travel about 3 million years ago. We launched our first interstellar craft about 2.7 million years ago. We quickly learned the universe's biggest secret."

"What secret was that?"

"We were not alone. Our mythologies never mentioned other species. They were Nibiru-centric. We thought we were the apex of creation—the lone sentient race in the universe. We believed The Father Creator manifested this universe just for the Anunnaki."

"The bass is delicious," said Maria. "What happened when you encountered other beings for the first time?"

"Some on Nibiru feared them—believing them a threat to our traditional ways. Others looked at their technology and abundance as a way to pull Nibiru forward into the future. Eventually, we created relations with a few other worlds and joined a small galactic confederation."

"The Anunnaki aren't the most advanced species around?"

"By the Seven Stars, no! Many races are far superior technologically. Other races are beyond the need of technology. They control their environments completely with thought. We filled a needed niche—a niche that eventually made us powerful and feared."

"What was that niche?"

"We are very sturdy creatures—strong and stoic—as you pointed out. We became the perfect hired military muscle in the galaxy. When planets went to war, they hired Anunnaki mercenaries. This allowed us to amass the best military technology from around the known galaxy. We used it to increase our influence and our power."

"It's fascinating how similar you sound to humans . . . in your flaws, I mean. Sorry, that came out the wrong way," said Maria, sipping and swallowing a bigger gulp of wine than she'd planned.

"No," waved Inanna, "It's a fair charge. The apple does not fall far from the tree. You have much of us in you. When our DNA became your DNA, many of our flaws became your flaws."

"What is life like on Nibiru? What are average people like?"

"The Anunnaki are extremely long-lived by human standards, but many lead unfulfilled lives," Inanna shared with regret.

"Unfilled? How?" Maria pursued.

"Living so long and having technology to do practically everything for you is no panacea. Over time, a sense of meaningless sets in. How many sunsets can you watch? How many books can you read? When you live that long in a single form, you've seen everything and done everything. Life becomes a bore."

"Sounds dreadful," Maria offered. "How long can you live?"

"Technically, there is no upper limit. The average lifespan is about 500,000 earth years. A few people have lived close to 900,000 years."

"That's incredible! How have you extended your lifespans so much?"

"We have the technology to synthesize organs as easily as you make a photocopy. An Anunnaki my age has worn out countless hearts, renal organs—practically every system in our bodies has been replaced many times."

"I would think," replied Maria, "that living so long would open opportunities to explore life's meaning or achieve every dream."

"There is that human optimism," Inanna complimented, "Marvelous! We Anunnaki do not view life in that way. Most Anunnaki are happy only when they are fighting or meditating," said Inanna.

"That's an odd combination. Most meditators on Earth aren't fighters."

"By fighters, I don't necessarily mean warriors—though that's one persistent manifestation. We have to be fighting for something or against someone. It's in our blood. We draw energy from dispute and the negative emotions it generates. We expected humans to share this characteristic, but conflict seems to decimate the human spirit. You seek ways around or beyond conflict."

"I don't know. We seem to thrive on conflict," argued Maria.

"You often find yourselves in conflict, but you do not relish it as we do."

"And how does meditation fit into the equation?"

"For the Anunnaki, meditation is means of spiritual and scientific discovery. We quiet the mind, tapping into the field of pure potentiality," Inanna said.

"What do you mean by the field of pure potentiality?"

"How shall I explain this?" Inanna wondered. "What is in our universe is, Maria. We refer to that experience as reality. However, everything that *is not* exists in the field of pure potentiality—always ready to become reality. Do you understand?"

"Hmm. Can you give me an example?"

"Reality is a realm for the senses. Potentiality is a realm of the imagination. Our minds are gateways connecting us to these realms. Consider the automobile or your ComTab. Before their invention, neither was part of reality. They existed only as potential realities."

"OK."

"The inventor, using imagination and mind, taps into that potential, and manifests a new reality. In the field of pure potentiality, both always existed."

"So, our minds transform potentiality into reality?"

"Precisely. It's true of things and ideas. One mind manifests a thing—making it real. Moving from real to transformative requires many minds. The *Book of Possibilities* says, 'One awakened mind begins a revolution. Many awakened minds begin an evolution.' The change we seek on our two worlds, Maria, it's an evolution."

"I've never considered the world in those terms before, Inanna. Not to be morbid, but you mentioned the exceptional Anunnaki lifespan. What does kill you?"

Inanna stopped. Maria was shocked to see a tear sparkling in her eye. "Of course, we can be killed by violent acts if organs are beyond repair. We are vulnerable to a few diseases. Eventually, even with replacement organs, we cannot keep the brain functioning. We've been unable to synthesize a brain capable of imbuing consciousness. When our brains die, we die."

Maria pondered Inanna's description of her people. "I always thought living forever would be wonderful. Surely, there must be ways for your people to find meaning."

"If you lived for hundreds of thousands of earth years, Maria, where would your motivation come from? Many of our people drift for tens of thousands of years simply because they have time to drift. There is no impetus to achieve anything. They readily lose themselves in the fiction of the synthworlds—"

"What's a synthworld?"

"A highly advanced and persistent virtual reality, running on a massive government computer called The Grid. My brother, the King, instituted synthworlds. Officially, they provide meaning and diversity in the lives of our people," said Inanna.

"And unofficially?" Maria questioned.

"They are a relentless indoctrination feed. Shortly after birth, we plug children into The Grid. Many lose the ability to distinguish synthworlds from the real world."

"That's shocking! Parents allow their children to be plugged into a network?" Nobody sees that as a problem?" Maria accused.

"My people have sold their souls to be perpetually entertained," replied Inanna.

"You call yourselves an advanced civilization? How do people act in the real world to change things or better life?"

"They don't. That's the beauty of it from my brother's perspective. When my government needs warriors, scientists, or someone for any purpose, they disconnect them. My people are conditioned to believe disconnection is a great honor. When they are disconnected from that grid, we function as normally as you."

"Is your crew connected?" accused Maria.

"Absolutely not!" Inanna bristled. "I have granted them complete freedom. They are here because they choose to be here."

"What about culture? Do you have music?"

"Music is for the young. How many times can you listen to the same songs?"

"Are your children educated?" Maria asked.

"They have access to all the carefully contrived knowledge their brains can absorb. The Anunnaki live in a benevolent dictatorship run by a small elite class and led by the royal family—my family," Inanna said raising her wine glass in mock salute.

Maria noted Inanna's sarcasm. "So, there is no free flow of information?"

"None. The average Anunnaki knows exactly what the elite wants him or her to know about any topic. Babies are 'ported' immediately following birth and the indoctrination begins."

"Ported?" Maria questioned.

"Babies—non-elite babies—have ports inserted into their necks. These ports create an interface between their brains and the synthworlds."

"What about news and entertainment?"

"The Anunnaki are force-fed synthworld entertainment to distract them from important issues of the day. They are experts on the trivial. They know every statistic from the games and the birthdate of every entertainer. Their minds are filled with all the information one could ever want along with the disinformation that keeps them under the thumb of our elite."

"I don't understand. Your government practices censorship?" Maria condemned.

"Censorship?" Inanna mused. "We don't practice censorship in the way you mean it. The elite tightly control the entire body of knowledge available to ordinary Anunnaki. Removing yourself from The Grid without government approval is a capital offense. When they are awake, the government is beaming approved synthworlds and information into the brains of every citizen. People even communicate with each other through The Grid."

"How do you eat, sleep, or complete other . . . necessary functions?"

"The port is a wireless *anywhere* connection. People move around in the ordinary world and interact with it. The synthworlds are beamed into their brains wirelessly wherever they go. All public and private communication must happen through The Grid."

"That doesn't sound very private."

"There's no privacy. All communication belongs to the government. Everything is monitored, tracked, and recorded. Thoughts and words can be crimes. Many of my crew came to work for me to escape The Grid."

"I'm not following, Inanna. How do you interact with the outside world while you're connected to The Grid?"

"The Grid has an internal and external setting. Internal begins the synthworld feed directly into your mind. External stops the synthworld feed, allowing you to interact with your environment. In this mode, The Grid becomes a listening as well as an analysis system. Our government records every word of every conversation. The speaker's inflection is analyzed and his thoughts scanned for hidden meaning."

"Who is analyzing this information and why?" asked Maria.

The government—actually the royal and noble class on Nibiru—uses The Grid to identify any subversive words or thoughts that might pose a threat to them. They sold The Grid to people as a security feature. Parents were promised someone would always know where their children were and what they were thinking."

"Talk about Big Brother!" Maria squawked. "Why don't people rise up against that kind of tyranny?"

"It is all people have known on Nibiru for millions of earth years. This is why The Human Question is so difficult to address on Nibiru. The Elites profit from humanity's current situation. They have used The Grid to convince our people humans are dangerous and need to remain controlled."

"Even if you can pull off your plan on Earth," worried Maria, "How do you plan to change things on Nibiru?"

"Plans are in place to address Nibiru. The first order of business must be to bring humanity out of the dark. We must have full disclosure."

"Your plan seems backwards to me!" Maria protested. "You can disclose all you want to humanity. What good is it, if Nibiru remains dysfunctional?"

"I'm happy to hear your passion for the topic," Inanna said, beaming with pride at Maria's tenacity, "but Nibiruan politics was not what I brought you here to discuss."

"Right. You wanted to talk to me about . . . God," offered Maria, not believing she was reminding Inanna.

"Yes. In our culture, we call him The Father Creator."

"You know he exists . . . and . . . and you believe in him?" Maria cautiously asked.

"He exists. Belief is not necessary," Inanna assured.

"Does everyone on Nibiru know he exists?"

"Many in my culture have pushed aside The Father Creator

and our connection to him. They believe science, technology, and mathematics solve the mysteries of existence."

"Maybe they do," Maria suggested. "I'm not sure we need God to explain this universe."

"It's true science and mathematics have simplified, extended, and added material comfort. Yet, they have failed to answer the primary questions of existence."

"And what questions are those?" asked Maria making direct eye contact with Inanna.

"Sentience. Consciousness. They don't explain the self-aware component of the universe, Maria."

"You mean they don't explain us."

"Precisely."

"So, that means God did it? I'm not sure I buy that logic, Inanna. If God breathed life into this universe, where is he? He seems like an absentee landlord to me."

"Do you believe mathematics did it, Maria?" replied Inanna.

"I don't have the answer and I don't know how to get it. I prefer questions with answers."

"Let's assume, Maria, mathematics can account for how the universe burst into being. How does it solve for our existence? What meaning can it add to that existence?"

Maria was digging at an odd bronze-colored vegetable she could not identify. "I don't know, Inanna. I mean, what if there's no meaning to our existence? What if we're here and then we're gone and that's it?"

"Do you really believe that, Maria?" asked a troubled Inanna.

"God hasn't exactly been a positive influence in my life, Inanna. Growing up, people judged me in the name of God. I watch people all over the earth killing and dying in the name of their God. I see good and decent people living in fear of God's judgment upon them and their loved ones. Based on that, I don't see how God can be the answer."

Inanna dropped her head and shook it. "I feared this was your view. That's why I brought you here this evening. I want you to have the answers you seek."

"That's not likely. I'm never going to—"

"You're all suffering under the delusion of false god images. It is so important you understand the next layer of this story and spread the truth among your fellow human beings. The worst sin we committed was not genetically engineering you to be slaves or not telling you about it thousands of years ago. Our worst sin was setting up our imperfect image in your minds as the image of God."

"I don't follow you, Inanna. You mentioned the false god concept the other day. What do you mean? How did you do it?"

"We clearly established your psychological relationship with God as servant-master. Let me be precise. We set the relationship as slave master and slave. This false Anunnaki God—angry, jealous, and judging—is still the one sold by most earth religions today. We taught you to approach God on your knees because we wanted you to approach us on your knees. Because of our actions, many humans walk around their whole lives damaged by feelings of worthlessness. Curse us!"

Maria saw Inanna's anguish as she spoke. "How did you substitute yourselves for God? People believe in a God who created the universe, not in you."

"Conceptually they believe in The Father Creator, but God's personality came from their ancestor's interactions with the Anunnaki. The Father Creator is not angry, jealous, or judging. He does not send anyone to hell or strike you down where you stand."

"How did you inflict this psychological scar?"

"Plainly and simply, we did it through fear. In the early days, after your creation, we physically punished humans who stepped out of line. We planted "the fear of God" in your minds so strongly that it lives on in your thoughts and actions today. Humanity is a broken species, Maria."

"Well, on behalf of humanity, thank you," Maria joked to lighten the air.

Inanna was having none of it. She wanted to make this point sharply. "I mean it. Your concept of who you are, what you're capable of being, and what God wants for you is perversely skewed—practically 180 degrees from the truth."

"Many people I know would argue with you, Inanna. Jack would tell you he doesn't worship ancient Sumerian gods. He worships the single God of the universe and he is obeying God's will."

"What is an analogy that will make this clear?" searched Inanna. "Think of a child who grows up in an abusive adoptive home. He grows up associating parents with abusers. The same way you and so many humans associate God with judge. Suppose that child grows up and in middle age discovers his adoption. He learns his birth parents were wonderful people who gave him up to give him the best chance in life. Would he suddenly view them as his parents and change his view, conditioned through his whole life of parents as abusers?"

"I don't know," replied Maria. "I suppose he could drop his relationship with his adoptive parents, try to form one with his birth parents, and change his views on parents."

"Come now, Maria, you're a student of human psychology. Is that how most humans would react, given this situation? The people around him, who have a stake in the situation, are telling the adoptee his adoptive parents are the only parents he's ever known. 'It is what it is, they say.' It doesn't matter if these saintly birth parents are out there somewhere, they weren't there for you."

"You're losing me, Inanna," frowned Maria.

"Humanity had step-gods, Maria. You have step-gods who abused you, but we are the only concept of God you have ever known throughout the history of your civilization. Your step-gods made you feel small, unworthy, and incapable. We punished those who tried to break free from that mindset."

"What are you telling me, Inanna?"

"I am telling you there is an actual Father Creator who brought this universe into being—humanity's long lost birth God. He does not see you as small, unworthy, incapable, deserving of judgment. He created the Anunnaki, what became human beings, and every other sentient creature in this universe to learn, grow, expand, and reach its potential. We locked humanity out of that equation and short-circuited your whole vision of what the spiritual dimension is."

Maria sat back in her chair. Her mind was churning. This information was profound and yet deeply disturbing. "OK. Even if what you say is true, many people are still not going to change their views to align with it."

"I know," said Inanna, "at least not right away. If we can restore the connection between The Father Creator and humanity, we break the Anunnaki grip. We can transform these negative visions of the human future ending in individual or collective judgment. It is damaging and diminishing people. It is damaging and diminishing your civilization. This lie's day is over!"

"And how do we do that?" asked a bewildered Maria. "You talk like you have some direct connection to The Father Creator."

"I do, Maria. I have for some time now. He has been working with me to restore the balance lost by the unjust Anunnaki actions toward humanity. He is eager to be connected to you."

"Inanna, you're scaring me a little bit. You talk to God?"

"Yes and so shall you."

Maria felt very uncomfortable, then terrified, then strangely intrigued. "You can make this happen?"

"Oh yes, Maria. If you are finished eating, I am prepared to prove it to you right now."

(20)
Maria and The Father Creator

Inanna led Maria into her Room of Ascension. Maria felt a sharp shift in the ambient energy, as she stepped into the pyramid-shaped room. Behind her, the massive gold doors sealed them inside this vault of a room. A barely audible buzzing sound filled the dimly lit room and the air felt statically charged. The images on the golden walls depicted Sumerian and Egyptian gods in forms familiar to Maria from her college days. Far above, she could see a small skylight. Individual stars were not visible, but the skylight seemed to combine, focus, and magnify the starlight. The vibrant shaft of light it created pierced the middle of the dark room and illuminated Inanna's royal seal in the center of the floor.

"Welcome to my Room of Ascension, Maria," Inanna said, spreading her arms wide apart, closing her eyes and lifting her head to the sky. "This is where I meditate and where I commune with The Father Creator."

An overwhelming sense of Déjà vu gripped Maria. "Have I been in this room before?"

"Of course not, Maria. Why would you ask that?" Inanna responded, looking circumspectly at Maria.

"I don't know. I just have this incredible sense that I've been here and done this before," Maria puzzled.

"This room magnifies thoughts and ideas and sends them out into the Universe. It is possible to make quantum connections across time, space, and beyond. Many wild and wonderful things happen here, but you have never been here before," assured Inanna.

Inanna moved around the room lighting candles and incense sticks. The earthy scent of Sandalwood filled the chamber. Maria loved that smell. It always caused her to feel relaxed and somehow in touch with herself. Inanna continued to light incense until the chamber became hazy.

"We are going to meditate, Maria. Please, be seated and begin relaxing yourself. Breathe deeply in through the nose and out through the—"

"I've meditated before, Inanna," Maria interrupted, somewhat rudely. In fact, so, rudely that she apologized. "Forgive me. I'm a little worked up."

"Just relax, Maria. Relax."

Inanna seated herself on the floor a few feet from Maria. "Lights out," she called.

The remaining electrical lights dimmed. Inanna closed her eyes and pressed her hands together. "Greetings, Father Creator. I call upon your wisdom to guide us in our endeavors. I call upon your strength to complete our tasks. Let your blessings rain upon all sentient beings, wherever they live in the cosmos. May our minds become one with your mind? Please welcome your beautiful child, Maria, into your presence."

The room was quite dark. Maria spied around the room waiting to see what was going to happen. She was trying to be covert so as not to offend Inanna into thinking she wasn't taking all of this seriously.

Suddenly Inanna shocked her back into the process, "Close your eyes and focus, Maria."

"Father Creator," Inanna spoke powerfully, "I have brought your daughter Maria to commune with you, to be one with you—

as I have been one with you. She seeks answers for herself and for her people. We await the boon of your wisdom."

Maria felt the ambient energy surge. The room seemed to be pulsating rhythmically. She peeked again and saw electrical pulses climbing the walls on all sides. The lens at the apex of the pyramid concentrated the energy and transmitted out into space. A deafening buzzing sound dominated the room. Maria saw Inanna still speaking, but she could no longer hear her words. Maria reached for and grabbed Inanna's hand.

The noise and the throbbing energy seemed to be reaching a crescendo and Maria felt her form rising and hovering above the floor. She closed her eyes again and discovered her vision enveloped by a purplish fog. In the distance, she perceived a rapidly spinning rainbow-colored wheel. Her stomach dropped and her heart raced as she accelerated toward the wheel. Faster and faster, she hurtled like an arrow aimed at a target. She winced as she was about to make impact. There was a blinding flash of white light then . . . nothing . . . literally nothing.

Maria felt her consciousness floating in an inky blackness with no sound, no dimension, no anything. She tried to speak, except she had no...mouth. Then she realized she could hear her thoughts . . . well not quite hear, but something approximating hearing. She spoke in her mind, "Inanna, where are you? Inanna?"

There was no reply. Maria felt a presence—a strangely familiar presence. She had that Deja Vu feeling again. She'd experienced this before, but she couldn't place it. Over and again, her words echoed through her mind.

"Is this all there is? Is this what it's all about?"

Then her questions stopped and a voice gentle like the evening breeze, but powerful like the ocean replied, "Now is the time, Maria, now!"

"The time for what?" she asked.

"The time for you to know, the time for you to act, the time for you to become."

"Father Creator? Is that you?"

"Bless you, my precious child. Bless you, my special Maria. Your answers are at hand."

"Are you The Father Creator Inanna told me about?"

"I am. I am that which is one—that which is all."

"Are you . . . God?" asked Maria.

"You ask as if you fear the answer," replied the voice.

"I'm not afraid," barked Maria. "I'm cautious. How can I be sure you aren't some kind of an illusion?"

"How can you be sure everything isn't an illusion?" replied the voice ironically.

"Answering my questions with a question doesn't inspire my confidence."

Father Creator chuckled. "The damage of your programming is evident, my child. You have learned to start from doubt, rather than from belief. That is a great disadvantage in life."

"When one lives in uncertain circumstances with uncertain outcomes, one tends to become that way," retorted Maria.

"Again, you start with the negative, my child. Why do you presume uncertainty—because you do not know the outcome? That does not make it uncertain. Maybe it just makes it interesting."

"I guess it's all in how you look at it," Maria agreed. "Still, you allow us to suffer through the pain of these outcomes and you do nothing. Why?"

"You moved quickly from doubting my reality to pointing a finger at me."

"If you are who you claim to be, you know the reason and the context for my question. Why do you allow suffering and uncertainty to plague us?"

"It's free will, Maria, free will. It's the greatest and most powerful gift I have given any of you."

"Free will is going to be your defense? Couldn't you make things easier on us?"

"If I solved all your challenges for you, what would be the point of your existence? How would you ever grow? How would you ever get better?"

"Is that the reason we are here? Are we here to grow and get better? And then you grade us?"

"My, my. The Anunnaki conditioning runs quite deep in you, doesn't it?"

"What conditioning?" Maria replied.

"This ridiculous notion you hold that God or the gods are going to judge and punish you. That's nonsense the Anunnaki imprinted upon your species to control you. It is why I am working with my child, Inanna, to put this right for my human children. These slave thoughts must end."

"You don't judge?"

"I love. I encourage. I want what every parent wants—the best for his children."

"So, no one gets punished? You're perfectly OK with evil people getting away with evil things? There's no justice in your universe?" charged Maria.

"Maria, my child, you make me feel like one of your interview subjects," Father Creator said patiently.

"Maybe you are," replied Maria.

"Of course, I have created a system of justice. It's built into the fabric of the multiverse—not doled out as punishment or reward at the end of your lives."

"I don't see the justice built into the system. I see bad people getting away with horrific acts. I see people wallowing in endless poverty. Where are you when these things are happening?"

"You choose *everything* that happens to you. It may not be conscious and you may not see the links, but they are there. Free will, Maria. Free will."

"You're blaming poor people for being poor?" argued Maria.

Father Creator sought to allay Maria's concerns, but also to challenge her to see beyond them. "I'm saying what seems unfair to your form seems imminently fair to your soul. Beyond the myopia of your forms, every experience has a purpose. You choose your experiences freely. Your soul has its reasons. I impose nothing upon you. I simply provide the canvass on which you create your realities."

"What about justice for the Anunnaki? According to Inanna, they have committed grievous wrongs against humanity. Will they be punished?"

"The same rules apply to the Anunnaki or any other species in my realm. Their thoughts and their actions create their outcomes. What they did violated one of the few basic tenants of my universe. One must never interfere with the development of a sentient species—even I refuse to violate that principle. They did and those outcomes are still coming to fruition. Our discussion right now is part of balancing those events."

"Why don't you just fix what they did? Why must humanity continue to suffer under these delusions generation after generation?"

"I cannot clear your delusions, Maria. The Anunnaki cannot clear your delusions. Humanity must clear its own delusions, but first it must have the truth. You have chosen to be an emissary for the truth."

"What did I choose? Inanna dragged me into this situation," pleaded Maria. "I certainly did not ask for it."

"Now, don't act like a child, Maria. Your form didn't choose, but your soul did. You came to right this wrong. You and everyone else, are precisely where they decided to be," instructed Father Creator.

"But it's not fair—"

"I didn't promise fairness. I promised freedom."

"Alright, what happens when humanity receives—I mean chooses—the truth?"

"That is the happy day when I welcome humanity into direct connection with me."

"What do you mean *direct connection?*"

"Humanity's consciousness was consumed by the Anunnaki ruse. Your minds were enslaved to perceptions of God so far removed from truth that you became unable to connect with me."

"If you're God, why can't you connect with us?"

"It doesn't work that way. You have free will. You can focus your attention on whatever you choose. The Anunnaki chose for you and misdirected your attention to them. It's as if you became focused on reflected sunlight, rather than the sun."

"There are people on my planet right now that would disagree with you. They believe they are connected directly to you and doing your will by hating and killing each other."

"That's a by-product of the Anunnaki delusion."

"Those are semantics! They believe they're doing God's will. That doesn't bother you? They pray for your blessing as they plot each other's destruction. You're detached from that reality?" demanded Maria.

"Maria, I accept your tone because I know you must release this anger before you can be a productive change agent. Of course, it bothers me. It devastates me. What would you have me do?"

"Make your intentions clear. Be the adult here. Correct them."

"My intentions have always been clear, if you pay attention

to the universe around you and the truths of nature. The problems you speak of are the direct result of the Anunnaki intervention. They misaligned your concept of God."

"Then show up. Set things straight," decried Maria.

"Maria," laughed Father Creator, "I can't show up in Time's Square proclaiming the truth. The fools who believe they do my will by harming others won't listen. They would call me a false god and find ways to discredit me. They recognize God only in their books. They would not recognize him in their streets. I'd probably be arrested or shot."

Maria chuckled and agreed that was probably true. "So, what then? What's this plan Inanna and you have cooked up?"

"I have no plans. This is Inanna operating under her free will. She's working to change history on two worlds and you are part of her plan to make it happen on Earth. Remember—"

"I know. Free will," Maria finished, seeing a pattern in Father Creator's responses.

"Most of all, I want peace for you, my child. Do you remember the dream on the planet? You were running and you jumped—"

"Off the ledge. That was you?"

"That was me."

"I thought you didn't intervene," Maria chided.

"Well, maybe on special situations," Father Creator admitted. "Do you recall what happened when you ran and jumped off the ledge?"

"I ran to the edge and I leaped. I thought I was going to die, but I didn't. Something, someone…you caught me and helped me land safely."

"That dream was a metaphor for this journey you are about to embark upon. Just remember, I am always here for you. There are no mistakes. Everything is for your growth and your improvement."

Maria felt a sense of playfulness suddenly overcome her. "How does one create a universe?" she asked.

"Well, that's complicated, Maria," confided Father Creator. "The best analogy, in your terms, is that I manifested a very, very advanced software program with amazingly complex holographic properties."

"So, we are all just imaginary beings in a massive computer program?"

"No. You are far more than that. My analogy was technically accurate, but it fails to communicate the true nature of this reality or your significance within it. If I am a great bonfire, then you are each sparks from that fire. Does that make sense?"

Maria puzzled. "Do you mean that we are all a part of you?"

"Nothing in my realm is apart from me, Maria."

"In your realm? Are there realms beyond yours? Are you the only one of your kind?" Maria asked in rapid fire.

"Everything you could possibly conceive of as being a part of existence is within my realm," explained Father Creator.

"But not everything that is?" Maria followed.

"The explanation might confuse you."

"Then confuse me," Maria agreed.

"My kind exists in a state that is beyond what you would refer to as reality. We live to create. Each of us creates according to the dictate of our being. We are completely sovereign over that which we create and our creation can take any form of our choosing."

"So, there are others like you who create other universes?"

"In a manner of speaking. What you consider a universe does not capture the complete essence of these creations. When you say others, you imply separation where there is none."

"But you said your kind."

"That is a limitation of your language. We are all manifestations of one and our creations, though diverse, are as well."

"You've done it. You've confused me," shared Maria. "Does it make sense to ask how many dimensions are included in your creation?"

"As you understand the concept of dimensions, there are thirty-three dimensions in my realm. Yet, the most highly evolved beings only occupy the eighth dimension. That is where the growth and the free come in, Maria. You are all slowly scaling a thirty-three-dimension reality. Humans and Anunnaki are operating only in four dimensions. There is so much more for you to know and to understand."

"Wait, I thought we lived in a three-dimensional universe," questioned Maria.

"That is a very common misconception. Your physicists long ago established that you live in four dimensions: height, width, depth, and time."

"How does the Anunnaki intervention in Earth history impact the path we are on?" asked Maria.

"The Anunnaki denied you your connection to me. Without that connection, you have become stuck in a three-dimensional paradigm that you take far too seriously and much too literally."

Maria had exhausted her questions for now. She had *some* of her answers. She now understood her questions and maybe her answers were going to change worlds.

"Thank you, Father Creator. Will I have a chance to speak to you again?" asked Maria.

"I guarantee it, my child. For now, I leave you with a vision—a vision of The Future Possible. Blessings to you and yours, my beautiful child."

Images now passed rapidly through Maria's mind—like a

slideshow moving too fast. She felt like the images were trying to depict an Earth at peace and living in harmony with others in the cosmos. She could feel each human being free to explore his or her full potential. Finally, there was an image of a baby. Maria felt warm and she felt satisfied for the moment.

As the last images faded, these words reverberated through her mind. "Trust, Maria, trust."

Maria jolted and again found herself accelerating rapidly— this time toward a bright white light. She wanted to shield her eyes, but she had no hands. Just before impact, the white light resolved back into the color wheel. She passed through the wheel and snapped back into regular consciousness, as she felt her body gently come to rest on the floor of Inanna's Ascension Room. She noticed she had been holding Inanna's hand through the entire experience.

"How was that?" asked Inanna.

Maria nodded her head. "That was . . . amazing."

"Did you speak to The Father Creator?" Inanna eagerly asked.

"Yes. I believe I did," said Maria. "I believe I did."

(21)
The Assignment

ANN CEO Pete Rogers paced back and forth before his massive office window overlooking downtown Austin. He had one hand raised to his forehead and a grimace on his face. Then both hands went back to his hips. His exercised body language evidenced his challenge to make sense of what he was hearing.

"Maria, the White House Correspondent job isn't something you can walk away from and then come back to. I handpicked you for this job. How can you do this to me?"

Maria knew telling her boss and old college friend wouldn't be easy. She anticipated theatrics and she knew she had to come ready with a "What's in it for Pete" message.

"Pete, I am on to a story—a big story—maybe the biggest story. I need a temporary field assignment to pursue it. Put me on special assignment. I'll come back to the White House job when I've nailed this story. It might even lead back to the White House. I don't know."

Rogers turned to face his star reporter.

"Back to the White House? OK, Woodward. Spill it. What's this all about?"

Maria grinned sheepishly and studied the tips of her shoes for a moment. Human beings genetically engineered by aliens thousands of years ago. Now those same aliens want to help humanity escape the grip of a silent global dictatorship. She was still having a hard time believing the story. How could she expect Pete to believe it?

"Pete, have you ever wondered where we came from? Where's the meaning behind . . . behind . . . all of this? What if you had a chance to find out?"

Pete involuntarily rolled his eyes. "Damn it, Maria. I don't have time—"

"Pete, I have evidence modern humans were genetically engineered by an alien species called the Anunnaki. Modern governments know about this and are actively involved in—"

"Geez, Maria. Just stop!" Pete glared at Maria with a mixture of anger and incredulity.

"Are actively involved," Maria continued, "in a cover-up of this information?"

"Forget it, Woodward. Maybe I should call you Dana Scully. Next you'll be telling me the Illuminati are involved and the smoking man is running it all behind the scenes."

"Well, Pete, as a matter of fact—"

Pete raised his hand in a stop gesture. He came around the desk to confront Maria face to face. He placed one hand on each shoulder and held her as he spoke. "Maria, listen to me and listen good. I want you to take a few days off—"

"I'm not crazy," Maria raised her voice. "I have evidence."

What evidence?"

"I've got an eyewitness, Pete. She has answers about the timeless mystery of human origins. Who we are and where we're going."

Pete released Maria, walked back around his desk, dropped dramatically into his chair, and placed both hands to his head.

"What you're telling me doesn't make sense. How can you have an eyewitness to the beginning of humanity?"

"Her name is Inanna—the Sumerian goddess Inanna. She contacted me in Hawai'i. She believes humanity is in great danger. She and her Uncle Enki are trying to help us."

"Help us? This is crazy!" Pete said. "Maria, this sounds like a story I'd read at the grocery checkout."

"Believe me. I know!" Maria agreed. "I've been living this craziness for weeks."

"Let's say I believe you for a moment about the genetic engineering. How could this woman be an eyewitness to the birth of humanity?"

"The Anunnaki are extremely long-lived. Inanna was a child when Enki created human beings as a worker race to serve the Anunnaki on Earth."

"Why did these Anunnaki need a worker race?" Pete asked, pretending to be taking this seriously.

"I don't know the whole reason. It had something to do with a hole their atmosphere. They devised a method of healing their atmosphere using tiny suspended gold particles. Nibiru lacked gold, but they knew Earth was gold-rich."

"So the Anunnaki are gold pirates and we are their slaves?"

"Well, yes. That is, we were their slaves. The Anunnaki are from a planet called Nibiru. It orbits our sun's brown dwarf twin."

"The sun's brown dwarf twin?" chided Pete. "Our sun doesn't have a brown dwarf twin."

"According to Inanna, we do. She can explain this better than I can."

"You know you're flushing your career down the drain, don't you? You'll be lucky if you're not committed. Look, Maria, we're old friends. I'm willing to forget this whole conversation. You take a few days off to consider things."

The thought had occurred to Maria many times in recent days. *Am I crazy? I'm finally where I want to be and now I'm going to risk it for this story. Who would believe it?*

"Pete, do you remember when Tim and you started this net-work? Do you remember back before ratings and advertisers? The two of you built a business plan in college for a network that would be an alternative to the mainstream established regurgita-tion of information. You sold that idea to investors and you cap-italized on the wave of public distrust of the big networks. The two of you wanted to change the world—"

"Maria," Pete looked at his old friend with pleading in his eyes. His look said, "Please don't go there," but Maria now knew she must.

"The two of you were going to change the world by changing media. You hired me and other journalists who shared that vi-sion. Do you remember?"

"We have to live in the real world, Maria. Advertisers pay the bills. Those advertisers have customers. Those customers don't want you to tell them they're the result of some age-old test tube experiment and members of a slave race."

"And what if it *is* the truth, Pete? Aren't the people of this planet entitled to that information?"

"Even if we *were* genetically engineered, who cares now? Comfortable lies sell better than uncomfortable truths. This isn't an audience for this truth. Why can't we leave it alone now?"

"I'd agree, if this story died in the Sumerian sand 6,000 years ago, but it's as fresh as this morning's headlines. Haven't you ever wondered why we have political system versus political sys-tem, economic system versus economic system, religion versus religion on this planet?"

"People disagree. They don't see eye to eye. It doesn't mean there's some vast conspiracy."

"Earth's real movers and the shakers set one group against another to maintain their greedy grip on this planet, Pete. When the Anunnaki left Earth, they placed these power brokers in charge. As long as they keep humanity in the dark and the revenue rolling to Nibiru, they can run Earth as they see fit. They're fabulously wealthy and powerful because of it, but they are controlled—we are controlled—from Nibiru."

"What proof do you have that any of this is true?"

"I have Inanna."

Pete chuckled. "Are you . . . ah . . . channeling this Inanna? Do you click your fingers and she appears?"

"She's here right now. Would you like to meet her?"

"If I'm going to explain to Tim why we're putting our whole enterprise at risk to pursue this insanity, she owes me that much."

"She's monitoring our conversation. Inanna?" called Maria.

"Great," said Pete, "a Big Brother goddess."

A shimmering, revolving light appeared in the middle of the office. It instantaneously assumed the shape of a woman nearly seven feet tall. In an instant, Inanna stood in front of Pete's desk. He sat back in his chair, a look of astonishment spread across his face.

"Pete, this is Inanna."

"Greetings, Pete."

"Hello, Inanna," Pete managed.

"You have questions."

"Um, yeah, a few."

"I understand. I will provide whatever answers you need. Shall we adjourn to my ship? Our communication will be more secure there."

"Your ship?" Pete repeated questioningly, as he eyed Maria.

"Yes. We have a matter-energy converter to ease transport. It is similar to those in some of your science fiction."

"Do you mean like a Star Trek transporter?" Pete clarified.

Inanna paused. "Yes. That's a good approximation."

"Pete, you might want to block out your calendar for the afternoon," Maria offered.

"Maria, you should find a suitable place outside the building to transport from. We don't want to raise suspicions," said Inanna. "I will see you aboard shortly."

"You've done this already, Maria?"

"Yes. I've done it a couple of times. It actually tickles."

Inanna returned to her ship to prepare for her guests. Pete and Maria left his office. He canceled his afternoon meetings on the way out. He and Maria rode the elevator down 23 floors in silence. Maria led Pete to the back of the building. A beam of light enveloped them and they vanished.

(22)
Pete and the Vimana

In an instant, Maria and Pete materialized aboard Inanna's royal tender. A human-looking officer was operating the transportation device. The ships ceilings were higher than ceilings on Earth. Short hallways led off in three directions from the circular transport room. Three doorways lined each side of the hallways. The main hallway was wider than the other two and ran toward the back of the ship.

The doors of the room at the end of the main hallway swished open. Inanna emerged and motioned for Maria and Pete to join her. They followed her into a well-appointed conference room featuring a long table accented with crystal. Over-sized chairs surrounded the table, but there were two human-sized chairs for Pete and Maria. The room's panoramic windows followed the arc of the ship's rounded shape. The Earth, slowly spinning below, provided a spectacular view.

"Welcome to my Vimana, Pete." Inanna said.

"Your Vimana?" countered Pete, "Your flying carpet?"

Inanna smiled at the reference. "Yes. Some of your ancestors called our small tender vessels flying carpets. You are familiar with the term?"

"Yeah, I've seen them discussed on The History Channel. They said Vimanas were ancient flying craft described in Indian myths."

"All true—except the myth part. Vimanas were and are quite

real."

Pete listened and observed, but Maria recognized the skepticism brewing on her friends' face. He was a skeptic at heart. He mistrusted the political system, religion, science—even other media. He built a media empire by riding the wave of his generation's skepticism and he wore that skepticism like a badge of honor. The sarcasm that accompanied it was another matter. He wanted to tone it down, but it just flowed out of him.

"Please have a seat," offered Inanna.

"Thank you. Quite a show you put on, Inanna," Pete said smugly with folded arms.

"What do you mean a show?"

"Yes, Ma'am. You've got advanced technology. Maybe you're even an alien. None of that proves you're the Anunnaki or that you engineered human beings thousands of years ago."

"Actually hundreds of thousands of years ago. Maria, you were right. Pete is skeptical," said Inanna smiling warmly. "What would convince you?"

"Home movies," Pete said dryly.

Inanna called out a command in a tongue Pete didn't understand. The wall at the far end of the room separated revealing a large video screen. Inanna spoke again. Headsets rose from the table and a video began playing.

"Please wear these headsets. The video will be translated into English for you." Inanna instructed.

Inanna narrated over the top of the video directly into their headphones. "This is video of our first Earth landing party after the Atlantean Ice Age—about 450,000 earth years ago. King Anu, my grandfather, commissioned the expedition. The two men are my father, Enlil, and my Uncle Enki. They commanded the expedition. That is Enki speaking."

Inanna paused to allow the video narrator to speak. The narrator spoke in an unknown tongue with an English overlay.

"By the grace of The Father Creator, we have arrived safely on the seventh planet. As Alalu promised, the air is again breathable. The fruits and the grains are edible and the water drinkable. We have set up temporary housing in the land between the two rivers. We have named our settlement Edin. The wildlife is plentiful. Most interesting among them is a bipedal species with a relatively large brain. We call them Lulu. They seem to have flourished in the absence of advanced humanoids on Earth. We have begun seeking gold in the southeast sea. Unlike Mother Nibiru, Earth has day and night cycles. This has disturbed our natural rhythms and sleep. The sun here is exceptionally bright and we have to wear eye protection over our eyes. The heat is nearly unbearable for Anunnaki."

Pete raised his hand, "Can you stop the video for a moment."

"Of course."

"The narrator called Earth the seventh planet. Explain how Earth is the seventh planet."

"Nibiru orbits the star Proxima Centauri. Unknown to your scientists, our two stars comprise a binary system. We consider Nibiru the outermost planet in our combined solar system. As we travel into the inner solar system, our ships encounter Pluto, Neptune, Uranus, Saturn, Jupiter, Mars, and Earth—the seventh planet. Earth is also referred to in our creation myths as the seventh planet."

"I see," Pete said. "Why don't our astronomers know about this linkage between, what did you call your star, Proxima Centauri—"

"Yes."

"And our sun?"

"Your scientists believe gravitational forces are the primary determinant of stellar motion and the interaction of heavenly bodies. Gravity is only the grossest force and among the least important. Trust me; our stars are part of one system."

"How can I verify this is a 450,000-year-old video and not a hoax?"

"Keep watching," Maria said eagerly.

"You've seen this before?" asked Pete.

"I had many of the same questions as you, the first time I came to Inanna's ship."

"Shall we continue," encouraged Inanna. She resumed the video.

A new clip began. Again, Enki was talking. "Lulu lives in family units. It is not as strong as the other primates we have encountered. It survives by wits not brawn. The males hunt in groups and use military-like tactics to capture and kill large prey. It creates basic tools and weapons. It is capable of using fire, when it occurs naturally. It seems to have rituals about the fire. Lulu is susceptible to predators at night. Fire acts as a natural defense. Lulu has made a god of the fire, indicating an ability to abstract and a willingness to obey unknown forces. I have gained the trust of one family group. I have tried to teach them to create fire without success. The creature is not able to utter words, but communicates with others through a series of grunts, chirps, and hand gestures."

Images of Enki interacting with Lulu appeared on the screen.

Enki continued. "The males can grow to roughly six feet tall. The females are generally shorter and lighter. They share a characteristic with other primates: they are not monogamous. A single male may mate with multiple females and they may live together. There is no indication they have the capacity for spirituality beyond the fire worship. Following is some raw video of them."

The hi-definition video left no ambiguity. A family of human-like creatures—but not human and not primate—appeared on the screen. Enki interacted with them like Jane Goodall with her chimpanzees.

Another clip began with Enki creating a video journal. "I fear our efforts to mine the Earth's gold and save Nibiru may come to naught. The latest group of Nibiruan conscripts sent to mine has rebelled. They refuse the hard work demanded in the mines, but mother Nibiru still cries out for gold to save her atmosphere. My brother, Enlil, arrives tomorrow. I have an unusual suggestion for him."

The clip cut again. "Brother Enlil, welcome," Enki is saying.

"Enki, my brother, how did you allow the mining to get out of control? Angered is our Father, King Anu. He commands a plan to quell the rebellion. Nibiru needs the gold. He orders me to control the situation or risk the intervention of Anunnaki warriors."

"Brother Enlil, our father's concerns are well-founded. For the sons of Nibiru, refuse to work the mines, and will not be coerced. Last night they came to my dwelling and threatened to put torch to it."

"This is not acceptable," said Enlil his voice rising in anger. Anu will move against us. The fires of battle on Earth will destroy our expedition here. Even now, Anu awaits my transmission of a solution."

"Brother Enlil, I have a plan to spare the wrath of our father and secure the gold. We will create a worker to mine the gold. We will give him only enough intelligence to work, but not to question our authority."

"How is this possible, my brother?" asked Enlil.

"Brother Enlil, by mixing our life essence with the Earth

creature's essence, shall it be accomplished."

"Enki, my brother, what right do we have to create a new being? Only The Father Creator holds the power to create life. Many at home will not support this kind of experimentation on spiritual grounds."

"Brother Enlil, it is not a new life form I propose. We would enhance the earth creature to make him useful to us. The workers we need can be created by mixing our essence with his essence. No laws of nature would we violate. Besides, my brother, the essence of the earth already runs through your veins and mine. We would simply be expanding the connection between Earth and Nibiru."

Enlil paused for a moment in thought. "Enki, my brother, your reasoning and your brilliance are beyond reproach. How will you proceed?"

"Brother Enlil, we must experiment to find the optimal mix of their essence and ours. It is not without risk of failure, but with the approval of our father, Anu, I can begin at once."

"Enki, my brother, I will transmit a message to our father, Anu, without delay. Let Anu and his council consider your proposal."

The lights came up. Questions filled Pete's mind and competed for his lips. Finally, he spoke. "Inanna, these videos portray a rather fantastic story. Even if I believe it, can you imagine the political and religious firestorm that would ensue from such a story?"

"Excuses, Pete. Such excuses only perpetuate the deception and delay the inevitable. Human beings have a right to know their true origins. They can handle the truth."

"Can we?" Pete cautioned. "People hold to their beliefs very strongly. They're willing to fight and even die for them."

"There may be a strong reaction, but you underestimate your

species. They must understand not only what there is to die for, but what they have to live for."

"You mentioned our governments. Are you telling me the governments of the world know aliens have been visiting the planet throughout history?" Pete asked.

"The governments you know—the ones run by politicians and bureaucrats—possess varied levels of knowledge on the topic. Such governments rise and fall. I speak of an unbroken line of power stretching back thousands of years. It swears an absolute allegiance to the Nibiruan crown—to my brother," said Inanna.

"Do you mean the Illuminati?" Pete asked.

"Your concept of the Illuminati is a close approximation. Their actual name is The Cadre. These people did not attain their status by merit or good fortune, but through absolute obedience to Anunnaki rule. They are highly hybridized humans with complete loyalty to the Nibiruan crown—to my brother. At the behest of the Nibiruan crown, The Cadre entered into agreements with some alien species."

"What kind of agreements?" Pete asked.

"Highly profitable agreements for Nibiru and The Cadre, implemented at humanity's expense. The two primary treaties govern the transfer percentage of Earth's GDP to Nibiru and the prescribed number of human abductions allowed each year."

Pete shook his head. "I'm sorry. I can't buy it. Are you saying our governments know about alien abductions and transfer part of our global GDP to Nibiru? Why would they allow that?"

"Pete, you're operating under the illusion your governments have a choice in the matter," replied Inanna.

"They don't? You're telling me Earth is covertly run from a planet four light years from here and there's nothing we can do about it."

"I'm telling you your planet is run from a far-off world and there's nothing you can do about it until the people of earth become aware," Inanna corrected. "That's where Maria and you come into the picture. We need to get this information to the people."

"I run a serious news organization, Inanna. We're already the outsider in Washington. You're asking me to broadcast tabloid content—things that will get us ridiculed."

"Pete, forget the ridicule," said Maria. "Isn't our first obligation as journalists to the truth? I observed an abduction firsthand. They took a Filipino man from his bed. Had it not been for Inanna, he might be dead now. How many missing persons on our planet are really alien abductees never returned?"

"Maria, I know you don't want to hear this, but I have a business to run. We do have advertisers and they have customers. Those customers go to a church, a temple, or a mosque every week. They don't want to be told their God is an alien or that men in shadows orchestrate their lives."

"I remember when people, not dollars, were your bottom line, Pete," Maria said disgustedly. "Is there no room in your bottom line to take some heat for what's right?"

"That's just great, Maria. Stand on our principles and we'll be standing in the unemployment line. I don't like it, but it is what it is," replied Pete forcefully.

"I hate that phrase," Maria said. "Maybe the audience would reward you for being the one courageous enough to speak the truth. Have you considered that?"

"Oh, sure, there's lots of precedent for that in media history. I'm not even sure I believe anything I've heard here today."

"You don't believe I witnessed the abduction?" asked Maria?

"I believe you believe you witnessed the abduction."

"You're feeling denial Pete," Inanna said. "It's human nature. You earn your living by reporting the news. It's a blow to your ego that this is going on and you know nothing about it."

"Hold it right there!" Pete stood and pointed at Inanna. "This is not about ego. You're asking me to believe governments have kept this secret through time. Governments aren't good at keeping secrets. People would have talked."

Inanna leaned across the table to emphasize her point. "People have talked, Pete. Your institutions simply have not been listening. This is no secret to millions on your planet. They have personally experienced sightings and abductions. They suffer in silence, waiting for their institutions to acknowledge them, rather than snicker at them."

"You want me to believe in conspiracy theories about shadow governments and powerful men in dark rooms running presidents and prime ministers." Pete said sarcastically.

"Yes!" Inanna affirmed. "Trust me. My government will not leave the fate of its Earth operation in the hands of human voters. The Cadre is real and very much in control, Pete!" Inanna urgently insisted.

"What my brother commands, The Cadre executes. Where The Cadre wants war, there is war. Where they want famine, there is famine. Where they want religious radicalism or ethnic tension, they plant it. Where they want human beings to live in fear, they manifest things worthy of your fear. This system has enslaved you to believe you are nothing, when you are much. It has taught you a scarcity mindset in a universe of abundance. It has told you God wants to limit you, when God created you to expand."

"If any of that were true, someone would have uncovered it and reported it," argued Pete.

"C'mon, Pete!" said Maria. "You say that, but Inanna is giving this to you on a platter and you're turning up your nose. She's giving you the scoop of all scoops and you're arguing that someone else should have broken the story already."

"If this is so urgent, Inanna, why don't you land this ship on the White House lawn and ask to meet with the president? That should prove your existence and no one could deny or twist that?" Pete questioned.

Inanna began to speak and then paused, as if to ponder her words. "My government is not prepared to engage in an open dialogue on this matter. That leaves me with only one course of action—to help humans uncover the truth for themselves."

"Let me see if I have this *truth* straight? Aliens created us. They continue to abduct us. They collect taxes and create wars through a group called The Cadre. Is that what you're claiming?" Pete persisted.

"That's part of the truth, but most thinking humans already accept alien life as a reality," Inanna replied with even greater urgency in her voice. "There's a bigger truth—a more dangerous truth. The video alluded to it, but didn't state it. My people genetically engineered modern human beings. We blended our DNA with proto-human DNA to create modern human beings. We have ruled your planet and you for nearly half a million years. This crime has been committed without the knowledge or consent of the vast majority of human beings."

When Maria said those words earlier, they had not sunk in. Pete thought Maria was speaking theoretically. Standing now on Inanna's ship made denying the possibility more difficult. He sat for a moment trying to process the full implications of that statement. "Are you saying that humanity is an experiment conducted by an extraterrestrial species and—?"

"Yes. By my people," inserted Inanna.

Pete looked at Maria and then at Inanna and began laughing. "This is insane. Do you expect me to believe this nonsense? Do you expect me to report it?"

"It's not nonsense, Pete." Maria said.

"Your points might make sense to a religious person, but I believe in science," said Pete. "Our modern science has clear evidence human beings evolved on Earth. They have the genetic and archaeological proof. Darwin's theory is accepted by the overwhelming majority of the scientific establishment."

"You have theoretical half-truths and a leap of faith," countered Inanna. "Your scientists cannot conceive of divine or extraterrestrial intervention and so they build theories that make the most sense, if you ignore those possibilities. They cannot account for the sudden emergence of the large-brained, hairless modern human. There is a steady progression in the evolutionary chain and then there is a quantum leap forward. That leap forward is you and we did it!"

Pete sat shaking his head. "It's not possible."

"Not only is it true," Inanna continued, "but our crime against humanity goes further. Let me list a few of our crimes. We inserted ourselves as your gods. We forced you to labor for us. We hardwired fear of us right into your DNA to control you. We confused your languages. We set culture against culture, race against race to keep you under our thumbs. We genetically limited your mental capabilities. We physically enforced these fear-based mindsets to keep you limited. We superimposed our imperfect, selfish, angry personalities into your conception of God. And finally, we left you to suffer under the delusions we created for you."

Maria saw Pete was teetering. "Listen to her, Pete," she encouraged, "This is important . . . for all of us."

Pete was out of arguments. It made perfect sense, but how

could he accept it? He rose and paced around the table trying to gather himself.

"So, you merged your DNA with the DNA of hominids to create a better, smarter slave?"

"Yes, and your ancestors worked for my people mining the earth's gold, during what you call prehistory. This went on for several hundred thousand years."

"Why is there no record of this," asked Pete?

"It's there, Pete," assured Inanna. "It's woven into your myths, but you fail to listen. Your scientific age is so smart it cannot read the simple verbiage in mythology around the world. It believes only in what it can see and measure. There is much you do not see and much you have not measured."

"How did we get from the gold mining era to recorded history?" Maria asked with eagerness in her voice.

"The Anunnaki elite, myself included, lived among the humans. We ruled the earliest human cities as patron gods and goddesses. Human labor supplied our needs and enriched Nibiru with raw materials. Other alien species viewed the new human race as breeding stock to rejuvenate their ailing DNA. King Anu signed the first agreements permitting these species to interbreed with humans. This era created the racial and ethnic variations in humanity. It was also the source of myths reporting beings from heaven mating with human women.

"For many millennia we justified our actions with the assurance that human beings were not a truly sentient species. My Uncle Enki, before creating you, convinced my government of this fact. However, Enki and I began to see evidence of humanity's sentience. We brought the evidence to my father, but he enjoyed being worshipped as a god too much. He made an official proclamation stating humans were not a sentient race. He decreed that educating a human was a crime punishable by death.

"Uncle Enki and I left our cities and took a small band of humans with us to caves in the desert. We were determined to educate the humans and prove their sentience. We succeeded brilliantly for a few years, until . . ."

"What happened?" Maria asked.

"We were caught. My father ordered the other Anunnaki involved and the educated humans executed. He spared my Uncle Enki and me, but exiled us to Nibiru. Soon after, he exiled all Anunnaki, save himself and my brother Ea. They stayed upon the earth and ruled it with an iron fist. They aided human tribes loyal to them. Tribes loyal to departed Anunnaki gods were conquered and chided for their belief in false gods. When my grandfather, Anu, passed into The Father Creator's realm, they abandoned Earth and left it under the control of The Cadre."

"So, what does this have to do with us today?" asked Pete.

"There was much debate on my world about how to handle The Human Question. Some thought we should just leave. Others believed we should eradicate humans and claim the earth outright. The first group had little motivation to do anything. The latter group had little support. For a while, nothing happened. We waited and we watched as tribalism and barbarism grew up on the earth. Belief systems arose. Humans fought wars over territory and resources. Abominations abounded."

"It sounds a lot like today," commented Maria.

"No, Maria. It was much worse. We did not build your species to stand on its own. You had no values to inform your course. We bred you to work and survive, not to grow and aspire. You were unable to overcome your defects. My brother and my father preferred you that way."

"Wow! You don't paint a flattering picture of us," said Pete.

"As I've told Maria, you are a broken species," countered Inanna. "You're conditioned beings."

"How are we conditioned?"

"You are conditioned to focus on negative and self-destructive things. You believe money creates things in your world. Money becomes your barrier to happiness. Those beliefs drive you to get a job to make the money, rather than do what you love and let the money come to you. You believe your God thinks you a lowly sinner rather than the amazing creation you are."

Maria wiped a tear from her face. Pete listened soberly.

"I digress. About this time, King Anu passed away. My father, as his eldest son, became King Enlil IV. He had little regard for humans and eventually came to support the idea of eradicating you. Earth's value was his obstacle. Your planet is one of the crown jewels of the known galaxy. As an Anunnaki possession, it granted him status.

"He wanted the humans gone, but he needed to maintain Earth's beauty. He launched a massive advertising campaign designed to convince the Anunnaki people that the moral thing to do was to destroy the defective human race for its own good. As this campaign neared fruition, my father suddenly died. My brother, Ea, ascended to the throne. He believed as my father believed, but he brought a new determination to the effort. Enki and I did not agree so we decided to take action."

"What kind of action, Inanna?" asked Maria.

"We knew from our previous activities, that humans could absorb culture and civilization. We believed humanity could overcome its programming and exceed it. We returned to the earth, in direct opposition to my brother, and gave the people of Earth written language, mathematics, agriculture, and other aspects of civilization. We lived among the humans who still insisted on worshipping us as gods. We helped the very earliest civilizations in your mythologies form."

"But King Ea was determined to put a stop to our efforts. He sent an occupation army, forcing us to leave the earth. He decreed put to death any human found practicing writing, agriculture, mathematics, or any other examples of advanced culture. This is the origin of your Tree of the Knowledge of Good and Evil story.

"Ea wanted to destroy the humans, but he still lacked support for it at home. He needed to create a reason. He secretly sent a provocateur to fool the humans into giving him his reason. The provocateur fostered rebellion among the humans and a desire to "be like the gods." Meanwhile, he sent examples of these human aspirations back to King Ea. My brother used this information to convince the Anunnaki people the humans were dangerous and a threat. The idea that these barbarians could aspire to be like the Anunnaki was outrageous. Support grew for Ea's plan."

Inanna was a wonderful storyteller and Maria was locked into her every word.

"Finally, my brother devised a strategy to destroy the humans and preserve the earth. He planned a deluge. Still, he needed his trigger to bring the Anunnaki people fully in line with his plan. The provocateur provided Anunnaki technology and helped the humans construct a spaceport code named Babel. My brother released fake information detailing human plans to build a spacecraft and invade Nibiru. Ea had his support."

"How could humans have had the technology to build spacecraft and attack your planet, Inanna?" asked Pete.

"They didn't, but photos of the spaceport, the long propaganda campaign, and writings of human dissidents frightened the Anunnaki people enough to give my brother his excuse to attack. The plan was to seed the clouds of the earth and create a storm of unprecedented proportions."

"Enki and I had to do something. We could not stop the attack, but we could act to preserve the human race. We approached a man known to history as Utnapishtim and later as Noah. We helped him prepare to save the seed of humanity and many of the animals present on the earth. When my brother's plan was executed, Utnapishtim and a handful of his followers survived."

"The carnage revolted the Anunnaki people. Guilt over their role in King Ea's attack plagued them. When news came that a few humans had survived, it was like a small moment of redemption. Political will forced Ea to pledge never to destroy humanity again. He signed a decree, delivered by Enki to Utnapishtim, cementing the accord. Resources were directed into helping humanity get back on its feet."

"One thing did not change. The relationship between Anunnaki and humans remained servant and master. We fostered an atmosphere of fear and awe about us among humans. Through your DNA and by our actions, we had frightened you into a state of utter submission. My brother lost the battle, but he was determined to win the war. He reinstituted and strengthened The Cadre, ensuring its complete domination over economic, physical, mental, and spiritual dimensions on Earth. The gold continued to flow and the tyranny blended into the background becoming the fabric of human life on Earth."

"Inanna, you told me Nibiru's contact with Earth went back further than the gold expedition. Can you explain? Maria asked.

"Can we come to a conclusion here?" Pete inserted. "I have a network to operate."

"There may be important information, Pete. Don't you have a desire to know?" Maria asked.

"Apparently, not as strong as yours, but OK," Pete rolled his eyes.

"There is much more to tell about the history and interaction between the Anunnaki and Earth cultures," Inanna said. "Everything I've told you happened during our third extended interaction with Earth. Our first contact with your planet occurred nearly 2 million earth years ago. At that time, a civilization sometimes called the Lemurians inhabited the earth.

"The Lemurians were a highly advanced civilization spiritually and mentally. An ordinary Lemurian was capable of moving massive objects solely with the power of thought. Their average life span was about 1,000 earth years. Their primary focus was the development of a spiritual resonance with the earth.

"Lemurians were a somewhat global civilization inhabiting much of what is now called the Pacific Rim. Some of their largest cities are now beneath the Pacific, as more land mass was exposed in their time. They possessed moderately developed transportation and communication systems. They lacked space travel and focused on spiritual development rather than technological or economic advancement. We developed a trading relationship with them. They showed us how to use the power of the mind to connect with The Father Creator. They were a peaceful race and our good friends.

"Among them were individuals so developed they could transport themselves from one place to another or one time to another, when in deep meditation. They were aware of nine previous advanced civilizations on Earth. Some possessed technological sophistication beyond what the Anunnaki have today. These civilizations made Earth one of the great technological and cultural centers of the known galaxy. This is why so many alien species are aware of Earth's existence. Eight of your ancient civilizations met cataclysmic destruction. Survivors rebuilt, but it usually meant starting from scratch. In the eighth cycle, leaders planned to preserve information and carry it over into the next cycle.

The resulting ninth civilization developed rapidly and became so technologically advanced they were able to move planetary bodies. They determined that having a moon orbiting the earth would be beneficial for colonization. They captured the object you now call the Moon and towed it into position around the earth. They also captured Tiamat's largest moon— the planet you now call Mars—and towed it into its own orbit around the sun. Again, the goal was colonization.

"Without its two largest satellites, Tiamat's orbit became unstable. It orbited too near Jupiter and Jupiter's gravity pulled it apart. This event hurled tiny planetoids into the inner solar system and devastated the civilization then on Earth. It also created the asteroid belt.

"The Lemurians were the direct successors to this civilization. The survivors swore off all but necessary technology in favor of a spiritual approach to life. For nearly 3 million years, the Lemurians lived peacefully upon the earth. A militant reptilian species invaded our solar system about 750,000 years ago. They attacked Nibiru first, but we were able to hold them at bay. They moved into the inner solar system and attacked our allies: the Lemurians. The Lemurians mental capabilities made them a surprisingly dangerous foe for the Reptilians until the invading species used a genetically-targeted bioweapon that precipitated a mass extinction of the civilization."

Maria sat spellbound by Inanna's tale. She felt empowered by the universe of insight flowing to her. Inanna promised her understanding and context for her existence and she felt closer than ever before. Pete listened politely, but he wasn't as impressed by Inanna's tour of earth history. He bowed to Inanna's storytelling prowess, but heard nothing provable.

Inanna continued her history lesson. "We were able to evacuate a few Lemurians and ferry them back to Nibiru. The Reptilians now turned their attention to Nibiruan bases located on Earth's moon and Mars. Again, they used bioweapons that killed the Anunnaki warriors stationed there. Their fleet headed back to conquer Nibiru. The bioweapons caught the Lemurians off guard, but now they used their mental capabilities to determine its components. King Shiva led a Nibiruan fleet out to meet the reptilians half way between Earth Space and Nibiru. The reptilian vessels were no match for our ships. They relied completely on their bioweapon, but the Lemurians had developed an antidote.

"After ingesting the antidote, King Shiva boarded the reptilian flagship to discuss terms. The reptilians served him wine laced with the bioweapon. He held the poison in his throat until his throat was blue and then swallowed it. When he did not die, the reptilians became very afraid. Shiva signaled his fleet to open fire on the reptilian ships. We forced them out of the solar system never to return. From then on, King Shiva was known as the blue-throated king.

"What about Atlantis?" Maria questioned.

"Atlantis was a joint venture between the Anunnaki and the remaining Lemurians. We established Atlantis to bring life back to the earth and mine abundant gold. By this time, the Lemurians had been fully absorbed into our civilization. A small group of Lemurians kept their genetic purity through intermarriage. They became our greatest clergy and healers.

"That civilization was slowed by the onset of an ice age. During a warming period, the catastrophic failure of a massive ice sheet caused a flood destroying the main city. It was thousands of years before we came back to Earth. When we returned, we were in need of gold for our atmosphere. A disgraced King Alau demonstrated that Earth was again habitable. We returned with a less ambitious mission this time—simply to get the gold we needed."

Maria noticed Inanna was losing Pete. "Inanna, can you share your plan with Pete?"

"I can provide witnesses with corroborating evidence for Maria to interview. Her goal is to build a case strong enough to confront President Paxton at his next news conference. She asks her questions on international ITV forcing the world to pay attention."

"It's risky. Maria hasn't asked a question for five straight press conferences. What makes you so sure she will even get to ask the question?" Pete asked.

"Trust me, Pete. I can make sure Maria gets to ask her question."

"Why is this so critical right now, Inanna? What's in this for you?"

Tears welled in Inanna's eyes. Maria hadn't seen such emotion from Inanna before. For the moment, Inanna turned away from Pete and eyed Maria. "Maria, do you recall the Bible verse that reads, 'To the Lord, one day is as a thousand years—' "

"And a thousand years is as a day," Maria finished.

"Yes. There is truth in that statement. Because of our advanced lifespan, we do not appear to age over the course of earth decades or even centuries. I am about 350,000 years old. I'm middle-aged, but I am dying."

"Dying," gasped Maria.

"Yes. I have a rare disease that is slowly killing me. I'm able to function because of my medication and meditation."

"Even with all of the technology you possess, there's no cure?" Maria asked with concern.

Inanna managed a smile, "There is always hope, but we have

our limits too."

"I'm sorry you're dying, Inanna," Pete offered, "but I need more than you're giving me to risk my network."

"Give me a chance to build the story, Pete," pleaded Maria. "This story puts ANN on the map and—"

"Or out of business," Pete cut her short.

"Think what this could mean for humanity, Pete," Maria petitioned. "Understanding the truth about our past opens a future of possibilities—maybe even access to technology that could transform our ills."

Pete shook his head. "I'm still not buying your story. I've read documents talking about secret government operations to fake ET contact. How do we know you're not part of such an operation, Inanna?"

Inanna looked at Pete ironically. "Do I look human to you? Does this ship look like something your technology could create? I am afraid your skepticism is clouding your judgment."

"Why do we even need this investigation, Inanna?" asked Maria. "Why can't I just release this information based on what you've told us?"

"People want to see the nail holes in the hands," said Pete.

"What are you talking about?" Maria asked.

"Proof, people want proof. Thomas had to see the holes in Jesus' hands to believe. Our modern scientific society is filled with doubting Thomases—people like me. Inanna knows it. Without hard evidence, no one will believe," said Pete.

"He's right, Maria," said Inanna.

"That's what she needs you to do, Maria. She wants you to find compelling hard evidence to make the case."

Inanna was through debating. She needed Pete's help and she was willing to do what it took to get it. "What's your answer, Pete?" Inanna asked.

Pete turned to face her. When their eyes met, Inanna held his gaze intensely. Using the power of her mind and the force of her will, she imposed her position upon him. She felt dirty for employing a technique the Anunnaki had used on humans to control them so many times. It was simply a utilitarian calculation. The good of too many was at stake for her to allow Pete's doubts to stand in the way of her plans.

As Pete stared into Inanna's eyes, he could feel his position softening. It was a strange feeling—almost as if Inanna was bending his will with her mind.

"All right, Maria," Pete finally said. "You are officially on special assignment. Bring me the big story. Let's make this happen!"

(23)
Walter Reed

The first lead Inanna provided to Maria was a Captain Lucas Biggs. Biggs was a veteran of the Operation Iraqi Freedom. He was now a full-time psych patient Walter Reed National Medical Military Center. Inanna said a man named Cutler—her contact in U.S. intelligence—secured the meeting. Maria researched Biggs before the meeting. Nothing in his background made him a candidate to know anything about the big truths she sought to uncover.

Cutler provided Maria with a digital pass. She displayed it on her ComTab for scanning. The surprised looks she got from the guards revealed the importance conferred by the clearance level. She knew of Walter Reed only from pictures. The massive complex served as ground zero for healing the physical and mental wounds that were the cost of persistent military action by the world's greatest superpower.

She approached the front desk of the hospital and flashed the pass. "I'm Maria Love. I'm here to see Captain Lucas Michael Biggs."

The male nurse at the desk glanced at her pass and snapped to attention. "Yes, Ma'am."

He looked up Biggs in the system. "Ma'am, Captain Biggs is in Ward 54, our inpatient psych ward. It's a rather dangerous place for visitors. Are you sure you want to go there?"

Maria thought quickly. "Is there a room where Captain Biggs

and I can speak privately?"

"Ma'am, I can have Captain Biggs taken to conference room 27 on his floor. It's often used for legal consultations. Will that be sufficient, Ma'am?"

"Yes. Thank you."

"Ma'am, Captain Biggs' chart indicates he is prone to violent outbursts. I recommend we have a guard posted in the room with you."

Maria's tension rose. "Yes, Lieutenant. Thank you."

The nurse turned to a nearby guard. "Corporal, please escort Ms. Love to conference room 27 on Ward 54."

"Yes, sir," responded the guard. "Right this way, Ma'am."

The guard showed Maria into a grayish blue room with an icy institutional vibe. The thick metal door featured a barred window and several large dents. The humming of the fluorescent lights partially muted the occasional screams and outbursts outside. She sat and waited for a man she knew little about, trying to prepare to interview him about . . . she didn't know what.

The door opened and large armed orderly stepped inside. "Ms. Love?"

"Yes. I'm Maria Love."

The orderly left and returned momentarily with Biggs. The orderly closed the door and locked it. He led Biggs—his ankles and wrists cuffed—to a chair across the table from Maria. Biggs' appearance belied his 49 years. He looked closer to 69. A difficult life had worn ruts into his face. The orderly then retreated to the corner of the room and stood at attention.

"Captain Biggs, my name is Maria—"

"Maria Love," Biggs completed her sentence. "I know who you are. I've seen you on ITV."

"You watch ANN?"

"Young lady, people who think they know the truth watch

Fox News or CNN. People who have experienced the truth and lived it watch ANN. I must say, though, you're looking more and more like the other two every day."

Maria ignored the barb against her network and proceeded. "Sir, I'm here to talk to you about something that happened a long time ago. I don't know if you even remember it. A man named Cutler helped me get a pass to come here and talk to you."

Biggs glared at Maria for a moment. "You know Cutler?"

"No, I don't know him," assured Maria, "I've never even met him. He is a friend of a friend and he is working to help some truth come out."

"That doesn't sound like the Cutler I met," retorted Biggs. "He was arrogant and all about him—a typical ABC agency operative."

"The two of you have met?"

"Only once. It was in Baghdad many years ago. He helped put me here, you know," Biggs shared and then stared off into space for a moment. "Exactly what kind of truth is Mr. Cutler trying to get out and how does he expect me to help?"

"Captain, this may sound . . . strange, but what do you know about UFOs?"

Biggs chuckled and then eyed Maria critically. "You're joking right?"

Maria hesitated. "No. I'm serious."

"Ms. Love, UFOs . . . and Mr. Cutler are the reason I'm here."

"Here at Walter Reed?"

"Yes and here on Ward 54. You do know about Ward 54, don't you, Ms. Love?"

"No, Captain Biggs, I'm afraid I don't."

Biggs nodded. "Of course you don't. Ward 54 is where they put people who can't quite function normally in the real world anymore. It's where they put you when they want you to be for-gotten."

"I'm sorry, Captain."

"Don't be, Ms. Love," Biggs made a waving gesture with his cuffed hands. "It's better this way. I probably am crazy. You want to know if I know anything about UFOs? Hell yeah, I do! Saying so put me in here and refusing to change my mind about it made them throw away the key."

"Is belief in UFOs or talking about them a crime?"

"It is in the military, Ma'am. It's not a misdemeanor or fel-ony. It's a thought crime. The smartest people in the military never share their UFO experiences. The smart ones share it once, get their hands slapped, and then shut up. I did neither."

"What was your experience, Captain Biggs?"

"Maybe you should be asking Mr. Cutler these questions. He probably has more answers than I do."

"Captain Biggs, please. I need your help. Part of the reason I'm here is because I was . . . I was abducted," Maria shared.

"You were abducted? Hmm. I think I was too," Biggs said carefully. "I think my men and I were abducted and healed of mortal wounds. My doctors keep asking me why I just won't ad-mit it never happened."

"Tell me more," Maria leaned forward compassionately.

"We were on a mission—Operation Original Sin. Can you believe that name? I was in Army Special Forces. I commanded a unit sent into Baghdad during Operation Iraqi Freedom to re-cover Mr. Cutler and some artifacts. This was before the Iraqi government had even surrendered. Dangerous . . . we must have been crazy, young or stupid . . . probably all three," Biggs mused.

"Just what happened, Lucas?" Maria asked, dropping the pretense of roles and speaking to Biggs human to human.

Tears welled in Biggs' eyes. "We, um . . . we went to the Iraqi

National Museum. We found Cutler holed up in the basement there. We recovered his arrogant ass and his box of artifacts and . . . um . . . we were making our way out of the museum when we came under attack by Iraqi Republican Guard. I have no idea why they were stationed in a museum. That's crazy. Anyway, one-by-one my men went down and we were overrun. I took multiple hits. Just before I passed out, I saw things freeze . . . the Iraqis . . . everything. Then I saw Cutler and the crate disappear in a bluish beam of light and I lost consciousness."

"A bluish beam of light," Maria gulped and repeated uncomfortably. She was now seeing the connection.

"Yeah," continued Biggs. "The next thing I know it's six hours later. My men and I are back out in the Iraqi desert in our vehicles—like nothing ever happened . . . you know. We didn't have a scratch—well except for Washington. We should have all been dead from our wounds, Maria, but we were perfectly healthy and alive."

"So, Washington was the only one with any injury that remained?" Maria queried.

"Yeah. Later, under hypnosis, he remembered what happened in the time between the museum and the next morning. They took us to some medical facility. Not a human medical facility, if you know what I mean," Biggs leaned forward and winked. "He heard them say to leave the scar on his hand as physical evidence. They healed us and they put us back in our vehicles."

"They?" asked Maria trying to seem incredulous.

"Don't play games, Ms. Love. You know who I'm talking about."

"I do," agreed Maria. "Sorry. Then what happened?"

"This military police unit shows up and arrests all of us for stealing the vehicles. I tried to show them my orders directly from CENTCOM. No one wanted to hear it. My men and I spent the next six months under psychiatric review because we couldn't remember what happened to us. Two of my men committed suicide within a year after the incident. They were 23 and 25, Ms. Love. One had a kid . . . a little girl. Two more of my men died before their 35th birthday. Only me and Washington are left . . . at least I think Washington is still around. I've been in here for two years this time. I don't think I'll ever leave again."

"Lucas, don't think that way. I believe we're a part of something amazing with the potential to transform humanity. The people around us who don't understand haven't been given that same gift."

"You know what, Maria? I'd trade this experience in a second. It was just dumb luck my unit was chosen for that mission. We did our jobs, damn it! We just reported what happened. Our government chastised, ridiculed, and drugged us for our service. My men were allowed to die thinking they were crazy. How can a government do that to men who bravely choose to serve?"

"I'm so sorry Lucas," Maria said grasping for Biggs' hands. "Do you even know what was in those crates?"

"I have no idea, but I sure would like to know. Six men gave their lives for that crate. Four are dead and two of us are walking dead."

"You said your friend, Washington, was not locked up right now?"

"Not as far as I know. Last time I saw him, he said he was going off grid."

"Do you know where?"

"Nope. No idea. He told me he would never come back here again and he meant it."

"How could I get in touch with him?"

"You don't, Maria. The man is trained Special Forces. He knows how to disappear, live off the land, and use a weapon. You won't find him. Even if you did, it would be way too dangerous."

"Lucas, I'm beginning to think doing nothing is the most dangerous thing for all of us. Do you have his full name?"

Biggs eyed Maria suspiciously. "I'm not sure I should trust you. I guess I have no choice, do I?"

"Lucas, I promise you. The only thing I'm after is the truth and to help people harmed by the lies."

"Williams, Reginald, P. DOB 11/18/1983. Dover, Delaware. He was a track and football star. He had a full-ride to Rutgers in football, but he gave it up to serve his country after September 11. He didn't deserve what happened to him. None of us did."

Maria recorded the information on her ComTab. "Thank you for trusting me."

"I don't . . . yet. Prove me wrong."

"Lucas, I'm going to do everything I can to find out who was behind this and what it's all about. Keep watching ANN. You're going to see some fireworks at the next presidential press conference."

Maria rose to leave. "Maria," called Biggs. "There was one other piece of evidence—an artifact of some kind. It was in my pocket the morning after. Washington and I have traded it back and forth over the years, depending on who was in lock up at the time. If he's out and you can find him, he may still have it. He's studied this stuff for years now. He's obsessed. He may know what the markings mean."

"If Washington is out there, I will find him," Maria promised.

"Thank you, Maria."

"For what?"

"For seeing me as a human being and not a crazy man. It's

been a while. Even the other patients in here think I'm off the deep end on this UFO stuff. Some of the younger guys have nicknamed me Martian Man. They haven't found out what it feels like when the military ceases to have a use for you. I pray every night that they never do."

"Thank you, Lucas. Here's my number. If you need anything . . . anything . . . you call me."

Maria left her meeting with Lucas Biggs perplexed. Inanna had Cutler set up the meeting. She neglected to tell Maria that Cutler was involved in Biggs' circumstances. The bluish beam of light also indicated Anunnaki involvement. Why had Inanna not given her the full story on this? Maria felt a connection to Biggs. She was angry with her government for the way it had treated one of its heroes. She left Walter Reed determined to help him.

(24)
Coffee at Starbucks

Sloane McKay walked up Arch Street, as she always walked, on a mission. The historic marker in front of The Betsy Ross House caught her eye. She was a New York girl, but she had always loved the historic feel of downtown Philadelphia. She stood still for a moment, paying silent homage to the 18th Century brick structure and the strong woman who once lived there. She always believed that women would make the difference in human civilization. That's why she went into science. She continued her speed walk up to North 3rd St. and entered the Starbucks on the corner. She ordered a latte and grabbed a window seat to wait for Richard Holcomb.

Sloane anticipated Holcomb would challenge her conclusions. He was bright—a real expert in his field—but conventional. She, on the other hand, stretched facts to the edge of credulity and she knew it. She believed scientific orthodoxy had become too rigid and dogmatic—more eager to debunk than to discover. Her intuition told her she was on to something—something important. Sloane was unique among her scientific colleagues. She followed her intuition and sought to use science to confirm it. She took seriously Einstein's admonition: "Imagination is more important that knowledge."

Holcomb entered the coffee shop and immediately saw Sloane. She was hard to miss. Her fiery red hair and beaming smile exuded an energy that filled the room. He ordered a black coffee and joined her at the table.

"Sloane, it's good to see you again. I assume from your email that you have something exciting to show me."

Sloane looked at Holcomb. He reminded her of so many professors she remembered from her grad school days—beacons in their fields that once had the audacity to shake up the status quo and then became the status quo. She was determined never to become that.

"I do, Richard. ComTab, find Holcomb images and display," Sloane ordered.

Sloane switched on her ComTab's back screen so they could both view the images simultaneously. "Richard, tell me what double helices mean in these images."

Holcomb slipped on his reading glasses and studied the image. "Actually, those are entwined snakes and they usually symbolize the god Enki."

"Entwined snakes?" Sloane queried. "Those look like DNA strands to me."

"Well," Holcomb smiled, "that's kinda like looking at a cloud and seeing an image, Sloane. The ancient Sumerians had no concept of DNA."

Sloane held her argument for the moment. She wanted Holcomb to review the ME images without her interpretation. "OK. What do you make of these images with the double helix and these ME symbols around them?"

"ME was often used to symbolize the special power or knowledge held by the gods. Enki was the holder of this knowledge."

"Can you clarify that, Richard? I'm not sure I understand."

"It was roughly analogous to the gifts of civilization to humanity—mathematics, writing, art, government."

"So, looking at these images as a whole, how would you

interpret them?"

Holcomb considered for a moment. "Obviously, it represents information about Enki and his ME power. I'm not sure there's enough context to say more."

"Do you see a connection between this information and the repeating pairs you asked me to analyze?"

Holcomb sensed Sloane was waiting to spring something on him, but he saw no connection. He prepared himself for the younger scientist to prove him wrong. "Not really, Sloane. I believe they are probably completely unrelated, other than the reference to Enki."

"I was able to make a connection," beamed Sloane. "If you look at these double helices individually, they appear meaningless. However, when you piece them together they are a crude, but accurate, representation of the human genome."

"Interesting," Holcomb commented, sipping his coffee and feigning interest in the people passing outside the window.

"Yes, but it was the ME symbols that caught my eye. ME is the scientific symbol for methyl. There is a genetic process known as gene methylation. This process modulates gene expression—turns it on or off—without modifying the underlying DNA."

Holcomb turned his attention to Sloane, continued sipping his coffee, and waited for her punch line.

"Because I had a representation of the entire human genome, I was able to run a detailed analysis of these images. Our science says either genes are methylated or they're not. These images indicate genes partially methylated—dialed up or dialed down. Theoretically, it's possible, but beyond our current technology."

What are you suggesting, Sloane?" asked a perked up Holcomb.

"I'm suggesting these images indicate a human genome artificially manipulated specifically to modify gene expression. More than that, my program extrapolated the physical and psychological impacts of the manipulation. I'm suggesting, Dr. Holcomb, that your pairs indicate the gods mixed their DNA with ours and these ME images are the recipe."

Holcomb was dumbfounded. "C'mon, Sloane. We've been studying these languages and images for 150 years. Every credible scientist in my field would interpret the entwined snakes and the ME symbol, as I did. You're saying these 450,000-year-old tablets show the blueprint for the modern human being?"

"That's only the beginning, Richard. My program took the DNA and extrapolated the appearance of a creature with this DNA switched completely on."

She swiped her screen to display the next image and she read the look on Holcomb's face. "Are you surprised?"

Holcomb moved closer and examined the image displayed on the ComTab's back screen. "That . . . that resembles a Sumerian depiction of one of their gods."

"Precisely! The physical analysis indicates this species is 120 to 150 percent taller and 50 percent heavier than the average human being is. How does that compare with the Sumerians' descriptions of their gods?"

Holcomb nodded. "I certainly see similarities."

Sloane continued. "The psychological comparison is even more startling. Based on our existing knowledge of DNA and gene expression, it draws some striking distinctions between these two races—humanity and their gods. Your Sumerian gods are egocentric, dominant, and warlike, with a strong need to be in control. In short, they are rulers by nature. Human beings, in comparison, are docile, fearful, and possessing the psychology of a servant."

"Sloane, that sounds like astrology cloaked as psychology. How can you possibility infer these generalized personality characteristics to gods and people?"

"It's a fair criticism. I, too, was concerned about overreaching. I went to Amazon and searched for books to learn more about the temperament of the Sumerian gods. I came across a book published in 1997 titled "Psychology of the Sumerian Gods" by Dr. Richard Holcomb."

Holcomb turned red. "Wow! I didn't know that book was still around."

"Oh, yes," said Sloane. "And I quote: 'The Sumerian gods set the template for gods throughout the cultures of the Near East. They were brooding, angry, arrogant; possessing an extreme desire for human adoration. They moved seamlessly between overt war-like behavior and overt sexual behavior. The myths describe their brutalities towards human beings who disobeyed the commands of the gods. These were gods that needed to be in control.'"

Holcomb swallowed hard. He admired Sloane McKay's enthusiasm, brilliance, and ingenuity in tying the two descriptions together. Yet, the scientific method ruled his thinking. You can't accept such wild assertions without proof. He had doubted his own conclusions about the god-man pairs he found on the tablets. This hypothesis, supported by more hypotheses, was somehow . . . unscientific.

Holcomb felt bad, almost unprofessional, for doing it, but he went into ridicule mode. "Sloane, you're mixing fields and seeing connections where none exist. I was explaining the characteristics of mythological beings, as described in Sumerian myth. That's a long way from putting those gods on the couch and conducting computer-extrapolated genetic psychoanalysis.

You're drawing conclusions based on images analyzed by an algorithm, and then extrapolated based on imprecise genetic information. I don't wish to be rude, but that would never stand up to peer review."

Sloane took the criticism in stride. "I'm not offended, Richard. I'm used to these kinds of responses to my ideas. I agree. It's apples to oranges and it's unscientific, but isn't it interesting how these two widely separated analyses of this data seem to describe the same race? I'm not seeking peer review. I'm here to help you solve the mystery of your tablets. Have you come to a different conclusion?"

Holcomb didn't respond to the question, but continued his questioning. "What about your "technique's analysis of human beings? Look at our history. We're warlike, greedy, and want to control over each other. I don't see servile as a primary human characteristic."

"The analysis is valid. If I'm right, the methylation of the genes in our genome is set to create a definite tendency to defer to authority. Your generalization is accurate in groups, but at the individual level, it's different. Think about how people defer to a god in the sky, the president, or even scientists like us all the time. They are willing to fight, die, or kill for concepts they were born into, never questioned, and never verified. Yet, they are certain of their truth because someone in power told them it was so. Frankly, that's the state of 90 percent of the people in this room or out on that street. They trust *their* experts to tell them what to believe and they rarely question it. When they encounter other people who listened to different authority figures, cognitive dissonance ensues. They see those people and their authority as a threat. That's how wars begin. Ninety-nine percent of those who ever rebel only switch to the paradigm of some countering authority figure. They don't opt out of the authority deference system."

Holcomb was again dazzled by Sloane's ability to articulate a point. "Your colorful and passionate exposition of human tendencies is impressive. Let's say, for the moment, you're right about the genes. Isn't manipulation too strong a conclusion? Maybe we just haven't learned enough about the methylation process to understand partially methylated genes. Maybe this is just the current outcome of natural evolution. You can't prove manipulation."

Sloane was surprised by how easily she was rolling over such a scientist as accomplished and articulate as Holcomb. Now she had to give him a point for going right to the weakness of her argument—the assertion of genetic manipulation.

"Richard, you're right. There are many unknowns. I can't prove it. Let's look at the preponderance of the evidence, though. You have tablets dated to a time well before any of the languages on them should have existed—even before humans should have evolved. Yet, someone had to have carved these tablets in those languages. You found a series of symbolic pairs 23 and 24 in number, matching the number of chromosomes in humans and primates respectively. The second pair was clearly delineated as special. This matches the presumed second chromosome fused in humans and separated in primates. The tablets seem to indicate the pairing of gods and humans. They further indicate DNA manipulation by a method unknown or unproven by our current science and clearly beyond our capability. Finally, my psychological analysis of the Sumerian gods, however I arrived at it, matches the characterization of them by one of the unchallenged experts in the field—you."

Holcomb felt momentarily checkmated. He stared out the window at the people walking by the coffee shop. He reveled for a moment in the implications of Sloane's conclusion to each and every one of them. Finally, he said, "Of course, I'll want to see the specifics of your analysis and how you arrived at these conclusions."

"Of course, I'm happy to make all of it available to you and your team. I've been trying to control my excitement, but I see this as a *real* breakthrough. For the first time, we have overt scientific evidence to support Intervention Theory."

"Or perhaps just symbols on a tablet that we are reading too much into," cautioned Holcomb. "So, what are our next steps?"

"Cutler contacted me yesterday. Has he been in contact with you? He said you would have more information about some reporter he wanted us to talk to."

"Yes. He told me he was arranging a meeting with a Maria Love next week."

"Hmm . . . isn't she the White House correspondent at ANN?"

"Is she? I'd never heard of her."

"What is the interview about?"

"All I know is Cutler has arranged an exclusive for her on our findings related to the tablets. I don't know what he's up to."

Sloane laughed. "Do we have findings that we can share?"

"You obviously do," Holcomb smiled. "Cutler mentioned other people being there as well. He usually keeps me in the dark."

"Have you worked with him before?"

"I've worked with him for more than 20 years. I confess I still have no idea what he does. How do you know him?"

"He approached me about three years ago. He told me he was the director of something called the Nanna Consortium. Apparently, they have an interest in supporting scientists pursuing hard data on speculative scientific topics. Cutler has been my only contact, but the grants keep rolling in and I get to do the work I love."

Holcomb connected with that. "I've been very fortunate, in the same way, over the years. In an odd way, Cutler has been responsible for much of my success too."

"Well," said Sloane rising. "I must be going. Thank you for the spirited conversation."

"I'm still a bit skeptical about your findings, but thank you for the time and effort you put into them. I guess I'll see at the Maria Love interview," Holcomb said holding her eyes for a moment.

"Would you like to share a cab?" she offered.

"No. Thank you. I drove. Besides, I rarely get to sit and people watch. I think I'll hang out here a while longer and ponder my fate and that of the rest of the slaves," Holcomb replied playfully.

"Good-bye, Richard," Sloane said as she brushed slowly past him on her way to the door. Her perfume hung in the air for a moment, leaving a lingering impression.

What an impressive woman, he thought. For a moment, Holcomb thought of Anne. Sloane McKay challenged him the way Anne used to challenge him. He missed the challenge. He was taken by Sloane's compelling presentation, but could any of it be true? He scanned the coffee shop crowd—drinking their coffee and working on their computers. He watched pedestrians and cars outside moving from one place to another like ants. Could everything we think we know be false?

A man came out of nowhere and bumped Holcomb hard. The man hurried off without an apology. Holcomb turned to get a look at him, but saw only the man's back hurrying out the door. When he turned back to the table, he found a folded piece of paper in front of him. He opened the note and mouthed words in a whisper.

Holcomb, stop the pseudoscience. Things are not what they seem. Meet me along the waterfront at the Adventure Aquarium. 3:15.

(25)
SCI

Holcomb found a bench along the Delaware River in front of New Jersey's Adventure Aquarium. He closed his eyes and turned his face toward the hot summer sun. He inhaled deeply and slowly exhaled. For a man used to spending his days locked in the laboratory working his mystery, today felt like an adventure. His planned meeting with the beautiful and challenging Sloane McKay now led to a secret meeting in a conspicuous place with an anonymous man.

Holcomb scanned the Philadelphia skyline across the river and then down the Jersey side, pausing on the majestic U.S.S. New Jersey anchored a short distance away. A suspicious man passed slowly by, eyeing Holcomb as he walked. Holcomb was about to speak to him when he felt a hand on his shoulder.

"Good afternoon, Dr. Holcomb," said a male voice, as a nondescript middle-aged man swung around the bench and slid into the seat next to Holcomb. The man stared straight ahead at the river, as if purposely to avoid eye contact.

"Good afternoon, Mr.—" Holcomb paused expectantly.

"My name isn't important. What's important is what I have to say to you."

"Well, if that's the way you want to play—"

"Dr. Holcomb," the man interrupted, "Would you call yourself a patriotic man?"

"You bet!" Holcomb replied.

"The kind of man who would do what needed to be done to protect this country?"

"I just said yes. What's your point?"

"I'm a colleague of Mr. Cutler's. I know he has you working on a special project. He's told you that the project involves U.S. national security. That's a lie," said the stranger.

"I've known Cutler for over twenty years. I've worked on several projects for him. Why would he lie to me?" questioned Holcomb.

"My superiors ordered me to look into Mr. Cutler's activities. I've learned he is part of a cult formed back in the 1990s. He and other members use their positions within U.S. intelligence to further the cult's agenda."

"Cutler doesn't strike me as the cult type," laughed Holcomb. "What kind of cult?"

"They believe the ancient Sumerian gods are real. They worship them and await their return to Earth."

Holcomb sat forward. This was the second time today someone had spoken to him about the Sumerian gods being real. He considered the Cutler he knew. The man was different, but nothing about him screamed cult. "Why do you believe Cutler is involved in this cult? As far as I can tell, he's married to U.S. intelligence."

"We've discovered Cutler was the leader of a group known as The Secret 7. Going back to the 1990s, this group was preparing for a momentous event." The man paused and looked at Holcomb as if waiting for him to fill in a blank.

"What kind of event?" Holcomb asked evenly.

"This group is comprised of ultra-insiders. They're fanatical followers of Enlil. They believe the return of the Sumerian gods—particularly Enlil—is imminent. Their goal is to position themselves as Earth's leaders when their gods return."

Holcomb scoffed, "Sounds like a conspiracy theory to me. I'm a busy man—"

"Dr. Holcomb, have you ever wondered why our government has such a fixation on Iraq?"

Holcomb had wondered many times, and he involuntarily blurted, "Iraq is Sumer."

"Precisely!" said the stranger. "The Secret 7 hatched a plan to demonize the Iraqi regime after the first Gulf War. Their objective was to control Sumer and present it as a gift to Enlil upon his return. For a decade, they built their case against Iraq within government and in the public consciousness. They waited for their moment of opportunity. When September 11 happened, they controlled the right people in the right places and they made their move."

"Made their move?"

"Their plan was to control Iraq. They believed Enlil would return on December 21, 2012. With his help, they planned to establish a new political order on the earth."

"December 21, 2012 was a joke," laughed Holcomb. "Those predictions were greedy people scaring the money out of gullible people."

"But the Sumerian myths do speak of the gods' return, do they not?"

"They do speak of such a return, but the operative word is *myth*."

"It's not a myth to these people. When the 2012 return failed to materialize, their fervor grew. They began execution of their back up plan."

"And that was?" Holcomb asked.

"They formed a foundation called SCI. Perhaps, you've heard of it?"

"Sure. That's the group committed to putting a manned colony on the moon by 2035."

"That's their public mission. Actually, they are a front created to funnel black budget dollars into some highly unusual projects."

"What kind of projects?"

"Do you know what SCI stands for, Dr. Holcomb?"

"I'm afraid I don't."

"It's an acronym for Second Coming Institute—as in Enlil's return to Earth. We believe they're funneling money into the building of advanced spacecraft. Since Enlil did not return, their goal is to fake his return and establish their new global system under this authority."

"That's quite a thesis, but I'm just translating some Cuneiform tablets for Cutler. None of this is my concern."

"What you're working on, Dr. Holcomb, is evidence to build their case."

"Build their case for what?"

"That their Sumerian gods were aliens responsible for the creation of modern humans through the hybridization of their DNA with that of primates. This would give the aliens claim to the planet and claim to us."

Holcomb went cold. For the second time today, someone was telling him aliens had merged their DNA with pre-humans to create modern humans. "What you're proposing is rather fantastic. How would my research help them prove such a thing?"

"Don't be coy, Dr. Holcomb. I know what your work is indicating and I know Sloane McKay is urging you to characterize your data. She works with Cutler. She is really the chief science advisor at SCI."

Holcomb liked McKay. Part of him wanted to leap to her defense, but she did say she got her funding from some consortium.

He thought for a moment about the enigmatic Mr. Cutler and all his delays and ruses over the years. He considered his recent words that now "the timing was right." Doubt was creeping rapidly into his mind. "You say they are going to fake a landing?"

"Yes. We believe Cutler has overseen the construction of several highly advanced craft—decades perhaps centuries ahead of what is publicly known."

"You asked me if I'm a patriot. I absolutely am. I don't know how you expect me to help you, but if what you're saying is true, you can count on me."

"I was hoping you would say that. We are concerned SCI is planning something with this reporter—Maria Love. They're using her to expose evidence that the Sumerian gods are our creators as prelude to their false invasion. I need you to convince Maria Love this evidence is pseudoscience and not something she should be reporting to the public."

"That's it? You arrange a secret meeting with me to persuade me to tell this reporter that I can't substantiate these claims about the Sumerian gods crossbreeding with humanity?"

"I know it seems mundane, but we believe Maria Love is a lynchpin in their plan to release this information to the public and begin conditioning them for this *alien* invasion. You would be doing your country a great service by helping us stop it."

"Well, I don't believe the tablets can truly substantiate those claims anyway. I will do all I can to make sure Maria Love understands the reality."

The stranger seemed satisfied with Holcomb's answer. He removed a small device from his pocket. It was cubed, about twice the size of a die, and translucent. "Dr. Holcomb, this is so important to national security, that I have been authorized to reward you for your success."

"Reward me? How?"

The man stared at the gadget in his hand. "How long has it been since you lost your wife, Dr. Holcomb? Six years? Her name was Anne, wasn't it?"

Holcomb tensed, as the stranger's knowledge was crowding his personal space. "How do you know about my wife?"

Without answering, the man continued. "Have you ever imagined visiting the Sumerian city-state Ur, rather than having to surmise it from tablets and artifacts? What if you could visit Ur in its prime and observe it first-hand? Imagine the leaps forward that would make possible in your field."

"You're talking about time travel. That would be amazing, but quite impossible."

"Would you like to see your wife, Dr. Holcomb?"

"Don't toy with me. I'll walk away right now!"

"I'm not toying with you. I'm offering you a taste of the gratitude you would receive for helping us in this matter. You see this device, well I'm not going to get technical, but it uses thoughts to tune into various times in our timeline—past and future. You can use it to go back in time and spend time with your wife—as much time as you want. You'd like that, wouldn't you?"

The thought of spending one more moment with Anne nearly overwhelmed Holcomb, but his scientific skepticism intervened. "That's nonsense. The universe does not work like that. We must deal with the reality of loss and not comfort ourselves with false hope."

"There's no false hope here, Dr. Holcomb. Take it for a test drive. If you like it, help us debunk Cutler and SCI and it's yours."

The man handed the device to Holcomb. "Put it in your hand and focus your thoughts on a moment in time you would like to visit."

Holcomb took the tiny cube and eyed it skeptically. "I feel like you're asking me to do an incantation. This is ridiculous."

"I assure you, Dr. Holcomb. This is real. Close your eyes and focus your thoughts on a moment."

Holcomb hesitantly closed his eyes and focused on that moment six years ago. He had not been present. Still, he endlessly played the possible scenarios in his mind. He began to relax and now was focusing on the moment right before Anne's car crash. He wanted so badly to be there with her. He felt his consciousness flicker. He opened his eyes and discovered he was in the car with Anne. She was driving and he was in the passenger seat. She looked over at him and smiled, as if it was perfectly normal for him to be there.

"I love you, Rich," she said and grasped his hand.

Emotions filled Holcomb. He choked back tears. Her hand was warm in his. Her pulse ticked vigorously with life. He noted the time on the car clock 9:21 A.M., just three minutes before the crash that took her from him.

"You look so beautiful today, Annie," he managed.

"Why thank you, Dr. Holcomb," she replied playfully, "You're not so bad yourself."

So many thoughts rushed to his mind. He was here. Could he change the timeline and the outcome? What if he warned her? As much as he wanted to try, he needed to know more about how this worked before he played with the timeline. Perhaps the man could tell him more about the limitations of this experience. He decided to hold her hand and be with her this time. He could always come back and change this moment once he had the device.

Suddenly, a car ahead and to the left blew a tire and swerved into Anne's lane. She let out a scream and then impact at 60 miles per hour. Holcomb felt the car begin to flip. He looked across and saw the horror on his lovely wife's face. Then there was another flickering of consciousness and he found himself back on the bench, shaking and weeping.

"I take it we have a deal?" asked the man.

Holcomb nodded, trying to regain his composure.

The stranger reached over and took the device from Holcomb. As he did, Holcomb noticed the most exquisite watch he'd ever seen. Large diamonds surrounded the face and laced throughout the band. It didn't seem like the kind of watch a government employee would own. Holcomb noted the word Mason engraved on the watch.

"That's a nice watch," commented Holcomb.

"Thanks," replied the man with complete disinterest. "I must be going. I will be in touch again after your meeting with Maria Love. Remember she must be convinced that this is absolutely fiction."

"I understand."

The man tilted his head, as if to indicate goodbye, and walked away up the waterfront.

Holcomb sat for a moment soaking in the river and the summer day. The stranger's story connected some dots. Why were Cutler and McKay so eager to persuade him of this Intervention Theory? Did they have a nefarious agenda? Maybe they were playing him.

He pondered the stranger's offer. Being with Anne again, if only for a moment, intoxicated him. Now, he knew there was a way in this universe to spend time with her. If the cost of having her back was to debunk a doubtful theory, so be it.

(26)

Maria Finds a Partner

"How long will this take?" Maria asked impatiently.

"Not long," replied Utu, Inanna's Chief Intelligence Officer.

Maria came aboard Rakbu for dinner. She needed Inanna's assistance. After her meeting with Biggs, she knew locating Reggie Washington off-grid would be a challenge. She was confident Inanna could help. Relying on people was hard for Maria, but she noticed her increasing dependence upon Inanna. All the while, Inanna encouraged her to be more independent. She constantly filled Maria's head with talk of The Future Possible and Maria's special role in it.

Maria and Inanna watched as Utu hacked his way through multiple U.S. intelligence databases, adeptly bypassing subroutines and firewalls until he reached a system called VetTrack. "We're in," he said proudly.

The screen displayed a crowded interactive map that seemed to be tracking thousands and thousands of targets. It reminded Maria of an air traffic control screen. "What are we looking at? Maria asked.

"Your Pentagon has inserted implantable chips in every soldier on active duty going back to the first Gulf War," Inanna replied. "The chip allows your government to track every active duty service person and veteran anywhere on the planet."

Utu entered all the information Maria had on Washington.

VetTrack automatically searched for his unique transponder code among the millions on the screen. Within seconds, the system identified his transponder code. Slowly it zoomed from a global view to a national view to a local view accurate to within a few feet. Suddenly,

"Got him," said Utu.

Washington's transponder code was located in a very remote part of Idaho in the Frank Church National Wilderness. A report displayed detailing his movements over the past 12 hours. Clearly, he was alive and living way off the grid.

Utu reviewed the area's topography. He determined it would take Maria at least two days on foot to reach Washington's location from the nearest trailhead. The mountainous and thickly forested terrain would be dangerous for an experienced hiker. That was not Maria. They had to get her closer. Inanna decided to transport Maria a few hundred yards from Washington's location. A scan revealed he was living in a well-constructed cabin with an unusually large radio signal.

Inanna expressed concern about Maria going alone, but offered no personnel from her ship to support. She reiterated that Maria—that the humans—must do this alone. Maria had maintained communication with Jaypee Escudero. She convinced Inanna to allow him to join the mission. Maria contacted Jaypee, who excitedly accepted. He joked that this would be his first scheduled abduction.

Inanna transported Escudero aboard Rakbu the following morning. Inanna personally showed him around the ship. Maria and he spent the afternoon with Security Chief Uruk learning to use the Anunnaki-provided equipment they were to use. Inanna invited them for a private dinner in her quarters. Her chef prepared Philippine Paella in Escudero's honor.

"This recipe is amazing, Inanna," commented Jaypee. "It almost tastes like my mother's recipe."

Inanna acknowledged the compliment. "Jaypee, circumstances have changed. I have a device called a TimeCube. It enables me to scan the timeline to gauge the likelihood of certain events occurring. We consult it as a guide in challenging situations."

Jaypee listened with peaked interest and a researcher's attention. "That's amazing, Inanna. When you say circumstances have changed, what do you mean?"

"This is important information for both of you," continued Inanna. "It appears your partnership is to play a critical role in disclosing the truth to humanity."

Maria and Jaypee looked at each other. Maria spoke, "Critical how, Inanna?"

"I'm not ready to share the details yet. It could interfere with the natural course of events."

Maria objected, "Inanna, I thought we moved beyond the secrecy between us."

"We are, Maria. I promise there will be full transparency in due time. For now, I still need you to trust me and follow your own instincts. That goes for you too, Jaypee. I am willing to help, as I am on this evening's adventure, but you need to do it yourselves."

Jaypee spoke up, "Inanna, would it be possible for us to see this TimeCube?"

Inanna looked at Maria and saw she could still use a confidence builder. "Computer, recognize my security voice print," said Inanna.

"Voice print recognized," replied the computer.

"Locate my TimeCube and transport it onto the table at my present location."

A tiny bluish beam appeared on the dinner table and deposited a small translucent cube.

Inanna picked up the cube and held it in the center of her massive hand. "In the time of my father, the Anunnaki royal family was given these devices by an unknown race. I believe my father knew who they were, but he would never share the information with me. My Uncle Enki told me these devices were given to us with a condition that we keep Earth and the human race under control."

"How were they used to keep us under control?" asked Jaypee.

"Enki was always cryptic about that. From an early age, he instilled that in me. He was more like a father to me than my father was. He told me he did not agree with the terms, but he took this device to stay on an even playing field. He knew my father and my brother would use it to keep humanity under their thumbs. He gave this to me when I embarked on this mission for Earth transparency."

"How does it work," queried Maria?

"We don't know," Inanna answered. "We've studied the device, but how it works continues to elude us. We do know it detects quantum vibrations in the timeline and calibrates possibilities and probabilities."

"If you don't know how it works, how do you use it?" asked Jaypee.

"Its use was demonstrated to us. You hold it in your hand and you think about an event: past, future, probable or actual. It projects visions of possible events into your mind. The images are very clear—like a lucid dream. The TimeCube provides a likelihood report for every observed event. This tells us how likely that event it to occur. Sometimes we can even tell when the event will occur. The accuracy is 98.2 percent. My brother, the king, has highly trained Seers. They use the device to pinpoint future events or trends leading to events. He uses these reports to guide policy and military strategy. These devices helped make the Anunnaki a formidable military opponent for anyone in the known galaxy—even races more technologically advanced. We could project battle scenarios and adjust our strategy and tactics to maximize our advantage."

"Fascinating," offered an enthralled Jaypee.

"Jaypee," said Inanna, raising a wine glass and pointing it at him, "By bringing you aboard my ship and sharing these things with you, I have taken you into my confidence. I recognize this information would be a coup for you in your field of research. I must insist that you share none of this."

Maria protested again. "Inanna, I'm confused. You keep saying you want disclosure and yet you keep demanding secrecy."

Inanna had come to expect Maria's objections. She rather enjoyed them. "Maria," she smiled, "I only suggest he not reveal it before the press conference. After that, he can share it with the world. In fact, I'm counting on it."

"Press conference?" queried Jaypee.

"It's a secret," laughed Maria, "I'll tell you later."

"Well, the two of you have an interesting night ahead. It is now dark over the western United States. You should get going. Dress warmly. Washington's cabin sits at about 6200 feet. It's going to be chilly, especially for you Jaypee, and very dark."

"You sound like my mother, Inanna," chided Maria.

"I have something else for you," Inanna handed a small device to each of them. "These devices allow us to track you. The large button on top is an auto-transport control. If you get into any trouble, simply press that button and you will instantly be transported back to the ship."

"Thank you, Inanna," replied Jaypee.

"Inanna, please don't worry. I've reported in war zones. Jay is an experienced hiker. We'll be fine."

Inanna grabbed Maria by her shoulders and looked down at her intently. "The TimeCube is very uncertain about the outcome of this mission. There is a reason a man lives in a place like this. He doesn't want to be found."

"If it's so dangerous, why don't you send some security officers with us?" retorted Maria.

Inanna released Maria and paced haltingly away from her, head down as if pondering. "No. You must do this alone. The Father Creator has been clear with me."

"The Father Creator?" Jaypee asked.

"I'll tell you about that later too," Maria smiled at Jaypee and turned back toward Inanna. "If it's that risky and you won't help us, why risk it? Do we need him?"

"You're interview with Biggs indicated he has a piece of evidence. If that evidence is what I believe it is, it's critical to your case."

Jaypee could see the concern on Inanna's face. "Don't worry, Inanna. I will bring her home."

Inanna smiled and hoped for the best.

(27)
Contacting Washington

Two bright blue beams pierced the pitch black of the Frank Church National Wilderness. Inanna outfitted Maria and Jaypee with highly advanced night vision goggles. They turned the darkness into an experience similar to wearing sunglasses at noon. They also had a special microphone that muted the sound of their voices in the air, while flawlessly transmitting it into the other's earpiece.

Maria scanned their surroundings and quickly spotted the cabin. Her built-in distance finder and altimeter indicated it was 100.3 yards ahead and 42.8 feet above them in altitude. It was perched atop a flat bluff overlooking a large valley. She motioned to Jaypee.

"I see it," he replied.

They slowly made their way along a narrow path, obviously cleared intentionally. The jagged path was steps from a sheer cliff on the left and crowded by a dense forest on the right. Jaypee led the way. He made sure to let Maria know where the path narrowed or where the footing was faulty.

Maria peered over the edge. Her goggles registered the 507-foot drop to the bottom of the canyon. Some pebbles gave way beneath her and she collapsed down to one knee. "Damn it!"

"Are you OK?" Jaypee asked.

"I twisted my ankle. I'm all right. This sure seems like more than 100 yards."

Clearly, this location didn't lend itself to a quick retreat. Maria checked her pocket for the transporter device—their emergency way back to Rakbu. Whew! It's still there. That might come in handy.

The night was still. The sound of Jaypee's breathing into his mouthpiece occupied Maria's ears. Jack's face flashed through her mind. She recalled the look of disappointment when she told him about this assignment. She hadn't even shared the danger or the details. Suddenly, she realized if something happened out here, he might never know. Inanna wouldn't let that happen, she comforted herself. Inanna seemed to need her.

As they reached the end of the path, Jaypee grabbed Maria's hand and pulled her into the forest on the right. They paused and knelt behind a patch of bushes. The cabin sat in the middle of the clearing beyond the bushes.

"How do you want to do this, Maria?"

"I was hoping you might have a good idea."

Jaypee shook his head. "I hadn't really pondered the logistics. My father was a Filipino Marine. I chose academia."

"I guess we walk up and knock on the door . . . carefully."

They rose and took two steps into the clearing when they saw a bright flash and the unmistakable boom of a shotgun. The sound reverberated off the canyon walls. The ground seemed to shake. Maria and Jaypee instinctively hit the ground. Maria looked up and saw a man standing on the front porch of the cabin. The second barrel was ready and aimed right at her.

"Mr. Washington," she shouted, trying to prevent her terror from reflecting in her voice, "Lucas Biggs sent me."

"Biggs?" Washington replied. "Biggs is dead."

"No, sir," assured Maria rising, her hands in the air, "He's alive. He's at Walter Reed. I spoke to him three days ago."

"Damn! I thought they probably killed him this time,"

exclaimed Washington. "He hasn't been returning my emails. I thought sure he was dead. How do I know you're not government here to take me back there? I won't go back there!"

"I'm Maria Love and—"

"The TV reporter?" asked Washington.

"Yes. You've heard of me?" asked a surprised Maria.

Washington lowered his gun. "Ms. Love, I didn't move out here without a plan. I specialized in electronic during my army hitch. I have a communication set-up here that would put some intelligence agencies to shame."

Maria began to brush the dirt off her. "This is Dr. Jaypee Escudero."

Jaypee smiled and waved, "Hello, Mr. Washington."

"Escudero," Washington thought for a moment, "you're that UFO guy. You were on that America Overnight show a few weeks ago?"

"Yes," Jaypee confirmed.

"I talked to you. I told you about something that happened in Iraq, while I was in the service."

"Yes. Yes, that's right."

"Mr. Washington, that event is why we're here. May we come inside?" asked Maria.

There was a momentary pause. "You're not armed are you?"

"We're not armed," Maria answered.

"Well, that's just crazy! Who in their right mind come out here unarmed? How did you get here? How did you find me?"

"Mr. Washington, I promise. We'll explain everything if we can just come in."

"Come on in," Washington waved the shotgun and sheepishly lowered it.

Maria entered the cabin, expecting backwoods rustic. Instead, she found a rather inviting living room with a roaring fire warming the late May night. There were the telltale signs that a single man lived here, but it was nice. Across the room, there was a spacious two-wall desk loaded with five large monitors. One monitor displayed what appeared to be a sophisticated and detailed air-traffic control screen. Another seemed to be crunching massive numbers. A third displayed an NBA basketball game. Images from UFO lore and Washington's military service adorned the walls.

Washington leaned the gun against the wall near the door and invited his guests to have a seat. "I don't get many guests out here. Oh, there's the occasional bear, mountain lion, or raccoon, but not people—and certainly not beautiful White House correspondents from major news networks and Filipino PhDs. What gives?"

Maria and Jaypee looked at each other uncomfortably, neither sure what to say next.

"No offense," Washington broke the silence, "but you don't look like the kind of hardcore hikers it would take to reach this cabin. Besides, I have motion detectors rigged in trees for hundreds of yards around this place. You just appeared out of nowhere and set off my alarms. That's damned unusual."

Maria played coy. "People don't just appear, Mr. Washington. We flew in by helicopter this afternoon and hiked the rest of the way this evening. Maybe your alarms are malfunctioning."

Washington's eyebrows raised and his forehead crinkled. "Now, don't BS me, young lady. There are only two groups that can make people appear out of nowhere. Them," he said pointing at an image of the Pentagon on the wall, "and them," he looked up emphatically and pointed to the sky.

"Them?" Maria feigned.

"Ms. Love, don't ever play poker with me. Ask the doctor here. He studies them."

"Look, Mr. Washington. I did see Lucas Biggs three days ago in Washington D.C. He explained to me what the two of you— your team—experienced in Iraq. Jaypee and I are working to help uncover the truth about your experience."

"My experience, Ms. Love, is that I was a patriotic young man who served my country. I signed up for the hardest assignments our military can dish out. Then I was laughed at, ignored, and left behind by my government. Do you know how that feels?"

"No, obviously, I don't," replied Maria, looking Washington right in the eye and hoping to gain his trust.

"It feels like a damn kick in the stomach. That's how it feels. They send recruiters into areas like where I grew up. They talk to young men about glory and fill their heads with that red, white, and blue baloney. Then they send you to some God-forsaken place all in the cause of some corporation's bottom line. Lieutenant Biggs, me, and the rest of our team were serving our country that night. We didn't ask for that assignment, but we showed up and we did our job. For our trouble, they called us thieves and lunatics. Two members of our squad took their own lives before they were 30. I wasn't going to let them win."

Jaypee was eager to jump into the conversation now. "I was intrigued by your case the night we talked on America Overnight. What else can you tell me?"

"I don't remember what I told you. I've called that show dozens of times. It's a place where someone like me can tell his story to thousands of people without being laughed at."

Jaypee tried to focus Reggie. "You told me you were in a battle with Iraqi soldiers. You said you were killed and came back to life. You said something about a bluish beam."

"Yeah, man. That's what went down," Washington paused and reflected.

Maria jumped in. "Biggs told me the two of you are the only survivors from your unit. He said they've kept both of you in and out of psych wards for the past 20 years."

"Damn straight and I'm not going back! Now, why don't you tell me how you really found me?"

Maria raised her hands in a calming motion. "We're not here to take you back. We're here to help."

"Really? How can you help me?"

"By bringing the truth to light."

"Ha! The truth and three bucks will buy you a cup of coffee in our current political system, Ms. Love."

"How did you find me?" Reggie insisted.

"We gained access to a sophisticated intelligence database . . ." Maria paused looking for the right words.

"Damn it! I have a tracking chip in me, don't I?"

"It would appear so," Maria said.

"I knew it! It was in those damn vaccines they gave us. Some of my buddies told me they were putting nanobots in the vaccines."

"Well, I don't know how they did it, Reggie, but that database tracked you right to this cabin as easily as if you were standing in Times Square. You think you're out here hiding and they've known where you are all along."

"Damn! I knew it. You can't trust those SOBs!"

Maria felt like she was getting through. "Reggie, Jay and I are working with some people to get UFOs, alien abductions, and situations like yours out into the open. We want the truth to be known so there's no more ridicule for heroes like Lucas and you."

Tears welled in Reggie's eyes. "They're real! Years after the incident I did some regressive hypnosis. I just wanted to know what I couldn't remember. We were on some ship. They were . . .

fixing . . . us. I know we were dead by our standards, but not by theirs. They healed us and they . . . they put us back in those vehicles and left us out in the desert."

"What else?" Jaypee prompted.

"They left this scar on my thumb as evidence," Washington answered, holding up his hand and revealing a four-inch scar, "I heard them say it during my regression."

"Lucas said something about an artifact the two of you have traded back and forth over the years."

"Yeah. That was the other piece of evidence."

"Did it come from the crate," Maria asked, "or from elsewhere?"

"I don't know. It was in the Lieutenant's pocket next morning. We managed to hold onto it while they interrogated us. They thought we stole those vehicles. That's all they wanted to know. They weren't interested in our orders, the crate, or the bluish light."

"Do you have it?"

"Yes, ma'am, I do. It's right over here. The artifact is strange. It's really old, but it has properties similar to modern electronics."

Reggie held the artifact in the light. At first glance, nothing about it seemed remarkable. The stone was roundish, flat, and about the size of Reggie's hand. Hieroglyphics covered the polished surface.

"It looks like an old stone," Jaypee commented.

"I know right?" Reggie responded. "Watch this."

He grabbed a hand-held x-ray reader and passed the stone in front of it. "Look at the dense circuitry inside it. If you could power up this baby, my guess is it has the computing power of your average ComTab."

"How old is it?" Maria asked.

"I don't know. *Old.*" Reggie replied. "You can't cut it either."

"What's the writing say?" wondered Jaypee

Maria suddenly realized she recognized the writing. "It's Sumerian. I minored in Near East studies in college. That's Sumerian. There's no doubt about it."

"Can you read it?" asked Jaypee.

"I recognize Enlil . . . Enki . . . Earth . . . There's a date of some kind. These look like they might be the other planets in the solar system. Each one has a number inside of it. Some of these numbers might represent fractions. That's Earth. It has a one within it. This body has 318. This body has 95 . . . 14 . . . 17 . . . 3."

Jaypee chimed in. "I am an amateur astronomer. Those numbers appear to be the relative masses of the outer planets in our solar system. Jupiter, Saturn, Uranus, Neptune. I'm not sure what planet has three times the earth's mass."

"I know what planet has three times—" The sound of two helicopters hovering above the canyon interrupted Maria. Powerful spotlights blinded them through the window.

Reggie instinctively reached for his shotgun. "I've never had anyone come here in three years," he said, "and now visitors twice in 45 minutes. Please tell me that's your ride."

"We didn't come in helicopters," Maria responded.

"Yeah, I figured that out."

They saw flashes coming from the helicopters and bullets riddled the front of the cabin. Maria, Reggie, and Jaypee hit the deck just in time. The copters crept closer and continued firing. The hail of bullets obliterated the computer monitors along the back wall of the living room.

Then the firing paused. Reggie looked through the shattered front window. He saw commandos dressed in black piling out of the helicopters, which had now landed in the clearing. They could hear voices and footfalls surrounding the cabin.

"We need to get out of here," he shouted.

There was another deafening round of fire coming from both the helicopters and the commandos.

"You're about to find out how we got here," Maria yelled. "Do you have the artifact?"

Reggie slithered across the floor and retrieved it. "I have it."

An explosion on the front porch banged Reggie's head hard against the floor, knocking him unconscious.

"Jay, I'll hold on to his right arm. You grab his left. Hopefully, this thing will take all three of us."

There were two loud slams into the front door and the commandos burst through.

"Now, Jay, now!" Maria shouted.

They hit the buttons on the auto-transport devices, but nothing happened. Only the dark and a few seconds separated them from a confrontation with the heavily armed commandos. Panic filled Maria's mind. Jack's image passed before her. Finally, she felt the familiar tingle of the bluish beam.

They materialized aboard Rakbu in their laying positions, covered in dust and glass. Maria and Jaypee coughed profusely. Reggie wasn't moving or making a sound.

Uruk greeted them, as he communicated with Inanna on the bridge. "We have them, Mistress, all three of them."

Maria stood and helped Jay to his feet. She staggered over to Reggie, nudged him, and called his name. There was no response. She noted a large wound on the back of his head.

"He needs help!" she shouted.

Uruk called Dr. Enti and had Reggie transported directly to the hospital. Maria picked up the artifact Reggie had left lying on the transporter platform.

The doors slid open and Inanna pushed urgently into the room and came directly to Maria. "Are you unharmed, my child?"

"I'm fine, but Reggie is severely wounded. What happened? Our devices malfunctioned. I thought we were dead!"

Inanna sighed heavily. "We were monitoring you carefully. There was a complication. I was worried this would happen."

"Worried what would happen?" Jaypee asked.

"We are able to detect certain types of interference in the timeline. When the helicopters appeared, we detected a variance indicating the timeline was being altered."

"I don't understand. We were out in the middle of nowhere. Who could have known we'd be there?" Maria asked.

"They didn't just know where you'd be. They knew when you'd be too. Someone tried to ambush you and stop our plan."

"Who?" Maria asked.

"I'm not sure. We will have to be much more careful going forward."

"They monitored the timeline using a TimeCube, didn't they?" Maria caught on quickly.

"Yes, but not a TimeCube like mine. My TimeCube predicts probabilities, but it cannot alter the timeline or insert people or things into it. Those helicopters were not supposed to be there. They were literally added to that moment in the timeline from some other moment. They appeared on our TimeCube and ship sensors simultaneously and without warning."

Maria's head was spinning a bit.

"That's a huge advantage. How do we counter it?" Jaypee asked.

"We don't know exactly how it works. We believe our adversaries have found a way to add someone's thoughts into the TimeCube equation. By reading the thoughts, they are able to see the person's plans—time and location included. Once they know when and where, they are able to take action to disrupt the timeline. "

"They're reading our thoughts?" asked Maria.

"Yes. We believe that must be the mechanism being used to pinpoint moments on the timeline."

A huge smile came across Jaypee's face. "This is so cool! I've waited my whole life to know things like this."

"This is a serious matter, Jay," Inanna warned.

"I know, but it is still so cool! How do we counter it?"

"Going on the assumption that our adversaries are able to monitor our thoughts, Dr. Enti was able to create an implant to scramble them to an outside source. My whole crew now has been testing them and incidences of timeline interference have dropped precipitously."

"How does it work?" Maria asked.

"The device is painlessly implanted behind your left ear. Dr. Enti tells me it transmits a low-level field that randomizes thoughts about past and future. We believe this confuses the mind-monitoring technologies. It's not fool-proof, but it's the best defense we have right now."

"I see," Maria nodded, trying to follow.

"Dr. Enti can explain it better than I can," confided Inanna.

"It makes sense," inserted Jaypee. "There have been studies showing definitive brain patterns when we are thinking of the past or the future. If an advanced mind-probing technology could read those patterns, it could indicate past or present. The intensity of those patterns might indicate the nearness of the event."

Maria objected, "Jay, how could any technology account for all the complexities of our thoughts?"

Jaypee smiled. "Ah, Maria! You're thinking like a 21st Century human. For our level of technology, it is quite impossible. Maybe not for a race far more advanced like the Anunnaki."

"Jay, I'm afraid you're giving us too much credit. This technology was given to us by an even more advanced race. We may understand the basics of how it works, but we are far from capable of replicating it."

Maria held the artifact up to the light. "This is what tonight's mission was all about, wasn't it?"

Inanna nodded. "Of course, you had to—"

"I know. Do it ourselves," Maria completed.

"Yes. Well, I recommend both of you see Dr. Enti immediately and receive the implant. We need to discuss plans for a meeting where you can put all the puzzle pieces together."

"Put the pieces together? Maria mused. "I don't even know what the puzzle is supposed to be yet."

"I am confident it will all become clear to you when all the right people are in the room. I am having that arranged right now. Keep the artifact. It will be important."

"If we're doing it ourselves, why does it feel like you are orchestrating the whole thing?" Maria wondered aloud.

"Maria, my child, I have simply rented the hall. The people in this meeting will play the concert leading to understanding."

"That's quite poetic, Inanna. Who will be in the meeting?" Maria asked.

"People able to piece this puzzle together—people with the knowledge, ideas, and evidence to see the truth."

"So Reggie, assuming he's OK, and Biggs—"

"Biggs will not be present. Mr. Biggs is dead," Inanna shared.

"Dead?" Maria gasped in shock.

"It is related to this evening's timeline corruption. The mission in Iraq is an important piece of this, Maria. Biggs and Reggie were the only two men alive who could corroborate that event. You need that testimony for your case. The TimeCube showed us Biggs' death just moments before the helicopters showed up tonight. Two men showed up in his hospital room and strangled him. Someone wanted to silence them both."

"Will Reggie make it?" Jaypee asked.

"Dr. Enti reported to me in my heads-up display. Reggie will be fine. He has a nasty cut and a concussion. I am ordering an implant for him too. We will erase his memory of coming to the ship and—"

"Erase his memory. Are we back on that again?" Maria protested.

"Maria, he is now the only witness to an important piece of this story. His testimony must not be tainted by memories of being here. We need him to share what happened to him in Iraq and present the artifact to the panel," argued Inanna.

"Those are all the reasons to keep his memory intact and keep him safely aboard the Rakbu. His cabin is a total loss. Whoever is after him will find him there. This is the safest place for him. When do we get beyond conveniently removing human memory when it suits your purposes, Inanna? Maybe we can just explain the situation to him and let him make the choice," countered Maria.

"It's too risky," Inanna shook her head. "We've come too far."

"Yes, we have!" Maria asserted. "We've come too far for you not to trust us!"

"His coming aboard was an unintended accident, Maria."

"The Father Creator told me there are no accidents, Inanna. Maybe this is all a part of the disclosure process."

"Inanna, you brought me into your confidence. Why not Reggie?" chimed Jaypee. "Tonight was the second time Reggie's life was placed in jeopardy as part of this grand scheme. Hasn't he earned the right to be a full partner in this?"

Inanna looked at the two determined humans. Maria had chosen her partner well. "Very well," she assented, "but you need to talk to him and make sure he understands the purpose of this panel and his role in it. Maria, the format for this meeting will be a roundtable. Your role is to draw out the evidence and fill in the blanks of the story. Not everyone in the meeting knows the purpose of it and not everyone shares our view of the world. Do you understand?"

Maria looked at Jaypee and smiled in victory. "I understand, Inanna. Thank you for letting us do it our way."

"Perhaps that is the only way we succeed. It is the Anunnaki way to control things. Old habits die hard."

"We can do this," Maria asserted, looking to Jaypee for assurance.

"Ni gawin ito Hayaan! Let's do this!"

"We have arranged a secure location for the discussion. Mr. Cutler will moderate," Inanna instructed.

(28)
Night of the Roundtable

Richard Holcomb sat alone and uncomfortably at a large old money dining table. Around the table were sixteen settings with a name displayed for each one. He scanned the names around the table. He recognized Sloane McKay and Maria Love, but the other names were a complete mystery to him. He was in the dark about the evening's agenda, other than a clearly expensive dinner.

His strange meeting on the Delaware River days before indicated he would face a moment of decision during this meeting. What kind of decision he could only imagine. All he could think about was the opportunity to spend more time with Anne. He might say anything or do anything for even a few fleeting moments with her.

The other guests filtered into the dining room of the massive Virginia countryside estate. The attendees politely sipped the wine poured by the highly efficient staff. Holcomb noticed many of the guests seemed at ease in this secretive, black-tie setting. He was used to similar academic affairs, but this crowd seemed a step up from that circle. His heart raced with anticipation and some trepidation. He was clear on his desired outcome, but cloudy on the expectations upon him.

Maria arrived, unsure how this evening was to unfold. She assumed Cutler would have more details about her role in the proceedings. Inanna revealed little. Maria gathered she was to interview the other guests relative to alien intervention in human history.

Reggie followed Maria to their seats. Jaypee worked his way around the table, introducing himself and sharing the wide grin he wore so comfortably. Maria smiled, as he seemed to be making fast friends with a middle-aged man seated at the far end of the table. The two of them began walking towards Maria and Reggie.

Jaypee's smile grew as he approached them. "Dr. Shawn Meyer, please meet Maria Love. She is the White House correspondent for ANN and this is Mr. Reggie Washington. He is an Iraq War veteran and a fellow contactee."

Meyer reached his hand out to shake hands, "It's a pleasure to meet you, Maria. I don't often see network correspondents at gatherings like this. Reggie, Jay was just sharing a high-level overview of your case. I've never heard anything like it. I'd love to talk about it in more detail."

Maria looked at Jaypee somewhat surprised by his openness in this unknown setting. Using her eyes, she encouraged him to share more information about his friend.

"Shawn is the director of the UFO Transparency Project and an alien abductee. His group works with governments around the world to promote transparency about the reality of alien contact. We have participated on panels at several conferences in the past."

Meyer's presence at the event baffled Maria. Obviously, there was more to this than the few people she had interviewed. The appearance of a tall young man and the ding of his knife striking a wine glass interrupted Maria's thoughts.

"Friends, welcome to my humble abode. My name is Howard Mason III. My father founded Mason Industries. Some of you may have expected Mr. Cutler to host this event. He was detained with other matters and he asked me to stand in for him."

Maria felt concerned. Inanna was not aware of the plan to change hosts. Maria wondered how much control Inanna really had in this process.

"Those of you who know me are aware of my deep and abiding passion for the topic of human origins. Our speakers this evening have groundbreaking information to share with us. With this guest list, I expect a spirited discussion to ensue."

Chuckles erupted from the far end of the table.

"In any case," Mason continued, "I assure you all communications in this room are secure and safe. Feel free to speak openly."

Maria scanned the faces around the table. They seemed a misfit bunch of intellectuals, policy makers, and business types. Her stomach tightened, wondering about their agendas.

"First, I have a surprise for you courtesy of Mason Industries. Your dinner this evening will be prepared to order by the world's first fully programmable commercial 3D food printer. Simply speak your seat number and your food selection into the ComTab at the center of the table. Your dinner will be "printed" directly onto your plate in less than three minutes."

A large apparatus descended from the ceiling with printer arms protruding from it. Each arm positioned itself above a plate and methodically created the requested dish. The room buzzed with conversation at the amazing technological display. The guests dined on everything from vegetarian lasagna to shrimp scampi.

When everyone had finished eating, Mason stood and spoke again, "Well, I hope everyone found the meal preparation fascinating and the food delightful. It's time to get on with the evening's agenda. Normally, these meetings involve long PowerPoint presentations. Tonight our format is a bit different. We have a world-class journalist in our midst—Ms. Maria Love. She's going to interview witnesses and researchers tonight to help us piece together a startling new mystery of human origins."

Holcomb stiffened and went cold, as the man he had met along the Delaware River appeared in the corner behind Mason and took a seat. The man eyed Holcomb and gave a nearly imperceptible nod. He then inconspicuously opened his palm so that Holcomb could see the promised time device.

"With that, Ms. Love, I will turn it over to you."

Without directions of how to proceed or list of guests and credentials, Maria was unsure how to begin. However, she told Inanna she could handle it and now was her chance to prove it. She decided to tell the story chronologically and hope other guests would jump in with their pieces of the puzzle.

"Good evening, ladies and gentlemen," Maria began. "We often hear this debate in our society between those who believe human beings are an act of intelligent design and those who believe in a strictly materialist evolution of our species. For the past month or so, I've been gathering evidence of a third possibility. I must admit to being skeptical at first. However, as I learned more about this third possibility, I have become convinced of its validity and reality. Tonight, with your help, I want to explore that third possibility—outside intervention in human origins."

A voice from the far end of the large table spoke, "Interventionism sounds like nothing more than a muddled new age intelligent design theory to me. I think what she's talking about is the repeatedly debunked ancient alien hypothesis."

Murmuring spread around the table. Maria sensed the energy flowing against her.

"Dr. Nagas," Mason inserted, "please let Ms. Love call her witnesses and make her case. You will have time to rebut her ideas."

"Thank you, Mr. Mason." Maria turned to the man who had spoken out. "I'm sorry, who are you, sir?"

"I'm Dr. Eric Nagas—director of the American Skeptics Alliance. My life's work involves helping people overcome their delusions about fairy godmothers, angels, and demons."

His snarky comment made Maria feel a bit combative. "Does the concept of intervention frighten you, Dr. Nagas?"

"I'm not frightened by words, Ms. Love. I'm frightened by the delusions people live under. Please continue. I'm eager to hear your riveting evidence of space gods."

"Let her present, Eric, and quit trying to bully her," demanded Shawn Meyer.

"C'mon, Shawn, I remember when you were a real scientist before your *encounters* began," Nagas retorted.

"A true scientist is not compelled to deny his own experiences as part of the evidence, Eric."

"A true scientist remains objective and does not allow his subjectivity to persuade him to believe in ETs," Nagas hammered Meyer again.

"What do you know about it, man?" Reggie piped up. "You laugh because it's never happened to you. You'd feel differently if it had."

"I'm sorry and who are you?" asked Nagas dismissively.

"I'm Reginald Washington, U.S. Army Ranger and veteran of Operation Iraqi Freedom."

"And what is your purpose here, Mr. Washington?"

"I was to be Maria's first witness before you so rudely interrupted her."

"Have you seen little green men, Mr. Washington?" chided Nagas.

In a different situation, Reggie was quite sure how he'd deal with someone like Nagas, but he gathered his dignity and continued. "I've had an experience. Back in 2003, they sent my Army Ranger unit, commanded by Lieutenant Lucas Biggs, God Rest his Soul, to Baghdad to recover some artifacts. We secured a large crate and Mr. Cutler, who I was hoping to meet again tonight. Our mission was code-named Operation Original Sin. You won't find any record of it. The mission was classified Top Secret."

Holcomb shifted in his chair and focused his attention on Reggie.

"We were attacked and overrun by an Iraqi Republican Guard unit. They cut us all down. Biggs, my CO, saw Cutler and the crate disappear in a bluish beam before he lost consciousness."

"I assume you have proof of that," Nagas retorted.

"Cutler can verify—"

"Mr. Cutler isn't here. I've known him for years. He'd never—"

Reggie ignored Nagas and pushed on. "The next morning we woke up in our vehicles 30 miles from Baghdad and all our wounds healed except this cut."

Reggie raised his hand to expose the unhealed cut running the length of his thumb almost to his wrist.

"Tales of a bluish light and a cut on your thumb—that is your proof for this story?" Nagas continued to badger. "Maybe you and your buddies were smoking something, huh?"

Reggie continued. "Years later, under regressive hypnosis, I remembered all of us being taken aboard a ship and having our wounds healed. I heard one of the doctors say to leave the scar on my thumb as evidence."

"What kind of a ship was it, Reggie?" Maria got a question in edgewise.

"It was a spaceship with a hospital way beyond anything I have ever seen on Earth. They brought us back to life. We were dead. All of us."

"Hypnosis is pseudoscience and chronically unreliable," Nagas asserted.

"What did the crate look like," asked Holcomb, surprising himself with the question.

"It was a large wooden crate. It probably weighed about 200 pounds. It sounded like it had glass or pottery in it."

"And you say Mr. Cutler disappeared with it?"

"That's right," Reggie confirmed.

"And when was this?"

"April 9, 2003."

"That was the crate he brought to me," Holcomb said aloud.

"Who are you?" Maria asked.

"I'm Dr. Richard Holcomb. I've been the government's top expert on ancient Near East artifacts for more than 30 years. Cutler brought that crate to me. I accused him of stealing it. You got it from the National Museum of Iraq?"

"That's right. The museum's where they overran us and where Cutler disappeared in the bluish light."

"Dr. Holcomb," a star-struck Maria began, "I read many of your papers back when I was in school. I minored in Near East studies at the University of Texas. I'm honored to meet you. You say Mr. Cutler delivered the crate Reggie is describing to you? What did you do with it?"

"We spent the next couple of years cleaning the artifacts, piecing them together, photographing them, and dating them. Then Cutler pulled the plug on the project and told me the timing wasn't right. I didn't see him for years. Then a few years ago he showed up again and asked us to continue the work using the high-definition photographs."

"What were your findings, Dr. Holcomb?" Maria queried.

Holcomb looked at the man seated in the corner and thought of Anne. "I would have to say they were interesting, but inconclusive."

"Were you able to decipher the Sumerian writing on the tablets?"

"That's classified. I can't answer that."

"Speak freely, Dr. Holcomb. Everyone at this table is granted clearance," said Mason.

"Dr. Holcomb?" Maria persisted.

"We found . . . anomalies . . . in both the dating and the writing on the artifacts."

"What kind of anomalies?"

"We discovered the tablets contained not only Sumerian, but many other ancient languages and protolanguages."

"Were all the languages from Mesopotamian civilizations?"

"No. They represented language families from around the world. Many depicted similar or identical mythological tales in these various languages."

"Are you saying these Sumerian cuneiform tablets had languages besides Sumerian on them?"

"Yes."

"Dr. Holcomb," Maria continued, "were you previously aware of any other ancient culture using cuneiform tablets?"

"Yes. Other related civilizations such as the Akkadians used them, but there is no evidence they were ever used elsewhere."

"Is that possible, based on your expertise, Dr. Holcomb, for these tablets to be the result of cultural interaction among these civilizations?" Maria asked.

"Not in that era, Ms. Love."

The man in the corner flashed the device in his palm again. "You said you dated the tablets. How old were they?"

"We used several dating methods. They seemed to agree, but my team has dismissed them because they cannot be correct."

"I don't understand. You're a very competent scientist. I'm sure you ran more than one test to verify the dates. Why couldn't they be correct?"

"The dates cannot be correct, Ms. Love, because they violate too much other established science."

"Is that a criterion for truth?" Maria blurted. "Skip that. What did the dating indicate?"

"The dates exceeded 400,000 years in each case."

There was some stunned whispering around the table.

"And those dates can't be correct, because?"

"Because we know modern humans didn't even exist 400,000 years ago, much less advanced writing and languages."

"And so you disregard hard evidence because it doesn't fit our current scientific paradigms of the human past?"

"Dating methods can be imprecise. There's always the possibility the samples are contaminated. Those factors must be considered when data is interpreted."

"Dr. Holcomb, are you invalidating archaeological dating methods as a useful tool?"

"That's ridiculous, of course not."

"Just in this case?"

"The dates can't be right. If a radar gun measures an accurate speed for a hundred cars, do we believe the driver who claimed it was wrong?" decried Holcomb.

"Sir, you're changing the subject. Do you believe the dating was wrong on these artifacts?"

"I don't know."

Maria couldn't believe she was grilling one of the most respected men in the field of Near East studies and a man whose work she admired. "How many dating methods did you use?"

"Several, Ms. Love," Holcomb replied, looking at her and the man in the corner.

"Those several methods all confirmed the 400,000-year date?"

"There was some variance."

"But they substantially confirmed the extreme antiquity of these artifacts?"

Holcomb nodded.

"Were you working alone in this analysis?"

"No. We had language and cultural experts from around the world working on this project."

"What did your colleagues think of the dating results?"

"We were all intrigued, but baffled. We know modern humans and languages could not date to that period?"

"How do we *know* that?"

"150 years of archaeology and anthropology demonstrates modern humans didn't appear until about 200,000 years ago. Advanced languages did not appear until the last 20,000 or 30,000 years."

"So, the multiple confirmations of the artifacts' date flew in the face of the established paradigm in several scientific fields?"

"Yes."

"Tell me about the situation when your colleague and you came across the evidence of human hybridization on these ancient artifacts."

"That's stretching the facts, Ms. Love. We found an interesting anomaly on the artifacts in Sumerian and Sanskrit. The meaning is up to interpretation."

"Perhaps, Dr. Holcomb, but what was your hypothesis about what you found—the part that ended in you consulting with Dr. Sloane McKay?"

"I didn't ask Dr. McKay for her unusual interpretations of

our tablets. Mr. Cutler arranged my meeting with her."

Maria turned to Sloane McKay. "Dr. McKay, why did Dr. Holcomb say he asked for a consultation with an expert in genetics?"

"Richard, Dr. Holcomb, and his colleague believed they had found a representation of human chromosomes being merged with the chromosomes of the gods," McKay replied.

"Did you concur with that analysis?"

"Ms. Love, my expertise is not in Sumerian writing. I relied on Dr. Holcomb to interpret the tablets. My role was to evaluate the genetic significance of their findings. Based on what he told me, the tablets seemed to draw a comparison between modern human and primate genomes. There was a special emphasis on the merging of the second chromosome."

"What is the significance of the second chromosome?"

"The primary genetic difference between modern humans and all other primates is that primates have 24 pairs of chromosomes and we have 23. When you compare the chromosomes, you find human Chromosome 2 contains roughly the same information as primate chromosomes 2 and 3. It appears they were merged."

Maria wasn't grasping something. "What is the significance of this information on the tablets?"

"Very simply this," McKay responded, "Dr. Holcomb has dated these tablets to over 400,000 years. How could artifacts of that age contain detailed information comparing human and primate DNA?"

"Ms. Love," Holcomb inserted, "what Sloane is saying is accurate to a point. I would remind you that reading ancient Sumerian is not like reading a sentence in English. There's significant interpretation involved."

"We all understand that, Dr. Holcomb. Still, the parallels are astonishing," said Maria.

Holcomb continued. "Let's be honest. We have a series of repeating hyphenated words. They *seem* to combine god and human and they *seem* to compare human to primate. The number of repetitions does correlate the number of chromosomes, but we're extrapolating upon extrapolation here. That doesn't prove anything."

"Richard, you're being too modest," McKay replied. "There was a second example in Sanskrit detailing the same information—gods merging with protohumans to form modern humans. Can that be mere coincidence?"

"You're far too predisposed to your theory, Sloane," cautioned Holcomb.

"What theory is that?" Maria queried.

"Dr. McKay believes in Intervention Theory," commented Nagas emphatically making air quotes. "It's why we in the skeptical community refer to her as Dr. Woo Woo."

Maria was determined to tune out Nagas' sarcasm. "What is Intervention Theory, Dr. McKay?"

"Can we use first names, Maria?" asked McKay "All this formality is driving me nuts."

"I think you were already there," demeaned Nagas.

"Go ahead, Sloane," encouraged Maria.

"It's a formal theory hypothesizing precisely what you're driving towards, Maria. We live in a world dominated by two views of human origin—Darwinism and creationism. There are various derivations, but these two broad paradigms constantly battle for minds of humanity in a zero sum game. Each must be completely correct and compromise is defeat. Interventionism can live with both the idea of a creator and with evolution. The theory simply states that, in the case of modern humans, the process was sped up through the intervention of some advanced external intelligence."

"It means, Ms. Love, that giant pink bunnies from Mars came to Earth in our distant past and mated with us," chided Nagas.

"Eric, that's enough," Mason warned.

"Howard, I just find it hard to sit here and listen to this nonsense."

"Maybe you could positively contribute to the conversation rather than attacking," Maria suggested.

"You're buying all of this, aren't you, Ms. Love? This is why scientists and not journalists should be the filter for information in our society."

"Sloane, why did you find Richard's artifacts so compelling?" Maria persisted undaunted.

"In addition to Richard's interpretation of the chromosomes on the tablets, I found information on the tablets that roughly represents the entire human genome."

McKay pressed a button near her and displayed a four-faced monitor that rose from the center of the table so that everyone could see her slides. "You see these intertwined snakes on many of the tablets. I believe these represent the double helix of a DNA strand. Around these symbols, you see a lettered symbol ME. This is the abbreviation for methyl. Over the past couple of decades, we have come to understand that the process we call methylation controls the on/off switch of genetic information. Current theories hold that methylation only switches characteristics on or off. However, I scanned these images and analyzed them against the human genome. The results indicate these configurations demonstrate dialed up and dialed down methylation. This is cutting edge 21st century genetics and would be a revelation in my field. Yet, these tablets are over 400,000 years old."

"While Sloane's interpretations are fascinating," Holcomb spoke up, "the entwined snakes represent the god Enki. He was the healer god and we continue to use this iconography to represent medicine and healing today. ME refers to a healing power possessed by the gods and kept by Enki."

"Dr. Holcomb, didn't Enki create human beings according to the Sumerian myths?" asked Maria.

"Yes."

"Why is he represented by a symbol that resembles DNA strands?"

"That's speculative, Ms. Love. Those in my field would argue this symbology relates strictly to his position as the healer god."

"What if you and your colleagues have been wrong about that? Sloane's analysis seems to point to a more significant connection."

"I've told Sloane, and I'll tell you, you're seeing connections that simply are not there. You're seeing shapes in clouds."

"Is that scientific analysis or your opinion, Dr. Holcomb?" asked Maria.

"It is the considered opinion of an entire field of research."

Maria turned to Sloane. "Sloane, how did you arrive at your analysis?"

Sloane pulled out her ComTab and walked the entire group through the steps of her image analysis. There were whispers and faces made around the table as she made her case.

"After I determined the images represented the human genome and degrees of methylation, I had the computer extrapolate the two extremes. Basically, I had the database turn all methylation of the DNA off and all methylation of the DNA on."

"And what did that tell you?" Maria prodded

McKay displayed an image that looked very much like a Cro-Magnon man. "This is what this DNA would produce if all of the methylation was switched off."

Next, she displayed an image of a modern human. "This is what the precisely dialed DNA, as described on the tablets, produces."

Finally, she displayed an image that looked just like Inanna. "This is the image of a being produced by this DNA, if it is switched completely on."

Maria, Jaypee, and Reggie sat forward in their chairs. Maria sensed Jay was about to speak, but she grabbed his wrist in restraint.

McKay continued. "This being, based on our knowledge of the impact of genetics and epigenetics, would be about 120 to 150 percent taller than a human being. It would possess double the raw intelligence and would have an extremely expanded life span. I was also able to extrapolate psychological factors and environmental factors that could produce such a being. I can't tell you where this being came from, but I can assure you it was not Earth. I have detailed my findings in a paper that I can provide to the whole group."

Nagas was the first to burst the balloon. "You have theory piled upon theory here. Your data has not been peer reviewed. This all your theory stretched to the nth degree by asking your computer to play along."

"Now," whispered Maria to Reggie.

"That looks exactly like the beings I saw on the ship in my hypnotic regression."

"Great," Nagas through up his hands; "we have Dr. McKay stretching the facts beyond credulity and your pseudoscience experience to corroborate it. That should give every UFO nut on the planet a whole new mythology to believe in."

Maria turned and eyed Nagas. "Dr. Nagas, we have a credible scientist using scientific means to analyze information on

400,000-year-old tablets—tablets containing information that is cutting edge science today. We have the testimony of a wounded war hero and a man of impeccable integrity. What kind of evidence would you accept?"

"Well, I'm not likely to buy any of this, regardless, but some indisputable scientific evidence extracted from these mythological tablets would be a start."

Maria pulled the palm-sized stone from her pocket and reached across the table, handing it to Holcomb. "Dr. Holcomb, what can you tell me about this artifact?"

Holcomb turned the stone over in his hand and scrutinized it. He placed it under the Bluetooth magnifying glass in front of him and projected it onto the screen, allowing everyone to see. "The writing is Sumerian. It's very old. It is reminiscent of the materials that comprised the tablets I studied."

"Can you read any of the writing?"

"On this side, there are some very long number strings written along lines emanating from a sun-like object in the center. I could probably decipher the numbers with some time and a magnifying glass."

"What about the other side?"

Holcomb methodically pointed out the magnified symbols on the stone. "There are symbols representing Enki and Enlil. These are the planets: Mercury, Venus, Earth, Mars, Jupiter, Saturn. . . . I don't recognize these last three symbols."

"What about the numbers within the planet symbols?" Maria asked.

"Five-hundredths, eight-tenths, one, one-tenth, 318, 95, 14, 17, and 3. These make no sense to me," Holcomb said.

"Do we have an astronomer in the room?" asked Maria.

Dr. Jill Meagher spoke up from the far end of the table. "Maria, I recognize those numbers associated with the planetary bodies. Those are the relative masses of the planets in our solar system compared to Earth."

There was some awed whispering around the table.

"Dr. Holcomb, do you have any reason to believe this artifact is a fake?"

Holcomb looked at the man in the corner of the room. He sat quietly, waiting for Holcomb's response along with everyone else in the room.

"Dr. Holcomb?" Maria urged.

Holcomb seemed nervous and began to sweat. "My initial reaction is . . . it seems to be . . . authentic. Where did this come from?"

"It came from the same crate as your tablets," Reggie shared. "It was in my CO's pocket the next morning. This artifact and the cut on my thumb are the only two pieces of evidence from our mission. The records of this mission are either highly classified or destroyed."

Holcomb cleared his throat. "We would need to have this dated . . . to confirm its authenticity."

Reggie pulled out several pieces of paper and handed them to Holcomb. "I had it dated last year, Dr. Holcomb. Here is the documentation of the results and information about the lab that did the test. They placed the age at between 410,000 years and 440,000 years."

"Dr. Holcomb, can you turn the stone over again?" asked Dr. Jill Meagher. "That diagram looks very familiar."

Holcomb turned the stone over and placed it back under the magnifying glass. Meagher studied the image for a moment. "That looks like the pulsar map."

"The pulsar map?" repeated Maria.

"Back in the 1970s Pioneer 10, Pioneer 11, Voyager 1, and

Voyager 2 spacecraft all were equipped with maps that employed information about nearby pulsars to show the way to Earth. This image looks almost identical to that map."

"There's more," Reggie interrupted. "When you view the stone with x-ray, there are millions of circuits inside it. Here are some x-ray images I took. You can confirm this for yourself."

The scientists around the table sat in stunned silence. The looks on their faces revealed the upset caused by the artifact.

Maria decided this was a good moment to go for her summation. "We have 400,000-year-old tablets with DNA information that can produce pictures of Cro-Magnon man, modern humans, and some kind of alien. We have an equally ancient stone with images of the planets and their relative masses and a map that quite possibly shows the way to our solar system. That stone has electronic circuitry comparable to our most advanced today. We have eyewitness testimony that these items came from a crate found in the National Museum of Iraq 21 years ago. We have eyewitness testimony that the crate and our friend Mr. Cutler disappeared in a bluish beam of light. We have a unit of highly-trained special forces troops who are apparently overrun and killed, only to awake the next morning miles from their previous location and with hardly a scratch—"

"I'll admit," Nagas interrupted, "the stone is a puzzling piece of evidence. The rest of it is a nice story, but hard evidence linking your evidence is lacking."

"I have one more witness," responded Maria. "Jay Escudero is a world-renowned researcher in the psychology of the UFO phenomenon. Jay's studied the brain chemistry of abductees and recently had his own abduction experience. He's going to share his evidence that the beings who created these tablets and that stone are still involved in life on Earth today. Jay."

"Ms. Love, the hour is late. Perhaps Dr. Escudero could

share his story another time," suggested Mason.

"Respectfully, Mr. Mason, we have this impressive group here right now. Jay's story is so important." Maria replied.

"I'm sure it is, but it's time to call it an evening."

"But we have not even discussed the implications of this information." Shawn Meyer voiced.

"I think each person here has enough information to draw his or her own conclusions. By the way, I would take the stone," said Mason.

"I'm sorry?" said Maria.

"Mr. Cutler has asked me to take custody of the stone. It belongs to U.S. intelligence. Thank you, Mr. Washington, for taking such good care of it," Mason replied.

"Sir, my brothers and I risked our lives and, I believe, actually lost their lives for that stone. I'd say that makes it mine," asserted Reggie.

"This is not a discussion, Mr. Washington."

Reggie held his hand up for Mason and everyone in the room to see. "Do you see this scar, Mr. Mason?" he asked, his voice choked with emotion. "Do you know what it is?"

"It appears to be a very nasty scar, Mr. Washington."

"This scar and that stone are the only evidence we have—I have—of a night my government says never happened. That same government who ordered us into that museum to retrieve this information. Now, I don't pretend to know the significance of this stone, but it was earned by the lives of four of my brothers!"

"Of course we respect your service—"

Reggie cut in, "That's BS! You say you respect my service, but you don't show it. You cheer today's battlefield hero and forget tomorrow's scarred veteran."

"You and your colleagues risked much, but you were not on

a privately funded mission that night. You were working for the U.S. government. The item belongs to the government," Mason's insistence became stronger.

Mason motioned two men into the room. They held Reggie, while the man who had been sitting in the corner came up behind Holcomb and took the artifact.

"You're going to destroy the evidence," Maria half shouted.

"We're going to preserve the evidence, Ms. Love," Mason assured.

"That's very interesting, Mr. Mason," Shawn Meyer called out from the far end of the table. "Your father is one of the three richest men on this planet and very vocal in his ridicule of the alien issue—far more vocal than a man in his position needs to be."

Mason glared at Meyer for a moment. "Dr. Meyer, my father is not even on the Forbes 400 list—"

Meyer laughed dismissively. "Let's be real. The Forbes 400 list documents some of the highest paid overseers on the planet, but not the real masters. Your father is a real master. He doesn't control interests in companies. He controls interests in nations."

"What a high opinion you have of my father, Dr. Meyer. That sounds like a conspiracy theory to me. Do you subscribe to conspiracy theories?"

"I'm all about the truth, Mr. Mason," Meyer replied with dead seriousness. "Why would the son of a man so vocal in his opposition to transparency on this topic be an advocate for it? I must admit that I was a bit shocked to see you appear this evening rather than Mr. Cutler."

"My disagreement with my father on this issue is well-documented, Dr. Meyer—"

"Documented where? I've heard you've held a number of these meetings . . . gathering information and then collecting the evidence. I've also heard that evidence never sees the light of day again."

"There you go again, Shawn, calling this evidence," accused Nagas. "You have artifacts and speculation—nothing more."

"If that's the case, Eric, then it should harm no one for our veteran friend here—Mr. Washington—to keep his battle relic."

Mason sought to take control of this conversation. "Mr. Cutler is an old family friend. He trusts me and I do have the clearance, and the authority, to act on his behalf and that of U.S. intelligence. I assure you that I have nothing but the best intentions on this issue."

"Then prove it," Reggie interjected. "Help us make this evidence public."

Mason smiled disingenuously. "Well, if it means that much to you, I suppose there is no harm in allowing you to keep it. It is just a stone after all."

"It's a stone with proof of a very ancient scientific knowledge of our solar system," Meyer asserted.

Mason waved his arm toward Reggie and the mysterious man in the corner placed the stone back in his hand.

"Perhaps," Mason conceded. "It's fortunate that Dr. Richard Holcomb—one of the few people on the planet who could actually interpret it—was present this evening."

Holcomb was distracted from the compliment by a hard stare from the mysterious man, who had returned to his corner seat. Suddenly, Holcomb began to convulse. He writhed spasmodically before his head crashed onto the table. The spasms continued and then ceased.

Sloane McKay rushed to Holcomb's side. "Somebody call 911!" she screamed.

"Richard! Richard!" shouted McKay in vain.

(29)
The Future Possible

Maria sat alone in her semi-permanent quarters aboard the Rakbu. Richard Holcomb's sudden and frightening death rocked her hard. She wondered how a man, so vibrant and young for his age, could suddenly die that way. Moments before, he engaged her in fervent discussion about alien intervention in human history. Then he was gone. Moreover, without Holcomb's interpretation of the evidence, who could corroborate this information when it came time to prove it?

Mason allowed no ambulance on his estate. His personal physician declared Holcomb dead right in the room where they met and debated. Mason's doctor used a handheld medical device that reminded Maria of a Star Trek medical tricorder to determine the cause of death—a sudden and catastrophic aneurism.

In the commotion, the disputed stone disappeared. Finger pointing and accusation ensued, but no one claimed responsibility for taking the artifact. Mason informed guests the county coroner was on the way and advised them to leave for their own anonymity. Maria was reluctant to leave without the stone, but Reggie worried the authorities might lock him up and Jaypee was in the United States illegally. They persuaded Maria to leave. Inanna transported Jaypee to the Philippines. Reggie returned to Rakbu for his protection since his cabin was heavily damaged and no longer safe.

The presidential press conference loomed just 36 hours away. Maria now faced it without a key witness and her most credible piece of evidence. She had Reggie's images of the stone, but that wasn't primary evidence. An image is easily altered and debunked. She had the dating documentation, but not the stone it purported to date. Part of her wanted to run and pretend she knew none of this. Who was she, to be humanity's messenger for this information?

Maria had comforted herself with Inanna's perceived control of the situation. Now Inanna had proved fallible. She was surprised by the helicopters at Reggie's cabin and surprised by Cutler's absence at the roundtable. Clearly, Inanna had limits. She was not all knowing and all seeing. Who knew if she could deliver on her promise to ensure a question for Maria at the press conference?

The door chime sounded. "Enter," Maria said.

Inanna entered the room and joined Maria at the window overlooking Earth. "Such a beautiful planet, isn't she?"

"Yes," replied Maria.

"If you knew how rare and precious Earth is in the known galaxy, you would understand why she is such a focus."

"I can't get Holcomb's death out of my head, Inanna. One thought keeps spinning through my mind—does any of this matter? Aren't we all going to die one day? Who cares?"

"Oh, The Belly of the Whale, is it?"

"I'm sorry . . . the Belly of the Whale?"

"Your mythologist, Joseph Campbell, talked about it in his concept of the hero's journey. It's the moment the hero experiences big doubt because she is about to cut ties with the world as she knows it and choose the new world."

"Haven't my actions already proved my commitment to this journey? Haven't I already chosen?" asked Maria.

"Yes, but until now you have been able work in the shadows—without having to be the face of these ideas. Tomorrow night you are going to take this information public. People will point and stare and call you the alien lady. The status quo is going to turn its back on you and you will have to continue this journey alone."

"I suppose you're right. What's bothering me more is . . . what's the prize? This started as a personal question. I feel like I have my answers. Is it really worth going public? Can't others find their own answers?"

"Maria, what becomes of humanity, if it continues on its present course? People continue to live in the dark without the information they need to make decisions about their lives. Is that what you want?"

"No."

"Your planet and your species are run by a few men from the shadows for a distant tyrant. Worst of all, much of humanity continues behaving like slaves before an all-powerful god— ready and eager to send them to eternal damnation. Being human is a crime. Can your species be free? Can progress be made while people believe such things?"

Maria stared down at the earth. Seven and half billion people lived down there. Most of them believe they are shaping their own destiny in a game rigged since the dawn of history. She turned from the window, paced to the middle of the room, and turned to face Inanna. "I guess the question is, why me?"

Inanna smiled as warmly as Maria had ever seen her smile. "That's always the hero's question, Maria. You see, the hero finds nothing special in her actions. She thinks she is like everyone else —only she's not. The hero has traveled beyond the horizon and back with vital information for the tribe. This is always the moment of decision for the hero. Do I share what I have learned or do I keep it to myself?"

"And where do you stand on the question, Inanna?"

"Hundreds of thousands of earth years ago, I faced a similar choice. My race perpetrated a grievous injustice upon a sentient species. My choice was to act or remain silent and go along. Acting meant turning my back on my father, my brother, and my position within the Anunnaki elite. My choice to act doesn't make me a saint, but it allows me to live with my role in this universe."

"So, help me make the right choice, Inanna."

Inanna shook her head. "The days of someone else making the decisions for you—for humanity—are at an end, Maria."

"I hope I'm ready."

"Trust me, Maria. Ready you are!"

Inanna walked right up to Maria. "I won't make the decision for you, but I can help make your decision easier. They say lies are best hidden in plain sight. Before your press conference, I need you to see the scope of the lies arrayed against you. You must understand the self-determination of your species hangs in the balance."

Inanna called out, "Commander, Enka, please prepare my Vimana for Maria and me."

"Right away, Mistress."

"May what I show you tonight outrage you and seal your determination."

Maria and Inanna transported aboard the Vimana. Inanna ordered the pilot to set course for Mars at 1 C.

"1 C?" Maria asked.

"Yes, C is the speed of light," replied Inanna. "It is the maximum safe cruising speed for this vessel within a solar system. The trip to Mars will take about 40 minutes. Let's adjourn to my observation lounge."

Maria had been aboard Rakbu several times but hadn't experienced actual space flight. Her mind boggled at traveling the speed of light. She felt a slight disorientation and a bit dizzy.

"It takes a few minutes to get adjusted," said Inanna, noting Maria's discomfort. "The ship deploys technology to offset the inertia created by high velocities, but it cannot fully compensate."

"So, why are we going to Mars?"

"I know. *Everyone* has been to Mars," Inanna replied, trying to affect some humor. "There's something there you need to see."

"What?"

"If I could tell you, I wouldn't need to show you."

The Vimana achieved orbit around Mars. "Mistress, what are your orders?" asked the pilot.

"Engage the heat shields and take us to the surface coordinates I'm transferring to you right now."

"Yes, Mistress."

The ship veered sharply and headed into the Martian atmosphere. "Hang on," Inanna instructed, "even though the Martian atmosphere is thinner than Earth's, it is rougher than spaceflight."

For the next several minutes, the Vimana jostled violently and the temperature rose significantly within the ship. As suddenly as it began, the shaking stopped. The ship glided gently a few hundred feet above the planet's surface. The iconic red surface rushed past below, but something seemed wrong. Maria noticed a bluish tint to the sky. The Vimana pointed toward a large flat plateau and came to rest atop it.

"Pilot," Inanna commanded, "prepare my surface vehicle."

Inanna led Maria to the Vimana's aft bay. The pilot was already seated in the driver's seat of a high-tech dune buggy. They climbed into the back seat. The bay doors lowered and became a ramp. The buggy eased down the ramp and out onto the Martian surface. For a moment, Maria forgot about tomorrow's presidential press conference and everything else back on Earth. She was dumbfounded to be rambling across the Martian landscape.

"Inanna, this is amazing! Thank you for bringing me, but why are we here?"

Inanna did not answer. Instead, she pointed to a series of large structures ahead. The buildings seemed purposely camouflaged to match the Martian surface. As they approached the massive complex, Maria could see they weren't made of dirt or rock. Their composition was a combination of metal, stone, and other materials cleverly mixed to blend into the landscape.

The driver pulled up in front of the largest structure. "Let's go inside," said Inanna encouraging Maria to follow her.

"Isn't it too cold?"

"It is summer," Inanna chuckled.

"What about oxygen? Don't we need space suits?"

"That's part of what I need you to know."

The top of the buggy slowly flipped open. Maria held her breath, not sure what to expect. Inanna was already outside the vehicle walking around. Maria followed her on a leap of faith. In the distance, the sun looked pale and bluish in the Martian sky. The temperature compared to an early spring afternoon in D.C. She cautiously opened her mouth and slowly inhaled and exhaled. To her surprise, she could . . . breathe.

"Pace yourself, Maria, there is far less oxygen than on Earth. You will tire easily, but it is breathable."

"It reminds me of my trek to a Himalayan base camp in Nepal," Maria shared. "How is this possible? Mars is not supposed to have a breathable atmosphere."

"Take your foot and scratch the surface," Inanna instructed.

Maria took her right foot and kicked the dirt beneath her

feet. The red dirt was only a few millimeters thick. Beneath the red veneer, the soil was volcanic black. She looked back up at Inanna in surprise.

"Do you understand the paradox, Maria? The red dirt is oxidized. Your scientists believe the oxidation occurred eons ago when—according to their theories—Mars had water and a more substantial atmosphere. Yet, the same scientists readily admit the planet is prone to huge dust storms. So, tell me, Maria, how does the planet maintain this thin layer of ancient red dirt when it's being blown around constantly?"

"I don't know."

"The oxidation continues. It's happening right now. There is less than when we first came here two million years ago. There is *far* less than when one of your ancient Earth civilizations built the structures you're looking at right now, but the rocks and the dirt continue to oxidize. There is breathable oxygen here!"

"This is astonishing, Inanna, for sure. I'm not seeing the significance."

"If the people of Earth knew their nearest planetary neighbor was more hospitable than they had been told, don't you think there would be a bigger demand to come here?"

"I suppose."

"To become a spacefaring race is the next natural step for humanity, but you have been purposely bottled up by planted paradigms rife with disinformation. The first paradigm holds Earth has too many problems to waste resources on space exploration. The second asserts there is nothing to see out here—just desolate, lifeless worlds."

"I don't understand the purpose of the deception."

"My government doesn't want humanity taking those next steps into adulthood or to understand its heritage. It immediately discredits the ideology, claiming Earth people are inferior. Because my government doesn't want it and it controls those who control your governments, your governments have followed suit—publicly at least—with this cover up."

"What do you mean publicly?"

"The public space programs on Earth are not the real space programs. They have been set up to perpetuate those two lies— that there are better uses of your resources and there is nothing to see out here. Meanwhile, governments have secretly been exploring the solar system and even trying to create small bases on the Moon and Mars. I know you were young, but do you remember the long string of 'accidents' on public Mars rovers back in the 1990s?"

"I remember reading something about them."

"Those American and Russian probes were destroyed because there was a virtual war going on around Mars. Your governments wanted to establish a covert presence here and my government was determined not to allow it. So, instead of the truth you were told stories like some grad student did the math wrong on a mission planned for ten years and the vehicle crashed because of that miscalculation."

Maria looked up and around taking in the view of the massive structure in front of her. She could see others grouped together in the distance. The color of the structures matched the Martian surface. The oddly shaped roofs caused them to blend with the planet's surface features.

"You said people from Earth built these structures?"

"Yes. It was one of the civilizations before Lemuria. These structures were built when Mars was still a moon of Tiamat. That civilization possessed highly advanced technology—technology beyond what the Anunnaki possess today. They towed Mars into its   current   independent   orbit.   They   also captured Neptune's moon Triton in the outer solar system. They towed Triton into orbit around Neptune. They were trying to test a theory to determine whether a moon orbiting opposite its planet's rotation would create enough pull on the moon to heat its core, warm its surface, and create a habitable atmosphere."

"Incredible!" Maria responded, taking note of the details around her as she listened.

"The changes disrupted the orbital balance in the solar system. Tiamat got too close to Jupiter. The gravity pulled it into an orbit causing it to collide with one of Jupiter's largest satellites. This created your asteroid belt and caused a rain of rocks to hurtle towards the earth and it wiped out that civilization."

"How do you know all of this?"

"The Lemurians were very aware of their history. They were capable of technology. They simply chose a different path for their civilization. Records survived the cataclysm and when remnants of their civilization merged with us, those records were taken to Nibiru."

Maria was awed. How could such a false paradigm be created and perpetuated? "Can we go inside?" she asked.

"Absolutely, this is part of your heritage. Be careful when you begin walking. You're going to feel rather light-headed. Deep slow breaths in through your nose and out through your mouth."

Maria stopped to catch her breath several times on the short walk to the main entrance. Inanna appeared unaffected.

"You should be able to breathe better once we are inside. We don't understand how, but the structures generate artificial oxygen bubbles that encase the entire building. However it was done, it still functions today."

The main entrance was massive. Maria estimated it to be nearly 100 feet high and 200 feet across. The stones forming the base of the building were Mars-colored and each the size of a large house. The entrance was open to the outside and revealed a long voluminous corridor running the length of the building and terminating in a similar entrance on the far end.

Maria immediately felt the difference in the air as they moved inside. Breathing became easier and she scanned the massive hallway. Being open to the elements, red dust covered everything. However, there were bare spots on the floor revealing exquisitely ornate tiles 10 feet squared. Catacomb rooms climbed the walls on either side of the corridor. There were 12 levels each containing dozens of rooms. The ceiling that seemed to blend with the Martian landscape from above was transparent from below. It magnified the Martian sunlight, giving it an earth-like intensity that filled the corridor.

Inanna caught Maria's mouth agape. "Astonishing, isn't it? People from Earth created this millions of years ago."

"Were they a completely different species or were they human?"

"They were an independently evolved humanoid species, but you carry part of their DNA."

"How is that?"

"After the reptilian invasion, the Lemurians were absorbed into Anunnaki society. The two species were sexually compatible and soon our two races became one. Through intermingling, their DNA mixed with ours and eventually became part of your DNA through our intervention with your species. This interbreeding of Anunnaki and Lemurian is revealed in mythological stories about the sons of heaven mating with the daughters of earth."

Maria shook her head. "Why would they want to keep this heritage from us? Why hide these truths?"

"My father and my dear brother have insisted on a policy of

human containment and control. They have used their function-
aries on earth to ensure you are deceived and denied this
knowledge. My Uncle Enki tried to share some of this knowledge
with humanity, but his attempts became demonized in your mythologies. From the beginning, human awareness of this information was considered dangerous by my government."

"This cannot stand! People must know!" declared Maria.

"That's why I brought you here. That's the indignation I
wanted you to feel before you go into the Belly of the Whale and
confront the president tomorrow night."

"Does President Paxton know about these things?"

"It's very unlikely. Powers above government have always
controlled this information. Some in government know enough
to carry out their functions. Presidents have been considered too
transient to be brought into the inner circle."

Maria spun around 360 degrees. "I don't want to leave here.
It's so beautiful, but I need to prepare for tomorrow night."

They climbed back into the buggy and drove back to the
Vimana. Inanna led Maria back to the lounge. Maria sat riveted
at the window as the ship pushed against the planet's gravity and
quickly ascended through the atmosphere. Within moments,
they were free from Martian gravity and racing back across the
solar system at 1 C.

Inanna's personal attendant appeared with two large coffee
mugs. Inanna drank tea, but Maria found her mug filled with a
delicious hot caramel macchiato. They sat in silence for a moment sipping their drinks and watching the distant stars slowly
pass. Even at the speed of light, the great distances to the other
stars caused them to creep across their field of view.

"You know, Maria," began Inanna, "what you're doing is not
just about uncovering the past. It is about creating the right future for humanity. I have heard The Father Creator call it The

Future Possible. He sees tremendous potential in humanity, if only you can awaken to your true potential."

"I want to believe that about us, Inanna. Yet, I look at events around the world every day and I see all the hurt we bring to each other. It's why Jack and I have not had a baby. I'm not sure I want to bring one into this world."

"I hope you will change your mind about that, Maria. You would make a remarkable mother. What you're choosing to do is so courageous. I'm not sure you even realize yet how brave you are."

"What is possible for us, Inanna, if we pull our act together?"

"The first thing is a clear understanding of your rich heritage. We are not the only race to intervene genetically in your species. We were just the first and we have remained the most involved in your development. You represent the best and the worst of several races in the known galaxy."

"Is that where our ethnicities come from? Is that the influence of various alien races?" Maria followed.

"There is some information you are not prepared to know yet, Maria. You would use it against each other in destructive ways, rather than understanding the true significance of it."

"OK. There you are hiding information from me again," said Maria only half kidding.

"This one is for your own good. Knowledge of your full history would only flame the fires of ethnic and religious differences. Some people would use it to claim ethnic or racial superiority for their group. I'm not going to tell you that whole story—not yet."

"All right," Maria huffed. "What would this change mean here and now?"

"One big benefit that would transform your planet is the advancement of energy on your planet. Cheap, practically free, and ubiquitous energy would drastically change Earth's economic dynamic. Energy cost and access are two of the greatest barriers to modernization and equalization on your planet. This ship literally runs by drawing energy right out of the vacuum of space. Some of your scientists identified a crude method for achieving this over a century ago. Knowledge of it remains hidden. Some people have referred to this as zero-point energy, but the name is a little misleading."

"Follow the money," Maria commented ironically.

"What?" asked Inanna.

"Nothing. It's just an old journalistic axiom. And what about The Future Possible? It sounds rather romantic."

"The sky is the limit for humanity. If you can see your true potential and transcend the psychological limits we have placed upon you, nothing is impossible for you. That's what worries my government and their allies most of all—human potential."

A tone sounded and pilot spoke, "Mistress, I'm sorry to disturb you, but a Z-vessel is following us. It is the same vessel we intercepted leaving Earth a few weeks ago."

"Course, distance, and speed," Inanna called out.

"They are on direct intercept course. Distance is 730,000 kilometers and speed 2 C. At our present speed, they will reach us in about 45 seconds."

"How long until we reach Rakbu?"

"18 minutes."

"Increase to maximum speed, raise our shields, and take evasive action. Rakbu, this is Princess Inanna. A Z-Alliance vessel is tracking and threatening us. Please move to intercept us at maximum interplanetary speed."

"Enka here, Mistress, acknowledged. We will reach your position in 7 minutes 50 seconds."

"Pilot, update!"

The Z vessel continues to close. It is now within 100,000 kilometers. It has raised its shields and activated its weapons."

"Ready a spread of torpedoes. Set them to detonate in their path and blind them. Open a channel to the Z vessel."

"Open, Mistress."

"Captain Kotz, this is Princess Inanna of Nibiru. You seem to be threatening aggressive action against a vessel carrying a member of the Nibiruan royal family. Break off your pursuit or face the consequences."

"Greeting, Princess, I didn't expect to see you so soon again. Now you claim your ties to the Nibiruan crown. From what I have heard, your brother the king would probably give a reward to the captain who destroyed you."

"This is your last warning, Kotz. The Rakbu will be here in minutes."

"In minutes, they will find only the debris of your craft. Target weapons on that ship," Kotz commanded.

"Fire," ordered Inanna.

The Vimana let loose five high yield torpedoes that exploded directly in the path of the Z ship, forcing it to adjust course. Meanwhile, Inanna ordered her pilot to change course to delay the Z ship's ability to locate the Vimana.

"Enka, how long?" shouted Inanna.

"Three minutes," came the reply.

"Pilot, set a direct course for the Rakbu—maximum speed. How long until we reach them?"

"Seventy seconds, Mistress. The Z vessel is closing and firing. Brace for impact."

The Vimana shuttered violently. Maria fell to the floor. She was still there when the second impact came.

"Mistress, our shields are down. One more hit and we will be disabled."

Inanna reached for Maria and pulled her off the floor. Smoke filled the lounge. "Target them with a full spread of torpedoes and fire!"

There was a slight pause, "Direct hit, Mistress, but their shields are still intact and they are firing."

The next impact made a horrific sound. The Vimana seemed ready to come apart. It listed and came to a stop—dead in space.

"We cannot withstand another hit!" said the pilot.

Inanna embraced Maria and shouted, "Rakbu!"

The Rakbu roared past the Vimana and toward the oncoming Z vessel, firing her weapons as she ran. The massive ship's firepower lit the surrounding space and pounded the Z vessel, forcing it to turn and run.

Kotz left still taunting and promising "We shall meet again, Princess. Perhaps next time you will not be so fortunate."

"I showed you mercy at our last encounter, Kotz. Don't count on it next time," Inanna shot back.

"Mistress," a worried sounding Enka called, "are you all right?"

"We're fine, commander, but I think they broke my toy," Inanna attempted some Earth humor.

"Mistress?" inquired a confused Enka.

"Nothing, commander." Inanna smiled at Maria, sharing the joke.

"Mistress, Earth Space is not safe. You must secure a fighter escort for your little adventures."

"I will take that under advisement, commander. Please tow the Vimana into a bay and transport us aboard Rakbu. Then make best possible speed to Earth. Maria has an important date with the President of the United States."

Maria's adrenaline rush slowly subsided from the battle. In the wonder of the visit to the ancient Martian structures and the terror of the battle, she forgot about the president. Inanna recovered from the excitement of the battle more quickly than Maria. She always seemed to transition more easily than a human did. Even in a moment that might have been their last, Maria noted how protective Inanna was of her. Inanna had wrapped Maria tightly in her arms, but with the gentleness and affection of a mother.

Inanna could see Maria was lost in thought. She verified Maria's readiness for the press conference. "How do you feel about tomorrow night? Did our adventure restore you confidence?"

"Restore?" Maria laughed. "I'm not sure I was ever confident about the press conference, but I am resolute. I see The Future Possible. I want that for humanity. I want that for my family and me. I want it for you, Inanna."

Tears welled in Inanna's eyes. Maria didn't even know if the Anunnaki cried, but Inanna appeared on the verge.

"You have come so far, Maria. Tomorrow night is not an ending, but a beginning. You have been in training for this moment for a long time. I believe in you."

"How can you be so sure?" asked Maria.

"Our *Book of Possibilities* reads *The Sun knows when to shine. The rose knows when to bloom. So, too, will you know when it is your moment.* This is your moment, Maria."

Maria choked up. "That's . . . beautiful, Inanna. Thank you."

The two women embraced. "The Future Possible," whispered Inanna.

"The Future Possible," repeated Maria.

Maria climbed onto the transporter and vanished in a bluish beam of light, still holding Inanna's gaze. She materialized in a D.C. hotel room. Tomorrow was a big day for her—for humanity. Was she ready to be a hero? She couldn't say. She only knew she was determined to do her part.

(30)
Maria Poses Her Question

Maria rose with conviction in her heart and shaking in her knees. She'd had June 3 circled on her calendar for weeks. Now the moment had arrived. There would be no questions about Valentine's Day gifts tonight. "Mr. President," she shouted.

"Maria Love ANN," President Paxton called to the surprise of most in the room.

"Mr. President when will the U.S. Government acknowledge the presence of extraterrestrials on our planet, in our history, and in our DNA?"

A stunned hush fell over the room. Had Maria Love really just asked the President that question? Heads, microphones, and cameras involuntarily turned to face Maria standing near the back of the East Room.

The President smiled and eyed his questioner. "Maria, isn't it?"

"Yes, Mr. President."

"Maria, the U.S. Government has long maintained such speculation is precisely that, speculation. I have no specific information that confirms or denies your assertion. Perhaps if you file a FoIA request—"

"Excuse me, Mr. President," Maria pushed on, "I think we're all aware of what a FoIA request yields on this topic. I'm asking you, sir. Are you aware of Operation Original Sin carried out April 11, 2003 in Baghdad?"

"Ms. Love, that predates my administration by—"

"Mr. President, a U.S. Army Special Forces team was sent into The National Museum of Iraq to extract a U.S. Government operative and a crate filled with Cuneiform tablets. That crate contained evidence about the true origins of modern human beings."

"Maria, that's a fascinating story, but I'm afraid I can't help you," replied Paxton.

"Will you commit to looking into the matter, Mr. President?"

"Ms. Love, that's enough," White House Chief of Staff Joe Bieber broke in, "You've asked your question. You've had your follow-up and the president has answered your questions."

"With all due respect, Mr. Bieber, the president has not answered my question," Maria retorted.

President Paxton gently nudged his Chief of Staff aside. He stood smiling nervously for a moment, sizing up the beautiful reporter who had turned his press conference into an inquisition.

"Ms. Love, I have no knowledge of the operation you reference or any other information that lends the slightest credence to your other assertions."

"Mr. President, we have the tablets," Maria blurted almost instinctively.

"You have the tablets?" asked the president incredulously.

"Well . . . sir . . . that is . . . I have images of the tablets and documentation confirming their dates."

"That's it," Bieber cut in again. "Ladies and gentlemen, I'm sorry, but no more questions."

The press corps rumbled with collective discontent. The Secret Service and staff rushed President Paxton from the room.

Maria stood in the back of the room. The enormity of what just happened settled in. Colleagues deprived of their questions glared. Cameras zoomed. A sea of microphones formed a semicircle around her. Colleagues fired a barrage of uncomfortable questions her direction. In an instant, she transformed from predator into prey.

"Maria, tell me more about this evidence," one reporter shouted.

"Is ANN dabbling in conspiracy theories now," questioned another?

The barrage caught Maria off guard. She failed to anticipate Bieber pulling the plug or her colleagues turning the tables on her. She had violated the cardinal rule of journalism. She had become the story. Covering her head, she decided on retreat. She pushed through the crush of reporters toward the door. Cameras flashed. The questions became more abusive and dismissive.

"Um, no comment," she responded to a question about whether she had been visited by little green men. She reached the White House East Room exit and found her crew waiting in the hallway.

"Let's get out of here," suggested Cathy Sebring. "You know how wolves can be when they're deprived of dinner."

(31)
The Oval Office

As Maria and her team sought an escape route, three secret service agents stopped them.

The leader of the trio spoke. "Ms. Love, will you please come with us?"

The two large men behind the leader each grabbed an arm and guided Maria away from her colleagues.

Cathy Sebring said, "She's a reporter. She has rights. Get Austin on the phone."

The agents led Maria down a corridor of offices away from the East Room circus. She realized they were headed to the West Wing. They ushered her into The Oval Office and instructed her to have a seat. She'd been in the White House many times, but had never been to the West Wing, much less the Oval Office.

"Wait here," said the lead agent abruptly.

Maria waited for several minutes. The Chief of Staff's office door opened. Joe Bieber entered. He dropped into one of the other chairs fronting the president's desk. He displayed no appetite for pleasantries.

"That was quite a stunt you pulled out there tonight, Ms. Love. Do you know there has never been a live televised presidential press conference ended abruptly like that? Were you trying to embarrass the president?

Maria felt some indignation simmer within her. "I did not end the press conference, Mr. Bieber. I simply asked a question.

You ended the press conference."

"What compelled you to ask President Paxton those ludicrous questions on national ITV? There can only be one reason. Someone wanted to embarrass him. Who put you up to it?"

"Why do I feel like I need to invoke the Fifth Amendment, Mr. Bieber? No one put me up to it. I've been investigating the issue of current and historical alien involvement in human culture and—"

"And what?" Bieber interrupted.

"And I have developed significant evidence of conscious, repetitive efforts by the U.S. Government to conceal and misdirect the public on this topic. Whether President Paxton was in office is irrelevant. He's the president now and he owes the American people some answers."

"You're swimming in dangerous waters, Ms. Love."

Suddenly the door opened the Paxton entered. Bieber rose almost to attention, "Mr. President."

Maria, too, instinctively stood and said, "Mr. President."

"Joe," Paxton said almost playfully, "I heard you were holding Ms. Love captive in The Oval Office."

"I was trying to explain to Ms. Love the gravity of the position she placed you in this evening, Mr. President."

"Yes it was quite a scene, Ms. Love," Paxton agreed.

"Well, sir—" Maria began.

"Joe, I think I'd like to have a word with Ms. Love too . . . alone."

"Mr. President, I advise strongly against that."

"I know you do, old friend," said Paxton, placing his hand on Bieber's shoulder."

"Mr. President, as Chief of Staff—"

"Joe, I'm not asking you as the president. I'm asking you as a friend. Leave us."

"Ron, Mr. President," Bieber corrected himself, "Is this wise?"

"Probably not. I'll talk to you in the morning."

Bieber looked questioningly at Paxton, glared at Maria, and left the room.

"Ms. Love, please have a seat," Paxton motioned, as he assumed his position in the chair behind the desk. "I hope you didn't take Joe's defensiveness personally. He and I were college roommates. In my political career, his advice has saved me more times than I can count. I respect his opinion. He knows my views on this whole alien issue. When you asked your question tonight, he was trying to prevent me from saying something stupid."

"Well, Mr. President, what are your views on the issue?"

"This is, of course, completely off the record?"

"Absolutely, Mr. President. I'm asking as a citizen—as a human being—not White House correspondent."

The President took a deep breath. "This is a little unprecedented, Ms. Love. May I call you Maria?"

"Please do, Mr. President."

"The truth is I've had a life-long, if rather secret, passion for this issue. Talking about it is the short road to political suicide, if not a straightjacket."

"Believe me, Mr. President, I've felt headed for that straightjacket many times in recent weeks. How did you get interested in the topic?"

Paxton blew out a big breath of air. "I didn't even tell my wife this for many years. When I was 17, I was on a camping trip with friends. The trip was a big pre-senior year rite of passage. We'd planned it all summer. We selected a remote lake in the Upper Peninsula of Michigan and . . ."

Paxton paused and stared off into space, prompting Maria to bring him back, "Mr. President?"

"I'm sorry, Maria. I don't talk about this much . . . well . . . ever. We were sitting around the campfire. It was late summer. The air was warm and muggy for that part of the world. We saw . . . uh . . . we saw a light in the sky. At first we thought it was a plane or helicopter, but we couldn't hear the damn thing," Paxton paused again.

"It hung in the sky for about an hour. Nothing was happening and we lost interest. Suddenly, that thing lit up like a Christmas tree and moved rapidly towards us. Now, we could hear it. I've never heard a sound like that. It's hard to describe—like huge plates of metal grinding against each other and echoing through the sky. The ground shook hard enough to knock us off our feet."

Maria leaned in to listen more closely, sensing the president's intensity.

"Then these bright beams of light began emanating from the UFO—"

"You would definitely classify it as a UFO, Mr. President?" Maria asked.

"I've never seen anything like it—before or since. It seemed to be conducting a patterned search on the ground. The noise became painful to our ears. We retreated into the woods. It followed us. It was gaining on us! There was a bright flash and . . ." Paxton stared off into space again.

"And what happened next, Mr. President?"

"I remember looking at my watch. It read 8:21 P.M. The next thing I knew, I woke up in the forest over a mile from our campsite. My damn watch read 2:13 A.M!"

The president looked right into Maria's eyes with distress. "I can't account for those six hours, Maria. I don't know where I was. I don't know what happened to my friends or to me. None of us could remember. Joe Bieber was there that night too. He never speaks of it and doesn't like to discuss the subject, as you saw. That partly accounts for his reaction tonight. It was as much personal as professional."

"How did you deal with the event, Mr. President? Did you seek counseling or a support group?" asked Maria.

"I set it aside because talking about it threatened all my goals—a fact Joe Bieber constantly reiterated. Do I wonder? Sure. I've always wondered what happened that night and what it meant."

Thoughts rushed to Maria's mind—information and experiences she wanted to share with the president. She couldn't believe how he opened up to her. The sincerity and passion in his eyes was compelling. Maria realized, more than ever, her journey wasn't just about her. It impacted every human being—from presidents to street people. We were all in the same situation. We were all stuck and without answers.

"You showed real courage asking those questions on national ITV tonight. Why did you do that?"

"Sir, I've been investigating the topic for a while. I've heard, seen, and experienced amazing things and uncovered incredible evidence. I work as a White House correspondent for a national news network. Why not go straight to the top?"

Paxton regained his presidential demeanor and professional separation. "I see. Well, Maria, I can assure you, on this issue, I am not the top."

"You're the President of United States. If you're not the top, who is?"

"I haven't exactly been able to figure that out. Joe Bieber is one of the few people on this planet present when I made the mistake of assuming the president had carte blanche to inquire about intelligence matters—particularly UFOs. You've heard the jokes in movies about the president not having clearance to know about this information. Essentially, that's true."

"What happened when you asked?"

"First I was delayed by assurances the information would be made available to me. I waited for weeks and nothing. I brought my entire national security team in Homeland Security, CIA, Chairman of the Joint Chiefs, NSA. I demanded to know everything they knew about the UFO issue. There was hemming, hawing, and more promises. Finally, I got a pile of redacted documents containing nothing new. I can confirm to you, though, that several of the well-known incidences were based in fact."

"Roswell?"

"Roswell. Yes, but it wasn't the first. There were several incidents before World War II. The Washington lights in 1952 and 2002 were a stunning example. We had UFOs confirmed over NATO positions in Europe during the Cold War. There were incidents where nuclear missiles were deactivated after UFOS were spotted in their vicinity."

"But, Maria, the reason you're here right now is that you mentioned tablets, a military operation, and a witness to human origins. Those are astonishing claims. What was the name of that operation again?"

"Original Sin, Mr. President."

"Tell me more about that."

Maria shared what she knew about the operation and the tablets that resulted from it. She brushed over her experiences with Inanna.

"You've seen the tablets?"

"I've seen photos of the tablets, Mr. President, but I held an ancient stone with advanced knowledge of our solar system. Unfortunately, we lost it."

"Lost it?"

"It was stolen. I've heard expert interpretations of the information on the artifacts. This is cutting edge genetics and astronomy. I have documentation dating these artifacts at more than 400,000 years."

Paxton whistled in astonishment. "That's amazing. And this can all be corroborated and verified?"

"Yes, sir," replied Maria with a dry mouth, "I believe I can arrange that."

"You mentioned a witness. Who could be an eyewitness to events that happened so long ago? That seems impossible."

"Impossible for us . . . " Maria began and then hesitated.

She knew that telling Paxton about her experiences was risky, but she'd asked the questions to get answers and here she was with the President of The United States offering more help than she'd ever imagined. She shared how Inanna had helped her to gather information to expose the off-world involvement in human affairs. She described the tablets and their interpretations in more detail. Finally, she shared a detailed account of the structures she witnessed on Mars.

She kept waiting for the president to stop her, call her crazy, and usher her out of The Oval Office. Instead, Paxton listened to the story soberly and asked probing questions. He felt like an ally—and a powerful one at that. The conversation lasted until quarter past midnight. He committed his support to finding the answers Maria sought. He committed Maria to silence about their discussion. They tentatively scheduled a meeting to view the evidence. Paxton ordered a car to take Maria home.

His final words to her were, "My people will be in touch with you. This must be off the record, Maria, all of it. Watch your back. President Eisenhower was not kidding when he talked about the Military Industrial Complex."

Maria knew the term Military Industrial Complex, but she

had never delved into it. The comment brushed past her. She felt a sense of accomplishment. Who knew the President of the United States would be a truth seeker, even a little bit of a conspiracy theorist?

Hard days lay ahead professionally, no doubt. All Maria felt at this moment was vindication and hope for the truth. This evening's embarrassment felt worlds away. She wondered what Inanna would think when she found out. Well, she probably already knew. She couldn't wait to tell Jack. Jack! Maria checked her phone messages. She had 41 missed calls and 38 voicemail messages. Five were from Jack. He was probably worried. Seven were from Pete Rogers. He probably wanted to fire her. The rest were from various news organizations including several tabloids.

(32)
King Ea's Reverie

King Ea of Nibiru sat quietly in his Royal Room of Ascension. . . waiting. He waited for word, for assurance from The Father Creator. Despite his best efforts, he never felt the presence of The Father Creator in his meditations anymore. On occasion, he received strange communications from entities claiming to represent a fifth-dimensional alliance threatening to conquer Nibiru. The messages never persisted and he believed them to be illusions created by a mind eager to connect to something, if not to The Father Creator.

Ea was a large and powerful man, even by Anunnaki standards, and a warrior through and through. He ruled Nibiru—the 27th king in a proud line reaching back nearly two million earth years. From earliest childhood, he lived to make his father proud. Few could live up to the standard set by King Enlil the Great and no one could live up to Ea's vision of his father. His name further fueled his feelings of inadequacy. He bore the name of his Uncle Enki—his father's younger brother and a man Ea viewed as weak.

Despite 10,000 earth years on the throne, the shadow of his father's greatness haunted him. Ea always felt the need to prove his strength and his power—to his people, his allies, and especially the humans. The smallest offense sparked his quick temper and he used that temper to intimidate and bully those around him. His impulse was to respond from strength—even aggression—so no one would doubt him.

Ea regretted the distance and animosity between him and his only sister Princess Inanna. Their estrangement wounded him, but he blamed her. Inanna's attempts to free humanity were dangerous nonsense. They placed her on the wrong side of history. Their father had believed the humans were a resource and not truly sentient. Ea agreed and made it the cornerstone of his Earth policy.

Ea often reflected on how his differences with Inanna emerged. They traveled to Earth as children after the premature death of their mother. Their father—still crown prince—ruled the Earth colony known as Edin. The Anunnaki walked among their human slaves as living gods.

Ea spent his days with his father learning how to be a god and soaking up all he could about how to dominate those around him—Anunnaki and humans.

"You are Anunnaki," his father often said. "You are to be the leader of a proud warrior race worthy to be called gods."

Prince Enki—their uncle—influenced Inanna. Enki genetically engineered the humans. While Enlil saw them as inferior beings, existing only to perform labor and to worship him, Enki increasingly saw the humans as sentient creatures wrongfully enslaved by the Anunnaki. This growing contention between the brothers resulted in several wars between them and forces loyal to them.

King Anu sided with Enlil and sent warriors and warships to Earth to support his eldest son. He ordered the complete destruction of several cities ruled by Enki as punishment for his disloyalty. Enlil's forces obliterated Enki's cities from space using state-of-the-art nuclear weapons. Enlil pushed for his brother's arrest, but Anu had a soft spot for his second son. He censured Enki, but spared his life.

The split between Enlil and Enki led to the rift between Ea and Inanna. Inanna tried to be like her older brother and to remain loyal to their father, despite her growing disenchantment with his treatment of the humans. Ea and Inanna vigorously debated the issue many times, but Inanna moved further and further from her father's position on The Human Question. The final straw for Inanna was her father's One God Decree. With the stroke of a pen, Enlil stripped the other Anunnaki of their status as gods to the humans and declared he alone was the God of humanity.

The campaign slogan read, "Enlil is the only God of heaven and earth."

With King Anu's health failing, Enlil brutally enforced his One God Policy upon the humans. He attacked his fellow Anunnaki, who challenged his supremacy, eventually sending the other Anunnaki—Enki and Inanna included—home to Nibiru. Only Enlil and Ea stayed upon the earth. For centuries, they dominated the planet, turning humans against humans. They gave help and advanced weapons to human tribes in their favor, and summarily executed whole cities that opposed them. They set up a group they called The Cadre comprised of Anunnaki-human hybrids and bred them as overseers with sworn loyalty to Enlil and his line.

Enlil loved to test the loyalty of Cadre members by putting them in stressful situations and demanding their obedience. Ea remembered one time when Enlil commanded a Cadre member to take his eldest son to a cliff and throw him off to prove his loyalty. Enlil observed to see whether the Cadre member would comply. At the last minute, Enlil intervened and stopped the execution. He praised the Cadre member for his devotion and gave him greater responsibility.

This incident imprinted on Ea's mind. This demonstrated power and the use of power to command what you wanted from others. His father was a master at it. Ea watched and he learned. He believed every word of his father's divine claims upon the earth and upon the humans. So complete was his indoctrination, he saw no reason for any self-respecting Anunnaki to question it.

When they received the word of King Anu's death, Enlil and Ea left the earth. Enlil installed The Cadre as permanent governors of Earth. Ea arrived home as Crown Prince Ea. He honed his kingship skills under his father for nearly 1,000 earth years. He served in the Nibiruan Senate along with his sister and uncle. Enki and Inanna constantly pushed legislation to loosen the restraints on humanity, provide more transparency, and encourage their development. Ea took a special pride in defeating their efforts by scaring the Anunnaki people with what he called the human menace. He repeatedly succeeded in maintaining the crown's free hand on what he called "The Human Question."

As he worked against them, he labeled their insistence on helping the humans as treason. He also began to see the Senate as an unnecessary check on the king's power. He lobbied Enlil to weaken the Senate, but his father was a traditionalist at heart. Unable to persuade his father, Ea vowed to reduce the Senate to a toothless debating society when he ruled. He also planned to deal with Enki and Inanna's treason.

Ea became king when Enlil died suddenly of a mysterious gene disorder. The doctors told Ea his father's genes were "undone." They degenerated into the genes of a small child. He died quickly and painfully. The illness defied explanation.

As king, Ea was so caught up in his political intrigues, that he never made time for a family and never produced an heir. In fact, neither he nor Inanna had offspring. As it currently stood, there was no heir to continue the line. Their family was at risk of losing the crown.

"Father Creator," called out the king. "I await your wisdom. I await your guidance. I am King of Nibiru. I demand to be heard!" bellowed the lonely king.

He sat and he waited, but nothing happened. He often had the technology in the room checked to ensure functionality. The technology worked fine. The Father Creator simply refused his calls.

Suddenly, a dark energy imposed itself upon him. He'd felt and resisted this force before, but now it insisted. He fell into a trance and awakened to a world of higher frequency where everything seemed more vibrant and alive.

A voice spoke to him. "Oh mighty king, The Father Creator denies your calls, but we hear and we answer."

"Who are you?" replied the shaken king.

"We are beings who are as you shall one day be. We exist in the fifth dimension and we can grant your every wish, if only you will align yourself with us," boomed the voice.

"The Father Creator does not deny me!" Ea shouted.

"Really?" retorted the voice. "When was the last time he was with you? You sit in that room waiting and still he never comes to you."

"Father Creator," Ea began again.

"He will not listen to you, oh mighty king, but you shall listen to us."

"Why would I listen to you? What's in it for me?" the king said confidently, regaining his warrior spirit.

"Your survival. Yes. We will ensure your survival."

"Is my survival at risk?"

"Oh yes, mighty king. You will soon find yourself on your knees begging for our help. It is a future fact."

"I would never bend my knee to you or anyone else!" declared an angered Ea.

"Your arrogance will be your undoing, oh mighty king. You will concede to us and then we will help you."

"Help me how?"

"Help you put your world back in order."

"I have it under control. Your help is not required."

"What of earth and the humans? Do you have that under control too?"

"What do you know of that?" Ea demanded.

"We warned your father and your uncle not to begin the human experiment. Now the humans threaten you and they threaten us in the far distant future. Our mutual interest is to get them back under control now."

"You spoke to my father and my uncle? What proof do you have of that?"

"We gave them the TimeCube technology that has helped your house remain in power on Nibiru. We gave you the ability to see the possible futures, at least some of them, and to act to protect your interests."

"I see no evidence in the TimeCubes that the humans pose any immediate threat to Nibiru. As for keeping them under control, I have seen to that."

"Your TimeCube data is . . . incomplete. We shared only a part of our technology with you. Our TimeCube sees a growing possibility these humans will continue to grow and advance— one day overtaking you and us. This cannot be allowed."

Ea paused to consider the words of the entity. He could not even be sure he was talking to a single individual. He saw shadowy forms in the light and the lone voice seemed to be coming from everywhere. "How will this take place?" Ea asked.

"We are not prepared to share those details with you yet. Just know that we know. Your sister will play a key role in your house's undoing. She must be stopped."

"My sister, The Princess Inanna," chided the king, "her meanderings are harmless and no threat to me or to Nibiru."

"Tell us, oh mighty king, do you have an heir?"

Ea's mouth ran dry. "What concern is that of yours?"

"We recommend you take that up with your sister, The Princess Inanna."

"Inanna is too old and too sick to bear a child."

"Oh mighty king, you really should think more creatively. Your sister has."

Worry began to grow in Ea's mind. He was middle-aged and vibrant, but having no heir was a concern. "What would you have me do?"

"You must reassert your control of the Earth and the humans. You have permitted your sister to do as she pleases. It's placed you and us at risk. Stop her or we will!"

"Meaning?"

"Meaning, oh mighty king, that we saw this dangerous outcome approaching the moment your father and your uncle created the humans. As long as they were your slaves, the future looked fine. When your Uncle Enki began sharing knowledge and culture with them, we warned him that we would intervene if our future took a turn for the worse. We gave him 6,000 years to prove they were not a threat to us. That time is up. He never spoke to you of this?"

Ea's temper was easily raised where his uncle was concerned, but Enki was considered an old wise sage and a hero to his people. This had prevented Ea from dealing with him in the past. "No! He has never shared your deal with me."

The entities knew just the buttons to push with King Ea.

"Oh mighty king, your sister practically rules the earth. Your uncle has deals that create danger for Nibiru. Your father would never have allowed such things to happen when he was king."

Ea was now in a fit of rage. "Tell me what I must do!"

"You must control the humans and change the timeline or we will deal a fatal blow to Nibiru on your watch, oh mighty king."

"What do you mean by a fatal blow?"

"The 26th king in your line challenged us. It was his undoing. Don't let it be yours, oh mighty king."

"My father was the 26th king," Ea shouted.

"Yes. He *was* and now is no more. Until we meet again."

Ea emerged from the trance with a jolt. He prided himself on never showing fear, but an undeniable chill ran through him. He felt personally threatened by the entities speaking to him in the trance. Was the threat real or was his barren relationship with The Father Creator making him crazy?

He steadied himself and began again. "Father Creator."

(33)
Message from Home

Inanna awakened to a tone indicating an urgent message from the bridge.

"Mistress, Commander Enka here. There is an urgent message coming in from Nibiru on the secure Royal Channel.

Inanna called out, "Lights," and rose to her feet. She winced in pain, as her condition caused stiffness and pain from lying in one spot too long. She took her hands and fidgeted with her hair.

"Put the message through, Commander."

"Yes, Mistress, sending it now."

King Ea's exaggerated image appeared on Inanna's monitor. He magnified his image in all communications to emphasize his power and gain psychological advantage.

"My sister," started King Ea, "Did I awaken you?"

"It is of no concern, my brother. How may I be of service to you?"

"Are you well, Inanna, you look a bit tired. Is your condition worsening?"

"Am I to believe my king contacted me at this hour to check on the status of my health?"

"You are always so perceptive, sister. Still, I am concerned for your wellbeing and that is my reason for contacting you."

"I am touched, brother."

"I received a visit from the Z Alliance ambassador today. He spoke of another incident involving you and one of their ships.

They were quite angry. I had to talk them out of sending warships to hunt you down."

"Then, I suppose, thanks are in order, brother."

"Still on this crusade for humans, are we, Inanna?"

"Does my brother disapprove?" Inanna asked smugly.

King Ea flashed anger, but managed restraint. "I am king,
Inanna. I decide our Earth policy. Not you!"

"What the Z are doing to humans is immoral, Ea! Even you
cannot be blind to that."

"We have lucrative trade agreements, Inanna. You know
Earth is vital to the Nibiruan economy. We cannot afford interstellar incidents over your personal grievances."

"My personal grievances? My views reflect the views of most
Anunnaki on the Human Question—that is when they are not
deceived by your deceptions."

Ea lost his cool. "I'm warning you, Inanna. Stop this dangerous course. Your human friends will suffer for your stubborn-
ness. How clever you were to have your Maria ask the American
president about alien intervention in a live press conference. He
has even promised to help her. I have put a stop to that too."

"You leave Maria out of this," bristled Inanna.

"Not to worry, my sister, your precious Maria is safe for now.
After all, she does carry royal blood thanks to you."

Inanna feigned ignorance. "What do you mean, Ea?"

"Don't play games, sister. I know all about Maria. I know
how you are conspiring to create an heir to the throne—to take
my power from me."

"You know nothing, Ea," shouted Inanna. "Maria—"

"Is safe for now, my sister, as are you. If you persist on this
path, her safety and yours may slip beyond my control."

"The *Book of Possibilities* states, "Be open to the power and
possibility alive in the uncertainty. I will take my chances,

brother."

"The *Book of Possibilities* is for old men and fools, Inanna."

"You place too little faith in The Father Creator, Ea. Tell me, does he still refuse you in your meditations?"

"I will waste no time on your trifles. If you stay out of my way, I will spare Maria and you. However, others you have involved are not so fortunate."

"Is that a threat, my brother?"

"That is a promise, Inanna. I have peered into the TimeCube. I have seen the future you are trying to create for the humans. I promise you it will never happen!"

"What are you going to do?"

"Go to the TimeCube, my sister, and see for yourself. In the meantime, I have dispatched a squadron of Nibiruan warships to Earth Space. They arrive in two days. If there are any more commerce-impeding incidents, I may give the humans what you want—proof of our existence. Do you think they would believe if we took out London, Washington, Beijing?"

Inanna swallowed hard, "And I will take any necessary action to prevent that from happening, but go ahead and try."

"You sound eager for me too."

"Maybe I am," declared Inanna.

"Be well, my sister. If you choose the humans, you seal their fate and yours. Ea out!"

As soon as the communication ceased, Inanna rushed to the safe embedded in her bedroom wall. She mentally transmitted the combination to the mind-lock protecting her most important possession. The door swung open and Inanna grasped the radiant cube within. It's barely audible hum harmonized the space around it. Its gentle vibration ran through her body, producing calm and clarity. This state prepared the user for "The Seeing."

The Nibiruan Royal Family obtained the TimeCubes from a mysterious source several Earth millennia ago. Despite centuries of effort, Nibiruan scientists had not determined how the devices worked. TimeCubes operated on a trans-quantum level and seemingly in multiple dimensions. They worked in concert with the operator's mind to produce visions of potential futures. Some people were natural seers. Others learned through practice. The Royal Family selected seers with certain aptitudes from the population to read and interpret the TimeCubes. Inanna was the only member of the Royal Family trained as a Seer and she was among the best.

While the TimeCube's operation puzzled, it demonstrated real world benefits time and again. The Royal Family employed TimeCubes to see possible threats to their rule, predict the outcome of battles, and even forge profitable trade agreements. The devices predicted the odds of future events, displaying outcome percentages and categorizing them as certain, likely, possible, or impossible.

A skilled Seer could explore alternative scenarios to increase or decrease the likelihood of events. Amazingly, a TimeCube could even scan the past for related events, conversations, and thoughts that led to the postulated eventualities.

Inanna closed her eyes and spoke, "TimeCube, show me the cosmic dreamer. Grant me access to the cosmic dream."

Slowly, scenarios appeared in Inanna's mind. Like animated storyboards, possible futures played and their outcomes displayed. The TimeCube interfaced with her brain, giving her a type of heads-up display for navigating the scenarios.

Inanna focused on Maria and looked 72 hours into the future. The TimeCube confirmed Maria's physical safety, but Inanna saw her experiencing anguish over an undefined event. She tried to bring the event into focus, but could not. She saw the event compelling Maria to tell Jack everything.

Then she checked President Paxton. Something was wrong! She saw bombs embedded in a broad European boulevard, but zeroing in on the location would take time. She saw the president's car driving over the bombs and exploding. Finally, she saw a headline reading, "President Paxton Killed in Terrorist Attack." The TimeCube put the certainty of this event at 98.6%.

"When?" asked Inanna.

The TimeCube displayed a countdown for the attack. The clock read 2:54, 2:53, 2:52. The president's car would explode in less than three minutes!

"Bridge," shouted Inanna.

"Yes, Mistress," replied Enka.

"Where is President Paxton today?"

"Checking, Mistress. He is in France for the 80th anniversary of the D-Day invasion."

"Can you get a fix on his current position?"

"He is in Paris. It may take a few minutes triangulate his position from this distance."

"We don't have a few minutes," said a now panicked Inanna.

The clock was now counting down 19 seconds . . . 18 seconds. The Probability meter had climbed to 99.7%.

"Scan the major streets of Paris for bombs and transport them to a safe location."

10 seconds. 99.9%.

"Mistress, we are out of range to transport anything from the surface."

The clock hit zero and the probability meter showed 100%. Inanna watched in real-time as Paxton's car exploded and flipped over three times. The massive armored limousine was no match for the bombs targeting it.

She turned her attention to the Nibiruan ships on their way.

She noted they had entered the outer regions of the Oort Cloud. Two days looked to be a good estimate for their arrival.

She scanned the timeline to view her brother's orders to the squadron commander. An image of Admiral Ninn sitting in a chair below the king appeared.

"Ninn," muttered Inanna with disdain. "Of course, you send your lap dog, Ea."

King Ea was giving orders. "Admiral, it's time to send the earth and my sister a message."

"I understand, Excellency."

"When you arrive in Earth Space, I want you to target one Earth city and destroy it. It is time for a refresher on who controls the earth. Let them know the gods of old have returned. When my sister shows herself, and she will, capture her and her crew. Tow the Rakbu back to Nibiru."

"Consider it done, my Lord," Ninn replied.

"TimeCube, display scenarios and outcomes for a battle between Rakbu and the Nibiruan fleet," Inanna ordered.

The returns startled her. No scenario she explored gave Rakbu greater than a five percent chance of surviving the encounter. The TimeCube calculated the odds of Rakbu defeating the fleet at virtually zero. She requested the odds of her survival, but canceled before they displayed.

It matters not, she thought. *The Book of Possibilities is clear.* "*No other liar is as convincing or seductive as the facts.*" *We don't need the facts. We need heart.*

Inanna deactivated the TimeCube and returned it to the safe. She knew Paxton's death would devastate Maria. She wanted to be there for her, but she now had problems of her own. Maria was strong. She had Jack. She would have to grieve alone.

"Commander Enka," called Inanna.

"Yes, Mistress."

"Please assemble the senior staff first thing in the morning. I want a battle readiness report from all departments, Inanna out!"

Inanna was exhausted by the emotion of the past 20 minutes. She returned to bed and tried to sleep. Tears welled in her eyes. For the first time in years, Inanna wept.

(34)
Sixth Day of the Sixth Month

The sixth day of the sixth month began with hope. The most powerful man in the world had agreed to help Maria on her quest to uncover and expose the truth. She awoke with an uneasy intuition.

She was officially on leave from ANN. Pete Rogers' tepid support for her pursuit of this story evaporated in the fallout from Maria's questions. Only Jack intervening with his old friend and fraternity buddy convinced Pete not to fire Maria. He placed her on extended leave until the firestorm blew over. What a firestorm! For two nights running, she had been the darling of late night ITV jokes. A cottage industry of Maria Love videos mushroomed across YouTube.

Neither President Paxton nor, surprisingly, Inanna had contacted her. She did have several standing invitations from UFO groups to speak at their conventions. Several major tabloids approached her about stories. The most interesting involved Maria secretly carrying an alien baby. She chuckled at the story's irony. Another involved Maria confirming she saw the frozen bodies of Michael Jackson, Elvis Presley, and Princess Diana aboard an alien ship. Maria wanted no part of undermining the credibility of her mission. The tabloids would run those stories with or without her.

"ITV. ANN," she called out.

She expected to see more stories about her and maybe something about the 80th Anniversary of D-Day taking place in Normandy, France. Right away, she knew something was wrong. Breaking News headlines scrolled across the bottom of the screen. Justin Cardone, one of ANN's up and coming young anchors was speaking. Behind him, images of Paris displayed. At first, Maria thought the report was about a massive car accident.

Then the chilling words crawled across the screen, "President Critically Injured in Terror Attack."

"Damn," Maria said. "Volume up."

Cardone was speaking, "President Paxton had just returned to Paris after visiting Normandy Beach to commemorate the 80th anniversary of the D-Day invasion. He was scheduled to meet for private talks with President LeGrand. The President's motorcade was traveling down the Champs-Élysées when a bomb beneath the road erupted as the President's car passed."

The video of the incident played and replayed in slow motion, as Cardone spoke.

"His car flipped several times and landed on its top. The force of the explosion destroyed two cars in the motorcade. There are reports of several dozen casualties in the crowd. They came to welcome this popular American President, less than five months into his second term. The explosion instantly killed Presidential Chief of Staff, Joe Bieber. Ambulances rushed the president and Mrs. Paxton to the hospital. The hospital lists Mrs. Paxton in serious condition with non-life-threatening injuries. President Paxton's condition remains a mystery at this hour. It is known he has been in emergency surgery for more than an hour to address multiple severe injuries."

Maria sank into a nearby chair. Tears came to her eyes. "No! No!"

"Vice President Chang was visiting his home state of

Oregon when news of the attack came. He has yet to comment. There has been a statement released from The White House Press Office stating that the 25th Amendment to the Constitution has been invoked and the Vice President has been sworn in as Acting President. This indicates, whatever the President's condition, he's unable to continue his duties at the moment."

Cardone paused for a moment, as he listened in his earpiece. "Yes. I understand," he said to the voice speaking to him. Gathering himself, Cardone looked somberly into the camera. "Ladies and Gentlemen, I regret to inform you that the 46th President of the United States, Ronald Paxton, is dead. This news comes from Reuters in Paris and other major news agencies are now confirming. The President expired on the operating table under the care of some of the top surgeons in France."

"The White House is now confirming that 38-year-old Anthony Chang has been sworn in as the 47th President of the United States. We understand the announcement of President Paxton's death was delayed to allow President Chang to return to the capital. Chang will speak to the nation this evening, but he has released a statement saying in part that, The American people are shocked, saddened, and outraged by this senseless act of terrorism. He vowed to use every resource at his disposal to bring those responsible to justice. Chang becomes the youngest man ever to hold the office. He is a second-generation American of Chinese-descent and a graduate of Oregon State University. He was an unknown political science professor when he authored much of the Democrat platform in 2020 and served as special advisor to President Paxton during his first term. Chang has never held elected office. His parents are practicing Buddhists, but he converted to Christianity during college."

Cardone continued, "Now we have footage taken a few minutes ago of the new President emerging from Marine One (the

Presidential helicopter) on the lawn of the White House. It is said he is headed into meetings with advisors to determine how to respond to the terrorist attack that has slain a president."

"We have ANN military and terrorism analyst retired General Mark Dixon with us. General Dixon, who is responsible?"

"Well, Justin. Even though we don't have independent confirmation yet, my sources are telling me that this is the work of the Brotherhood for Globalization of Truth or B-GOT. This is a network of nationalists with a mission to disrupt all international commerce, dialogue, and cooperation. They have been increasing their activity in recent years and have been threatening a big attack."

"General, Why President Paxton, and how did they, apparently, plant a bomb in one of the busiest avenues in the world?"

"Justin, we've got clear intelligence that B-GOT has sympathizers working in nearly every country in the world. These people are determined to undermine international norms. I don't know how they got a bomb in that street without detection, but I know it means we are going to have double down on all of our security efforts to keep the people of the world safe."

"And why President Paxton?"

"Well, Justin, if you're going to send a message to the people of the world in general and the people of the United States in particular, what better target than an American president?"

"That makes perfect sense. Thank you, general. Recapping President Ron Paxton was killed today . . . one moment. Sorry, folks, this is live ITV. This is right on cue with what you were just saying, General. Sergey Mitchell—the purported leader of B-GOT—has posted a video on the Internet. He has claimed responsibility for the attack in Paris. He warns Americans and all the people of the world that this is just the beginning unless the governments of the world respect national sovereignty and stop pushing what he calls a 'globalist agenda.' The CIA released the video and the agency has confirmed its authenticity. U.S. Officials sought and received UN authority to use the so-called global Internet Kill Switch to shut down the website where the video was posted."

Maria had seen enough. She turned off the ITV. The president was dead and so was the only other human being who could confirm she had spoken to him three nights earlier. She was so close to victory and now the unbelievable events of this day had changed everything. Just days after President Paxton had promised his help to expose the off-world involvement in human civilization he's dead.

"How can that be?" she said aloud. "That's quite an incredible coincidence."

She'd learned from working with Inanna that few coincidences are just coincidences. Maria's mind flashed back to Paxton's last words, words of warning, about the Military Industrial Complex. She turned ITV back on and went to YouTube. She typed Eisenhower Military Industrial Complex. She watched President Eisenhower's farewell address to the nation. She'd watched the speech back in college, but now every line seemed to ring with new meaning.

"Great! Now I sound like a conspiracy theorist. Let's take this one step at a time," she half-whispered aloud as she retraced the past three days.

Paxton brought up the MIDC. Did he believe that the investigation into off-world involvement on the earth might invoke its wrath? Was today confirmation of his fear or was it just a coincidence? Why did it happen on this day of all days? Had someone created this event right from the context of their conversation as a warning? Days after agreeing to help her expose the alien cover-up, the president is assassinated while celebrating the 80th anniversary of an invasion led by the same man who gave the MIDC speech.

As the coincidences came together in her mind, the questions piled up. Why would the MIDC care about alien involvement and a president willing to help expose it? How could they have heard us speak?

"We were in the Oval Office. That has to be one of the most secure rooms in the world," she affirmed to the four walls of her living room.

Over the next few hours, Maria immersed herself in articles and videos discussing the military's role in UFO history. She soon realized there was a host of powerful interests with no desire and, in fact, outright opposition to exposing the topic or the untruths used to marginalize and conceal it for decades.

Still, Maria was perplexed. Was this a rabbit hole or was it possible they would kill the president to keep the secret hidden? Then, more coincidences began to happen. Maria's ComTab rang—Pete Rogers.

"Pete," Maria began, "Can you believe about Paxton?"

"Listen, Maria, we've been friends for a long time, but—"

"Pete, don't do this. The shareholders will get over it. This is too important. We have to stick to our—"

"Damn it, Maria," Pete said strongly in a hushed tone, "This is not about shareholders anymore. The FCC raided us this afternoon. There were FBI agents and some other people who wouldn't even identify themselves."

"The FCC? The FBI? What do they want?"

"They're threatening to take our license away, if we don't play ball."

"How can they do that? What do you mean play ball?"

"They want you out, Maria, permanently."

"On what grounds? How can they do that it's unconstitu-
tional? For God's sake, Pete, file a First Amendment challenge."

"Maria, listen to me, this is gone way beyond that. If we don't
have a license, we don't have a company!"

"Why are they doing this, Pete?"

"I don't know, but I can put two and two together. Obviously, someone didn't like your stunt the other night."

"Pete, you met Inanna. You've been on the damn ship! Why
are you rolling over like this?"

"If Inanna is who she claims to be, why doesn't she just show
herself to the world? Why all the games? For all I know and for
all you know, she is part of some advanced government program
and you are just a pawn in her game. Have you heard from her
since the other night?"

"No, I haven't. There's something I didn't tell you the other
night, Pete."

"Maria, I don't want to hear it. Look, you're an old and dear
friend, but you're out. I'm sorry. We have shareholders and 6,000
employees and—"

"And what?"

"And I received a call . . . an anonymous one . . . after the
raid. Someone described Jeremy walking home from school.
They detailed his clothes and his route home."

Jeremy was Pete's son. Jack and Maria witnessed his birth.
He was as close as Maria had to a son. She hesitated and then
said, "Pete, I'm sorry. I can't believe they'd stoop that low."

"You say they, Maria, like you even know who they are. You
don't know who they are, but they know who Jeremy is."

"Pete, I spoke to Paxton after the news conference the other
night. The Secret Service came and pulled me out of the mob
scene. The crew can verify it. They saw it. He was interested,
Pete. He has been trying to uncover all of this and he offered his

help."

"Who else was there?"

"Bieber."

"Great, Maria. Paxton and Bieber are both dead. Maybe that's a sign to stay away from this."

"His last words for me were to watch my back. He mentioned the Military Industrial Complex is always watching. Three days later he's dead, celebrating the anniversary of an invasion—"

"Maria, I can't risk the network. I can't risk Jeremy."

"The invasion is led by the man who made the Military Industrial Complex speech. Then they kill him on the anniversary of that invasion. Don't you think that's a message too?"

"Maria, you're grasping at straws. I'm sorry. I love Jack and you like family, but I can't protect you. I'm sorry you're out."

"Are you going to report that B-GOT is responsible for the attack?"

"That's what every credible source is saying. They took responsibility. Not everything is a conspiracy."

"Maybe not, but that doesn't mean that nothing is a conspiracy. Who are the credible sources? They release a grainy, shadowy video and then kill the website and you take that as irrefutable evidence?"

"Maria, I have to go. Tell Jack I'm sorry. Watch your back, Maria."

Pete hung up. Maria felt rage and sympathy. She wanted Pete to use the power of his network to challenge the "Powers That Be." At the same time, she understood. They threatened all he held precious and he was scared.

"Fear is always the tool used to keep humans in line," Inanna had told her. "It's worked for thousands of years. They divide and separate you until you feel like you're alone against the system. It will continue to work until you awaken to who you really are."

Just then, Jack came in the door. He looked dejected. He emphatically embraced Maria and they kissed.

"How was your day, beautiful?" he asked.

"I've had better. How was yours?"

"I tried to call you when I heard about Paxton. I kept getting a call cannot be connected message."

"I understand, honey," said Maria. "I just got off the phone with Pete. He fired me, Jack. He's getting heavy pressure from the government. They were threatening to pull ANN's license. The cost of keeping it was to get rid of me."

"What a coincidence," said Jack, "I got fired today too."

"Why did you get fired?"

"I got a message this afternoon to see Hawking. He told me Chang called him personally and ordered him to fire my whole team and me. It seems arms control talks are not so popular today."

"Why didn't Hawking fight for you? He's the Secretary of State and a family friend."

"Well, it seems like two family friends let us down today. Hawking couldn't save me. He's out too. Chang is shaking up his entire national security and foreign policy team. He wants his own people in place."

"Jack, I'm exhausted and I'm not feeling well. I'm going to bed. Tomorrow I need to tell you something, OK?"

"Get your rest. We'll figure this out," replied Jack with a kiss on the forehead.

The sixth day of the sixth month ended with a series of heartbreaking coincidences and utter defeat. Maria's mission and her career lay in ruins. Inanna called The *Book of Possibilities* the most sacred book of the Anunnaki. She gave Maria an electronic copy. Maria reached for the ComTab.

"Search *Book of Possibilities*. Find and read random motivational quotes," Maria instructed.

"Working," the ComTab replied. "Breath is hope. Hope is possibility. Possibility is everything. Many wait for The Father Creator to act, while The Father Creator waits for them. Fear is a tyrant. Love is the great emancipator."

Maria put on her headphones, closed her eyes, and listened. The quotes talked her down from the ledge.

"A thousand universes from now love will still be all that matters. Someone is going to create your reality. It might as well be you. To emancipate yourself, emancipate your mind. To emancipate your mind, emancipate your heart. Obstacles are signs of progress. The universe rarely challenges mediocrity. Change either transforms or it destroys. Your thoughts decide."

Change is certainly happening, Maria thought. *How can I transform this situation?*

"Your heart is mighty. Your mind is limitless. Your soul is infinite. A river has hope because it never stops moving forward."

That's it. I'm a river. I keep moving forward. Jack and I keep moving forward. We are limitless and infinite. We're not here to live as slaves to anyone or any circumstance.

"The truth is out there, but the path is in you. You can be a victim of your past or a builder of your future, but you cannot be both at once. Which do you choose?"

Maria felt a powerful shift happening within her. She always believed circumstances ruled us. She suddenly realized it was all a choice—her choice. Was she a builder or a victim? Her mother was always the victim. Most of the people she knew were always the victim or looking for a crutch to hold them up in tough times.

What if we could hold ourselves up?

"Thank you, Father Creator," she whispered. "Now I see. I'm here to stand on my own two feet and I will!"

Maria drifted toward sleep. Her last thought, *where is Inanna and why haven't I heard from her?*

(35)
Are You In or Are You Out?

Inanna assembled her senior staff in the Rakbu's main conference room. Twenty of her top officers and advisors were present and dressed in full uniform. Inanna sat at the head of a large table, wearing her sunray crown symbolizing her Royal authority.

"Ladies and gentlemen," she began, "the day I have long expected has arrived. My brother, the king, has dispatched Royal Battle Cruisers under the command of Admiral Ninn to Earth Space."

"Mistress," asked Commander Enka, "Do you know how many RBCs?"

"I have viewed the TimeCube, Commander. Ninn's force consists of 11 RBCs. King Ea authorized the task force for two missions. The first is to lay waste to at least one important Earth city. The second is to capture this vessel, tow it back to Nibiru, and deliver me to the hand of my brother, the king."

Hushed whispers circled the table. Finally, Commander Enka spoke. "Mistress, what is your command?"

"I do not intend to allow them to attack Earth. We will meet the task force and engage it."

"Mistress," offered Enka sheepishly, "Rakbu is a fine vessel. She is a match for two, maybe three RBCs, but eleven—"

"Commander, the task force has no carrier and that means no fighters. They don't know about the upgrades to the Rakbu and the fact we carry five fighter squadrons."

"Still, Mistress, they outgun us at least three to one."

"The fighters give us the element of surprise, Enka. Do you doubt my capabilities in battle?"

"Of course not, Mistress, but—"

"But nothing, Commander! We will establish an Earth Space perimeter. I will permit no Anunnaki vessels inside the orbit of Neptune. Ninn is an experienced and competent battle commander, but many of his ship commanders are young and inexperienced. If we can destroy or disable Ninn's flagship, the other ships will run for home.

"That's a bold assumption, Mistress," chimed Colonel Nurnta who commanded Inanna's fighter wing.

"Bold perhaps, and precisely what we must be if we are to succeed, Colonel. You shall conceal your fighters on the backside of Neptune. You will attack the taskforce from the rear. Squadrons 1 and 3 will join our attack on the flagship. Squadrons 2 and 4 will harass the other ships and keep them busy, ensuring our victory over Ninn. We shall hold Squadron 5 in reserve."

Nurnta replied, "Mistress, your leadership is not in question. Everyone here is loyal to you. We all signed up for the mission of helping to guide the humans to a better civilization. We all agree certain wrongs must be righted. But now, you are asking us to fire upon our Anunnaki brothers and sisters to protect the humans. That is unthinkable to some of my pilots."

Inanna sensed the uncertainty, even outright opposition to her proposal in the room. She knew she must have not only the obedience and loyalty of these people, but also their commitment. She removed her crown and set it on the floor. This was such an unprecedented gesture that it focused all eyes upon her.

She now spoke to her officers as one of them. "My friends," she began with a smile, "We all knew this day might come, didn't we? My brother, the king, is determined to keep the humans afraid and in the dark. He schemes to maintain their obedience to a divine personality we instituted to enslave their persons and their minds. Even now, he has dispatched Admiral Ninn for the express purpose of re-establishing an open relationship with the humans based on Anunnaki belligerence and domination. He would subdue them and usher in a new era of Anunnaki tyranny. How can we say we stand for a different future on the Human Question, if we stand by and do nothing to oppose this aggression?"

Bardo was Inanna's chief advisor on spiritual matters. "Mistress, you make a powerful case. But candidly, I am not convinced the humans are capable of the spiritual progression you seek for them."

"Why do you say that, Bardo?" asked Inanna.

"Mistress, they are not like us. They do not have a connection to The Father Creator. They murder each other over god paradigms, economic and political systems. Even now, the new American president is plotting an act of revenge against those he believes are responsible for the attack on President Paxton. How can we condone such acts? Where is there redemption for a species capable of such horrors?"

"And what of us, Bardo?" Inanna asked, trying to keep her blood pressure in check. "We created inferior beings and commanded them to serve our whims. We commanded them to worship us as gods. We filled their minds with fear of our anger and visions of our judgment. We—"

"Respectfully, Mistress, that was centuries ago," Bardo offered.

"We denied them their rightful connection to The Father Creator? Even as we speak, we send warships to rain destruction upon them to keep them under our thumb?"

"Mistress, you know they were not created for a link to The Father Creator. It's not in their DNA. They may not even be capable of it," declared Bardo.

"Do we deny them the opportunity?" shot back Inanna. "Do we fail to acknowledge their right to explore their existence and its meaning on their own terms?"

"I fear, Mistress, that you see more in the humans than is there. They're not capable of the higher thoughts you attribute to them. You expect them to reason and you expect them to feel like Anunnaki. They were not bred for it."

"They can and they will!" Inanna thundered. "Why did you sign up for this mission if you think so little of the humans, Bardo?"

"Mistress, whether they are capable of true spiritual thought or not, the humans do not deserve to be harvested by other species. It is an affront to the dignity of life. I signed up to help you put a stop to it."

Uruk spoke next. "Begging your pardon, Mistress, but maybe King Ea is correct. The humans are violent and rebellious. Perhaps they need a reminder of the order of things."

Inanna turned and glared at her security chief. "The order of things, Uruk?"

"Yes, Mistress. The Anunnaki are a proud and powerful race. We are superior to the humans. They are the product of our genius. What is wrong with using them as we see fit? I agree with Bardo. I do not think they are capable of true spiritual connection to The Father Creator."

"I am not pleased, gentlemen. I brought you here this morning not to debate the Human Question, but to plan our strategy for dealing with the Anunnaki task force headed to Earth Space. Instead, I find my crew channeling the words of my brother the king."

"Mistress, your crew is loyal. We will follow your command," asserted Enka.

"That is not enough, Commander. Without your passion for this mission, you may not be willing to pay the price necessary to see it through to completion."

"Mistress," began Bardo in his calming voice.

"Stop, Bardo," said Inanna raising her right hand. "I have not shared this with you. I have not shared this with anyone. As you all know, my sickness is rapidly advancing. As it has progressed, I've experienced the most profound meditations of my life. It has allowed me amazing clarity on life and on what we must do on the Human Question. I have had direct contact with The Father Creator."

A collective gasp reverberated around the conference table.

"The Father Creator has been clear with me. We, the Anunnaki, are responsible for what has befallen humanity. We created them to be dependent, warlike, and obedient to us. We designed them without their natural connection to the true order of the universe. We must fix this!"

"Mistress," Bardo began carefully, "You mean you've seen visions of The Father Creator?"

"No, Bardo. I have been in His presence."

"How have these contacts happened?"

"During my meditations, I pierce the veil of existence and I come to a place where I am able to connect with Him, commune with Him. It is an amazing feeling."

"Do you see Him," queried Bardo?

"No. He speaks to me in my mind and He plants visions of what can be . . . of what He calls The Future Possible. He is determined to find a direct connection with the humans. He has told me it is possible. They *are* capable. He refers to them as His grandchildren."

"Mistress, your medications are strong," said Dr. Enti, "They could be causing hallucinations."

"Are you saying I am delusional, doctor?"

Enti backtracked carefully. "Of course not, Mistress. Only hearing The Father Creator is . . . well . . . worrisome."

"Why worrisome? Why do you all look as if I am crazy? Bardo, you are one of the great Seers of our people. Do you think it inconceivable that The Father Creator can communicate directly with us?"

"Mistress, there are stories in our past, but—"

"And do those stories speak of Anunnaki having direct communication with The Father Creator?"

"Yes, but they are only stories."

"Then how do you know The Father Creator is real, Bardo?"

"Faith, Mistress. We must believe without having seen."

"And yet, if one sees, one is crazy?"

"No one is saying you're crazy, Mistress," said Dr. Enti. "Perhaps, you are just tired."

Inanna swallowed hard and she felt tears welling in her eyes. *I must not lose control in front of them,* she thought.

"Gentlemen, I wish I had the proof you seek. I wish you could see and hear what I have seen and heard. Then you would understand why the humans must no longer be subjugated and why we must protect them. Our people, despite our willingness to make excuses for it, have committed a crime of historic proportions. Maybe we had our reasons for it, but the time has come to decide. Are you in or are you out?"

There was silence and uneasiness around the table.

Inanna continued, "I will take your silence as assent. I don't want to go to war with our brothers and sisters either. I will do my best to avoid it. I fear it will not be possible. Commander Enka, set a course for Neptune. Colonel, prepare your fighters."

Inanna reached for her sunray crown and placed it back atop her head. She scanned the room with her regal glare and exited the room like a goddess—gracefully and with power.

(36)
Five Principles

The stress of the confrontation with her senior staff had tired
Inanna. She returned to her quarters. She required rest and space
to think. The tone of the meeting surprised her. She failed to
realize the level of resistance and confusion that still existed
about the Rakbu's mission. Her leaders and her crew needed a
common vision. Each person aboard the ship had reasons for
being there, but those reasons differed. The crew lacked true
commitment to a common cause.

For the first time, Inanna recognized The Future Possible
must be more than a concept in her mind. It required definition
and articulation to become actionable for her crew, the humans,
and others drawn to the cause. She also needed to prepare the
crew for the possibility of open rebellion. Engaging the Anunnaki taskforce might mean a battle. A battle meant open conflict
with Nibiru on The Human Question. Clearly, her senior staff
was hesitant. Her crew might be as well. What she needed was a
manifesto that declared the reasons for the actions she was prepared to take against King Ea.

"Computer. Dictation," she said.

Inanna spoke The Future Possible into life:

> For millennia, we have debated The Human Ques-
> tion on Nibiru without resolution. The Anunnaki re-
> gime has failed to take responsibility for its actions in
> genetically engineering a sentient species to serve the

interests of the Nibiruan Crown. That regime has persisted in hiding the truth and denying that species a complete understanding of its origins.

The King of Nibiru has willfully substituted himself and his predecessors for the true Father Creator of the Universe. He has imposed this false vision of God upon the people of Earth through fear and intimidation, as well as through religious and political systems. He has orchestrated the physical, psychological, and financial slavery of the human species. He has profited from the trafficking of human beings and from non-consensual experimentation upon them.

King Ea has thwarted all attempts to address these wrongs through peaceful political channels. He has denied open discussion on The Human Question and has allowed the good people of Nibiru to operate under the false impression that humanity is a threat to Nibiru.

For these reasons and many others, I declare King Ea's rule over Earth Space null and void. The Future Possible for humanity declared to me by The Father Creator is hereby established and ordered.

This decree establishes five immutable principles.

1. Human beings have a right to know their origins and the totality of their history.

2. Human beings have a right to be safe and secure in their persons. All interstellar human trafficking and experimentation must cease immediately.

3. Human beings are a sentient species entitled to self-determination in the future of their planet.

4. Every human being has the right to pursue his or her potential without physical or psychological limitations.

5. Human beings are a spacefaring race ready to join the galactic community and deserve to be treated as such.

From this moment forward, humanity's path is forever changed. It shifts from top-down control and disinformation to self-realization and transparency. Let every human being seize the opportunity to become all he or she was destined to be.

Signed,

Inanna, First Princess of Nibiru, Queen of Heaven and Earth, and Protector of Humanity.

Inanna asked the computer to read back the dictation. She paused for a moment. This was the big step. She was formally declaring her rebellion against her brother. She was drawing a line. Either humanity would be freed or she would die in trying. She sent the message to her crew and then she transmitted it over the interstellar governmental frequency. Governments used this frequency to communicate throughout the known galaxy—a kind of emergency channel. Today the entire galaxy would know The Future Possible had answered The Human Question.

(37)
The Situation Room

"Mr. President, B-GOT is a direct threat to American national security," said DHS Secretary David Fitch, "Were we not to respond, it would invite future attacks."

President Chang sat forward in his chair. He knew there were many in this room who doubted him—doubted his ability and qualifications to be Commander-in-Chief. They doubted the willingness of this young academic to make hard decisions. After all, his national security experience consisted of tough talk on the campaign trail. He felt their eyes upon him. He knew they would view any hesitation as weakness in this room and beyond. His hurried search for a highly qualified national security expert and vice-president was ongoing, but there was no time to wait for his new number two. The people around this table, all Americans, and people around the world were waiting on his next move. Terrorists had challenged American security and supremacy and he knew his political future, if he was to have one, hinged on what he did next.

"Sir?" urged Secretary of Defense Dan Hackett expectantly.

"Take me through this, gentlemen," Chang said. "How do we know that B-GOT is responsible?"

"Mr. President," said Chairman of the Joint Chiefs General John Cortez, barely able to contain his impatience and not trying hard to do it, "We have agreement across the intelligence community that B-GOT is responsible. We have a video confession from Mitchell."

"General, you have a grainy recording and a shadowy face," replied Chang testily. Cortez glared and dropped his head, pretending to review the documents in front of him.

"Sir, our voice experts have confirmed Mitchell's voice on the recording," offered CIA Director Sheila Gordon.

"I see." replied Chang. "How sure are you?"

"95% certainty, Mr. President," replied Gordon.

"Sir, that's as certain as this gets," said Hackett trying to keep the momentum going towards action. "Mitchell has motive, capability, and he's confessed. We have voice recognition. You have all the justification you need to act, Mr. President."

"I'm not looking for justification, Mr. Hackett. I'm looking for facts. I want to see the recording." Chang said.

Fitch spoke, "Mr. President, we ... uh ... we lost the video."

"Lost it?" queried Chang.

"Yes, sir. Our first priority was to take down the website. When we did, there was a technical glitch and the file containing the video was lost."

"How did you do the voice analysis, Mr. Fitch?"

"We were able to get what we needed by compiling excerpts broadcast on various news outlets. However, my people were able to transcribe the entire recording before we lost it. Mitchell clearly takes responsibility twice and decries America for leading what he calls 'the insurgency of globalization.'"

"Mr. President," followed Hackett, "We've known for a long time that Mitchell wanted to strike U.S. interests. It was just a matter of where and when. It fits B-GOT's pattern of going for a big attack. For God's sake, he took down an American president. The American people are demanding a response."

Cortez jumped back in, "Sir, we will broadcast weakness to

the whole world, if you allow this heinous deed to go unpunished. If someone is allowed to kill an American president without reprisal—"

"I know the argument, General," interrupted Chang, "I'm not against acting. I want to make sure we punish the *right* people with the least risk to our forces and minimal collateral damage. I'm not interested in taking down even a known enemy just to feel good. Let's make sure to punish those who killed President Paxton."

"With respect, sir," Cortez engaged, "We have Mitchell dead to rights. We have a confession and a reason to take him out. That's a win-win in my mind."

Chang felt the burn again of Cortez's stare. He met it with the best he could muster. He turned to his, well Paxton's, National Security Advisor Bradley Sheldon. Chang had worked with Sheldon for a few months on Paxton's national security team and he was the closest thing to an ally in the room. "Brad, do we even know where Mitchell is, if we decide to hit him?"

"Mr. President, we're working on that right now. Russia has been forthcoming with their intelligence. He's been a thorn in Moscow's side too and they are more than happy to help us get him. They believe he has a stronghold somewhere in the Caucasus Mountains—probably in Georgia. We have several strong leads that are helping us pinpoint his location."

"And the Georgians?" asked Chang.

"Mr. President," Hackett said, "If they're harboring terrorists—"

"We don't know they're harboring anyone," Chang corrected.

"If the terrorists responsible for murdering an American president take refuge on their soil, they must expect us to strike. Under the circumstances, the Georgian government has offered its help in order to maintain some control and consent to our actions."

"General Cortez," Chang turned with an air of assertiveness, "What are our options for striking?"

"That's the best part, Mr. President. Once we pinpoint Mitchell's location, we don't even have to put American forces at risk. We can conduct surveillance with stealth drones and strike with those same drones. We will operate in Georgian airspace without the Georgians even knowing it."

"And if we can't get him with drones?" asked the president.

"We can conduct ground reconnaissance and search and destroy missions with robotroops."

"Wait! What are robotroops?"

"They're a new toy, Mr. President," inserted Hackett. "They're battle-ready robots controlled remotely like drones. They're stronger and faster than a soldier is and are equipped with an M-16 and a small rocket launcher. We've been looking for an opportunity to test them. This could be it."

Cortez nodded to the Secretary of Defense and continued. "We drop them near the target and unleash them like a pack of wolves on Mitchell. I have three platoons and trained operators ready at a moment's notice."

"And collateral damage?" asked Chang.

Hackett eyed Cortez knowingly—sensing they almost had Chang—and spoke, "Sir, General Cortez has assured me that we can act swiftly, decisively, and with minimal civilian impacts. We've tentatively named the operation Burning Bush."

"It sounds like a win-win," said Chang with a troubled smile and a quick scan of the table for reassurance. All he found were looks of expectancy waiting for his word. That's when the power and the burden of his office struck him. Whatever happened next was on his word and his watch. History was going to judge him, not the others in the room, for the success or failure of what came next. Then a feeling of ultimate power overcame the self-doubt. He was President of the United States. No one on the planet could stand against an American President determined to see justice done.

"Ladies and gentlemen, make it happen," ordered Chang feeling for the first time like the president. "May God bless our efforts."

"Thank you, Mr. President," said Hackett with a fatherly pat on the shoulder. Hackett was almost twice Chang's age and had lots of experience in these matters. "You've made the right decision for the country and for President Paxton. The American people are behind you, sir."

Chang was both heartened by Hackett's support and a little uneasy about the father-son vibe. *Let's all hope so*, Chang thought as he was whisked out of the room by the Secret Service. As he emerged from the Situation Room, his Chief of Staff Doug Birch and White House Press Secretary Jessica Cohen fell into line behind him.

"Mr. President," said Cohen, "President Paxton's service has been scheduled for Saturday morning at the National Cathedral."

"Mr. President," chimed Birch, "I've arranged a press conference for tomorrow afternoon after the service. The American people and the media are going to want to hear from you."

"No questions," ordered Cohen.

"Got it, Jessica," replied Birch.

Chang's entourage moved down the hallway away from the situation room. Hackett grabbed Fitch's arm and pulled him back for a private conversation. "That went well, David."

"Yes. Better than I expected. I was worried he wouldn't pull the trigger," offered Fitch. "He's bright. I didn't know if he would buy the story."

"I had him all along," replied Hackett, "He relies on me. He doesn't even know how much yet."

"Well, you did a great job of convincing him to get Hawking and Love out at State," credited Fitch.

"Hawking was a dove. We don't need doves right now. This is a moment of opportunity for us. We must show the world that American supremacy is still intact. No one must doubt it. Sergey Mitchell is going to be an example of it."

"Dan, you know I'm with you," assured Fitch.

"Just out of curiosity, what are your teams in Paris finding?" asked Hackett.

"It's a damn conundrum. They embedded the bombs in the street, but there's no evidence of street work. It's as if they materialized in there or something. Honestly, we can't figure it out."

"Just make sure your findings stay . . . nebulous," warned Hackett, "We've got our opportunity to get Mitchell. Let's not cloud the issue with any uncertainty."

"Not to worry, Dan. I've already put a national security blanket over this investigation. The emotional outrage will ensure no one asking how the bombs got there."

"Well, maybe the conspiracy theorists," chuckled Hackett, "In fact, let's contact some of the scandal papers and plant a story about aliens embedding the bombs that killed President Paxton. That should provide a great disinformation cover."

"Beautiful! Consider it done," laughed Fitch.

(38)
The Neptune Line

Inanna impatiently tapped the armrests on her throne. From her vantage point in the center of Rakbu's bridge, she observed her crew monitoring their stations waiting for contact with Anunnaki task force. Anticipating a difficult day, she increased her medication dosage. Its effects were palpable, but her powerfully focused mind mitigated them. She sat robed in full royal garb—a long, flowing dress made from something similar to cotton and covering her from neck to toe. Its ruby red color offset the dazzling precious stone inlays. Her personal servant buffed and polished her crown for her big meeting with Admiral Ninn. Its golden surface glistened almost as brightly as the blinding rays of light it emitted.

"Time," she called out.

"The taskforce has slowed to light speed, Mistress," replied Commander Enka. "We should have a visual any moment."

"Have they detected us yet?" asked Inanna.

"There has been no change in their course or speed to indicate they have spotted us, Mistress. Wait, they are altering course now. They're now on an intercept course. They will be in communication range in about 10 seconds."

"Open communications," ordered Inanna.

"Admiral Ninn, this is Princess Inanna in command of the Rakbu."

At first, there was only silence and then an image of the formidable Admiral Ninn appeared on the screens circling Rakbu's bridge. "Mistress, Inanna. This is Admiral Ninn commanding the Tiamat and this taskforce. What a pleasure to see you again. It has been too many years."

"Not enough years for me, admiral," Inanna scowled. "Welcome to Earth Space. I am well aware of your mission. Perhaps, we should skip the niceties and get to the matter."

"As you wish, Mistress," Ninn replied.

"King Ea has dispatched me to Earth Space—"

"To bring me home and terrorize the humans," finished Inanna.

Ninn smiled in a moment of recognition, "Of course, you have a TimeCube. You are well aware of my purpose. The king has sent me to Earth Space to restore . . . order."

"I remember your kind of order, admiral. I could not stop you back then, but I will stop you today. Please inform my brother, the king, that Earth Space is secure and crime free at the moment and give him my regards."

"I'm afraid that's not satisfactory, Mistress. We have reports of pirates interfering with lawful commerce—commerce authorized and guaranteed by King Ea. His Majesty has sent me here to ensure that his views on this matter are clear to the humans and to you, Mistress."

"If by commerce he means the abduction of human beings by the Z Alliance, then I must admit I have interfered with the king's commerce."

"You see, Mistress, this is precisely the kind of thing the king has sent me here to stop," retorted Ninn smiling with a diplomatic stiffness.

"I will not allow Anunnaki warships into Earth Space, admiral, and I will not allow you to murder more humans."

"Princess Inanna, are you really going to set Anunnaki against Anunnaki for the benefit of the humans. It doesn't have to be this way."

"I agree. You can turn your taskforce around and leave Earth Space. Otherwise, I am prepared to take whatever steps are necessary to ensure the sovereignty of Earth."

"I hear your vessel has astonishing capabilities. Tell me, Mistress, did your TimeCube estimate your chances in battle against 11 Royal Battle Cruisers? Those seem like long odds."

Inanna stiffened, but maintained her poker face. She had run numerous scenarios through the TimeCube. Every scenario ended in the destruction of Rakbu or at least one Earth city. A majority of the scenarios ended in both.

"Surely, my brother, the king, did not send you here to make idle threats, admiral. I suspect you know I am not coming with you, nor will I allow you to attack the humans."

"Inanna, your brother only wants you home," smiled Ninn. "He has a TimeCube too. He knows you are sick. He only wants you to come home to Nibiru and die the death of a Princess, rather than that of a renegade."

"Admiral," Inanna insisted. "I have established a defensive perimeter around the earth system here at Neptune. I will fire on any warship that crosses that boundary."

Ninn's face now lost all objectivity. "Really, Inanna, how can you establish a defensive perimeter with one ship? By decree of his Majesty the king, I order you to drop your shields and transport aboard my ship."

"I am the Queen of Heaven and of Earth. I am First Princess of Nibiru. You do not order me to do anything," declared Inanna.

"I regret you will not listen to reason," Ninn responded.

"Reason? Is that what my brother calls me coming home as

a slave and the wanton destruction of innocent humans?"

"This is not about you, Inanna. This is about what is best for Nibiru. His Majesty makes those decisions, not you. He has merely sent me to remind you of that—"

Inanna realized this conversation was headed nowhere. She spoke two words into her mouthpiece, "Now, Nurnta!"

Sixty fighters screamed around from the backside of Neptune, catching Ninn and the Anunnaki ships off guard. Ninn's face soured and he cut off communication.

Colonel Nurnta personally commanded the fighters. "Squadrons 1 and 3 follow me in. Let's strike the Tiamat. Squadrons 2 and 4, break up those other ships."

The fighters streaked in and swarmed among the RBCs, strafing the massive ships with gamma ray torpedoes. From Rakbu, explosions could be seen lighting up the exteriors of several RBCs. Three of Anunnaki ships broke off and ran, but the others stood firm and turned their main and auxiliary batteries on the fighters.

Inanna gave the order and the Rakbu surged towards the Tiamat. Rakbu's main batteries hit the flagship with devastating accuracy and overwhelming power. "Target their main batteries and their engines," commanded Inanna as they closed on the Anunnaki flagship.

"Mistress, Tiamat has enhanced shielding and weaponry. She easily matches the Rakbu. Their shields are holding and they are returning fire," said Enka.

A massive jolt rocked the bridge. The ship's electronics momentarily faltered. The crew regained their positions after being knocked to the ground.

"Rapid fire with all weapons," commanded Inanna. Rakbu pounded Tiamat, but still Tiamat held her ground.

"Mistress," declared Enka with urgency in his voice, "Two

other RBCs are pinching us from starboard and port and firing."

The force of the weapons was not nearly as powerful as the Tiamat's weapons. Rakbu's shields held. "Mistress, the other RBCs have standard weaponry and shields."

"Target the engines of the other two RBCs and fire at will."

The Rakbu's unleashed a fury at the two RBCs. The first round of fire damaged their shields and the second round punched right through them, knocking the engines of both ships offline. The ships were immobile, but still able to fire and now they joined Tiamat in a combined barrage upon Inanna's vessel. Rakbu took multiple hits and shuddered mightily.

"Where are Nurnta's fighters?" Inanna called out desperately amid the smoke now stifling her bridge,

"They are just about to strike Tiamat," shouted Enka above the noise of alarms and impacts.

As Colonel Nurnta approached the Tiamat, he could see that the Rakbu was engaged in a devastating firefight with three warships. She appeared to be on fire. All three Anunnaki warships were ablaze, but all three continued to pound the Rakbu. Nurnta had once commanded an RBC and he knew the single weakness of the great vessels—a weapons blind spot running perpendicular to the ship above and below the bridge. It provided a fire free corridor just wide enough for his fighters to attack unhindered. He only hoped they had not redesigned the Tiamat to overcome that disability.

As his squadron raced toward Tiamat, the fighters attracted part of the flagship's massive firepower away from Rakbu. Thirty fighters peppered the hulking vessel with torpedoes.

"All right, let's come back and hit the bridge with the big boys," Nurnta ordered. "Remember to stay within the perpendicular corridor above the bridge. Just the way we practiced it."

Nurnta led the way. He adjusted his heading to target the center of Tiamat's bridge. He began his run at 400,000 kilometers and accelerated to 10% C. At about 200,000 kilometers, he came under fire from Tiamat's weapons, but none of them had the angle to strike him. Twelve seconds into the run, Nurnta released his antimatter torpedo at point blank range, pulled up, and accelerated to 50% C. A massive explosion shook Tiamat. The ship was listing precipitously.

"Direct hit," he shouted over the intercom. "You're clear. Stay within three degrees of perpendicular and they can't touch you."

One-by-one Nurnta's fighters hit the defenseless flagship with antimatter torpedoes. Meanwhile, having destroyed the other two RBCs, Rakbu turned its full firepower on Tiamat. The two massive ships exchanged blow after blow. Crews were now fighting fires throughout both ships.

Smoke choked Rakbu's bridge. Inanna continued to sit on her throne and give commands. "Enka," she called.

"Mistress, Commander Enka has been taken to the hospital with a concussion," answered a junior bridge officer.

"What is the status of the other Anunnaki ships," queried Inanna.

"Mistress, four destroyed, three contained by our fighters, and three have broken through the perimeter."

"Broken through the perimeter?" coughed Inanna with alarm in her voice.

"Yes, Mistress, three RBCs have broken off and set a course for Earth."

"What is their speed?"

"They're at 2C, Mistress. ETA to Earth is one hour and fifty minutes."

Scenarios ran through Inanna's mind. Three RBCs could

obliterate anything on Earth. She had her fifth fighter squadron on alert. They could match the RBC's 2C, but lacked the range to reach Earth.

"What is the status of Tiamat?" asked Inanna.

"Tiamat still has weapons and life support, but her propulsion system is down," responded the tactical officer.

Disengage the Tiamat," commanded Inanna. "Set a course for Earth maximum speed."

"Mistress, what about our fighters?" asked her acting executive officer.

"Advise Colonel Nurnta of the situation and lay in a pursuit course, commander."

"Yes, Mistress."

Tiamat got a few parting shots at Rakbu, as it backed off and turned to pursue the other RBCs. Nurnta's fighters continued to pound the Anunnaki flagship.

"Mistress, this is Commander Ur in the engine room."

"Go ahead, commander."

"Mistress, one of our engines is damaged. Our best possible speed at the moment is 1C."

"I need 3C, commander!"

"We should have 3C capability in about an hour, Mistress."

Inanna quickly did the math. "Commander, if we don't have 3C for an hour, those RBCs will arrive at Earth 15 minutes ahead of us."

"Mistress, we will do our best to have full power as soon as possible, but I must warn you that 3C is hazardous within a solar system."

"I am well aware of the perils, commander. You just get my engines functioning."

Inanna spun around to view her decimated bridge. "Tactical, what is our battle status when we do catch the RBCs?"

"Mistress, our two forward batteries are completely destroyed. Six more batteries are damaged. Our effective fighting power is about 50% and we are not capable of a frontal assault. Overall, we are no match for three RBCs right now."

Inanna tried to keep her spirits up. None of her TimeCube scenarios unfolded this way. Perhaps, there was still a chance. Her opponents aboard the Anunnaki ships were inexperienced commanders. She was ready to capitalize on any mistake or hesitation on their part.

"Mistress, there's an incoming message from one of the RBCs enroute to Earth. It's Admiral Ninn."

Shock and concern filled Inanna's mind, but she hid it from her crew. She thought Ninn was aboard helpless Tiamat. "Ninn? Put him on screen," she ordered.

"Greetings, Mistress. Your Rakbu certainly lived up to her reputation. I trust you now have a greater respect for the king's new flagship."

"I do," admitted Inanna. "Still, she sits adrift in space, on fire, and soon to be finished off by my fighters."

"Perhaps," said Ninn. "I anticipated your tactic. I relayed my communications through Tiamat to make you think I was aboard. However, I am aboard Shiva. I am headed to Earth to complete the first objective of my mission. I note you are in pursuit. It is kind of you to simplify my second objective."

"I will be there to stop you, Ninn. You murdered once. You won't again."

"Doubtful, Mistress. My hasty calculation puts us at Earth an hour ahead of you. How many cities can I destroy in that time?"

"Ninn," shouted Inanna completely losing her cool, "How can you take pleasure in this?"

"I take pleasure, Mistress, in serving my king and in serving the House of En. I take pleasure in serving Nibiru. I take pleasure in ensuring the rightful order of things. Vengeance is mine sayeth the Lord. The humans have forgotten that little nugget of wisdom. I plan to remind them today."

(39)
Burning Bush

"This is Justin Cardone with ANN breaking news. As the nation remembers a fallen president this Saturday, questions continue about the tragic explosion that killed the president and eight other people two days ago. First, a grateful nation says goodbye to President Paxton. Let's go inside the Washington National Cathedral to our new White House correspondent, Michele Monroe. Michele."

"Thank you, Justin. That's right the Washington National Cathedral is filled with nearly 3,000 mourners at this hour. They're here to say goodbye to a popular second-term president taken from us by a premeditated terrorist attack on Thursday."

"Describe the scene to us, Michele."

"Well, Justin the air is heavy with incense and the standard pageantry involved when church and state come together. There are many military people here in full dress uniforms to honor the president, as well as church officials in their formal funeral regalia."

"Is it true, Michele, that Mrs. Paxton is not in attendance, but that the president's two grown children and their families are?" asked Cardone.

"That's right, Justin," Monroe answered. "Mrs. Paxton remains in serious condition in a Paris hospital. However, the family did not want to delay the nation's opportunity to grieve for the president and so agreed to today's service."

"Of course, President and Mrs. Chang are present as well?"

"Yes. In fact, if you look behind me, you can see President Chang seated in the front pew. He's just to the left of the altar."

"The Right Reverend Bishop Leslie Mann is presiding over the service and is giving a brief sermon. Let's listen in," said Cardone.

"God is good. God is righteous. We are not meant to know the reasons for the awful things that happen in our world sometimes. We must accept that God's will is unfolding and that He has a plan we cannot see or understand. God is also just. He stands with us when we seek justice in this world. God is merciful. He offers us salvation from our sins through our Lord Jesus Christ. God is love. He has given us all we need to be happy in this life and in the next.

"Let us pray. Lord God most merciful, please welcome your son Ronald into Heaven. He has been your loyal and faithful servant here on Earth. Hear our prayer for our brother who has done much to make this Earth a better place. Grant us your peace at his passing. May the blessing of God Almighty, the Father, the Son, and the Holy Spirit be with you and remain with you forever. Amen. Let us go forth in the name of Christ."

[Somber organ music playing in the background]

"You can see," whispered Monroe, "the pallbearers consist of a special cross-service military detail. These men are highly trained just for this sort of situation. They will carry the president's casket to a carriage parked in front of the cathedral. The United States Marine Band is posted outside. They will play "Hail to the Chief," as pallbearers carry the flag-draped coffin to the carriage for the procession through the streets of Washington. President Paxton will be transported to the Capitol building where he will lie in state for three days."

"Michele, we're hearing now that President Chang will make

a statement this afternoon about the search for the terrorist leader Sergey Mitchell. Can you confirm that?" asked Cardone.

"Yes, Justin. We heard rumblings out of the Pentagon this morning that something big may have happened in the search for Mitchell."

President Chang made his way out of the cathedral, blanketed by Secret Service agents. Secretary of Defense Hackett waited for him on the sidewalk.

"Mr. President, a moment please," said Hackett.

"What do you have, Dan?" asked Chang.

"Good news, Mr. President," confided Hackett, trying to conceal his exuberance.

"You got Mitchell?"

"Not Mitchell, sir, but his second-in-command, Eduard Gelashvili. A Georgian informant tipped us off to a B-GOT meeting happening in Poti, Georgia. We were able to track vehicles leaving the meeting and we struck using drones. You have a victory against the terrorists, Mr. President. Congratulations!"

"What's your confirmation that we got Gelashvili, Dan?"

"We had eyes on the ground and they were able to verify that it was Gelashvili."

"Have you released this to the media?" asked the president.

"I will announce it in about 20 minutes, but we have been leaking indications to key news sources," Hackett replied.

"Anything from Mitchell?"

"Not yet, sir, but he's belligerent. I'm sure the response will be violent. Gelashvili was one of Mitchell's oldest and dearest friends. We must stay after him. I have a recommendation, Mr. President."

The president looked at his feet for a moment. How had he wound up making these decisions? A year ago, he was a political philosopher. He was quickly learning the burdens of command were far greater. "What do you recommend?"

"Well, sir, it seems I was misinformed. We have a full battalion of robotroops at our disposal. General Cortez briefed me this morning. The Joint Chiefs recommends inserting the robotroops on Georgian soil on a search and destroy mission. We're ready to launch Burning Bush on your order, Mr. President."

Chang hesitated again. He turned his back to Hackett and walked about ten steps, his head down in thought and his hands behind his back. Hackett not only had all the answers in these nebulous circumstances, but an action plan ready for execution. He seemed to be ready to hand a gun to Chang and send him into a room to shoot a stranger. Still, this was no time for him to appear weak to Hackett or the nation.

He turned back toward Hackett. "And what of the Georgian civilians caught in the crossfire of this action?"

The Secretary of Defense squinted at President Chang, as if he was sizing him up. "Mr. President, an American president, my friend and yours, is dead. Some people, like Sergey Mitchell, have forgotten the natural order of things on this planet. We must remind them. If you screw with the United States, then you have to pay. We have every right. The Georgians will complain to the U.N. Hell, the Russians may protest in the Security Council, but they won't do anything. We will find Mitchell and deal with him. This will be over in a couple of weeks. You'll be a hero."

Chang had doubts about the whole story and the easy culprit so quickly identified by the Pentagon and intelligence agencies. He had questions about Hackett and his motives. He felt bullied by the older, more experienced man and he didn't like it. Most of all his self-doubt crept in and infected his thinking. He had almost enough doubt and almost enough courage to demand Hackett find more facts and more justification—almost enough.

"Very well, Mr. Hackett, make it so."

"Thank you Mr. Presi—"

"Wait! I have one condition," Chang cautioned.

"Of course, sir," Hackett replied with an involuntary grimace.

"I want Mitchell alive!"

"Mr. President, this is going to be a messy business—"

"We have no actual troops at risk, Dan. I don't care how messy it is. I want him alive! I want to put him on trial before the world for his crimes. I don't want a repeat of the Bin Laden burial at sea. Are we clear?"

"Of course, Mr. President," Hackett huffed. "I have things to attend to. Excuse me, sir."

(40)
Telling Jack

Friday was a blur for Maria. She spent the whole day in bed, depressed and not feeling particularly well. Jack let her be. Besides, he needed time to analyze his next move.

Maria awoke Saturday morning to the sounds of a robin singing outside her window. For a moment, she experienced a blissful forgetting of events. She recalled a day in her childhood. She couldn't quite remember when. She was at the park with her mother. Robins chirped their happy song and then the owl appeared.

The owl—she hadn't thought about that in a long time. The owl showed up in the strangest places in her childhood and then . . . and then Maria couldn't remember things. This day was different. The owl appeared and all the living things around her froze for several minutes, as the owl spoke to her. The owl told her things that made no sense. She'd long ago written off the event as childhood fantasy.

Maria rolled over to find Jack gone. She needed to talk to him. He needed to know about Inanna. He needed to know why they'd really lost their jobs. His response worried her. She wanted to believe he'd jump to her side, but this new paradigm challenged his most cherished beliefs.

"Jack," she called out.

"I'm in here fixing some lunch, beautiful."

Maria smelled Jack's famous grilled cheese sandwiches.

"I know yesterday was a rough day for you. So, I let you sleep," said Jack.

"Thanks. I appreciate that, honey. It was a difficult day for me—more difficult that you know," said Maria.

Jack recognized that look on Maria's face. She had something to tell him. He walked over and wrapped his arms around her waist. "What is it? What's going on?"

Maria looked up into Jack's eyes. Those eyes always calmed her, but for some reason they made her feel cautious right now. "I don't really know where to begin. This alien thing . . . it's a bit more than just a story I was working on."

"I get it, honey. It's the X-Files with a little Indiana Jones thrown in," Jack smiled as he squeezed his beautiful wife closer.

Maria's head was down. *Do I really want to tell him this?* She questioned. *What if he thinks I'm losing it?*

"Jack, I need you to listen to me. They're really . . . you know, here."

"Who's really here," Jack was not catching on.

"The aliens are really here and one of them contacted me," Maria gushed.

"An alien contacted you? What like in ET or something? C'mon, honey. I know we're in a difficult spot, but let's keep it together," Jack coached her.

"I'm serious, Jack. Do you remember that day back in Hawai'i when I drove down to Honolulu?"

"Yeah, Pete wanted you to meet the new Honolulu bureau chief?"

"Yes, except I didn't meet the bureau chief. I met a woman who contacted me on Twitter. Her name is Nanna . . . Inanna."

"That's a strange name. Why did you meet her? Why didn't you tell me?"

"I'd been having these dreams and these lingering questions

about who we are . . . who I am . . . and why I'm here. I tweeted the question and she responded saying she had answers for me, but she wanted to tell me in person."

"Meeting strangers from the Internet doesn't seem like good judgment to me, Maria."

"Maybe not," Maria breathed deeply. "Jack, have you heard of the Anunnaki?"

"Um, yeah, somewhere," he responded, his agitation growing.

"Some scholars have interpreted the name as 'those who from heaven to Earth came'. Some believe the Anunnaki were . . . are . . . a race of space aliens that genetically engineered human beings."

"That's quite a story, but the Bible tells us we were created by God; not space aliens," Jack asserted.

"Who is God, Jack? Who is it that we call God? What are God's personality traits?"

Jack's eyebrows raised and he looked somewhat shocked at what he was hearing. "God is the being who created you and me. He created all of us. You know my beliefs on this. Why are we having this conversation? It's easy."

"It's always been easy for you, Jack. It's never been easy for me," Maria exclaimed in a voice laced with frustration.

"I thought we were on the same page on this topic," Jack maintained.

"I've gone along. I love you and I love your family. I didn't want to make waves, but I've never really agreed. You never really asked me. So, I'm asking you now. Does my view count?"

"C'mon, Maria," Jack said trying to calm her. "You know your views are important, but we have a lot to think about right now. We're both out of work and living in a costly city. Maybe we should focus on reality and leave these philosophical discussions for another time."

"This can't wait," persisted Maria.

"OK. Let's hear it. You don't believe in God?" Jack asked harshly.

"I do, Jack. Just not in the same way you do," said Maria carefully.

"What does that mean? It sounds like new age psychobabble to me. Either you do or you don't, Maria. There's no gray area."

"Who is that we've been calling God, Jack? I mean, the Bible describes God as angry, jealous, and vengeful. Why would the creator of this universe describe himself that way? If a human being has those traits, we'd send him to counseling. Why do we accept that's God's nature?"

"God is in control, Maria. It's not up to us to question His authority or His self-description. Our duty is to obey Him and His commandments to us. He loves us and he knows what's best for us."

"Why would the creator of the universe want us to give him the first ten percent of everything we earn? Doesn't that seem like a business arrangement unworthy of a being who manifested this massive and diverse universe? Why did he try to keep knowledge from us? Doesn't he want us to grow, to understand, to get better?"

"I don't know, Maria. I'm sure God had his reasons. That's enough for me."

"I've been to their ship," Maria suddenly blurted out.

"Whose ship? The aliens?"

"Inanna's ship." She's—"

Jack raised his hand to stop the next word from leaving Maria's lips, while shaking his head in disbelief, "That's just insane, Maria. You've imagined going to this ship."

"I didn't imagine it, Jack!" Maria retorted angrily.

"OK. Let's say I believe you've been to some 'ship'. How do

you know they're space aliens? They could be demons or something else. Satan is always trying to tempt us and pull us away from the truth."

"Does Satan fly a space ship that orbits the moon? Does Satan fire weapons at ships from other species abducting human beings from their beds?"

Jack was without words. Hands laced behind his head, he turned away, Maria grabbed his arm and turned him toward her. "I've been to her ship several times. She brought Pete and me aboard her ship. That's how we convinced Pete I needed to follow this story. She told me things about my father, my mother's pregnancy, and me."

Jack was about to respond, when the ground shook under them. The windows rattled violently. There was a five-second pause and another rumbling tremor. The second caused Maria to lose her balance and fall into Jack's arms.

"Earth quake?" asked Maria.

"I don't think so," replied Jack.

They came around the corner into the living room. Their eighth floor Arlington apartment had a beautiful view of the Potomac and the D.C. skyline across the way. Looking across the river, they viewed a horrific site. The Capitol dome was mangled, almost beyond recognition, and ablaze. As they watched, a fireball raced from the sky and struck the Capitol Mall near the Washington Monument. The ground again shook violently.

"What the hell!" Jack exclaimed.

Maria raced to the Internet Television and logged on to ANN. "Nothing yet," she said.

The network was running its normal Saturday programming. Then, as if on cue, Justin Cardone interrupted with breaking news.

"This is Justin Cardone at the ANN news center in Austin.

We are getting reports from Washington D.C. that several fiery objects have fallen from the sky and struck the U.S. Capitol Building. We're trying to get footage. We have confirmed that at least one of the objects has struck and damaged the Capitol dome. Our Michele Monroe, who was covering the procession of President Paxton's casket towards the Capitol, is on the scene. Michele, are you OK and where are you?"

"Thank you, Justin. We are OK. We were just blocks from the Capitol Building when we clearly saw two fireballs streak across the sky and strike the Capitol dome. As you can imagine, chaos broke out as everyone along the funeral route scrambled for cover. About 30 seconds later, we heard a third explosion from an object we are told hit near the Washington Monument."

"Michele, it's Saturday and Congress was not in session. Do you have any word yet on casualties at the Capitol?" asked Cardone.

"Nothing yet, Justin. You can see the mangled dome over my shoulder. Congress was not in session, but there were bound to be tourists in the building today, as well as people preparing for the arrival of President Paxton's body to lie in state. Obviously casualties are—"

"Excuse me, Michele," interrupted Cardone. "This is incredible! We are now receiving a report from Moscow that the Kremlin was also hit by fiery objects matching the description of those that struck Washington . . . and now . . . similar objects have hit the Great Hall of the People in Beijing and The National Diet Building in Tokyo."

A shocked Maria and Jack sat glued to the ITV. They set aside their argument about God for the moment.

Cardone turned to welcome to ANN national security consultant, General Mark Dixon. "General Dixon, thank you for joining us."

"My pleasure, Justin."

"What do you make of these attacks on four of the world's most important cities in the past 15 minutes? Clearly, important political buildings are the target. Could this be the work of B-GOT? We know that B-GOT's number two man was taken out yesterday. Could this be retaliation?"

"Justin, of course, that's one possibility. It's really too early to say for sure that B-GOT is responsible, but they have to be the prime suspect. The buildings and the nations targeted were clearly carefully chosen by the attacker to send a political message."

"The word fireball appears extensively in all these reports. What kind of weapon could B-GOT be using?"

"Well, again, it's hard to say. We'll have to review the video of these attacks and analyze it. However, a supersonic missile could create something that might look like a fireball to the un-trained eye."

"That's patently ridiculous," blurted Maria, "they're already speculating on the culprit, the motive, and the weapon. They don't know anything."

"I don't know. It's pretty obvious this guy Mitchell wants to do harm to us and governments around the world," countered Jack.

Maria continued staring at ITV and carefully avoided Jack's gaze. "I just can't believe how they start conditioning us before they have any facts. This could have been many things. They don't know Mitchell had anything to do with it."

"Like what?" Jack asked, feeling uneasy with his wife's militant attitude.

"It could be meteors," said Maria.

"Meteors? C'mon, Maria. What are the odds that four capital buildings on three continents get hit on the same day by meteors?"

Maria had to admit the chances were small. Where was Inanna? She would know the answers. Inanna had gone on silent running. Maria hadn't heard from her since before President Paxton's news conference. Maria felt alone and isolated. Normally, she counted on Jack for support. In this case, every word seemed to increase the rift between them. She hated it, but she had to follow through and speak the truth.

(41)
Approaching Earth

"Mistress, we are approaching Earth," said a recovering Commander Enka.

"Slow to 1C," ordered Inanna.

"Mistress, the Shiva has opened fire on the surface!" shouted Lieutenant Commander Ur.

"What are its targets?" demanded Inanna in an urgent tone.

"Washington . . . Moscow . . . Beijing . . . Tokyo," responded Enka.

"Time to Earth orbit?" asked Inanna.

"Seven minutes, Mistress. The Shiva continues its attack on the surface. The other two RBCs are on an intercept course with us," reported Ur.

"A delaying tactic, Mistress." reasoned Enka.

"Right," agreed Inanna. "Are our forward batteries repaired?"

"No, Mistress," replied Ur.

"Launch Fighter Squadron 5. They will be our forward batteries. Have them plow a path right between the two RBCs. We will take the Rakbu straight through to the Shiva."

"Yes, Mistress."

As the Rakbu and its fighter escort approached the two battle cruisers, the Anunnaki ships opened fire."

"Return fire with all weapons as we pass between them and take us straight through," Inanna instructed.

Squadron 5 blazed a path between the two RBCS with their torpedoes and then broke into two attack groups, one targeting each Anunnaki ship. The Rakbu fired her lateral batteries as she split the two ships and headed straight for the Shiva.

"Mistress, the Shiva is adjusting its orbit and appears to be targeting another location in south Asia," said Ur. "I believe it is New Delhi. They're firing!"

Dr. Sanjay Singh was just finishing another late night of work on his tablets, when he stopped and looked in awe at a fireball racing across the New Delhi night sky. Sequestered in his office all day, he was unaware of the other attacks. He puzzled at the fireball, but held his ground. People around him were screaming and running.

As a woman ran passed Singh, she grabbed Singh and shouted, "Shiva! Shiva! Shiva seeks revenge for our sins."

Suddenly, Singh realized the fireball was going to strike the ground. He had no time to take cover. The explosion's massive orange glow illuminated the city. The ground rumbled and shook violently, nearly knocking him off his feet.

"Mistress, the Shiva hit the Secretariat Building in New Delhi. It's adjusting orbit again and targeting a city south of there . . . probably Sydney," said Enka.

"How long until we're in weapons range," asked Inanna?

"30 seconds, Mistress."

"Target the Shiva and fire as soon as we're in range!"

Singh could see a massive undefined shape adorned with many lights. It appeared to be sitting in low Earth orbit and moving rapidly across the city to the southeast. Then he saw a second, larger shape appear at a similar altitude. The second shape hit the first shape multiple times, with what looked like lightning bolts. The sky roared and the ground shook with a fearful thunder. The smaller shape began to ascended rapidly with the larger shape in pursuit. Singh watched until the two shapes were tiny dots of light in the sky.

"Mistress, the Shiva is attempting to leave orbit! She's running!" reported Ur.

"No escape for you today, admiral," muttered Inanna. "Finish him!"

The Rakbu hit the Shiva with devastating fire. The Shiva managed to get off a few meaningless shots, but it was over quickly.

Singh observed a bright flash in the sky above the southern horizon. It reminded him of videos he'd seen of nuclear tests. The New Delhi night momentarily became the brightest of middays. A pressure wave followed the flash, blowing out windows and crumbling aging structures, and knocked Singh to the ground. Finally, a massive wind gust swept the city, collapsing a few more structures. Then there was nothing except the sounds of people screaming, car alarms going off, and sirens throughout the Indian capital.

"We got him, Mistress!" Enka celebrated.

"Yes!" Inanna exclaimed. "Take us into a higher orbit and project a scattering field to mask our presence."

"No doubt, Mistress," said Enka, "the human ground-based and satellite stations already have footage of the Shiva and of us."

"Obviously, but let us do what we can to minimize the damage. Initiate an orbital pattern to scan the attacked cities for damage," Inanna commanded.

"Yes, Mistress."

"Where is Maria?" asked Inanna.

"Scanning, Mistress," replied Ur. "She is in Washington and her life signs are strong."

Inanna sighed in relief. She turned to Enka. "That's very

good. I am fatigued, commander. I require rest. When your damage assessment scans are completed, find those other two RBCs and make sure they will not trouble the Earth further. Pick up our fighters here and then make best possible speed to pick up Colonel Nurnta and his fighters. I want to be back here in Earth orbit by Sunday morning Washington time."

"Understood, Mistress," replied Enka with a slight bow of the head. "Good night."

Inanna headed for her quarters, weary from the battle and the effects of her illness, but happy with the day's result.

If only I could have stopped the attack on the earth's surface, she thought. *Still, we defeated 11 front line Anunnaki warships and foiled Ea's plan for the moment.*

Maria flashed through her mind. "Father Creator," she whispered, "Please take care of my Maria."

(42)
Pentagon Strategy Session

Saturday's events sent a shock through humanity's collective nervous system. The world mourned its losses and wondered. What could explain the strange fireballs that struck five capital cities and severely damaged the world's most recognizable political buildings? Speculation ran wild through the echo chamber of the 24/7 news cycle.

For Secretary of Defense Dan Hackett, it was a working night. He'd made his position in the world by being the left hand while everyone watched the right. He summoned DHS Secretary Fitch and Joint Chiefs Chairman Cortez to his office for a late-night meeting. In Fitch and Cortez, Hackett found kindred souls who understood the necessities of American national security. It was time to test their trustworthiness.

Hackett learned early in life there are two kinds of people—those who create reality and those controlled by the realities others create. He always positioned himself firmly in the first group. Being in control ensured things got done your way and you get control by placing a stake in the ground, when others hesitate. His charm belied his ambition and he made all the right friends—in government and beyond government. He'd advised six presidents—Democrat and Republican—and held nearly every significant national security post.

A quick study, Hackett understood the world's power structure had little resemblance to the system people pushing buttons in voting booths believed. There were offices like president, vice-president, senator, ambassador, but they were not the planet's decision makers. The officeholders carried out the decisions of people who never made headlines. These people operated out of the limelight and controlled through sheer wealth and raw power. In the public mind, these controllers existed only in the realm of conspiracy theories—precisely how they liked it. Hackett had worked for decades to be indispensable to the controllers.

There was a knock on Hackett's office door. "Come in," he said in a commanding voice.

Secretary Fitch and General Cortez entered Hackett's office together, escorted by Hackett's personal Marine guard.

"Thank you, Jeffrey, you're dismissed," Hackett said to the guard. "Take the rest of the evening off and lock the door on your way out."

"Yes, sir. Thank you, sir," said the Marine, who saluted and left.

"Gentlemen, please have a seat. I've called you here this evening to discuss current events and how they can fit into our plan."

"Dan," Fitch began, "what do you make of these fireballs?"

"What do you make of them, Dave?" shot back Hackett.

"That's the damnedest thing I've ever seen," admitted Fitch. "I don't have an explanation. Some of my underlings are urging me to find a way to blame B-GOT for it. Others say the public would never believe that story and are urging me to call them rogue comets. I'm not sure I can believe that story."

Hackett looked calmly at his friend and said, "Dave, never worry about what the people will believe or won't believe. They'll believe what we tell them to believe. They'll blame whom we tell them to blame. All they ask in return is an entertaining story, a grain of truth, and something that plays into what they want to believe. It's human nature. Unless we self-actualize, we are born to defer to authority and expertise. Only those who escape that conditioning get to know the truth and make the truth."

The DHS Secretary had only known Hackett for a few months. Fitch was not a Washington insider. His appointment surprised everyone including Fitch. He was smitten with Hackett's vision of the world and rants like that one made him a kind of Obi-Wan Kenobi in Fitch's eyes. Still, he didn't see how this could work.

"Dan, I just don't see how we persuade people B-GOT has capabilities like that and I don't think people are going to believe the incredible coincidence of the comet story."

"General, what are your thoughts?" asked Hackett.

"Well, sir, I agree with Secretary Fitch. I don't see how we can sell either of those stories to the public."

"Is that it, gentlemen? Are these the only two possibilities you can think of that might explain today's events? Perhaps the reason neither makes sense is because neither is the truth."

Cortez and Fitch looked at each other with uncertainty and then back at Hackett for the big reveal.

"The reason you're not seeing it, gentlemen, is you're thinking only in conventional, flat Earth terms. The truth lies beyond the envelope. What happened today is readily apparent, if you're willing to see things in a way you've never seen them before."

"I'm not following you, sir," said Cortez.

Hackett was enjoying the game, but he really wanted his new confidants to understand. "What if I removed the two options you have put forward—a natural phenomenon or the action of a terrorist group? What other possibilities are there?"

"I don't know, Dan, another government?" offered Fitch.

Inside Hackett was laughing. So strong was Earth-centric conditioning that even these highly placed, well-educated, well-informed men couldn't grasp the obvious answer.

"Lights off, screen down," called out Hackett.

The lights in the room went dark and a large screen descended from the ceiling. "Gentlemen, what I am about to show you goes far beyond top-secret. You would do well never to mention this to anyone and never share it with the president, Congress, or even your families. I spent much of this afternoon making absolutely certain that what I'm about to show you is the only copy of these images and that anyone who might have seen these as part of his job won't be sharing them."

Hackett displayed an image of the Shiva on the screen. "General Cortez, can you identify this craft?"

Cortez put his glasses on an eyed the image for a moment. "I cannot, sir. Is it a submarine or some kind of a satellite?"

Hackett smiled, "John, what if I told you this ship is four times the size of FedEx Field? What if I told you it appeared in Earth orbit this morning moments before the fireball barrage?"

Cortez was a battle-hardened veteran and a professional soldier, but the recognition of what he was seeing elicited an unexpected response in his childhood tongue. "*Santa María Madre de Dios!*"

"My God, Dan, what is it?" queried Fitch as he leaned forward for a closer look.

"It's a spacecraft, gentlemen. Play," called out Hackett.

The screen displayed a rapid-fire series of images showing the craft maneuvering and firing.

Hackett narrated, "This spacecraft was imaged by four separate orbital intelligence cameras and tracked by high-definition radar. It entered orbit this morning at 11:17 A.M. EDT. You'll note the flashes and pulses emitting from the craft. We captured these images as it maintained geosynchronous orbit above Washington D.C. this morning. Those flashes are your fireballs, gentlemen."

Hackett continued, "Over the next 29 minutes, the craft maneuvered and established orbits over Moscow, Beijing, Tokyo, and New Delhi, firing its weapons on each city's seat of power."

"Is it still orbiting?" asked Fitch.

"No. It gets better! Seconds after the craft fires upon New Delhi a second craft of similar design, but twice the size, entered Earth orbit. It immediately attacked and destroyed the first ship. The destruction of that ship is what caused the blinding light in the sky and the corresponding shock wave in India."

"Do we have any idea why the second ship destroyed the first ship? Was it protecting us?" asked Fitch.

"There's no way to know," replied Hackett. "Less than 45 seconds after destroying the first ship, the second vanished from all cameras and radar screens. We have not detected it or any other ship since."

"Lights," called Hackett and the lights came back up in the office. "There's one more thing. The attacking ship broadcast a message. Our orbital and moon-based listening posts picked it up. It was transmitted in the language of each country just before the ship opened fire on that country."

"What was the message, sir?" queried Cortez.

"It's a derivation of a Bible verse. Deuteronomy, I believe. Vengeance is mine sayeth the Lord."

A stunned silence filled the room. This occurrence astonished even Hackett, an insider on the UFO issue for years.

"So, you can see, gentlemen. We can't tell the truth. We can't tell our lies, at least not as the only version of the truth. We are left only with misdirection, disinformation, and distraction."

"What kind of distraction do you have in mind?" asked Fitch.

"Sergey Mitchell," replied Hackett.

"I'm not tracking with you, Dan. How does Mitchell help?" Fitch asked. "We were after him anyway. How does he change the equation?"

"Because there is no Sergey Mitchell. He's fiction," replied Hackett.

"But I've seen the intelligence reports on him . . . his bio . . . his terrorist lineage . . . his record," argued Cortez.

"All fiction, general," Hackett said with pride. "As fear of Muslim terrorists dwindled, we needed a new threat. The anti-globalist movement was a perfect candidate—angry, committed, and easy to infiltrate. The man you know as Sergey Mitchell is a U.S. government plant. He infiltrated the movement 15 years ago and we helped him come to prominence. The goal was to make him the face of the anti-globalist movement. Then, when it was convenient, blame him for an event that would give us justification for some action."

Cortez felt out of the loop. "Excuse me, sir, but are you saying that Mitchell is not responsible for President Paxton's assassination?"

Fitch jumped in, "I didn't know who Mitchell really was, but I knew he probably wasn't responsible for Paxton's death. It just seemed like a win-win. We give the American people the justice they seek and we rid the world of a terrorist."

"That was my thinking too, Mr. Secretary, but to risk men and material to go after a fictitious figure. Why?" demanded Cortez.

"I like you, John," said Hackett, smiling at Cortez. "You're honest and a credit to the uniform. Chairman of the Joint Chiefs is your entry card into the club, but now that you're in the club, you need to understand how we play the game. I see big things for you. You could be the next Secretary of Defense."

"Yes, sir. Thank you, sir."

"Having a Sergey Mitchell around is a convenient tool of state. He creates a threat that keeps the American people just afraid enough not to question our defense and security expenditures. He provides an alibi for the things we must sometimes do to keep The United States safe and strong. The plan was to use him as an excuse to create a Georgian stronghold on the border with Russia. Paxton's assassination gave us the perfect opportunity to move forward with that strategy."

"So, why change that plan?" asked Fitch.

"Those ships, Dave. We need a distraction, and a damn big one, to deflect the questions we're going to get about those fireballs. Mitchell is demoted from star to distraction."

"How does that help us, sir?" asked Cortez.

"The capture and killing of Sergey Mitchell, who 350 million Americans blame for Paxton's death, is just the story to squeeze these fireballs out of the top spot on newscasts around the world."

"But how do you produce Mitchell?" asked an incredulous Fitch.

"We release footage of Mitchell's capture and of him being placed aboard a military transport bound for the United States. But . . . the plane crashes and all aboard are lost, including Mitchell."

"But, sir, what about my men flying that plane?" asked a wary Cortez.

"General, every soldier who wears the uniform must be willing to die for this country. That's exactly what the crew will be doing. The alternative is you go on national TV and explain to the American people that those fireballs were actually weapons fired by an alien vessel the size of four football stadiums and there is nothing you can do to protect them."

Cortez dropped his head, pondered for a moment, and then responded half-heartedly. "Yes, sir."

"John, I went out on a limb to bring you into the club. Don't make me regret it," warned Hackett.

"Dave," Hackett said turning to Fitch, "I will produce Mitchell and the video tomorrow. I need you to leak the story to all the right people in the media and make sure they understand that this story needs to dominate and the fireballs need to disappear."

"Got it," replied Fitch.

"You might also call that director friend of yours and get some help telling the story of these American heroes. Make sure people cry when they hear about brave soldiers who gave their lives to bring home the man who killed our beloved president," Hackett schemed.

"What about Chang?" Fitch asked.

"I will handle Chang. By the time I'm done with him, he'll think he's George Washington on a horse accepting the British surrender at Yorktown."

"You're a genius, Dan," Fitch applauded.

"But, sir," Cortez interrupted. "What are we actually going to do about those ships? What if they come back?"

Hackett smiled, "Why, I'm going to have a conversation with America's foremost expert on alien craft and alien intervention, Maria Love."

The three men chuckled and called it an evening.

(43)
Frozen Moment

President Chang's doubts and concerns about Burning Bush interrupted his sleep. He raided the White House kitchen for a midnight snack and headed toward the Oval Office to capitalize on his insomnia by getting some work done. The office transition was a work in progress. Circumstances left little time for a moving day. He felt like a renter. Many of Paxton's belongings remained.

As he approached the office, the youthful Marine guard saluted and said, "Good evening, Mr. President."

"Good evening," responded Chang, returning the salute. He was pleased to encounter someone younger than him.

Normally the lights to the Oval Office came on automatically. Chang entered and closed the door, but no lights. He tried the old-fashioned approach by flipping the switch, but nothing happened. Frustrated, he turned towards his desk and confronted a large figure sitting in his chair. Light through the window behind outlined the figure's shape.

"Guard!" shouted Chang.

"I'm afraid the guard won't hear you, Mr. President. Please don't be alarmed. I am not here to harm you. I am here to help you," said the figure in a gender-neutral tone.

"Guard!" Chang screamed again. He tried the door, but it was locked.

"How did you get in here?" demanded Chang.

"Please, Mr. President," encouraged the figure, "I have information for you . . . important information."

"Who are you?"

"That's not important. Only the information is important."

Chang composed himself. "What kind of information? How can you help me?"

"There are people in your inner circle, Mr. President, who don't have the same agenda that you do," replied the figure.

"And what is my agenda?" asked Chang suspiciously.

"I believe you want to do a good job as president. I believe you want to do what is right. I believe you want the truth. But there are those in your inner circle who feel safe only when lies and fear are the order of the day."

"Yeah, well, we did just have a president assassinated. Maybe a little more security is a good thing," countered Chang.

"Whom do you think killed President Paxton, Mr. Chang?" asked the figure, in a tone with less deference.

"I don't know. It was probably Sergey Mitchell."

The figure chuckled and repeated Chang, "Probably Sergey Mitchell. Is that why you authorized Burning Bush?"

"That's classified. How the hell do you know about that?"

"I'm in a position to know many things, Mr. President, but let's start slowly. Secretary Hackett has no intention of following your directive to bring Mitchell in alive."

"And how do you know that?"

"Because . . . there is no Sergey Mitchell. There is no B-GOT. It's an intelligence fiction created to support agendas and now called into service as a major distraction. Something far more important is happening here. Don't be distracted."

"What is happening here?"

"A conspiracy to keep humanity in the dark about its past and its future."

"That's a pretty big claim to—"

"Knowledge of it is what killed your predecessor, not Sergey Mitchell."

"I've had my doubts about the Mitchell story," admitted Chang, "but all the intelligence points to him."

"They're parrots in an echo chamber, Mr. President. Most of your intelligence community doesn't even know Mitchell is a cover, but Hackett does."

"How do I know I can trust you?"

"Some time tomorrow Secretary Hackett is going to contact you. He's going to tell you he has Mitchell. He's going to put him on a plane bound for the U.S., but that plane is going to crash. Meanwhile, Hackett and the other parrots are going to crowd the airwaves with the story of the brave soldiers who got Mitchell and gave their lives to avenge an American President. ITV will be so choked with news about Mitchell and the plane crash that today's events will be forgotten."

"Are you saying that these fireballs are the real story?"

"Yes."

"Why don't you just tell me what happened?"

"I can't do that. You must figure it out yourself. I can only tell you where to look. I can't, I won't, force you to see."

"Where should I be looking?"

"Talk to Maria Love. She is the key. The conversation she had with President Paxton after the press conference last week was the reason he died."

"Are you saying I'm risking my life by talking to Ms. Love?"

"We are all risking our lives for the truth, Mr. President. Watch Hackett tomorrow. That will be your proof that you can trust me."

A bright light flashed, temporarily blinding Chang. When he looked back towards his desk, the figure was gone.

The Marine guard burst into the Oval Office. "Mr. President, is everything OK, sir? I heard you call for me, but the door was jammed."

"I'm fine. How long was the door jammed?" the president asked curiously.

"Two seconds, sir. I will be more prompt next time," replied the private.

"Thank you, Marine. That will be all. I am going to bed. To-morrow may be a long day."

(44)
Sunday Morning Jack

Like the rest of the United States and the world, Maria and Jack spent their Saturday focused on ITV. Throughout the day, images poured in from around the world detailing the damage caused by the mysterious fireballs. Speculation ranged from meteors to a terrorist attack to some strange weather phenomenon associated with global warming, but there was no consensus.

Jack woke up about 6 A.M. Sunday morning. He left the apartment planning to attend church and left a note for Maria letting her know. On his way, he decided a run would put him closer to God this morning than a sanctuary. He wanted to feel closer to God right now.

My faith buoys me in difficult times, he thought. *Whom am I kidding? I've lived a pretty charmed life. I haven't really experience difficult times. Why now, God? Why have you shattered my personal and professional life? What have you allowed Maria to become involved with?*

He crossed the Potomac into D.C. and headed unconsciously for the National Mall. Even by D.C. standards, the crush of military, police, and media stifled movement. He found a place to park and stealthily changed into the running clothes he always kept in the car. The summer heat and steam oppressed. He donned his earphones and began his run near the Washington Monument. A massive crater scarred the Mall about 100 yards from the base of the monument. In the distance, the mangled Capital dome formed a silhouette against the rising summer sun.

Jack decided to mix the church and the running. He tuned his Internet Radio to THE WORD, a Christian radio station from back home in Texas. The Reverend Dr. Randy Peters was preaching his Sunday morning sermon. Jack had listened to him a couple of times before. Peters reminded Jack of the kind of Bible-based preaching of his childhood.

Peters was decrying the state of the world and imploring his congregation to stay on the path leading to the Lord. Jack approached the Capitol Building end of the Mall. Temporary safety fences and a strong security presence blocked Capitol Building access. He stood and jogged in place, viewing the still inconceivable sight of the smashed icon.

As Jack stood staring at the Capitol, Peters was reaching the crescendo of his sermon. "We live in a world that has turned its back on God. More than that, we live in a country that has turned its back on God. Yesterday's events simply prove God is watching. God is in control not man! Nothing happens unless it is God's will. When we are wicked, God chastens us for our own good. Let us show Him we have heard Him this Sunday. Remember the words of Deuteronomy 32:35: "Vengeance is mine, and recompense, at the time when their foot shall slide: For the day of their calamity is at hand, and the things that are to come upon them shall make haste!""

Jack looked at the Capitol and listened to Peters' words.

Is God punishing us? Are our sins coming home to roost? He wondered.

He needed his faith right now, but he needed Maria too. The two seemed to be in conflict. He struggled to understand why his perfect wife has gone off the deep end with this alien stuff. For all she knew, these could be demons. At best, she was tangled up with dangerous people in some super-secret government program. She needed to let it go and he needed to convince her. He worried for her soul and he worried for their future.

Jack stopped and said a little prayer, "Heavenly Father, please watch over my Maria. Help her to see your way and to let go of these dangerous ideas. I ask this in the name of our Lord, Jesus Christ. Amen."

Jack turned and began his jog back to the car. What he heard blew him away.

"This is Dr. Randy Peters. Thank you for listening. Please join me again next Sunday morning for the first in a special two-part sermon on the false alien second coming. As you know, I have many friends who sit in positions of power in our nation. For years, they have been warning me there would be an attempt by government and those beyond government to use aliens to fake the second coming of Christ and take over the planet. Like most of you, when I first heard these claims I thought they were fantasy. Now, I have tied these stories directly to Bible prophecy and I will share how you can prepare yourself for the deception at hand. Join me then, won't you? Every faithful follower needs to be warned about how the end times are coming to be."

How many more signs could God send him that Maria was on a dangerous path? He knew now that he had to turn Maria from this dangerous course. If not, he would lose her.

(45)
Wanted Woman

Maria awoke about 8 A.M. Sunday morning. She stopped to look at Jack's note and then turned on the ITV. She expected to hear more about fireballs. Instead, the news was wall-to-wall about the capture of Sergey Mitchell, the supposed mastermind of the Paris terrorist attack. Footage of the raid that secured Mitchell's capture played and replayed on every ITV news network.

The footage showed guards escorting a restrained Mitchell onto a plane bound for New York. Maria's journalistic suspicions were triggered by repeated close-ups of Mitchell's face and a comparison to wanted posters of him. She flipped through the news channels and every one of them showed the same close up and comparison to his wanted poster. It was as if someone wanted to make sure that no one doubted it was Mitchell.

Jack returned from his run. They were not used to tension in their relationship, but it remained palpable. Maria believed it would pass. She was more concerned about Inanna. Maria craved Inanna's steadiness and reassurance right now.

What were those fireballs? Were the Anunnaki responsible? She wondered.

Another newsflash interrupted her reverie.

Justin Cardone reported, "The plane carrying Sergey Mitchell and eight members of U.S. Special Forces has disappeared over the Black Sea. Those soldiers were escorting the world's most wanted man back to the U.S. Search and rescue efforts are underway, but unconfirmed and preliminary reports indicate they collided with a small plane flying the area without authorization. Witnesses reported seeing and hearing an explosion offshore. Stay tuned to ANN for the latest on these unfolding events."

Jack and Maria called a momentary truce to hug each other. "I just can't believe all of this is happening," Jack shared. "Why would God allow it?"

Maria managed a smile and was about to respond when there was a loud knock on the door. Jack sprang up to answer the door. Three men in suits and ties stood outside the door, flashing badges.

"Mr. Love?" queried the lead agent.

"Yes," answered Jack with surprise.

"I'm special agent Dalton with the National Security Agency. Is Mrs. Love here?"

"I'm here," answered Maria as she came up behind Jack.

"Mrs. Love, you are going to have to come with us."

"Why?" Jack protested.

"She's wanted for questioning. I can't divulge more than that, sir. This is a matter of national security, Mr. Love."

Jack looked back at Maria as if he didn't know her. "Maria, what is this about?"

"I don't know, Jack" Maria replied in a shaky voice.

"Ma'am, please come with us," demanded Dalton.

"She's not going anywhere without a lawyer," Jack responded.

Dalton was losing his patience. "Mr. Love, get out of the way or we will charge you with obstructing a federal investigation."

Jack reluctantly stepped aside and allowed the two men behind Dalton to grab Maria's arms and escort her out of their apartment and down the hall. He watched as they entered the elevator and his wife was gone.

He stepped back into their apartment, pondering who could help him. He picked up the phone to call Hawking. Surely, he had some favors he could call in. As he looked for the number on his ComTab, there was another knock on the door. Jack hoped for a minute that Maria had come back. He opened the door to find several men in dark suits and sunglasses.

"Mr. Love?" asked one of the men.

"What do you want?" Jack asked in frustration. "You've already got my wife. Are you here for me now?"

"Sir, I'm with the Secret Service. President Chang sent us here to ask Ms. Love for a meeting. The president has some questions."

"What do you mean? You don't have her? There were just three guys here from the NSA 10 minutes ago. They took her away."

"Do you know where, sir?" The lead agent asked.

"They were pushy and short on details," Jack replied testily.

One of the Secret Service agents got on his ComTab and made a call. Jack overheard part of the conversation. "Yes, sir. The NSA picked her up 10 minutes before we got here. No, Mr. Love doesn't know where. Yes, sir. Yes, sir, Mr. President."

The agent returned to Jack. "We're sorry to have disturbed you this morning, sir."

"That's it?" Jack said in frustration.

"Sir, I can tell you the president did not know that NSA had plans to pick her up this morning. The president really needs to talk to your wife. We are making inquiries. We will let you know what we find out."

The agents turned and left. Jack closed the apartment door and leaned against it in frustration. He lifted his head and said a little prayer. "Dear, God. Please protect my Maria. Amen."

Jack picked up his ComTab and began making calls. Hawking was sympathetic, but could not help. He seemed odd on the phone—not at all the man Jack had come to know. He seemed afraid for himself and his family. He made a few other calls and found no one able to help.

"Uncle Tony," he said aloud, "Uncle Tony will help me."

"Call Tony Love. Video." Jack spoke into the ComTab. His device connected and Jack's uncle appeared on the screen.

"Uncle Tony, how are you?"

"Jack, my boy, I'm a little rattled by these asteroids, but I'm doing great. How are you?"

"I need your help. Maria's in some trouble. Some men came to the apartment this morning—I think they were NSA. They took Maria away. A few minutes later, the Secret Service showed up and wanted to escort her to the White House for a meeting with President Chang. They wouldn't tell me anything. Can you help me?"

"NSA, you say? Why would they want Maria?"

"I don't know. I don't even know for sure they were NSA."

"I have some friends who still sit on some powerful Senate committees. Let me make a few calls and see what I can find out."

"Thank you, Uncle Tony. Um . . . "

"Is there something else?"

Jack hesitated. "I don't know if this is important or not, but Maria claims she met with Paxton after the press conference, a few days before he died."

"Did she tell you what they talked about?" Tony asked.

"Umm . . . UFOs," Jack sheepishly replied. "She thinks Paxton's death was some big conspiracy . . . and . . . she claims she's been aboard an alien spacecraft . . . several times." Jack half-expected his gregarious uncle to break out into laughter.

There was silence on the other end of the phone. Jack was certain Uncle Tony thought that he and his wife were losing it.

"Uncle Tony?" Jack finally said.

"Jack," his uncle began in a guarded tone, "let me make a few calls. I know you're worried about Maria. You need to be there if she comes home, but I need to talk to you about something . . . soon . . . and I've been putting it off. It's something your grandfather told me before he died."

"Can you just tell me?"

"No. I can't tell you. I need to show you."

"Uncle Tony, can we get Maria back and then—"

"I'm not sure, Jack. This may have something to do with what's happening to Maria. I don't wish to discuss this over a phone connection," Tony said with more paranoia than caution in his voice. "It's Sunday. If you leave now, you can be in Camden in two hours."

Jack shook his head in frustration. He couldn't imagine a secret his grandfather shared with his uncle that had anything to do with Maria and intelligence agencies.

"Does dad know about this?" asked Jack.

"No, and it concerns him too."

"Uncle Tony, I really do want to hear whatever you have to tell me, but right now I just want to get Maria back."

There was a pause on the other end. "You're right, Jack. Let's get Maria back. We can discuss this later, but it's critical. We must talk about this soon!"

"Fine, Uncle Tony. Thank you for your help!"

"I will let you know if I learn anything."

(46)
Meanwhile Back on Nibiru

A chime burst the dark silence inside the Royal bedchambers. King Ea awoke in a start and groggily called out a gruff, "Yes!"

The king's cousin and War Minister Edin appeared in a hologram at the center of the room. "My apologies for disturbing your sleep, Majesty, but we have news from Earth."

The king sat straight up, eagerly anticipating news of victory over Inanna and a message sent to the humans.

"And how is my sister, the Princess? I hope she is on her way home and not among the dead?" King Ea questioned.

"I'm afraid, Majesty, that things have not gone as planned. Mistress Inanna lives and remains in command of the Rakbu. Admiral Ninn is dead. Four of your ships were lost, including the Tiamat and the Shiva. Four others are disabled in Earth Space and three are limping back to Nibiru."

"And Earth?" thundered King Ea.

"Admiral Ninn was able to fire on five capitals before the Rakbu destroyed his ship in Earth orbit. There is heavy damage to governmental buildings in Washington, Moscow, Beijing, Tokyo, and New Delhi."

"How did Inanna defeat 11 of my finest ships, Edin?"

"Majesty, she has refit the Rakbu to carry at least five fighter squadrons. They ambushed the task force. Admiral Ninn employed a brilliant strategy of commanding from the Shiva rather than the Tiamat. The Shiva broke off with two other RBCs and headed for Earth, but Mistress Inanna disabled the Tiamat, disengaged, and gave chase. She caught and destroyed the Shiva, but not before Ninn had attacked the surface. There's something else, Majesty."

"What?" The impatient king demanded.

"Admiral Ninn transmitted a message before he attacked each city. He translated the message into the appropriate Earth language each time.

"What was the message?" King Ea asked.

"He said, 'Vengeance is mine sayeth the Lord.' Our sources tell us the human intelligence satellites definitely picked up the transmission."

"Masterful!" extolled the king. "How are the humans accounting for the events?"

"Our sources indicate that the Americans have managed to distract global news cycle. They staged the capture and death of the terrorist blamed for President Paxton's assassination. They have also put experts on all over the airwaves calling the attack on their cities coincidental asteroid strikes. They have created false evidence for the claim and are busily distributing it."

"Insolence!" decried King Ea.

"Majesty, I've had my best readers working with the TimeCube. They shared some disturbing data with me. As the result of these events, the TC now shows a 51.9 percent probability that full disclosure of the human past and our role in it will occur within the next 10 earth years. This is the first time simulations have ever shown a greater than 50 percent chance of that happening."

"That must never be allowed," King Ea stubbornly exclaimed, as he circled Edin's hologram image like a caged cat. "Two generations of our people have worked tirelessly to create the humans, build a civilization dedicated to our economic interests, and create prestige and standing for the Anunnaki in the known galaxy. I refuse to relinquish what we have achieved!"

"Respectfully, Majesty, as long as my cousin and your sister, the Princess Inanna is allowed to spin her plans for disclosure, our achievements will remain at risk."

"She may have won this battle, my cousin, but her time is short and she will not win the war. I require counsel. Assemble the senior ministers and the members of the Upper Chamber with royal blood. We must find a way to get control of this situation and quickly."

"Shall I include Senator Enki, Majesty?" inquired Edin.

"Yes," said the king slyly. "My uncle must be made to understand what his arrogant and traitorous behavior is costing us. If nothing else, perhaps he will tip us off to Inanna's plans."

"I understand, Majesty."

"And set up a quantum field conference bridge with Earth. I want to put The Cadre on notice that their incompetence is to blame for this situation. They must double their efforts to make disclosure so ridiculed that no one will risk their credibility to be involved with it."

"It will be done, my Lord. Please return to your slumber. I will convene the conference tomorrow."

(47)
The Tortuguero Lights

"I'm Chip Benson and this is ANN News. As if this weekend wasn't strange enough, there's a remarkable report this morning coming from a remote part of the Central American country of Costa. ANN's Heidi-Ann Holden reports."

A recorded report played with Holden describing events. "Tortuguero is a small remote town on Costa Rica's Caribbean coast. They call it 'The Little Amazon.' People come here from all over the world to escape technology, but some tourists are saying it was the site of a high technology encounter Saturday night."

"Katrin Meier, a German tourist, was part of a tour group on the dark beach last night watching sea turtles lay their eggs. She described what she saw."

"We were standing on the beach watching the turtles. They don't allow lights on the beach and it was very dark. Then the ocean lit up. It reminded me of Christmas."

"American tourist, Bob Nester, continues the story."

"The ground shook so hard that it was tough to stand up. The entire ocean glowed from lights beneath the surface. I counted five massive objects lifting out of the water a quarter to a half mile offshore."

"How big were they?"

"I'm not joking. These things were the size of football stadiums. They seemed to be roughly triangular-shaped with multicolor lights. Once they cleared the water, the rumbling stopped and they were absolutely silent."

"What happened next?" Holden asked.

"We forgot about the turtles and we all stood there and watched these things lift slowly up for about 30 seconds. I'd say they reached about 2,000 feet and then they shot off to the east-southeast over the ocean. They were gone in two seconds," said Nester.

"What do you think they were?"

"I'm a retired Navy Seal. I've never seen anything like that in my life, but I've heard stories from buddies who spent more time at sea than I did."

"What kind of stories?" Holden asked.

"These things were classic USOs."

"And what is a USO?"

"Unidentified Submersible Objects. Navy ships and cargo ships see these things at sea more often than you might think. I'd never seen one until last night. Now I've seen five."

The screen cut to a split screen between Kelly and Holden.

"Heidi-Ann, are you convinced these people saw what they say they saw?" asked an incredulous Chip Benson.

"Chip, everyone I spoke with was shocked, but certain about what they saw. There is one more piece to this story that adds some credibility to it. Around the same time as the report in Costa Rica, the Colombian government announced a breach of its national airspace. Several fighters were scrambled, but the objects dropped off the radar before the planes could reach the area."

"We certainly live in interesting times, Heidi-Ann Holden. Thank you."

(48)
The Cadre

When the Anunnaki left the day-to-day operation of Earth Corp and converted it into an economic vassal state of Nibiru, they created a small group of Anunnaki super hybrids to run their business for them. These human hybrids ran the earth for the Anunnaki. They called themselves The Cadre.

William De Berg, like dozens of generations of his family before him, was taller, better looking, more articulate, smarter, and more Anunnaki than the average human being. Though few people knew his name and fewer knew his face, perhaps because of that fact, De Berg answered to no one on planet Earth.

Along with a shockingly small group of men, he made and broke presidents and prime ministers, industries and their captains. He commissioned wars and famines. He stood silently behind a myriad of *separate* brands people thought competed for their business in the *free* market. He set trends and convinced the people of the planet they had created them on their own. Everything from toothpaste to motor oil to drug cartels all led to De Berg and his colleagues. He didn't measure his wealth in billions or on the Forbes 400 list, but on the scale of global GDP.

Before the past few hundred years, De Berg's family and few others had been first priests and then kings over the peoples of the earth. Their direct connection to the gods gave them spiritual and temporal power over humanity. They intermarried to maintain their genetic advantages over their fellow humans.

As finance became the source of power on Earth, De Berg and the others transitioned their power base into the financial system. They didn't run the financial system or the governments it controlled. They *were* the financial system.

The Cadre's role was simple and twofold. They managed Earth, Inc. for the Anunnaki crown and sent the first ten percent of everything produced to King Ea. They kept the arrangement secret from the rest of humanity. For thousands of years, they exacted this ten percent through spiritual control and the fear of judgment by the gods upon death. As human civilization evolved, fewer humans felt compelled to give their ten percent to the priests. The Cadre's strategy shifted to coercive taxation using the power of the state.

Like all smart intermediaries, this small group of hybrid humans became the brokers between human labor and the profits expected by their Anunnaki masters, ensuring massive wealth and power for themselves. Some grew arrogant and rebellious. They sought an Earth free of Anunnaki control, but replaced by their own. As long as they kept the wealth flowing to Nibiru, they had full autonomy upon the earth.

The Cadre's heavy-handed tactics created a human civilization suspect of power and rebellious against taxation. Devised as a means of ultimate control, the Internet proved their biggest blunder. It provided humanity a place to compare notes, share ideas, and dispel fear and prejudice. It became a platform for liberation and self-expression. As connectivity expanded, collective human consciousness awakened a sense that something wasn't right on planet earth.

Truths were twisted. Transparency was a façade. People questioned the power and legitimacy of church, state, and financial institutions. Most of all, the species felt oppressed by a huge lie it could not quite put its finger on. People began to seek a deeper meaning for their existence.

To King Ea, this was The Cadre's fault. They were failing their mission and putting at risk the earth that laid the golden egg for Nibiru.

De Berg was awakened by the one sound in his life he hated—the one person he did have to answer to—The King of Nibiru. "Mr. De Berg, you have an incoming quantum communiqué from Nibiru," began the message. "Please secure your location to hear the full message."

De Berg rolled out of bed and pressed a button on the wall. A highly advanced communication scrambler, penetrable only by a message transmitting on the Royal Channel, instantly secured his room. The Message was from Nibiru's Defense Minister Edin. It ordered De Berg to join a quantum conference bridge at 6:00 P.M. GMT. In a life where he generally gave the orders, he despised these summons and the Anunnaki that commanded him.

He called out to his ComTab, "Call Mason . . . Howard."

Howard Mason was another member of The Cadre and De Berg's closest confidant. De Berg's device understood to establish a secure link—one not traceable by the damned TimeCubes. The King often used the TimeCubes to monitor The Cadre. After decades of development, The Cadre had devised a way to speak without detection.

Mason answered, "Good morning, Bill. What time is it anyway?"

"Too damned early!" replied De Berg. "Did you receive the summons from his Majesty?"

"Yes. What the devil is this about?"

"I'm certain it has to do with that ill-advised attack yesterday. We have matters under control. Why can't he calm himself?" complained De Berg.

"Our king is a hot head," agreed Mason, "Unfortunately, there are no better options right now than to continue our arrangement."

"There is always . . . the opposition. I received another message from Senator Enki a few days ago," De Berg floated. He had secretly been working with Enki for years, but had never risked telling any of his Cadre counterparts. He always thought Mason was the one who might eventually go along with him.

"Damn it, Bill. He's been reaching out to us and making us false promises since the time of our great-great-grandfathers."

"Did you see the orbital images, Howard?"

"I saw them and I put Hackett in charge of making sure they were properly disposed of."

"That's good. We can't let people see those images, but that was an Anunnaki ship that destroyed the Anunnaki vessel attacking Earth." De Berg reminded. "Maybe Enki and Princess Inanna are ready to challenge the King . . . openly."

"Bill, what are you saying? Enki is an old fool with no respect at home and Princess Inanna is a rebel with her own agenda. For all we know, that was her vessel attacking us yesterday and a Royal Battle Cruiser that stopped her."

"Come on, Howard. You're no happier than I am with the status quo. I'm saying that maybe there's an opening to change things. Don't you want that?"

"If there was a way, certainly I would take it. King Ea is not as reasonable as his father was. Still, our arrangement is the only thing keeping this planet safe. What becomes of us, Bill, in this idyllic world you propose? What will the people of Earth do to us and take from us, when they find out we have been the guards on their cells?"

"Safe? How can we be safe, my friend, when the king makes deals with the Z to abduct humans? When he sells human DNA on the open galactic market? How can we be safe when the cancer rate among abductees is 500 percent above normal?"

"Don't forget, Bill. You're Anunnaki too. We're not like other humans. We have to think of the good of both civilizations."

"We are 33 percent Anunnaki, but we are 67 percent human, by decree of the king. Your arguments were fine when abductions were rare. Now, millions are abducted without even the knowledge of their elected officials. Three dozen men in a smoke-filled room give their OK to terrorize our species."

"Acceptable losses for the preservation of humanity and its protection," Mason argued.

"If the king cares about human wellbeing, why does he deny us technologies that would allow us to travel between stars, cures to simple and common diseases, and the oppor-tunity to become part of the larger galactic community?" demanded De Berg.

"He's given us so much. Look at how technology has advanced. We've received hundreds of years of technology in the past 30 years. These are old arguments, my friend. We have no options. The status quo is our protector. I'll see you on the conference call. Be careful with whom you share these . . . ideas. Not everyone is as accepting as me," Mason cautioned. "I'll see you on the conference."

Mason hung up. De Berg hoped to share his plan with his friend, but Mason offered no opening. He would have to hear about De Berg's plan along with everyone else.

(49)
Abduction

Inanna sat in her quarters reading from the *Book of Possibilities*—her favorite scripture among the holy books of her people.

In the vast expanse of time and space, your problems are small and your opportunities many. In those moments when courage would fail you, focus on the highest possible good as the outcome.

"May it be so, Father Creator," whispered Inanna as she pulled the book to her breast and tightly embraced it.

A message from the bridge interrupted her beautiful moment. "Mistress, we are entering Earth orbit," alerted Commander Enka.

"Scan for Maria," ordered Inanna.

"Mistress, she appears to be in a detention cell in a secured part of the Pentagon. We can transport her."

"Hmm," uttered Inanna, "is she alone?"

"No, Mistress"

"Hold. I'm on my way to the bridge."

"Ms. Love, thank you so much for coming to see me this morning. I hope I didn't interrupt a keynote address at MUFON," chided Dan Hackett.

"I'm honored that the Secretary of Defense would spend his Sunday morning personally interviewing me," replied Maria smartly. "Why have you brought me here, Mr. Hackett?"

"Is that really such a mystery, Ms. Love? You've openly admitted to cavorting with known enemies of the United States of

America," Hackett retorted.

"What known enemies?"

Hackett projected the images of the spacecraft on a screen in front of Maria. "Do you recognize this ship, Maria?"

"No," Maria replied, "Should I?"

"This isn't the ship you've publicly admitted to being aboard?"

"When have I publicly admitted to being aboard a space-ship?"

"You didn't tell Pete Rogers that you had been aboard an alien vessel on several occasions?" demanded Hackett.

Damn you, Pete, thought Maria.

She shifted in her chair. "I have been aboard a ship, Mr. Hackett, but I never saw the outside of it. I don't recognize your ship."

"Tell me about your conversation with President Paxton," Hackett continued.

Maria hesitated, surprised. "That was a private conversation in the Oval Office. How would you know about that?"

Hackett didn't respond. He knew about the conversation from his benefactor Howard Mason. As one of the top members of The Cadre, Mason had technology capable of listening in on conversations, even in highly secure places like the Oval Office. Hackett thought he ran Mason—well—he thought he ran everyone. In truth, Mason made Dan Hackett to serve his purposes. He had no compunctions about breaking him, if that served his purpose. The Cadre needed people like Hackett—people to convert their orders into government policies, while keeping them out of the spotlight and their hands clean. Hackett only asked the question to demonstrate that he knew many things and to intimidate Maria into answering. He loved interrogation. It was a game and the winner was the person who broke first.

"You killed Paxton, didn't you?" Maria shouted. "You and all your shadow buddies. You think you know what's best for the people, but you only do what's best for you!"

Hackett could tell his comment had the desired effect. He was getting under her skin. He calmly looked at his notes and continued. "Didn't it ever occur to you, Ms. Love, that going aboard such a ship and discussing issues that touch on U.S. national security might not be appropriate?"

"People get abducted all the time, Mr. Hackett, but then I'm sure you know all about that. Most abductees wind up on the front page of tabloids, not being detained at the Pentagon."

"You better take this more seriously, Maria. That ship was photographed in orbit around Earth yesterday. Watch this video."

Maria watched aghast as the series of photos clearly showed the ship firing at the earth multiple times.

"Those fireballs that devastated our Capital Building and five other world cities yesterday, Ms. Love, were actually weapons fired from this spacecraft. Historic structures were devastated and the latest estimate is 676 people killed and more than 13,000 injured in the attacks. Now, what do you know about these ships?" Hackett nearly shouted, as he leaned forward across the table.

Maria looked down and slowly shook her head. Tears now flowed down her face. *Would Inanna do that?* She considered. *Of course she wouldn't. She was trying to help humanity.*

"I can't help you, Mr. Hackett."

"Can't or won't, Ms. Love?" accused Hackett.

"The ship I was aboard is here to help us, not hurt us."

"Help us? Is firing on defenseless civilians helping us?"

"I told you. I can't confirm it's the same ship," Maria said fighting her tears.

"So, you admit it could be?"

"I don't think so. Inanna wouldn't . . ." Maria stopped knowing she had made a mistake by mentioning Inanna's name.

"Inanna?" queried Hackett. "Who is Inanna? You're on a
first-name basis with these . . . these aliens?"

"You can't hold me!" argued Maria trying to change the subject. "I have rights."

"This vessel has been classified as a terrorist threat, Ms.
Love. Your connection to it allows me to hold you under the
Patriot Act and throw away the key. You had better start talking.
Perhaps, we could be lenient, if you tell me what you know."

"I've told you all I know!" shouted Maria.

"And I've told you I don't believe you! Hackett replied ven-
omously.

"I have nothing more to say to you, Mr. Hackett."

"I can see this is getting us nowhere, Ms. Love." Hackett
summoned the guards, "Take Ms. Love back to her cell. She can
consider her stance for a while."

Two large guards grabbed Maria roughly and led her to the
door.

"Oh, Ms. Love," Hackett said matter-of-factly, "That ship
was destroyed. I sure hope your . . . Inanna was not aboard."

Maria went cold. "How was the ship destroyed?" she asked
cautiously.

"Oh. We don't know. It's so hard to say with these aliens,"
Hackett lied.

The guards led her out of the room and into the hallway. As
they reached the first turn in the corridor, the familiar bluish light
caught Maria. She materialized on the Rakbu and collapsed to
the ground in exhaustion.

"Maria," Inanna rushed to her. "Are you alright?"

"Inanna?" asked a confused Maria. "I knew it wasn't true.
They told me you were dead. I was heartbroken. They told me

you attacked Earth. I knew it wasn't you."

"No, my child, I am quite alive. Transport us both to Dr. Enti's office," ordered Inanna, as she lifted and cradled Maria in her arms. "You're safe now, Maria. You're safe."

(50)
DNA Destiny

Maria rested comfortably under light sedation in the Rakbu's medical facility. Enti had been Inanna's personal physician since childhood and she trusted him implicitly. She was concerned about Maria's physical and mental condition, given the stressful events of the past week. She asked Dr. Enti to do a complete mental and physical analysis on Maria. Enti conducted a full body molecular scan. The scan literally analyzed the wellbeing of every molecule in the body and provided recommended treatments, based on the results.

Inanna rested nearby while Enti awaited the results. True to her custom, Inanna fell into a reverie and pondered the big picture and her plans to change it.

She recalled the day she shared her DNA strategy with Enti and enlisted his help to make it a reality. Known as one of the great medical minds on Nibiru, King Enlil handpicked Dr. Enti for The Cadre DNA project. He developed a revolutionary technique to limit Cadre member Anunnaki DNA to 33 percent. His technique broke nature's 50/50 rule of inheritance. He determined that Cadre DNA must be capped at 33 percent because beyond that level the DNA became additive.

Inanna knew Enti's genius could transform her vision of DNA Destiny into reality. DNA Destiny was Inanna's program to merge the Anunnaki and human species into a single race with the best features of both. She planned to put an end to The Human Question by making species parity a political and genetic fact.

She recalled their conversation, "I want you to create a human-appearing hybrid with 49 percent DNA."

"Mistress, 49 percent DNA would make the being's DNA additive. If that person mated with a normal 17 percent human, the resulting offspring will have 66 percent Anunnaki DNA. In four generations, a full-blooded Anunnaki could be produced."

"Precisely, that's the goal," Inanna enthused.

"Mistress, that violates Anunnaki law and several executive decrees by your father and your brother."

"I'm well aware of that, Enti. Do you have an opinion on The Human Question?" Inanna asked.

"I'm a scientist, Mistress. I try to stay out of politics," Enti replied.

"Do you believe the crown's actions on Earth are appropriate?"

"That's not for me to say, Mistress."

"Do you believe the humans are sentient?"

Enti hesitated. "I don't know. I'm agnostic. I must admit the possibility troubles me. The blood of that planet runs through my veins. I'm concerned its current inhabitants are being denied their full potential."

"Help me create this hybrid, Enti. We will change history together. We will make right the wrong done by our government."

That day Dr. Enti became the first recruit for Inanna's mission, but engineering a 49 percent Anunnaki proved challenging. Inanna demanded the hybrid appear completely human to the eye and to human medical scans. To accomplish this feat, Enti switched on DNA activators within the human DNA deserts and controlling RNA expressions of the DNA blueprint.

For earth decades, the Rakbu abducted humans and

conducted experiments trying to create the perfect mix. Some of the abducted human females lacked the mental and physical fortitude to handle the stress of abduction and the procedures. Inanna dropped them from the program. There were a few genetic misfires—babies that appeared to Anunnaki or had other issues—only a few of them survived. The survivors were raised aboard Rakbu and they became part of Inanna's crew. They looked human enough to conduct ground reconnaissance, but could not fool human medical scans.

Irene Gomez became the first subject to make it through the process and produce a viable 49 percent baby—Maria. Maria became the prototype 49 percent Anunnaki and the lynchpin of Inanna's DNA Destiny strategy. Something else made Maria different. She had two mothers and no father. Her modified chromosomes were 51 percent from Irene and 49 percent from Inanna. Enti used Inanna's chromosomes to fertilize the egg in place of male chromosomes—a first in Anunnaki genetics.

Because of Maria's unique status in Inanna's plans, Enti monitored her development throughout her childhood. These check-ups required frequent abductions. Maria remembered nothing of these abductions except the screen memory of a wise old owl. To eliminate problems with the missing time, they abducted Irene along with Maria.

Inanna's strategy was ingenious. A 49 percent Anunnaki, who mated with a typical 17 Anunnaki percent human, produced an offspring with 66 percent Anunnaki DNA. That child would produce offspring with 83 percent DNA. Finally, that child would produce a 100 percent Anunnaki DNA human being. Inanna planned to *evolve* humans into human-appearing Anunnaki in four generations, giving them all the benefits of both species.

With the DNA limitations out of the way, Inanna believed a

powerful dose of historical truth and humanity's resiliency could overcome the millennia of slave conditioning. Human DNA parity would force King Ea to acknowledge humanity and change his earth policies. Inanna planned to undermine the genetics of Anunnaki dominance right under her brother's nose.

Inanna's envisioned a merging of the two species, giving each the best of the other. Long ago, the Anunnaki recognized their human creations exceeded them in certain areas. Humans possessed an innate curiosity, the ability to express love and compassion, and to excel in spiritual pursuits.

As a highly stoic race, the Anunnaki struggled in these areas. Anunnaki thinking forced a centralized, top-down mentality. Humans were open to asynchronous paradigms producing freedom of expression for the individual. Despite its technology, these limitations   stifled   social   development   in   Anunnaki culture.

Democracy, which readily took root among the humans, was utterly foreign to Nibiru. While he would never support it at home, King Ea viewed democracy on earth as a great opiate. It revolt-proofed his secret order by giving the humans a false sense of empowerment. Inanna hoped the infusion of human DNA and thinking might free the minds of ordinary Anunnaki.

Inanna once hoped to transform humanity spiritually, rather than biologically. She believed establishing a connection to The Father Creator would override the false Anunnaki god conditioning. She remembered two teachers who showed potential to ignite humanity's reconnection.

The first appeared in the shadow of the Himalayas. He preached a doctrine of self-discipline and direct connection to the divine. Inanna tested him twice. She appeared to him in the garb of Mara the destroyer, tempting him three times to deny his realization. Each time he refused.

Later she projected herself as several students seeking wisdom. She approached the teacher during mediation.

"Are you a god?" she challenged.

"I am not," replied the teacher.

"Are you the reincarnation of a god?"

"I am not."

"Are you a human being?"

"I am no mere human being," replied the teacher.

"What are you then?" asked Inanna.

"I am awake."

"Awake to what?" Inanna followed.

"Awake to who I truly am and to why I'm truly here. Once that awakening happens, there is no going back to old delusions."

The second teacher walked the dusty hills of Judea. Right away, Inanna sensed his intense connection to The Father Creator. He inspired her hope for humanity. The TimeCube indicated a challenging path for him. She appeared as the deceiver to test his resolve.

"Long has been your fast," said Inanna. "Use your wisdom to convert these stones into bread and satisfy your hunger."

The teacher refused, saying, "The food of the Father grants ongoing happiness and life. The food of the world grants temporary refuge from hunger pangs."

"If your faith in the Father is so strong, throw yourself from this cliff. Surely, the Father will come to your aid," tested Inanna.

"The Father does not respond to frivolous dares, but to the real needs of our lives," replied the teacher.

Finally, Inanna took the teacher to her Vimana and showed him the entire Earth. "Simply, say that I am The Father Creator and I will grant you everything in your view."

"There is only one Father of this universe," replied the

teacher. "My connection to Him is unbroken by your foolishness."

"How can you be sure, you are connected to the true creator?" Inanna questioned.

"He is the one who remains when all concepts dissolve. He is I and I am he. Wherever I am, there is He also. Wherever He is, there am I also. Cease your attempts to delude me, evil one, and leave me."

Taken together, these two teachers represented Inanna's ideal human being—self-realized and with a direct connection to The Father Creator. In each case, Inanna believed humanity's transformation was at hand. In each case, she watched as The Cadre expertly manipulated the teachings and folded them into the same old disempowering messages that had enslaved humanity for so long. That's when she knew the answer lay in biology, not spirituality.

An audible gasp from Enti interrupted her reverie. "What is it, Enti?"

Enti stood staring in astonishment at the full-color molecular scanner screen before him. The technology allowed a doctor to zoom into the anomaly for a visual and deeper analysis.

"You better come see this, Mistress," Enti said. "You won't believe it!"

(51)
The UFO Poll

"Thank you for watching ANN and welcome to Sunday Sound Off. I'm Justin Cardone. This week's tragic asteroid strikes around the world are already growing a cottage industry of conspiracy theories. The most radical claims that space aliens attacked the earth. A recent survey shows that 53 percent of Americans believe in UFOs. Fifteen percent believe they have seen a UFO. And eight percent even believe an alien attack on Earth is actually possible."

[Image of ET appears behind Cardone]

"But would ET really attack us and could ET even get here? Several experts join us today to discuss this issue. General John Cortez is Chairman of the Joint Chiefs of Staff. Dr. Iwo Yoshida is a professor of physics at Texas A&M University. Gary Sheer studies the UFO phenomenon and has been a vocal advocate for the disclosure of all the government knows about this topic."

"General Cortez, welcome to Sunday Sound Off."

"Thank you."

"Let's get right into it, general. Was Earth attacked by extraterrestrials yesterday?"

Cortez laughed. "Grant, I can assure you that there is no proof that yesterday's events were caused by an extraterrestrial attack."

"Are you saying it's not possible?"

"Well, I would defer to Dr. Yoshida's expertise in any speculation about what is possible. I can simply confirm that there is no proof that aliens caused yesterday's events."

"And what do you say to Americans who believe that is what happened?"

"We live in a free country. People are free to speculate all they want," replied Cortez.

Cardone dug further. "You have used the word proof twice, general. Are you suggesting that there is evidence pointing in the direction of an alien attack?"

Cortez shuffled in his chair a bit, measuring his reply. "I am saying that we don't know what caused yesterday's explosions, but we are exploring every explanation. Several reputable scientists have come out and said that, despite the unlikeliness of the strikes, the evidence points towards asteroids. The leap to aliens attacked us is just not provable by the facts. But, in our age of conspiracy theories, it's not surprising."

Cardone turned to Yoshida. "Dr. Yoshida, the general pointed in your direction as the referee on whether it's even possible for alien ships to reach the earth. Is it?"

"Grant, thank you for having me on the show. Everything we understand about the Universe indicates that it is simply impossible to transport mass, like a spacecraft, across the vast distances between the stars. Remember the universal speed limit is the speed of light. The energy it would take to approach the speed of light is practically unfathomable."

"Is that true or is it only true based on what we know about the Universe?" queried Cardone.

"Grant, I'm not going to sit here and say we have a complete grasp on the workings of the Universe. However, the things we do know have stood up to scientific scrutiny for decades. We have no reason to believe that any civilization, however advanced, could overcome these distances, given the challenges posed by the laws of nature."

"So, you would agree with General Cortez that an alien spacecraft is not a feasible explanation for yesterday's events?"

"Well, I would leave it to General Cortez to discuss our national defense assessment. Scientifically, I do not believe an alien ship could reach the earth to engage in such an attack."

"Mr. Sheer, why do Americans continue to believe in this phenomenon when our science and national security experts continue to hold to its impossibility? Have Americans watched too much science fiction?"

"Of course not, Grant. Americans are responding to a real phenomenon. UFOs are here and they are real. However, I agree with my colleagues that yesterday was not the result of an alien attack," Sheer concurred.

"I'm a little surprised to hear you say that, Mr. Sheer. If you believe the UFOs are here, why don't you believe they attacked us?"

"The species visiting us are extremely advanced. They're not aggressive. Every bit of evidence indicates they are trying to help us through this dangerous time in our development. They would not attack us."

Cardone eyed Sheer with surprise. "The UFO literature is filled with accounts of aliens doing horrible things to people. Are you saying those stories are untrue?"

"I am saying some people have misunderstood the phenomenon. If we tag a bear in the woods to track it, we do it for the bear's benefit. These beings may be doing things that seem intrusive to us, but they certainly have their reasons for doing them."

"Dr. Yoshida, Mr. Sheer says the aliens are here. You say it's not possible. How do you explain the abduction experiences people claim to be having?"

"Grant, I'm a scientist. I don't know the answer to that question. I believe the scientific data indicates a psychological response some kind of event we don't yet understand."

"A mass hallucination of some kind," offered Cardone?

"Perhaps . . . I'm not saying the experience isn't real for people. I'm simply saying that what I know about physics tells me there are no ships visiting Earth. Therefore, I must look for another explanation."

Mr. Sheer responded with emotion. "Dr. Yoshida, I believe exactly the opposite. The evidence says they are here. We know it. We've had contact with them. Maybe what we need is a scientific community that figures out how they got here, rather the continued stonewalling saying that it's impossible."

"Saying that they are here, Mr. Sheer, violates everything I know about physics and it violates logic too."

"How does it violate logic?" charged Sheer.

"Gary, the experiences abductees describe simply aren't part of the everyday world that most of us experience."

"That's true except for the 53 percent of Americans in the poll who say they do believe in UFOs," Sheer pointed out.

"In the absence of physical evidence to corroborate these experiences, it is merely another belief system," retorted Yoshida. "100 percent of eight-year-olds believe in Santa, Mr. Sheer. That doesn't make him real."

"Gentlemen," cautioned Cardone. "General Cortez, is the United States military prepared to encounter an alien attack, should one ever materialize?"

"It's hard to defend against the unknown, Grant. We take seriously the defense of the American people. Certainly, we are developing capabilities to protect this nation against any threat. Despite what you have seen in the movies, though, we haven't found a way to defend ourselves against asteroids."

"Gentlemen, we will have to leave it there. Thank you all for a spirited discussion."

(52)
De Berg

William De Berg stood on his private helipad waiting for his personal helicopter. His vast and opulent northern Maryland estate spread out before him. He owned islands and mansions around the world, but he grew up here—this was home. Few knew and nobody particularly cared—except those he paid to care—that he turned 82 today. He looked and felt half that age thanks to his Anunnaki blood and the gold dust longevity pills ingested by Cadre members. Many of his recent ancestors lived into their 120s. Until today, De Berg expected to as well.

Once, Cadre members were even larger, stronger, and longer-lived. Many lived 500 to 1,000 earth years. Their feats of strength and courage lived on in myth. Their disdain for their gods and two open rebellions persuaded King Ea to limit them. In the Decree on Genetic Minimization (DGM), he ordered all Cadre members genetically modified to reduce their Anunnaki DNA from 50 percent to 33 percent. Size, strength, intelligence, and longevity all fell among The Cadre.

Even so, modern Cadre members stood head and shoulders above ordinary human beings. The Cadre's slow aging, exceptional intelligence, and remarkable skills owed to Anunnaki DNA double that of other humans. Large areas of so-called DNA deserts were activated among The Cadre, but lay dormant among ordinary humans. These factors allowed them to manage the human race as easily as a zookeeper manages a zoo. Their

RNA was massaged to express as far more human than other Anunnaki. This allowed them to blend easily in among their subjects.

De Berg scanned the hundreds of acres of pristinely manicured lawns and gardens. He loved nature, but had so little time to enjoy it. The burdens of his position wore on him. His vast wealth and power seemed glorious and glamorous from the outside, but inside he felt as empty, lonely, and uncertain as the next person did.

A faraway tyrant and a father who eagerly served that tyrant shaped De Berg's destiny. Born to control a planet, he controlled nothing of his own life. His father mercilessly groomed him, from an early age, to take his place among Earth's crown princes. Winning wasn't enough. His father demanded domination of everything and everyone.

"A lion has no time to be anything else," his father once said. "You're first among men. Only your Cadre brothers are your equal. The world worships athletes, politicians, and celebrities. They, in turn, gravel before us. We make them and break them. The price we pay to have whatever we want is undying allegiance to our Anunnaki sovereign."

However, De Berg learned the hard way, even a young lion must conform. His sophomore year at Yale he fell in love with Andrea—a Wisconsin farmer's daughter. His father learned of the relationship and warned him to end it.

"I love her and it's my choice," he told his father.

"It is not your choice. You do not belong to you. You belong to King Ea and to your duty. Our DNA must not mix with a commoner DNA. That would dilute us and leave us unable to fulfill our responsibilities."

De Berg ignored his father's warnings. One Monday morning he woke up and Andrea was gone. Not just physically gone, it was as if she never existed. Yale had no records of her and mutual friends had no memory of her. His father made her vanish. For the first time, De Berg truly understood the scope of his father's power—the power that would one day be his.

He married a third cousin and a fellow Cadre member. Their marriage was a loveless co-existence punctuated by fake smiles and plastic waves at public events. They lived at opposite ends of a house so colossal the word mansion seemed inadequate. They dined together only on holidays and for show when they entertained guests.

De Berg vowed to break the grip of an arrangement made a hundred generations ago with a distant despot. He would use his power, however carefully, to move humanity in the direction of freedom and self-determination. To achieve his ultimate end, he must maintain his cover as a loyal Cadre member. That role compelled him to orchestrate brutal acts of inhumanity at the king's behest. Those atrocities turned his stomach and ravaged his soul. He spun so many lies and built so many false truths he could scarcely tell the difference anymore.

One lie dwarfed the others. It represented his ultimate act of rebellion against a system he wanted to tear down with his bare hands. The birth of an eldest son was a sacred event within The Cadre. The eldest son inherited the family's power and propagated it into the next generation. Eldest Cadre sons sat on The Earth Council—the body responsible for covertly running every aspect of life on Earth.

With the birth of his son, De Berg's rebellion boiled over. He resolved his son would never grow up as a well-dressed water boy for King Ea. His son would choose his own wife and live his own destiny.

By tradition, a first-born Cadre son was presented to King Ea and consecrated to his service. The ceremony was to be performed before the child's first birthday. An Anunnaki priest came to Earth to officiate the ceremony. The priest consecrated the pledge by marking the child with the king's seal and implanting a tracking chip. The king and his intelligence agencies used the chip to track and control Cadre members. They laced the tracking chip with a micro-explosive device. The device detonated when exposed to open air. Once a Cadre member you were always a Cadre member.

De Berg concocted a plan to protect his son and subvert the system. He boldly risked everything by contacting Senator Enki. He knew the Anunnaki supported disclosure on The Human Question. He asked Enki's help to fake his son's death and strike a blow for disclosure. Enki used his influence to handpick the high priest to perform the ceremony. The priest was a longtime friend and trusted advisor to Enki. His Anunnaki name was Emuq-Enu—meaning "Power Change."

While Emuq-Enu was on Earth for the ceremony, De Berg worked with him and with Enki to stage an accident—an accident that supposedly killed De Berg's only son. The high priest validated the death and reported to King Ea. Even the king would not question a high priest in such a matter.

De Berg befriended the Anunnaki priest and nicknamed him Cutler for his ability to knife through red tape. For decades, Cutler served as a secret envoy between De Berg and Enki. De Berg used his influence to place Cutler deep inside the global intelligence community. When a job called for dirty or faceless work, Cutler always stepped up. Cutler's commitment to the Enki and Inanna's opposition was so strong he went to work for De Berg, a mere human hybrid. Cutler often played the heavy hand needed to prod humans towards the truth.

De Berg entrusted his son to J. Michael Love III his best friend from Yale. Love was a member of a wealthy and well-connected New Jersey political family. During their college days, De Berg shared bits and pieces of his unique status with Love. The two men were like brothers. Love didn't blink an eye when De Berg approached him with the unusual request to raise his son.

Love raised Jack Sr. alongside his son, Tony. Tony grew up to become a U.S. Senator. Jack lived his life oblivious to his princely lineage. He moved to Texas, married the woman of his dreams, and had three children—the youngest his namesake. To limit, the dilution or concentration of The Cadre's Anunnaki DNA, the Anunnaki employed a technique to freeze their percentage of Anunnaki DNA at 33 percent. This meant De Berg's grandchildren carried the same percentage of Anunnaki DNA as him.

De Berg never acknowledged his children or his grandchildren. He knew of them only through Mike Love's anecdotes. Though he had access to a complete dossier for any person on the planet, De Berg never looked into their lives. The risk of exposure was too great. Their ignorance of him kept them safe.

Five years ago, with his lifelong friend on his deathbed, De Berg finally shared the whole truth with Mike Love. In all those years, Love never asked. He did what a friend—what a brother—would do. He loved Jack Sr. and his children as if they were his own. Tony and Jack knew of De Berg and had met him a few times during their childhood. At their father's urging, they referred to him as "Uncle Bill."

De Berg's wife never knew what really happened to her son. She knew only her powerful husband was responsible for his disappearance. She never forgave him for it. She refused to have more children with him. De Berg was fine with that decision. He had no intention of subjecting Jack or any other child of his to the king.

Recent events, though, made even De Berg's purposeful attempts to ignore his progeny impossible. He watched the presidential press conference the night Maria Love asked her question of President Paxton. He knew Maria by name only and he knew she was married to his grandson. What he didn't know is why Maria looked so Anunnaki. Only an Anunnaki hybrid would even notice, but Maria's features expressed strongly Anunnaki DNA.

Had his grandson unknowingly married another member of The Cadre? He wondered.

His desire to know overcame his caution. He pulled her file. The file indicated she was fully human. He was puzzled. Had someone discovered his secret and sent a hybrid to marry his grandson to keep the bloodline going? He definitely needed to find out and yesterday's events had made it paramount. He sent Cutler to the White House the previous night to set that wheel in motion.

The sound of a helicopter approaching from the south broke De Berg's preoccupation with his past. As commanded by the king, he was headed to the quantum conference. There were only three super secure, advanced technology sites in the United States and nine worldwide where members of The Cadre could attend a quantum conference. The nearest one to Bill De Berg was nestled safely and secretly in the mountains of West Virginia.

Some researchers and conspiracy theorists had located this heavily guarded facility and dubbed it the home of the shadow government. Indeed, they were not far off. Cadre members built these sites to house them and senior members of human society in the event of global emergency. The purpose was to insure the continuity of the existing power structure. This strategy allowed that structure to quickly recover and reconstitute after a catastrophe.

De Berg didn't understand the science behind the quantum technology, but the Anunnaki had found a way to tap into quantum fields to allow for virtually instantaneous communication between Nibiru and Earth. With advanced Anunnaki technology, the visual and audio quality matched a human video call, even across more than four light years.

He climbed aboard the helicopter and it headed west-southwest toward the West Virginia facility. Despite being among a handful of men running Earth, meetings with the king usually concerned him. Always he worried about exposure of his secret and his true allegiances. He was a man with much to lose, but not on this Sunday. Today he planned to challenge the most powerful person in his universe and he planned to win. He knew more about the attack than he shared with Mason. He knew an RBC attacked Earth and he wanted answers from the king about it.

Cutler called on De Berg's secure videophone.

"Good morning, Mr. De Berg. I visited the White House last night as you suggested," said Cutler.

"Excellent, Mr. Cutler. Was the message delivered?"

"Loud and clear, sir. I definitely spooked Chang. There's only one problem."

"And what's that?" De Berg asked, studying his notes for the meeting with the king.

"DoD agents picked up Maria Love this morning and delivered her to Secretary of Defense Hackett for interrogation."

"You must get her out of there. Hackett is Mason's minion and I don't trust him any farther than I can throw him."

"Mistress Inanna has transported her aboard the Rakbu, sir."

"Inanna?"

"Yes, sir. She sent a message asking that you transport aboard. She has news to share with you," Cutler said.

"That's serendipity, Mr. Cutler. I need to talk to Inanna too. I'm en route to an audience with his Majesty. Can she meet right now?"

"She stressed the urgency of the matter."

"That's odd. I haven't spoken directly to Mistress Inanna in years. How much does she know about our project?"

"Sir, my loyalty is to you. She knows nothing."

"Cutler, what do you know about the attack yesterday? Was Inanna involved?"

"Yes, sir. The ship that fired on Earth was a Royal Battle Cruiser—the Shiva. It was part of an 11-ship armada sent by the king to attack Earth. The Rakbu intercepted the armada. The Shiva was the only ship to reach Earth. The Rakbu chased the Shiva and destroyed her in orbit after the attack had begun."

"Inanna actually attacked Anunnaki ships?"

"She did, sir."

"I had no idea she would ever consider going that far for humanity. I think it's time I had a discussion with her. I'm on a helicopter headed for the West Virginia facility. Have her transport me aboard. She can send me straight to my meeting from the Rakbu."

(53)
The Alliance

De Berg materialized aboard the Rakbu.

"Mr. De Berg, welcome to the Rakbu. I am Commander Enka. I am Mistress Inanna's executive officer."

"Thank you, commander," replied De Berg.

"Mistress Inanna is waiting for you in the hospital."

"Is the Princess ill?"

"Mistress Inanna will explain. Right this way, sir."

Enka led De Berg to the hospital. There he found Maria Love sedated on a bed. Princess Inanna and Dr. Enti poured over some highly advanced medical readouts.

"Mistress Inanna, I present Mr. William De Berg."

De Berg reached out to shake Inanna's hand. He was normally one of the tallest people in a room. Among the Anunnaki, he felt like he was standing in a hole. "Princess Inanna, it's a pleasure to finally meet you in person."

"Mr. De Berg, welcome to the Rakbu," Inanna replied.

"She is an impressive ship, Princess. Cutler told me what you did for Earth yesterday. On behalf of humanity, thank you."

"It is strange, Mr. De Berg, to hear one of my brother's top leaders on Earth thanking me for destroying an Anunnaki vessel."

"I'm an inhabitant of the earth, Princess, and two-thirds human. His Majesty's attack assaulted my home. I didn't appreciate his lack of warning."

"Is that the only reason for your displeasure, Mr. De Berg?"

"There may be other reasons," De Berg smiled. "Please call me Bill. May I call you Inanna?"

Inanna assented with a wave of her hand.

"Inanna, why have you asked me here? I have a meeting with your brother in 40 minutes."

"Bill, do you know the woman lying on the bed?" Inanna asked.

De Berg recognized Maria immediately, but wanted to hide his familiarity. He turned, as if intensely studying her. "I believe it's the reporter . . . Maria . . . Maria Love, isn't it?"

"Mr. De Berg, I am Mistress Inanna's Chief Medical Officer Enti. Maria is pregnant."

De Berg maintained his well-practiced poker face. "That's nice. Did you invite me here to share this news?"

"Dr. Enti ran a DNA scan on the baby. Do you know who Maria is married to?" asked Inanna.

"Should I?" De Berg asked.

"Dr. Enti," encouraged Inanna.

"Sir, I scanned the baby and found that it has 82 percent Anunnaki DNA."

"Eight-two percent," De Berg blurted involuntarily.

"I ran the baby's DNA against our Earth database," continued Enti. "I found one match."

"Who matched?" De Berg asked.

"You matched, sir. Maria's baby is your great grandson," replied Enti.

"How's that possible? I have no children," asked De Berg trying to preserve his secret. "You know any child of a Cadre member must be reported and presented to the king."

"Indeed," said Inanna. "Yet, this baby, his father, and his grandfather were never made members of The Cadre. Why?"

De Berg froze for a moment, considering whether to trust Inanna or continue his charade. She had gone to battle against an Anunnaki ship to protect Earth. Maybe it made her a trust-worthy ally.

"Inanna, I believe we've been fighting in a common cause for many years, but on separate fronts," De Berg said. "Your actions yesterday proved to me that you're on humanity's side. I'm going to trust you with the truth, well, my truth."

Inanna listened intently, as De Berg recounted the story of his son's birth and his deception. When he finished, she said, "I am not aware of any human in the past 5,000 years having the courage to go against the Anunnaki crown so overtly."

Now it was Inanna's turn to test De Berg. "You must hate us."

"I don't hate the Anunnaki. I'm one-third Anunnaki. If the Anunnaki people knew the truth about humanity, I doubt they would condone their king's actions on Earth."

The passion in De Berg's voice and the determination in his words reminded Inanna of her own. "Yes. There has been a mas-sive historical injustice done to humanity. I have made it my mis-sion to set it straight."

"Mr. Cutler shared some of your activities with me, but I had no idea you were prepared to do battle with Anunnaki ships in defense of humanity."

"Are you familiar with the Anunnaki *Book of Possibilities*, Bill?"

"I've heard of it—never read it."

"That book flows with the wisdom of The Father Creator. It says, 'Pray for peace. Work for peace. Injustice is not peace. To achieve justice, you may have to break the peace.' I've spent much of my life embodying those first two phrases in that verse—hoping my brother would see reason on The Human Question. Yesterday it became necessary to invoke the last."

De Berg eyed Inanna with admiration. "Well, your actions

change the equation and my thinking."

De Berg shifted gears again. "Why are you so interested in my great grandson?"

"Because your great grandson is my grandson," confessed Inanna.

"He's *your* grandson?"

"Yes. Maria is biologically my half-daughter. She is 49 percent Anunnaki. That is why her baby and your grandson's baby is 82 percent Anunnaki."

"I knew it!" enthused De Berg, "When I watched Maria on TV, she looked so . . . Anunnaki. I suppose this practically makes us family."

"I suppose it does. What should we do about Jack . . . I mean your grandson?" asked Inanna.

"He must be told nothing! I'm about to embark on a course that will place Maria and him in great danger, if his true identity becomes known."

"I think that requires some explanation," Inanna said, concern growing on her face.

"One day you can tell him, Inanna, but not now!"

"Shouldn't you be the one to tell him, Bill?"

De Berg ignored the question. "Your brother proved yesterday he's capable of anything. I've wanted to challenge him for a long while. Finally, I'm ready."

"Challenging my brother is a dangerous course. Even I did not choose it without trepidation," said Inanna.

"Nor have I, Mistress. That's why Jack's identity must remain our secret. If Jack's exposed, I'm exposed. If I'm exposed, a project vital to Earth's defense is in peril," De Berg cautioned.

"What project is that?"

De Berg hesitated. "Inanna, Mr. Cutler is ardent in his loyalty to me. He's helped me many times in my quiet struggle for humanity. About 15 earth years ago, he stole a schematic from you. I've invested $2 trillion of my own money in its design and construction. It's the most highly classified project on Earth."

"What did he steal?"

Again, De Berg dodged Inanna's question. "Your actions have proven you a worthy ally. I have a gift for you, Inanna, actually 20 of them. They strengthen your hand and shift the balance of power in Earth Space. These gifts are yours. The price is your promise not to reveal my secret."

Inanna paused and calculated. She wondered what this Cadre member could offer her to change the balance of power. She knew that without help defending Earth Space was impossible. "If it is for the protection of humanity, then you have my word."

"I've been summoned into a meeting today with King Ea. I plan to deliver an ultimatum to your brother. I don't expect to survive. You will have delivery of the gifts within the hour."

"How will I recognize the gifts?"

"Trust me. You will recognize the gifts and you will know what to do with them. Those who are delivering them have been informed that you are to take possession immediately."

Inanna reached out and held both of De Berg's hands in hers. She purposefully gazed into his eyes. "Thank you. I will put your gift to good use, Bill. I will make sure your contribution to this cause is known far and wide."

"Promise me that you will not tell Jack and Maria about me or about their genetics of their baby—not yet," requested De Berg.

"Jack has strong doubts about this entire situation," Inanna said. "He must know at some point. I have looked into the TimeCube. He becomes indispensable to our cause."

"Perhaps he will, Inanna, but no yet. Please honor my wishes."

Inanna was tired of secrets, but honoring sacrifice must come first. "Your generosity has changed the destiny of our cause. I give you my word. I will not share this with them now. At some point, it may be necessary, but for now I promise my silence."

"That's all I ask. I must be going. I don't want to keep your brother waiting. If this is my death sentence, I'll go memorably. Let it attract help and resources to our cause. Please don't interfere with my death."

"Send my regards to my brother," smiled Inanna knowingly.

De Berg smiled back and vanished in the bluish beam.

(54)
Score One for the Humans

King Ea was in a particularly bad mood and he planned to take it out on The Cadre today. In his mind, their inability to maintain his brand of order on Earth had forced him to attack. The mission's failure only raised his ire. Again, his sister and her magnificent ship stood in his way. He was determined to change the situation and change it now.

In the king's mind, a state of war now existed between Nibiru and Inanna, along with her human allies. He was angry and embarrassed by his taskforce's inability to deliver a decisive victory. He planned to make Inanna and Earth pay.

The king's chief of staff appeared in front of the throne on De Berg's video screen first. "All rise and make known your allegiance to King Ea."

Everyone in the room and on the videoconference was expected to stand and recite the loyalty oath to the king.

O mighty king—protector and defender of Nibiru
Grace us with your wisdom and strength
Sworn to your allegiance am I!

De Berg stood and recited the oath as he had hundreds of times before. He placed his closed fist over his heart on the last line in unison with everyone else. The words seemed empty and hollow and he wondered how many of his colleagues felt the same way. It mattered not. Today his blind allegiance ended.

He anticipated King Ea would meet his rebellion with the most final of responses. A few other Cadre members had challenged the king in the past. They paid with their lives. However, those members were all bark. De Berg had come equipped with a bite.

The king seated himself upon his throne. De Berg saw the usual cast of characters on the Nibiruan side of the conference, with one exception. Oddly enough, his old friend Senator Enki was present. On the human side, only the most senior Cadre members were present—including De Berg and Mason.

"Ladies and gentlemen," began the king with a conciliatory smile, "I have called you here today to speak with you about our Earth problem. This past week I dispatched a taskforce to Earth. By my command, the taskforce was sent to restore order in the Earth system. As an Anunnaki protectorate, key to Nibiru's economic success, Earth must honor all trading agreements with our trade partners."

"Majesty," interjected Mason, "The Cadre has and continues to act in good faith on all trade agreements. I assure you—"

"Mr. Mason, I received a formal complaint from the Z ambassador. One of his science ships, operating legally in Earth Space, was fired upon and driven from the system."

"Majesty, as you know, we lack ships or weaponry to challenge a Z vessel. It could not have been an Earth ship," offered Heinrich Ruthmeister, The Cadre Council President.

"I'm not accusing you of attacking the ship, Mr. Ruthmeister. I realized your pitiful resources are inadequate to do so. My sister, Princess Inanna, was the culprit. I blame The Cadre for permitting conditions on Earth that allow my sister to believe there is hope for her little rebellion. You've allowed too much openness and too much discussion of off-world matters. This fueled the fire leading to my attack. I acted to protect trade and to remind everyone on this call who is in control on Earth."

De Berg had heard many blustery speeches by the king over the years. He bided his time, waiting for an opening.

"Our taskforce was brutally attacked by the Rakbu. Several of my finest warships were lost. An honored war hero and my friend—Admiral Ninn—died."

"Before Admiral Ninn died, he bravely fired upon five Earth capitals. With the glorious words, 'Vengeance is mine sayeth the Lord.' He reminded humanity to honor and respect their gods. As in the days of old, sin has gone unpunished for too long. Human beings have become too free, too loose, and too sure of themselves. We have fostered a false sense of entitled self-esteem. These are not traits leading to productive workers and growing bottom lines."

Ruthmeister began, "Majesty, if I may say—"

"No, you may not say anything, Mr. Ruthmeister. I'm not here to hear your opinions. I'm here to give you your opinions. The Cadre is responsible for the economic performance of Earth, Inc. Fear of the gods—well fear of my father and me—worked for thousands of years. You have created a system where fear of the gods is no more. You have attempted to remove me from discourse by replacing me with science and reason. Don't think I don't know what you're doing! By placing science, reason and economics before me, you have made yourselves the center of attention."

Murmuring filled the room and the conference bridge.

King Ea continued. "Mark my words. Despite Inanna's temporary victory, I will restore the rightful distinction between Heaven and Earth, between gods and humans. Either The Cadre will support that goal and execute against it or there will be no more Cadre."

"Perhaps, Majesty, if we had known of these concerns, we

could have acted," suggested Mason.

There was silence in the room and on the conference bridge. King Ea sat and seethed. Suddenly he swiveled his throne around to face Senator Enki, seated behind him and to the left.

"We have with us today the man who created humans and never lost his soft spot for them—my uncle—Senator Enki."

Mumbling again filled the room.

"Since the beginning, uncle, you have sided with the humans. You gave them technology and culture when Kings Anu and Enlil expressly forbid it. You preserved them when we destroyed the world with a flood. Now you side with my sister and against Nibiru. What have you to say, old man?"

The smart conference camera centered and zoomed in on Enki. He was exceptionally aged, even for an Anunnaki. He gathered his wisdom and his dignity and responded, "What is one to do, oh king, when the laws of nature and of The Father Creator counter the king's wishes?"

King Ea flew into a furor. He pointed his finger in rage. "You are the one who disobeyed the laws of nature by artificially creating this species! You are the one who has consistently violated this crown's key directives against helping them. They were built to be a servant race and you have tried to break them of their servant mentality. You and Inanna have convinced them they can aspire for the heavens and become our equals!"

"It is true, nephew," said Enki dropping titles, "I violated the primary rules of nature. That sin is mine alone. My redemption has been to work tirelessly to correct the fallout from those actions. Rather than admit our error, we continue to compound it. You did so again this week by attacking the humans. They are a sentient race ready to join the galactic community."

"Are you or are you not in league with my sister, the Princess? Have you or have you not sanctioned her attack on Anunnaki ships?" Ea demanded.

"Inanna sees the wrong as I see the wrong," Enki responded. "I have worked to change things in my way and she has worked to change them in hers. All the might of Nibiru does not and can never make this right, Majesty."

"That is your admission of guilt, old man! Guards," called out the king, "take my uncle into custody."

Two guards grabbed Enki roughly and yanked him from his seat.

"By my decree, a state of war now exists between Nibiru and Earth. Royal blood or not, any Anunnaki defending the humans is a traitor. You will be dealt with as such."

De Berg watched with anger. To see is secret friend and ally of many years arrested, was the last straw.

"Now that I've handled him," started the king, "Let's get back to the incompetence displayed by The Cadre."

De Berg interrupted, "Majesty—"

"I am not finished, Mr. De Berg. Do not worry. You will get your chance. If The Cadre were doing its job properly, we would not have these problems. I give you all the resources you need to keep Earth, Inc. running smoothly and this is thanks I get—a planet out of control."

"Majesty, we understand your frustration. If you had made us aware of your displeasure, we could have abated your wrath," Mason said.

"Do not play word games with me, Mr. Mason," Ea retorted.

"Your handling of the attack proves again your incompetence. I am trying to deliver a message from the heavens and your planetary spin masters have everyone believing it was an asteroid."

Mason tried again. "Majesty, it's not my intention to play word games with you. Your non-disclosure policy is crystal clear. The Cadre has worked tirelessly to deflect and ridicule all assertions of your existence, as you have commanded. Then you surprise us with this attack. What were we supposed to do, suddenly admit the existence of an extraterrestrial civilization laying waste to our cities?"

"Do not place this on me, Mason. That is a dangerous course."

De Berg's patience burst. "Perhaps if his Majesty had let The Cadre know about the attack beforehand, rather than allowing us to find out along with everyone else—"

"How dare you, De Berg! Do not overestimate yourself in my eyes, hybrid. You run planet Earth for me. I allow you power and riches in return, but I have no more regard for you than I do any other human."

"That's been crystal clear to me for some time, Majesty." De Berg shot back. "That's why I have taken action to change it."

"Do not trifle with me, De Berg. I have no compunctions about ending you."

"Then I'll be direct, Majesty. Over the past 20 years, I've diverted trillions of dollars of my personal wealth and the resources of several of my companies to the most top-secret project in Earth history—secret even from you, Majesty. I obtained the blueprints of Princess Inanna's ship—the Rakbu. We have constructed five Rakbu-Class vessels. As of about an hour ago, they are under the command of Princess Inanna and patrolling Earth Space. Within three days, she will receive fifteen more. I trust, after last week's events, you understand the prowess of these vessels. I believe one defeated 11 of the kings' finest ships."

"Bill!" pleaded Mason.

"It's enough, Howard. We've put up with enough. We've been repressed and diminished over and over again."

"Who are we, Bill? You have a good life and so do I," Mason responded.

"Humans, Howard. Perhaps, you can forget your human side, but I won't. We live at the expense of our fellow humans. We withhold technologies that could end poverty and cure disease to pad our wallets. We walk into these meetings and swear allegiance to a king who would swat us like a fly."

"Security!" shouted the king, "Find De Berg. I want his head! You will be an example, De Berg, of what happens to a humans or hybrids who challenges this government."

De Berg rose. "You want the earth and I deny you the earth. You want me dead, but I deny you the pleasure of killing me. If this is war, Majesty, then let me be the first casualty."

De Berg took a knife from his pocket and sliced himself below the right collarbone, exposing his Cadre implant. "Score one for the humans!" he shouted.

There was a short delay and then an explosion. De Berg's conference connection went black.

An enraged Ea stormed from the conference room. One of his aides, uncomfortably, ended the conference.

De Berg's mangled body materialized on a bed in the Rakbu's hospital. "We have him, Mistress," said Dr. Enti.

"How bad is he?" questioned Inanna from the bridge.

"He has massive damage to multiple organs and systems. I can fabricate replacements for much of the physical damage, but he has severe brain trauma and is in a coma."

"Can he be saved?"

"I will do my best, Mistress. May I remind you that his explicit instructions were for us to let him be a martyr for this cause?"

"I know," reflected Inanna, "but I need him. Despite declaring war on my brother, he still has vast resources, connections, and experience. Our cause needs him. Do your best, doctor."

(55)
In the News

"Thank you for watching ANN. I'm Chip Benson. Let's take a look at today's headlines."

"Mason Industries, the world's largest defense contractor, today announced a $30 billion contract with the Pentagon to develop an orbiting asteroid defense system. The announcement comes in the wake of last week's devastating asteroid hits around the world."

"Government watchdog groups are criticizing the deal. We have ANN's Pentagon Correspondent Steve Benson with us. Steve, what are watchdog groups concerned about?"

"Good morning, Chip. Several Pentagon watchdog groups are complaining about this contract, citing a conflict of interest on the part of Secretary of Defense Hackett."

"What is the perceived conflict of interest?" asked Kelly.

"Well, Chip, by law, Secretary Hackett's assets reside in a blind trust. However, his consulting firm regularly does work for Mason Industries. Hackett served as Chief Operating Officer at Mason for the three years leading up to his appointment as Secretary of Defense."

"Steve, what is the secretary saying about these accusations?" Kelly asked.

"Mostly, Secretary Hackett has avoided directly responding to the issue, other than to say he's too busy working to keep the country protected to pay attention. Pentagon spokesmen have come out over the past 24 hours and defended Hackett's ties to Mason Industries."

"And what are his intermediaries saying?"

"They argue Hackett has divested all financial interest in Mason Industries and that he no longer has any formal ties to the company. They have also said Mason Industries is the only company possessing the technology needed to build these systems. They are not going to let the appearance of conflict of interest prevent them from keeping Americans safe."

"Thank you. That's Steve Benson at the Pentagon."

Kelly went on to the next story. "Senator Clare David made headlines yesterday by announcing she plans to ask former ANN White House Correspondent Maria Love to testify before her committee. She wants to ask Love about a purported conversation she had with President Paxton before his assassination.

"We are joined by Senator David, Republican from Indiana. She chairs the Senate Homeland Security and Governmental Affairs Committee. Thank you for joining us, senator."

"It's my pleasure, Chip."

"So, you have asked our former colleague—Maria Love—to testify before your committee. Why? Do you put stock in Ms. Love's claim of a government cover-up on the issue of aliens?"

"Chip, Ms. Love asked a President of the United States a question about an issue clearly impacting national security. It's my understanding she later met with President Paxton and discussed the issue further. I want to know whether this information is valid and what threat it poses to U.S. national security. It's really that simple."

"Senator, and forgive me, you have a reputation for being somewhat of a . . . rebel. Do you believe the U.S. government is covering up knowledge of UFOs? Isn't that . . . kind of . . . out there?"

"Chip, if people want to call me a rebel because I'm always searching for the truth, so be it. I don't have an opinion on Ms. Love's information. In fact, I've seen no documentation and I haven't spoken to Ms. Love. She made provocative statements and asked provocative questions. The American people have a right to know whatever she thinks she knows."

"Good enough. Senator Clare David, thank you for your time today."

Kelly continued. "Speaking of UFOs, a new study published this week by the International Psychological Council discovered something fascinating. The study reports that human beings tend to believe bizarre things, however unlikely, when they fit into their life narratives. Dr. Bernard Gearhart, the lead researcher, cited this week's asteroid strikes as evidence."

"Gearhart insisted and I quote, 'Humans like to put a reason to events. The randomness of asteroid strikes is psychologically frightening. A reason—any reason—is preferred over the randomness of the Universe.' His statement comes amid a proliferation of polls showing large majorities of the world's people believe their governments are hiding facts about last week's asteroid strikes. Those same polls show 25 percent of the world's population believes last week's events were some kind of alien attack."

"Finally, something for the good news file. The Global Missing Person Network reports that instances of reported missing persons have dropped precipitously in the past eight months. In a press release, the group noted the decrease is global and they can point to no reason for the reduction. Perhaps, we have to accept good news sometimes and not ask why."

"Those are this morning's headlines. I'm Chip Benson. This is ANN."

(56)
The Next Realm

De Berg regained awareness in a bizarre place. He floated weightless and dimensionless in a pitch-black void. The only things punctuating the darkness were two exceptionally vivid bodies spinning in their orbits around their equally colorful stars. These were not models, but dynamic living representations of these bodies, or perhaps the actual worlds. He immediately recognized the large rust-colored Nibiru and her brown dwarf star and the smaller, but more beautiful, Earth chasing her Sun.

"Well, I didn't expect this," he muttered aloud. His voice made no sound in the environment, but he heard it in his mind.

"What did you expect, Mr. De Berg?" came a voice beaming into his mind from every direction.

"Who is that?" De Berg asked.

"I am that which has made all of this," the voice replied.

"All of what?" De Berg thought, realizing he could now speak in his mind as well.

"All that is, my child. What did you expect?" repeated the voice.

"I don't know, really. I think I expected there to be nothing . . . no continuation of me . . . an ending. I activated the micro explosive below my collar bone and . . ." De Berg said reaching for his collarbone, only to realize his disembodied state.

"Yes. There are so many philosophies about what happens after your physical deaths. Generally, I try to play along with your beliefs and give you what you expect."

"You never really answered me. Who are you?" De Berg asked again.

"I am that which created all of this. In your terms, I am The Father Creator."

"And where am I?"

"You are in an exceptional place, Mr. De Berg. Your selfless action moved an issue near and dear to me significantly forward. I thought you deserved to have a catbird's seat to watch how it plays out," Father Creator said.

"You mean the conflict between Earth and Nibiru?"

"Yes."

"Do you have the power to help Earth; to help break free from Nibiruan yolk?"

"Of course I could. Everything is possible to me."

"If you have the power to change the situation between Earth and Nibiru," De Berg began angrily, "Why haven't you? Why have you allowed this abomination to continue for so long?"

"Your anger is a residue of your long stay in time and space," said Father Creator. "It will pass soon enough. You will gain control again."

"No, I choose to be angry," De Berg confirmed. "How can you be our . . . our God . . . and permit this?"

"And what would you have me do, Mr. De Berg? What would be fair in your terms?"

"Stop the Anunnaki exploitation of Earth! For goodness sake, stop allowing them to masquerade around as . . . as you."

The Father Creator laughed.

"This's not funny," protested De Berg.

"Mr. De Berg, your unusual position on Earth has stilted your view of power. You think power is about manipulating those in your sphere of influence. It is not."

"That's just double-talk for inaction."

"You see, there's this little rule in my universe and even I refuse to violate it. You call it free will. As sentient beings in my universe, you all want it. However, few of you really understand its implications."

"Free will? A true leader does not allow his flock to choose what is bad for them. Is that to be your excuse?"

"Yes!" Father Creator strongly and loudly affirmed. "Every sentient being, indeed every molecule, in my realm has free will. It is my gift to you. Free will grows and advances all things. Free will *is* evolution. Without it, the universe would just be me catching your fly balls for you."

De Berg was a big baseball fan and he smiled at the reference. However, he would not allow these silver words to sidestep his righteous indignation. "Your gift of free will has allowed technologically superior races to enslave the human race. How can a species have free will, if it is manipulated and the truth is hidden?"

"You see free will as the problem, when I know it to be the solution," Father Creator said.

"The solution to what?"

"It's the solution to every puzzle facing humanity, the Anunnaki, and every other sentient race in my realm. Where you see a problem, I see a challenge."

"You said my actions changed the situation between Nibiru and Earth. How? By giving humanity weapons that create the potential for these two races to destroy each other?"

"That's the negative view, Mr. De Berg. What you have actually done is given everyone a choice. You have given them the gift of free will. They may use it to destroy each other or they may use it to change."

"That's an awful big risk to run. Why don't you just intervene and fix it?"

"I anticipated your questions and concerns, Mr. De Berg. You believe using my power to intervene and to fix things is a black and white issue. You're about to learn how difficult it truly is."

"I don't think it's difficult at all," De Berg answered. "You simply have to be clear on what you stand for."

"Then let the class begin," Father Creator said.

"What class?"

"We're going to test your theory. I've granted you a bird's eye view the standoff between Nibiru and Earth. I'm giving you full power to intervene in this situation however you choose."

"By full power, I assume you mean there are no limits on my actions?"

"None save the consequences. Remember, every action has consequences. Consequences are free will in action," Father Creator instructed. "Even God cannot avoid consequences. Choose wisely, Mr. De Berg."

"Great! Let's get started."

"There's information you need before you begin. Things are not completely as they seem," Father Creator warned.

"Debrief me. I'm ready."

Father Creator smiled. "Your race and the Anunnaki exist on the fourth dimension. Your dimension—"

"You mean third don't you?" De Berg interrupted.

"I mean fourth. In your dimension, you can manipulate height, width, and depth. Time—the fourth dimension—acts upon beings in your dimension. You have no control over it. It flows in one direction."

"I'm having flashbacks to calculus classes at Yale," smiled De Berg.

"You think the Anunnaki completely control the dynamics

between Earth and Nibiru. They do not. There is a fifth dimension race called the Savestran. They have chosen to interfere and are threatening both Nibiru and Earth."

"So, what's the fifth dimension?"

"In the fifth dimension, time becomes fungible the way height, width, and depth are in your dimension. Beings occupying the fifth dimension arrived there one of two ways. Spiritual races evolved their minds and their souls to the point of ascension. Races like the Savestran achieved this level through eons of technological advancement. However, they arrive there without having resolved their selfishness, anger, and possessiveness. This makes them a great danger."

"How do the dimensions interact with each other?"

"Fourth-dimensional creatures are at a huge disadvantage against fifth dimension beings. The ability to manipulate time is a game changer and they can do it in the fourth dimension as well. What's an analogy? Remember time is action and movement. Think of a keyboard and computer screen. A third-dimensional being is able to observe the screen, but lacking time, he cannot type on the keyboard. The first three dimensions are static realms. The fourth dimension is the first dimension where movement, change, and action are possible. You can type on the keyboard, but you have no delete key. Once you type something, it remains. The fifth dimension adds the delete key. Fifth-dimensional beings can see the screen, type on the keyboard, and erase what they have typed."

"So, theoretically the Savestran could change the history of the fourth dimension?" asked De Berg.

"Change, undo, erase," replied Father Creator.

"Wow!"

"For our experiment, I'll place you in the sixth dimension. From there, you possess virtual god-like powers in both the fourth and fifth dimension. Be warned, though, the Savestran are highly developed fifth-dimensional beings. They have developed new technologies placing them on the doorstep to sixth-dimensional transition. They are a formidable adversary and you are operating in realms you won't completely understand."

"I'm up for a challenge," De Berg boasted. "Tell me about the sixth dimension."

"Ah, the sixth dimension," mused Father Creator. "The sixth dimension is the first dimension where everyday reality becomes a paradox. Sixth-dimensional beings are no longer stuck in a single timeline. They are capable of recognizing and existing in multiple timelines—even timelines that contradict. They are aware their choices create new timelines, but conscious control of this process does not come until the seventh dimension."

"How does that work?"

"You must experience it to understand. Let's go visit your next realm. There will be disorientation at first."

Reality seemed to blink off and on again. When De Berg's vision returned, he viewed strange images.

"What do you see?" Father Creator asked.

"I see two clocks with fast-moving hands. One clock is moving clockwise and the other counterclockwise. I see the seven colors of the rainbow separately and all at once. I see two equations. The first reads two and two equals four. The second reads two plus two does not equal four."

"Your fourth-dimensional mind is interpreting what you see very literally. It's trying to make sense of the contradictions. Your vision will improve," promised The Father Creator. "I've delivered you to the sixth dimension. I've given you absolute power in the situation concerning Nibiru and Earth. Good luck."

"But . . . wait . . . how will I know what to do?" De Berg felt The Father Creator's presence departing.

"You won't. Follow your principles. Trust free will," answered The Father Creator's disembodied voice.

De Berg thought, *this could be the end of everything or the beginning of something amazing.*

The outcomes of both ideas immediately manifested before him. He focused on canceling the two thoughts and they vanished. He asked for the power. He bragged how we would use it. The Father Creator obliged. He sat and he watched Earth and Nibiru waiting for his chance to intervene.

(57)
Ea and Enki

Enki sat alone in his cell. He sensed the ravages of age sneaking up behind him, ready to snatch him without notice. Fatigue was his constant companion.

I have fought the good fight, but my time is at hand, he thought.

Enki found no absolution to escape his central role, his responsibility in the drama between the Anunnaki and the humans. Creating the worker race had been his idea. His genetic brilliance, after much trial and error, finally brought the race to life. He was first to recognize human sentience. He had invested the past 30,000 earth years into helping the humans, where and when he could. He tirelessly campaigned against his father, his brother, and finally his nephew for disclosure and transparency on The Human Question.

Now, finally, his support of human beings had landed him in this cell—disgraced as a traitor by his nephew's controlled media. In the old days, he had the resiliency to rebound and fight back. Now he longed only for a reunion with The Father Creator.

The fate of Disclosure—his life's work—now rested in Inanna's hands. She was capable, but her illness limited her window of opportunity. He feared for the cause and for the species of his creation. King Ea and the Anunnaki elite were determined to allow humanity to labor under misguided perceptions of the universe and of God.

A clamor arose outside his cell. He recognized the metal-on-metal sound and the cadenced marching of the king's Royal Guard. They dressed in ridiculous ancient garb and carried swords and shields. They were the personal security detail for the king. The sound stopped and the cell door slid aside with a *whoosh*.

King Ea entered. He gave orders to secure the door and it swished closed behind him. Ea's imposing frame hovered above Enki, who lay curled up on the floor against the wall.

"I would speak with you, uncle," Ea began with a carefully affected arrogance.

"I have nothing to say to you, Majesty," replied a disinterested Enki, purposely averting the king's gaze.

"Come now, uncle, certainly you are angry with me for incarcerating you. You could at least acknowledge that anger."

"Is the King of Nibiru now my counselor?" asked an amused Enki.

The king's face sobered. "You don't need a counselor, old man. What you need is justice and you shall have it soon enough."

"Justice? From you, Majesty? I have no such expectation. It is almost a contradiction in terms."

"You knew about De Berg's fleet, didn't you?" accused the king.

"I have no intention of telling you anything, Ea," declared Enki dropping ranks. "You might as well send your interrogators in to beat it out of me."

"You know, uncle," Ea softened, "You need not die. I can still spare your life, if you will only help me do what is best for Nibiru."

"I have watched you for many years, Ea, and we do not agree on what is best for Nibiru. I base my philosophy on freedom and transparency at home and on Earth. You base yours on secrecy and control. Those ships—"

"Those 20 ships will make no difference in the outcome," promised the king.

"Twenty Rakbu-class warships provide Earth Space with a significant deterrent to your aggression, Ea."

"You don't have all the information, uncle. You think I refuse movement on The Human Question because I am stubborn and selfish. It is to protect Nibiru that I maintain my policies."

Enki let out a hearty laugh. "How is your continued domination and deception of the humans protecting Nibiru? I think it protects your profits and that of your friends," asserted an incredulous Enki.

"There are . . . forces . . . very powerful forces that have threatened Nibiru, if I change course on The Human Question."

"Who has threatened Nibiru? The Z?"

"No. The Z Alliance is no threat," replied Ea.

"Then who?" demanded Enki.

"Uncle," began a now clearly shaken Ea, "Have you ever had communication with anyone besides The Father Creator in your ascension room?"

Enki stared at his nephew puzzling over the question. "Inanna is the only one who has a direct connection to The Father Creator. No one else has for a thousand shars."

"Perhaps, but I mean from other life forms?"

Enki squinted at his nephew. "I've never known the ascension rooms to open doorways to any reality, but an experience of The Father Creator.

"You and my father never had communication with a fifth dimension race that warned you not to create the humans?"

Enki stared at the ground and then back at the king. "The Savestran?"

"Yes. The Savestran."

The king paused, studying his elderly uncle. "You know, uncle, despite my father's differences with you, he always respected your judgment."

"Do you require my judgment, Majesty?" Enki asked.

"I require your loyalty. I require your trust. I require your help to prevent catastrophe for our people. You must help me stop Inanna from disclosing the truth to the humans."

"I will never abandon—"

"Let me guess—your principles? Don't be so quick to deny me! The fate of Nibiru is at stake." interrupted Ea.

"Nibiru is not at stake. The Father Creator would never allow it."

"The Savestran warned my father and you. They told you they had an interest in keeping the humans in the dark and controlled. My father recognized the wisdom in it. You, however, have worked much of your life to undo that control."

"I didn't take them seriously. I wasn't even sure they were real. Enlil believed it more than I did."

"They are quite real," assured the king. "After you helped the humans gain culture and technology, they warned that you had 6,000 years to persuade them that humanity did not threaten them. The 6,000 years are up and they are not persuaded."

"Humanity is no threat to them! They are delusional," Enki argued. "The Father Creator assured me that by advancing the humans spiritually and technologically and putting them in direct contact with him, the Savestran would be no threat. But—"

"But you failed! And now the comeuppance has arrived."

"You have prevented their natural progression. Still, we are very close, Ea. The Savestran fear humanity. Together we can defeat them."

"It no longer matters. The Savestran are energetic beings. They benefit from the energy generated by humanity. They view earth as their . . . feeding ground . . . in a matter of speaking."

"What do you mean they are benefiting from the energy of the humans?" Enki implored.

"They feed on negative energy somehow . . . on fear. They like the humans afraid. Our system of setting one group against another has made humanity perfect for their needs," relayed Ea.

Enki thought for a moment. "But if we move to Disclosure and the mood lightens, they lose their energetic feeding ground. That's all the more reason not to cave into these beings and their evil intentions, Ea!"

"They are concerned that Disclosure of our activities may expose theirs as well. They are willing to help us maintain our control over the earth. If we refuse to comply, they promise to destroy Nibiru by undoing the very timeline that brought us into existence. I will not lose all we have accomplished on my watch!"

"The Father Creator will not allow it," Enki declared.

"It is free will, uncle, free will. The Father Creator will not interfere. When I began receiving these messages, I implored The Father Creator for his help. He will not come to me."

"Are you proposing that we keep the humans in the dark and continue to allow these beings to feed upon them?"

"Don't be dramatic! They are not actually feeding on the humans. They merely feed on the negative energy generated by all the anger, hatred, and violence on Earth."

"It's the same thing, Ea. If we must keep the humans miserable, weak, and in the dark to satisfy them, we are responsible for the slavery of a sentient race."

Ea absorbed that comment and moved on. "There are many advantages to being in the fifth dimension, when interfering on the fourth. Past and future . . . any point in our space is an open door to them. They have capabilities far beyond any adversary we have ever faced."

"How do you know this is real and not just the figment of your imagination? Maybe they are bluffing." Enki probed.

"They gave me . . . they downloaded into my mind the specifications for a space gate technology far beyond our current capabilities. I am having it built. Where I can send a few individuals through one of our current gates, this technology allows me to put an entire army on Earth or Inanna's ship for that matter. De Berg's new fleet would be useless in defending the earth."

"You're mad. You cannot do that," Enki pleaded.

"I can and I will. They have shown me things too—events that are to be. Not probabilities like our TimeCube technology. These are guaranteed events that cannot be altered," Ea said with satisfaction. "Cheer up, uncle. You are to be a great-great uncle."

Enki looked at Ea with confusion. "What do you mean?"

"Come now, old man. There is no reason to hide your involvement in this plot any longer. The Savestran have told me everything. They told me about Inanna's and your plan to produce an heir that could take over the crown when I am no more. They told me about your scheme to reveal the truth to the President of the United States on live ITV. I put a stop to that too. I'm virtually omnipotent with their help."

"I don't know what they have told you, Ea, but I am telling you that all we want is transparency for the humans. We want them to be free to decide their own course and free of the fear we have kept them in all of these millennia. We have no interest in taking the crown from you."

"Don't lie to me, old man. I could have you executed right now for your traitorous acts. Maria Love is having a baby that is 82 percent Anunnaki with half Inanna's DNA and that of Bill De Berg's grandson. By Nibiruan law, that baby could become my heir, if I took him and raised him."

"What are you scheming, Ea?"

"I'm not scheming, uncle. I'm strategizing. I'm going to ready my new gate technology. I'm going to grab the child and ensure the proper future for Nibiru and Earth. We are working on the story about how I discovered he was my son right now. Then I am going to put an end to Inanna's little resistance movement. Finally, I am going to be the biggest hero in Nibiruan history—even bigger than my father—when I announce how I saved Nibiru and made us invincible through a new alliance with these fifth dimensional beings."

"Be careful, Ea. The one who rides the tiger often winds up inside. The Father Creator will never allow it. Inanna's connection to Him is strong."

"I'm beginning to wonder if The Father Creator isn't a figment of someone's imagination. The Savestran are real. Their threats are real and their promised rewards are real too."

Enki felt the frailty of his advanced age and felt helpless to stop the clandestine plans of his nephew. His only chance was to make Ea question the Savestran. "What if they are lying to you? What if we could defeat them together with the humans?"

"That is ridiculous. How could the humans help us against the Savestran?"

"There must be a reason the Savestran fear the humans. Maybe if we worked to help the humans move quickly forward and changed Earth's vibration, it would force the Savestran to lose interest."

"You forget that they know all our possible futures. Their fear is because of the distant future, not the present. That is why I am going to take control of the present to ensure that future never comes and our new alliance with the Savestran is secured."

Enki sunk to the cell bench, feeling old and defeated. "Your father and I should never have made that 6,000 year bargain with them. I only half-believed they were real. I certainly did not think they would carry out their threats against us or against humanity."

"We are where we are. It is either humanity or the Anunnaki. I intend to make sure Nibiru survives. I have initiated an operation to re-establish direct and firm Anunnaki control of Earth. Cheer up, uncle! My sister and you are going to get precisely what you want—full disclosure. You and your human allies may discover, however, that ignorance was bliss."

"What are you going to do, Ea?"

"You will see soon enough. For now, I have you where you can no longer interfere, old man. Guard!" shouted the king.

King Ea exited the detention room, Enki laid down on the stone bench that served as the cell's bed. He laced his bony and aged hands behind his head and closed his eyes.

"Father Creator," he said quietly, but aloud, "Why are you allowing all we have worked for to be destroyed? Have not Inanna and I faithfully pursued positive change for humanity? Why are you ignoring us now?"

An Image of De Berg passed before Enki in his imagination. His longtime friend and ally had sacrificed everything for the cause and now it was all for naught. De Berg reappeared and his image lingered, as if he was imprinted on the inside of Enki's eyelid. He was mouthing something, but Enki could hear nothing. He seemed to be mouthing the same words repeatedly.

Now Enki felt a powerful static charge in the air around him. His consciousness began to swirl faster and faster around a center point. He opened his eyes, but the intensity of the sensations grew stronger. A purple vortex filled his vision and encased him. De Berg's image appeared randomly on the inside of the vortex and he continued to mouth his message.

A massive suction grabbed Enki and pulled him through the

bottom of the funnel and into a long tunnel. He felt his form and his consciousness being pulled and stretched by the force pulling him through the electrically charged conduit. It seemed to go on to infinity. De Berg's words were becoming almost audible and then suddenly they boomed like the sound of thunder.

He was saying, "Change the game!"

(58)

And Baby Makes Three

Maria awakened in the Rakbu's hospital. She recognized her surroundings, but couldn't remember how she arrived there. She remembered Hackett detaining and interrogating her at the Pentagon. Beyond that, things seemed foggy.

Dr. Enti's smiling face appeared above her. "She's awake, Mistress," he said.

"Welcome back, Maria," said Enti.

Descended from Earth's Lemurian civilization, Enti differed from other Anunnaki Maria encountered—Inanna included. The man possessed a Zen quality that created palpable serenity in his presence. His warm smile seemed more human than Anunnaki. His family had largely intermarried with other Lemurians after their exodus to Nibiru. Enti retained the best qualities of the ancient Earth civilization.

Inanna didn't even take the time to walk down to the hospital. She appeared in a bluish beam of light and was instantly at Maria's side. She grabbed Maria's hand. "How are you feeling?"

"I'm a bit out of it. How long have I been here?"

"Three days."

"Three days! Jack is probably worried sick."

"He believes you are being detained by your government."

"I have so many questions, Inanna. Why did you disappear after they killed Paxton? I tried to contact you, but you didn't respond."

"My brother, the king, sent eleven warships to attack the earth. I was busy with them."

"Did that have something to do with the fireballs?"

"Those were not fireballs, Maria. One of the warships broke through and arrived at Earth ahead of me. They managed to attack five capital cities before I arrived."

"Why did King Ea attack Earth?"

"He sent the taskforce to bring me home and to remind humanity who was in charge. The commanding officer of the taskforce was ordered to attack Earth and demand humanity's unconditional surrender."

"I was able to stop them, but barely."

"Will he try again?"

"I'm sure of it. I shall be more prepared next time. We got help from an unexpected source today. I now have 20 Rakbu-class ships to defend Earth Space. That should cause him some hesitation."

"Defectors?" asked Maria.

"Not for you to worry about right now, my child," comforted Inanna.

Inanna smiled at Maria. Maria smiled back. Maria could feel the pulse running through Inanna's hands.

"What?" Maria finally asked.

"I have some good news. You are going to be a mother, Maria."

Maria laughed, thinking Inanna was kidding.

"Dr. Enti confirmed it."

"That's correct, Maria." said Enti, "You would have known soon, but I have the ability to determine it immediately after conception."

"Inanna, you know how I feel about bringing a baby into this world," Maria said, making an unsuccessful attempt to sit up.

"I'm not sure I want this . . . for me or the baby."

"Maria, The Father Creator has blessed you with a child. How can you say no to such a gift?"

"I'm not saying . . . no. I guess I'm just in shock."

"Do you want to know the sex?" Enti queried.

"I suppose so," replied Maria.

"You're going to have a boy," Inanna gushed, not waiting for Enti.

Maria smiled and thought of Jack. Then she remembered their blowup over her story and her experiences with Inanna. "Jack doesn't believe in . . . any of this, you know. He believes you're some kind of fallen angel and a threat to his belief system."

Inanna wanted to comfort Maria. She wanted to share what she learned about Jack's future in the TimeCube and share his DNA lineage. Instead, she smiled and said, "I know, Maria. You are just going to have to convince him. Now you have a reason to persuade him your path is creating a different world for your child."

"The timing of this baby . . . it's just not good for us," Maria managed, as she struggled to sit up again.

"The *Book of Possibilities* states, 'The Father Creator brings all things into being at just the right moment for the fulfillment of the universe's perfection.' I believe that, Maria. I know you will find a purpose in this happy event."

"I hope you're right. What about our mission? Paxton's dead. I'm pregnant. Your brother is trying to destroy Earth cities. Can we achieve The Future Possible?"

Inanna shook her head, "The TimeCube is unclear. It only indicates some big event is about to occur. What it is or its significance remains hidden from us."

"What do we do next?" asked Maria.

"You head home. You share your good news with Jack. The birth pangs of this big event may already be stirring," Inanna said.

"What do you mean?"

"Senator Clare David has taken an interest in your information. She has subpoenaed you to appear before her committee to share what you know about Paxton's death and aliens. The hearing is in a few days. It will be broadcast on international ITV."

Maria sighed. "Is this a good time with your brother targeting Earth? I hoped for a break in the action."

"Maria, this is an opportunity to open more people to the truth. That must always be our foremost goal. Let me worry about my brother."

The two women smiled at each other. With each encounter, Maria felt her connection to Inanna grow. She almost considered her a second mother.

"Dr. Enti," called Maria, "Am I cleared to go home?"

"You are indeed," Enti assured.

Inanna and Maria walked to the transporter room. They embraced warmly. "Keep thinking about The Future Possible, Maria. Keep the faith. Focus on that new day upon the earth."

"Got it. The Future Possible," Maria repeated.

Maria stepped onto the transporter and disappeared.

Inanna lingered for a moment, thinking of Maria. An urgent call from the bridge forced her back to reality.

"Mistress, we have an intruder alert!"

"Where?" Inanna demanded.

"In the hospital, Mistress."

"Transport me and a security team to the hospital now."

Inanna materialized in sickbay. There she found an aged Anunnaki with his back to her and leaning over De Berg's comatose body. There was something familiar about the man. He turned to face Inanna.

"Greetings, my niece, the Princess Inanna," said Enki

"My uncle!" Inanna enthused. "How did you get here, My Lord?"

"Him," said Enki pointing to De Berg. "He and The Father Creator brought me here."

"How could De Berg—"

"I don't know," Enki shrugged his shoulders, "but he did. He must be working with The Father Creator."

"But I heard my brother, the king, had imprisoned you, My Lord."

"You're correct, Inanna. Our king came to visit me in my cell. He shared his plan to undo all we have accomplished with the humans. All seemed lost. That's when De Berg appeared. I was pulled into a vortex, through a tunnel, and finally appeared here on your ship."

"My uncle, we are pleased to have you as our guest. I will have someone prepare quarters for you. We will plan a feast in your honor, My Lord."

"There is no time for that, Inanna. We have been too passive. We will lose Earth and humanity, if we are not bold. The Father Creator appeared to me during my transit. His message to me, Inanna, was 'change the game' and change it we must!"

(59)
Maria Comes Home

Maria materialized behind her apartment building. She gathered herself and prepared to tell Jack the good news. He'd be happy. His mother would be happy. How sweet to finally please her!

Then a defiant thought passed through her mind. Why should she have to live up to anyone's expectations? Wasn't that part of the reason she embarked on this accidental journey? Didn't she want to know what lay beyond what society dictates?

Maria wanted this baby, but she wanted it for what it represented—The Future Possible. Despite everything she'd been through, she was now clear—the world did not have to be as it always had been. Humanity could aspire and achieve greater things. This baby could grow up in a world not constantly reliving past scars or cowering before future catastrophe. It could live as a free, reasoning human being completely connected to its universal source. These ideas exhilarated Maria, but she wanted Jack on the same page. More than anything, she wanted him to take her hand and walk willingly into this new world.

She jogged up the eight flights of stairs to their apartment. She paused outside the door, took a deep breath, and turned the doorknob. *For The Future Possible*, she thought.

"Jack?" she shouted, as she opened the door.

Jack came rushing around the corner into the living room in stocking feet, slipping and nearly breaking his neck. He gained his balance and rushed to Maria.

"I have never been so worried in my life," Jack said hugging her tightly and then kissing her softly. "I've pulled every string I had to pull, but no one knew where you were."

Maria absorbed the connection between them for a moment before speaking. "The men at our door were with the Defense Intelligence Agency. Hackett brought me in for interrogation."

"Hackett? Why would Defense want to interrogate you?"

Maria took Jack by the hand and led him over to the couch. "Jack, I need you to listen to me and hear me. This is important to me . . . to us. Hackett wanted to talk to me about some images taken by defense satellites during the attack on Saturday."

"What attack? Why would he want to question you about it?"

"Jack, the fireballs were not asteroids. A spacecraft entered orbit around the earth and fired weapons on the five capitals. This was a deliberate act of—"

"Maria, I agree," Jack interrupted. "We need to talk about this whole 'alien experience' you're having. I'm concerned about it. I'm worried you might be involved with something more sinister than you realize."

"Jack, please let me finish. The ship attacked the five capitals and then a second spacecraft entered orbit and destroyed that ship. That explains the flash in the sky and the shockwave felt in India."

"Maria, you've been indisposed for a few days. They have been showing satellite images of the asteroid that hit us. It broke up into several pieces in the atmosphere and—"

"And what, Jack, hit the capital buildings of five nations on three continents? Does that sound reasonable to you?" Maria lobbied.

"They've also debunked this space alien stuff."

"Oh, I'm sure they have!"

"Maria, they've had physicists all over the news talking about the impossibility of faster-than-light travel. Even if there is alien life out there, they could never reach us."

"It's all lies, Jack."

"They've shared an unprecedented amount of intelligence on this—highly-classified information."

"I'll bet they have! They're sharing highly-classified lies in the hope that people will not see the plainly obvious truth."

"Maria—"

"Jack, Hackett showed me the images they had of the spacecraft orbiting and firing. He wanted to talk to me because I claimed to have been aboard an alien spacecraft. He thinks I aided the aliens that attacked us."

"While I was looking for you, I talked to Pete. I thought you might have contacted him. He doesn't believe this alien stuff either. He said one of the alphabet agency types who harassed him tried to link you and him to a false flag alien event."

"What do you mean a false flag alien event?" asked Maria.

"The guy told Pete some secret government or extra-government organization is planning to fake an alien landing to gain control of the United States, perhaps the world. They believe you might be somehow involved with this group. Maybe these spacecraft and the people you've been interacting with are part of that conspiracy."

"Jack, Inanna helped me escape from the Pentagon. I've been aboard her ship for the past 72 hours recovering from fatigue and dehydration."

Jack continued, as if he didn't hear her. "Maria, I was so worried about you that I couldn't sleep. I downloaded a series of videos by Dr. Randy Peters. He's a minister and a well-respected authority on Bible prophecy. He says there's a demonic-human alliance. He also believes they're going to fake an alien landing to simulate a false second coming of Christ. I know you wouldn't do it on purpose, but maybe you are mixed up with something like that."

"Inanna is not a demon. She's as flesh and blood as you and me. She's not part of a fake government conspiracy!"

"Don't you see, Maria? She could just be using you to further her agenda," Jack warned.

"She's my friend, Jack. She is not deceiving me. She's trying to help me—all of us."

"How is she going to help us?"

"We're a species without a memory. We're here, but we don't know how or why. They—"

"Who are they, Maria?"

"They," Maria continued defiantly, "have purposely muddied the answers to control us. Inanna wants us to know our origins and our past so we can build our future on the truth."

"I know the truth about my origin and my destiny, Maria. It's right there in the Bible. I'm not going to let an outsider—of dubious origins—dictate my truth!"

"You don't get, Jack! We already allowed outsiders to dictate our truth a long, long time ago and we're still living with the repercussions. It doesn't matter how old a lie is or how sacred we hold it, it's still not the truth. What if all our holy books have misled us about who god is and what god wants for us? What if we have been conditioned to think of ourselves as helpless and bad? What if the anguish, the divisions, and the unhappiness in the world are all because we have believed that lie? What if it was on purpose?"

"Maria, I love you, but you are more confused than I thought. Someone is deceiving you. Truth doesn't change. The truth is always the truth. God's commandments are the truth. Jesus dying on the cross for our sins—that's the truth!"

Maria paused for a moment to consider her options. It was

clear the love of her life was not on the same page with her. He would find almost any excuse for what was happening, except for the obvious one. He seemed willing to hold onto his old paradigms, despite the facts.

"Jack, Inanna told me something else—something about us."

"Maria, I really think you should ignore what this Inanna tells you for your own good."

"She told me I'm pregnant."

Shock flashed across Jack's face and then he transitioned into a softened look of love. "We're pregnant, beautiful?"

"Yes," Maria said, the emotion running down her cheeks in a stream of tears.

Jack reached out and pulled Maria to him. Then he swallowed her in his arms. She had always felt warm and safe there. For a moment, she felt that way again.

"You're certain?" Jack sought confirmation.

"Absolutely certain."

"How? When?"

"It probably happened in Hawai'i."

"I'm so happy, beautiful! I love you so much! That's even more reason for you to untangle yourself from this nonsense. Let's get things back to normal and raise this baby."

Maria pulled away and looked up into Jack's eyes. "That's exactly why I can't stop, Jack. Humanity's future must change—now more than ever. I don't want our child growing up in a world filled with false truths and false limits. I want our child to grow up understanding his full potential. I want him connected to his true place in this universe. The work I'm doing with Inanna gives us that chance. I must be a part of it."

"Maria, our world doesn't need new ideas. It just needs to recommit to the old ones and we'll be fine. Let's forget all this nonsense about the aliens. Let's sell this place, move somewhere, and begin anew—just the three of us."

"I need to see this through, Jack. I want you to trust me."

"And I am asking you to trust God."

"I am trusting God, but in my own way."

"Maria, there is only one way to trust God and that is God's way. Your way is going to be flawed."

"That's the kind of thinking that needs to change, Jack. We need to let go of this idea that we're a broken species. We need to see our true potential. That's what The Father Creator wants for us!"

"Who is The Father Creator?"

"That's how Inanna refers to God and now I do too. I spoke with him, Jack. The Anunnaki have the capability to let us speak to God."

"False prophets, Maria! God speaks to me in the Bible and in prayer. I don't need to have a real conversation with him— that's delusional."

"Why is having a conversation with God in the 13th century B.C. acceptable, but having a conversation with Him in the 21st century delusional?"

"The bottom line is, Maria, you don't know who you're dealing with. Now we have a child on the way. You can't continue to place yourself at risk."

"The Father Creator wants us to be happy and we're not. He wants us to become all we're capable of being and we're not. He's not interested in judging us or punishing us. Inanna told me those ideas were planted in our minds by the Anunnaki when they genetically engineered our species to be their slaves."

"God created us the way Genesis says he created us. We're not the victims of some alien experiment. We're not slaves."

"Then why do we act like it? Why do we grovel, lowly and ashamed, before our images of God? Why do we concede to even the most corrupt authority? The Anunnaki created us to be slaves and they still run our planet to this moment from afar. They taught us to be afraid and they used our temporary nature and the afterlife to threaten us into submission in this life."

"We *are* a flawed, sinful species, Maria. God gives us rules because we need them. We need to know our limits. Look at us! Even with those limits, we find ways to hurt ourselves and each other."

"No, Jack! We're a species trained to feel unworthy and we demonstrate that we are at every opportunity. Inanna is trying to help us right this great historical wrong done to our species. The Father Creator wants us to have true and direct connection with him. I intend to help them."

Maria was drawing a line and Jack could not, would not cross it. "You're asking me to choose between God and you, Maria."

"I'm asking you to believe in what I'm doing and that I have good reasons for doing it."

Jack shook his head. He couldn't believe it had come to this. "Then I think we need to take some time to consider our positions. I will never stop loving you, Maria, but I will never replace my belief in God with this alien nonsense."

Maria went cold. "What are you saying, Jack?"

"My family's having a family reunion in Texas. I think . . . I think I should go alone. I'll send your regrets. I think I'll stay there for a couple of weeks and give us some time. Should I tell them about the baby?"

Maria sat down on the couch, her face in her hands. "That's up to you."

"I'm not against you. I just think you're mixed up in something that could be dangerous—physically and spiritually for you. I can't support it. My faith won't allow it."

"Fine then . . . "

"OK. I'm going to pack. I leave in the morning. There's a courier message for you on the kitchen table."

Maria sobbed. She thought of the child within her. She could see The Future Possible—taste it. *Am I so determined to make is so that I would lose Jack in the process?* She wondered. *I don't want this to be a deal breaker for him, but I must continue.*

She saw the letter on the table. It looked official. As predicted by Inanna, the letter came from Senator Clare David's office. Maria opened the envelope and found a note requiring her to appear before David's Homeland Security Committee to discuss aliens and the death of President Paxton.

(60)
Chang and Hackett

President Chang sat at the Oval Office desk signing bills and executive orders. He was up early and trying to get a little work done before the morning's first meeting. His mind kept drifting to that meeting's other participant—Secretary of Defense Hackett. Hackett intimidated Chang. He was older and more experienced. Chang sensed Hackett's unabashed arrogance around him. He knew Hackett respected the office. He also knew that Hackett had little or no respect for him. *This morning*, Chang affirmed, *that would change.*

"Mr. President, Secretary Hackett has arrived," Chang's executive assistant interrupted his affirmation.

"Thank you, Madeline. Please let him know I'll be with him in five minutes. I have a few things to finish."

"Yes, Mr. President."

The situation reminded Chang of the famous showdown between President Truman and General MacArthur. He stood ready to channel his best Truman this morning. He finished reviewing and signing three more documents. He sat up straight behind his desk and said, "Madeline, please show Secretary Hackett in."

Hackett burst into the room as if he owned the place, as was his practice. Chang sat behind his desk pretending to study a document and, without looking up, invited Hackett to have a seat. "I'll be with you in just a moment, Dan."

"Of course, Mr. President." Hackett sat somewhat uncomfortably. The kid was showing some toughness. Hackett liked it, but he was determined not to allow the dynamic between them to change in Chang's favor.

Chang looked up and without ceremony asked, "Do you know why I've called you here this morning, Dan?"

"If this is about the article in the Times, I can explain. I was misquo—"

"It's about Sergey Mitchell and those dead soldiers," Chang butted in with a practiced stone face.

"Mitchell? Thankfully, that episode is over. The loss of our brave troops was such a tragedy."

"Did you know Mitchell's plane was going to crash, Dan?"

"Well, I'm sorry, Mr. President, but I'm not psychic. Why do you ask?"

"Because I was told Saturday night, you knew that plane would crash."

Hackett feigned ignorance, "Mr. President, I have no idea what you're talking about. Were you seeing a psychic? I don't mean to make light of this, but how could I have known what was going to happen?"

"My source told me you planned an operation to ensure that the plane would crash. He told me what would happen and how you would explain it. This was 12 hours before the accident."

"Your source was wrong, Mr. President," Hackett declared.

"I was told," continued Chang, "those fireballs were the real story and the plane crash was used to move them out of the news." Chang observed closely as Hackett shifted in his chair and his mouth seemed to go dry.

Hackett reacted with indignation. "What are you accusing me of, Mr. President?"

"I want to know what you know about the convenient and

timely capture of Mitchell the day after the fireballs. I want to know what you know about that plane crash and about the fireballs."

"I know we captured the world's most wanted terrorist. I know I had to write several letters to the families of the American heroes on that plane. I know those fireballs hit five world cities. Now, you know everything I do."

Chang seethed at the arrogance, but remained calm. "I was told that I should talk to Maria Love to learn more about the fireballs. Imagine my surprise when the Secret Service informed me she had been picked up for questioning by you."

"Ms. Love was wanted for questioning regarding her involvement with entities seeking to do harm to the United States."

"Really? Do you mean she's connected to terrorists?"

"It's an ongoing investigation, Mr. President. I wouldn't want to provide you with a premature report."

"Do you expect me to believe that a woman who has been coming into the White House for years is suddenly a national security threat?" Chang asked incredulously.

Hackett now leaned across the desk with a barely concealed look of disdain, "I don't care what you believe. I'm telling you. She's a threat to national security. She hid information that put the United States at risk and I am going to pursue her."

"What information is she hiding?" Chang demanded.

"I'm not at liberty to divulge that."

"I'm your Commander-in-Chief and I'm giving you a direct order, Mr. Hackett. Tell me what she's being investigated for."

Hackett folded his arms and stared defiantly at Chang.

"Are you still holding, Ms. Love?"

"No. She escaped."

"She escaped from a Pentagon holding facility?"

"That's right."

"How did she do that?"

"We're investigating that as well. We know she must have had outside help—perhaps from the people she's working for."

"You have no idea where she is?"

"She's been missing since she escaped Sunday," Hackett said.

"Senator David has contacted me. She's holding a hearing to look into Ms. Love's claims in the Paxton press conference. I intend to support her on these hearings. When Ms. Love resurfaces, I'm going to provide her with Secret Service protection. Senator David has been threatened over holding these hearings. I can only imagine that Ms. Love could be a target too."

"Forgive me, Mr. President, but you're really going to put your credibility on the line to support hearings about UFOs and conspiracy theories?"

"I have suspicions about what's going on here. I can't count on my advisors to tell me the truth. Therefore, I'll support anyone who can help me to find out. DIA is not to harass Ms. Love anymore before these hearings. Are we crystal clear on that, Secretary Hackett?"

"That's risky. She could be working with destabilizing elements. You could be protecting a national security threat."

"I doubt it. I think she's a victim of someone else's games. Senator David has also requested me to provide a witness to present our intelligence on the circumstances surrounding Paxton's death and their relation to Ms. Love's questions. I volunteered you, Dan. You'll be on the panel with Ms. Love."

"I don't think I can make the hearing, Mr. President."

"I haven't even told you when it is yet. These are your options, Dan. I need your experience in your role right now, but I'm not willing to compromise in an effort to get to the truth here. Bluntly, I think you're withholding information from me. Here are your choices. You can either participate in the hearing or you can tender your resignation effective immediately."

Hackett eyed Chang. "That would be a colossal mistake. You're already down a vice-president."

"I'm not going to negotiate this with you. Either you agree not to touch Maria Love and to participate in the hearing or you're out. It's that simple."

Hackett stood and pressed his knuckles upon Chang's desk. He could not stand that the nation had been entrusted to this young, inexperienced fool. "It's not in the best interest of the American people that I resign at this time, Mr. President. I'll participate in the damn hearing and leave Ms. Love alone until after the hearing. But, if that hearing reveals she's a threat to the American people, I'll have her arrested and held under the Patriot Act."

"You will do so only on my orders!" responded Chang, his voice shaking with anger.

Hackett squinted and squared his jaw. "I've been in this town since you were in junior high. I've seen them come and I've seen them go. When you're gone, I will remain. You're a footnote in history. A man made president by a poor nomination and a tragedy. You know it and I know it."

"That may or may not be true, Mr. Hackett. The American people will have to decide. Maybe you're just an old man clinging to a failed paradigm. You control through manipulation and domination. A new order has come to town and I represent that order. I was born in the age of digital democratization. Secrecy and concentrated power are yesterday's news in this administration. Humanity will no longer swallow them."

"Humanity doesn't change. We advance technologically and we become better at hiding our true impulses, but we are the same selfish species. We must be ruled with an iron fist or there will be chaos," Hackett argued.

"I choose to see our potential, rather than our flaws."

"You're naïve."

"I may be naïve, but I *am* President of the United States and *I* set policy in this administration."

Hackett sneered. "You really think sitting in this office puts you in charge, don't you? That only proves you really don't understand how things work."

"I think the Constitution—"

Hackett became more heated and personal. "The Constitution, Tony? The Constitution died when people decided they would rather be safe than free. And when men like you and I realized that they would make that trade, we knew we must forever keep them afraid."

"Don't group me with you. I would never—"

"You would never what? You've been responsible for the security of this country for less than a week. I've been at this for decades. Given the right situation, you'd become me just like that—to protect your power and to protect all we hold dear."

Chang shook his head, "I would never become you. I have a different value system. I see a future propelled by our promise not polluted by our past."

"When the power of your office meets the pressure from the media, meets competing interests, meets the right crisis, you will change. Count on it!"

Chang saw this conversation was going nowhere. "You are free to believe as you wish. You are not to harass Ms. Love in anyway. Are we clear?"

"Very clear, sir."

"That will be all, Dan, you're dismissed."

Hackett did a sharp 180 and left the Oval Office.

Chang wheeled around in his chair and considered Hackett's warning. This showdown reminded him why he decided to make the leap into politics. He didn't have Hackett's experience or his political baggage. Chang saw a humanity that could change, advance, and improve. He was in a position to make it happen and he was ready to make it so.

(61)
Senator Clare David

Senator Clare David arrived at the Hart Senate Office Building early, as she did every morning. She was the accidental politician—a woman who parlayed her father's distinguished military career into a political juggernaut in Indiana. She served as Republican chair of the Homeland Security and Government Affairs Committee. Some within her own party resented the appointment of a second-term senator to head such a prestigious committee. A few colleagues wondered aloud whether her appointment represented their party's attempt to look more female.

Tenacious and independent, Clare David ruffled feathers by asking questions no one else in D.C. dared. Critics called her irresponsible, but her well-orchestrated rebellion on specific topics won her praise from America's growing anti-establishment movement. This made her regular target practice for left and right media and earned bipartisan scorn from members of her committee.

"Truth is the first casualty of war, Clare," her four-star general father often said. Her time in Washington convinced her it was also the first casualty of Washington politics.

The senator reclined in her chair, back to her desk, staring out the window. The rising sun illuminated the mangled Capitol Dome across the way. Long a symbol of American power and freedom, the dome sat twisted almost beyond recognition.

"Damn it!" she muttered in frustration. "Who attacked us?"

Something extraordinary was going on—she could feel it in her bones. She suspected the asteroid story was a cover, but a cover for what? Her country was under fire. She planned to learn the truth behind it. Maria Love held the key to this puzzle. She just knew it.

A tone on her ComTab interrupted her reverie. "Senator, your first appointment has arrived—Dr. Randy Peters of the National Christian Coalition and Dr. Eric Nagas of the American Skeptics Alliance," said her administrative assistant.

Senator David spun her chair around, rose, and prepped herself to meet her guests. She remembered seeing this meeting on her calendar and pondered the oddity of this pair. Normally these two groups diametrically opposed each other. She wondered what gave them common cause. She knew Peters. His prominence in the evangelical community gave him long tentacles within the party. Those tentacles reached deeply into Indiana politics. His organization worked unsuccessfully to unseat her during her last primary. She hadn't forgotten, but the appearance of conciliation seemed politically wise.

The door burst open. The flamboyant Peters pushed past David's aide and approached the senator. With an outstretched hand, and homespun Texas drawl he said, "Clare, it is so good to see you again. How have you been?"

"It's good to see you, Randy," replied David motioning to her aide to close the door behind her. "I don't think we've seen each other since the primary debates a couple of years ago. As I recall, you were supporting a more family-friendly candidate to take my seat."

"Now, Clare, we all do what we have to do. But, I'm pleased as punch the good people of Indiana saw fit to send someone of your caliber back to the senate."

"Who is your friend?" David asked.

"This is Eric Nagas. Eric is the President of the American Skeptics Alliance."

Senator David reached out and shook Nagas' hand. "Glad to meet you Dr. Nagas. Please have a seat, gentlemen."

David's father always taught her to take the lead in an uncertain situation. She got right to the point. "I must admit to being a bit confused by your request to meet me together. I don't suppose you gentlemen often find yourselves in agreement. What has created common cause today?"

Nagas and Peters looked at each other like kids caught with their hands in the cookie jar. "Clare, that's what I like about you," Peters replied. "You always cut through the bull."

Nagas spoke up. "Senator David, Randy and I share a mutual concern about your intention to put Maria Love on national ITV, lending credence to these wild assertions about UFOs and aliens."

"Oh that!" David dismissed. "Gentlemen, it's my position that this is a matter of national security. Ms. Love may have information pertinent to my investigation.

"What, exactly, are you investigating?" Peters asked in a derisive tone. "I've heard you plan to bring up aliens."

"Play along with me, Randy. Here's the timeline. Maria Love goes on national ITV and asks the President of the United States about alien intervention in human history. Then, I have it on good authority; she had a secret meeting with Paxton to discuss the matter in more detail. Someone assassinates the president three days later. On the day of his funeral, five world capitals were attacked," said the senator as she motioned with her arm at the Capitol Building behind her.

"Attacked?" Nagas broke in. "Senator, surely you're not subscribing to these conspiracy theories that aliens attacked the earth?"

"You're the skeptic, Dr. Nagas. Does it seem plausible to you that an asteroid selectively hit the seats of power of five of the world's leading nations?"

"I assure you, senator, there is a rational explanation for what happened. The uncertainty of that explanation does not confer credibility on conspiracy theories."

David turned her gaze to Peters and smiled. "Randy, what's your position on this hearing? Why are you against it? Surely, you don't concur with Dr. Nagas that nothing supernatural can account for these events."

"Clare, I think we need to be careful here. While I do not share Eric's faith in science to resolve all matters, it's politically perilous to ascribe acts of God to extraterrestrials. I assure you my political base feels the same way. I urge you to drop this."

David refused to be bullied or rushed in her deliberations. She sat back in her chair and pondered the statements of these unlikely political allies. "And what of the truth, gentlemen? What if there is something valid behind Ms. Love's claims? What happens if American national security is at risk? Should I ignore that possibility?"

"Senator," Nagas lifted his nose in an almost involuntary gesture of his presumed intellectual superiority, "I'm a physicist. I can assure you that spaceships traveling across the galaxy are a pure flight of fancy. The laws of physics preclude this possibility. Even if some species figured out a way to breach the light barrier, traveling at relativistic speeds within this galaxy would be deadly to a spacecraft. I can state emphatically *they are not here*."

David eyed Nagas. "Dr. Nagas, are we not a civilization still reliant on the internal combustion engine?"

"Your point, senator?"

"My point, Dr. Nagas, is how can a scientist representing a

civilization with such primitive technology make definitive statements about the possibility of space travel?"

"Apples and oranges, senator. There's no way—"

"No way?" David interrupted. "How can you say what's possible for a civilization 10,000, a 100,000, or a million years ahead of us?"

David peered back to Peters. "Senator David," he began more formally this time, "I may not agree with Eric on whether or not there's a God. However, I agree with him that Ms. Love's story is just not credible. More than that, it's not Biblical. I recommend your committee spend its time dealing with legitimate threats to national security and stop encouraging this nonsense."

"I've seen your video series, Randy," replied David. "You seem to believe that a faked UFO landing or alien contact is inevitable. Why would you believe in the possibility of that and not the real thing?"

Peters' face turned three shades of red. Clearly, he was working to hold his anger. "It is exactly the kind of hysteria created by people like Ms. Love—and you, Clare, if you hold these hearings—that makes the use of alien contact for world domination possible for world governments."

Now Nagas turned on Peters. "Randy, you're not helping our case by spouting your own conspiracy theories. Let's stick to the facts here. The facts are these hearings contribute to this UFO mythology and keep people locked in the dark ages by replacing a fictional God with a space alien."

"Now just a minute, Eric," Peters retorted. "The fact that we share a common desire to stop these hearings does not mean that I am going to sit idly by and allow you to demean the faith of millions of Americans. Our faith is an experience every bit as real as any scientific evidence."

David smiled inside, satisfied at driving a wedge in this ridiculous alliance, but now she intended to make herself heard. "Gentlemen, this morning I received a communication from Secretary of Defense Hackett urging me to stop my plans for these hearings. I responded to him with a subpoena to appear before my committee along with Ms. Love. The fact that everyone seems to be against these hearings is as good a reason as any, in my mind, to move forward with them."

"If you do that, Clare, I assure you that NCC members in Indiana will view your attempts to create a theology of space aliens before God as an assault on their faith. That cannot bode well for you at the polls next time around," threatened Peters.

"That's fine, Randy. The NCC worked against me last time and I still won. I am going to do what is in the interest of the American people and the truth—wherever that leads. Look at that Capitol Dome! Asteroids did not hit it. Now, either some power on this planet has weapons way beyond the United States or there is another explanation. Ms. Love indicated she has information and I plan to expose it."

"Senator," Nagas responded, "If you pursue this course against the dictates of reason, you will be ridiculed among educated Americans. You are destined to become Senator Tabloid."

"Bring it on, Dr. Nagas. Maybe it's your unwillingness to see beyond what you can prove is a fatal flaw. My predisposed notions of how the universe might work won't blind me. These hearings are going to happen, gentlemen," Clare exclaimed in a near shout as she leaned across the desk and eyed her two guests.

"It's science fiction, senator," decried Nagas.

"Well, Dr. Nagas, when you have facts that can explain what happened, I will listen. Until then, I am going to get to the bottom of this *fiction*."

Peters, recognizing the meeting was over, stood, and gently

knocked his fist on David's desk. "I will see you on the campaign trail, senator."

(62)
Maria Testifies

Maria passed through security at the Dirksen Senate Office Building. She had attended a number of senate hearings as a reporter, but she never foresaw being the star witness at one of these proceedings. A man with a friendly smile was approaching rapidly.

"Ms. Love, I'm Tim Addler—Senator David's chief of staff. Right this way. I will show you into the hearing room."

There was a kind of carnival atmosphere in the hallway and as she stepped into the hearing room, the circus magnified ten times. Cameras flashed in her face. ComTabs zoomed from every angle to record the moment.

"Maria," one reporter shouted, "What do you intend to tell the committee today?"

"I intend to tell the truth," Maria responded with a quiet confidence.

She heard Addler ask security to clear the aisle and allow Maria to proceed to the witness table. As she approached from behind, she observed the back of a familiar head—Secretary of Defense Hackett.

"Mr. Addler," Maria halted, pointing at Hackett. "My understanding is that I am testifying alone."

"Ms. Love, Senator David wants to get to the bottom of this . . . mystery. She believes Secretary Hackett may have information vital to this investigation."

"Of that you can be sure, Mr. Addler," Maria responded as he pulled her chair out for her.

Hackett casually turned, feigning surprise at Maria's appearance. "Why, Ms. Love, we meet again."

Maria only nodded and sat down in the chair next to Hackett. She scanned the room before her. The senators formed a half-moon configuration at the front of the room. Senator David and the Ranking Member sat in the middle. The Democrats were seated to the right of the chair and the Republicans to the left. Senator David was holding her gavel and waiting for her colleagues to finish their conversations.

Senator David struck the gavel on the desk. "Ladies and gentlemen, please take your seats and cease your conversations. I hereby declare this hearing of the Senate Homeland Security and Governmental Affairs Committee in session."

David began her prepared remarks, "I am deeply troubled by recent events—"

"Madam Chair," interrupted the Ranking Member.

David stopped, "Yes, Mr. York?"

"Madam Chair, as I have stated to you privately, I am highly dubious of the value of this hearing. Due to the dubious nature of these claims and the nation's understandable sensitivity at this moment, I move that we adjourn this hearing and dismiss the witnesses."

"I appreciate the Ranking Member's concern, but—"

"Madam Chair," York inserted again. "I believe I have a bipartisan majority of this committee's members who support my desire to stop this hearing."

David now turned to face the Ranking Member and covered her microphone. "What are you doing, Jim? It is my intention to have this hearing with or without you."

York stared back and covered his microphone, "Clare, I've

been on this committee for more than 20 years. I'm telling you having this hearing is a mistake. It makes a mockery of this committee's charter and of the Senate."

"Senator, you are free to excuse yourself, but I intend to proceed."

The two senators faced forward again, their disagreement written across their faces.

"As I was saying," David continued, "I am deeply troubled by recent and unusual events that have left five world capitols damaged and an American President dead. I am concerned for the national security implications of these events. Heck, I'm concerned for global security. Moreover, I'm not convinced the American people are receiving a full accounting. Therefore, I have—"

"Madam Chair," interrupted Republican Senator Dennis Wilcox—past chairman of the committee. "Perhaps, the Ranking Member has a point. If you will not consider stopping this hearing, perhaps you would consider moving to a closed session where these sensitive matters could be discussed in greater detail."

David noted a knowing glance between Wilcox and Hackett seated at the witness table. "Senator Wilcox, what are we trying to hide from the American people here?" David demanded. "It was the people's Capital Building that was damaged. Their president that was assassinated. I think these matters concern them and deserve an open airing."

David, flustered but determined, continued, "I have asked two people here today that I believe can shed light on these matters—Secretary of Defense Dan Hackett and Ms. Maria Love. I would invite them to make their opening statements. I would ask my colleagues to withhold their objections and let the witnesses proceed."

Hackett emphatically grabbed his microphone and pulled it towards him, "Madam Chair, I have no opening statement. We have determined the culprits responsible for President Paxton's assassination and we are taking appropriate actions against those responsible. We have some of the best scientists in the world working to determine what happened with the asteroid and how we can better protect the earth in the future. None of this has anything to do with Ms. Love or her fantastic theories. I would respectfully urge you to consider the advice of your colleagues and end this hearing."

Hackett pushed his microphone away and glared menacingly at Maria as if he was sending a warning to be careful what she said.

"Thank you, Secretary Hackett, for your concern about this hearing. I would respectfully suggest that you do your job and allow me to do mine. Ms. Love?"

Maria felt herself shaking inside and she wondered if those around her, including Hackett, could see it. "Thank you, Madam Chair. Some months ago a woman claiming to be the Goddess Inanna of the ancient Sumerian myths approached me—"

"Madam Chair, really—" Wilcox called out and threw his hands in the air.

David was quick with her gavel and crashed it hard on the table. "Senator Wilcox, you will allow the witness to proceed. If you're not able to act professionally, I invited you to leave the hearing room. Please continue, Ms. Love."

Maria gathered herself. The heated atmosphere added to her nerves. "She—Inanna—informed me she had come to Earth on a mission vital to humanity's future. She referenced a tremendous historical wrong—a wrong committed against everyone in this room and every human being on this planet. She spoke of her determination to undo this wrong."

Maria paused. Whispers, giggles, and camera clicks filled the hearing room.

"Of course at first I was skeptical. Who wouldn't be? She showed me advanced technology, took me to her spacecraft in orbit, and showed me evidence that her people (The Anunnaki) had genetically modified humanity for their own purposes some 400,000 years ago. At first, I thought she was part of some secret government operation. Slowly, I began to understand she was completely serious."

Maria paused, swigged some water, and continued. "She told me her mission involved exposing this age-old travesty here on Earth and on her home planet. We have historically referred to that planet as Nibiru. It orbits the brown dwarf star in the Centauri Proxima system. The Anunnaki have manipulated and controlled our history from the beginning. They have allowed other races to abduct and experiment on human beings. Their government and our governments—particularly the major powers—have to one extent or another participated in this charade against the people of Earth. You see, the Anunnaki have demanded for thousands of years that we worship them as gods. They have undermined our direct connection to and understanding of our place in the universe. Inanna is determined to put an end to this."

Maria turned and looked right at Hackett, "Last week King Ea of Nibiru sent a taskforce to Earth Space to defeat Inanna, bring her home, and show all of us once again who is in control here on planet Earth. Inanna's ship, the Rakbu, engaged the Anunnaki fleet at Neptune. One of the Anunnaki ships—called the Shiva—broke through and fired upon the earth. That, ladies and gentlemen, is what caused the damage to our capital cities. The Rakbu caught the Shiva and destroyed it in earth orbit. This explains the massive fireball witnessed in India. There is so much more to this story and I welcome your questions."

The hearing room was abuzz with whispers and the synthesized sounds of cameras coming from the ComTabs. David slammed the gavel on the desk and called the room back to order.

David began, "Ms. Love, that's quite a tale. In all my years in public life, I don't think I've ever heard someone so convincing about something so inconceivable."

"Not long ago, Madam Chair, this would have been inconceivable to me too," Maria replied.

"I'm told that after your rather memorable press conference performance you were called to the Oval Office for a private meeting with President Paxton. Is that accurate?"

"Yes, Madam Chair. Actually, Joe Bieber pulled me into the Oval Office to scold me for putting the president on the spot like that. President Paxton intervened and we spoke for more than two hours."

"What did you discuss with President Paxton?"

"I shared with him the evidence I had compiled about Operation Original Sin and an alternative explanation of human origins. We discussed the alien and UFO issue and . . . " Maria paused.

"Continue, Ms. Love, you are under oath."

"Madam Chair, the president confided in me that he had a UFO encounter and a missing time incident while camping in his teens."

"Missing time?" David questioned.

"Yes, Ma'am. I knew nothing of it either. I've learned that UFO abductees often experience a gap in their memories after the incident. Inanna confirmed this for me."

"Inanna confirmed it? She has participated in these abductions?" David pushed.

Maria could feel the cameras in the room zooming in for a tight shot. "Yes. She has participated in both the abductions and the memory erasures in the past. Now, she stops ships from abducting humans and I have persuaded her not to erase any more memories."

"She doesn't sound like someone trustworthy, if she's kidnapped people and erased their memories," David led Maria.

"Inanna is trustworthy," Maria persisted. "She has our best interests at heart. She wants there to be transparency about our past."

"Madam Chair," interrupted Senator Clay Baker of Oklahoma, "Are we going to sit here and accept this ludicrous testimony into the record?"

"Excuse me, senator. I am telling the truth," protested Maria.

"I'm sure you believe you are, Ms. Love," Baker replied with a look of pity. "But we all know this can't be true, don't we?"

"And how do you know that, senator?" Maria demanded.

"Both religion and science tell us that aliens visiting Earth is an impossibility. Religion makes no mention of them and science confirms that, even if they are out there, they could never get here. Perhaps you're suffering from hallucinations? Have you been checked?"

Maria felt her blood beginning to boil at the insinuation. She breathed deeply to maintain her center. "Many spiritual traditions, Senator Baker, claim that civilizations all over the planet were given the tools of culture by beings from the sky. Why don't we trust our ancestors to be accurate witnesses to history? Why are we so sure we know better today?"

"Because we live in an age of scientific fact, Ms. Love, not myth and fantasy," inserted Senator Alton of Maine. "Our ancestors lived afraid of nature and the elements. They made up stories to explain those forces and to comfort themselves. Science eliminated the need for such stories."

David slammed the gavel again, "May I have order among

the committee members please. I have not completed my questioning. Ms. Love, what was the outcome of your discussion with President Paxton?"

"President Paxton had tried to secure more disclosure on the UFO and alien topics, but they thwarted him."

"Is that the big *they* with a capital T?" Baker chided.

Maria stayed focused on Senator David. "He promised me we would meet again after he returned from France. Of course, as we all know, he never returned."

"Are you implying something, Ms. Love?" Senator David asked.

"I believe President Paxton was murdered to prevent him from helping me."

Whispers turned to noisy discussion in the room and the incessant sound of synthetic camera clicks.

"You sound like a genuine C-O-N-spiracy theorist, Ms. Love," Baker asserted.

"You might be too, Senator, if you'd seen what I've seen," countered Maria.

David maintained her calm and commanded the room to order again. "That's a strong accusation, Ms. Love."

"I know, Madam Chair. President Paxton's last words to me that night were 'beware of the Military Industrial Complex.' He said discussing and pursuing these topics was dangerous."

"All the evidence this committee has seen indicates President Paxton was killed by BGOT not the Military Industrial Complex," David replied. "Am I correct, Mr. Hackett?"

"Indeed you are, Madam Chair. Ms. Love's accusations have no basis in reality—at least any reality I'm in touch with," Hackett chuckled.

The room broke into sporadic laughter.

"We have a confession from Mr. Mitchell. Several brave

American soldiers lost their lives capturing Sergey Mitchell and bringing him here for justice. I am outraged that Ms. Love would even make such assertions and I am sure the American people are too."

"Ms. Love?" prompted David.

"I believe that President Paxton was killed through cooperation between on-world and off-world forces."

"Off-world?"

"Yes, Ma'am. Inanna told me the Anunnaki King and his operatives on Earth are responsible for President Paxton's assassination."

"Oh, well, if Inanna said so!" Hackett berated her. "Madam Chair, I was more than happy to take part in this hearing, but I thought we were going to discuss the real issues surrounding President Paxton's death and what we can do to prevent such terrorism in the future. I'm not going to participate in this charade any longer."

Hackett stood and began gathering his belongings, as if he was going to leave.

"Secretary Hackett, you are under subpoena by this committee. Please sit down." David warned. "Don't make me hold you in contempt."

Hackett hesitated, eyed Maria, and sat down.

"Perhaps, Madam Chair," Maria charged, "Mr. Hackett would like to explain how Sergey Mitchell was so conveniently captured on the day after the supposed asteroids struck Washington D.C.?"

"What exactly are you implying?" Senator Wilcox asked. "Dan Hackett is a great American with a distinguished military and political career. What are your credentials to be questioning him, young lady?"

"I'm not implying anything senator," Maria replied eyeing

Hackett with dare in her eyes. "This isn't about my credentials. It's about the truth. News about the fireballs striking the capital cities dominated world news before the Mitchell capture and the accident happened so conveniently the next day."

"Ms. Love, you're out of order," gaveled David.

"Why did you want the fireballs out of the news, Mr. Hackett?" continued Maria undeterred. "Is it because you know for a fact they were not fireballs?"

"You're way out of your league, Ms. Love," Hackett scolded so only Maria could hear him. He pointed his finger squarely in Maria's face. "Madam Chair, do something!"

"Ms. Love!" shouted David.

Maria went for broke. "Tell them about the ships in your pictures, Mr. Hackett. Tell them how you rolled out the Mitchell capture when you did to distract from what those supposed fireballs really were."

"Ms. Love, I'm going to hold you in contempt of Congress if you don't cease your argument with your fellow witness."

"Ask him! Ask him, Madam Chair about the pictures!" Maria shouted.

An uneasy chaos rolled through the room. Maria was scoring points fast and the emotions evoked by her statements were palpable. She felt the cameras and the eyes in the room upon her. Beyond the cameras, were billions more watching eyes. With every statement, she changed minds and maybe history.

David was hammering her gavel, but emotions overpowered senate decorum.

One of David's aides appeared behind her and whispered something in her ear. Almost simultaneously, a concert of alert alarms went off on ComTabs all over the room. There was an awkward silence while everyone attended to the alerts on their devices.

David looked white as a ghost as she listened to her aide. Finally, she uncovered her microphone and spoke, "Ladies and gentlemen, clearly we are in the midst of a very passionate hearing. However, there's something unfolding over at the White House. Apparently, an unknown aircraft has penetrated the controlled airspace over the Capitol. It appears headed toward the White House. All government buildings are being evacuated immediately. I am suspending this hearing. The witnesses are dismissed."

(63)
The White House Lawn

Maria was ushered to the car that brought her to the hearing. "To the White House," she said. "Hurry!"

"ComTab," Maria said, "text message. Cathy Sebring. Sebring, are you at the White House? Send."

"Receiving a response from Cathy Sebring," the ComTab spoke. "Yes. I'm here."

"ComTab, text message. Cathy Sebring. Do you need someone to hold a camera or a light or something? Can you get me in? Send."

"Receiving a response from Cathy Sebring. LOL. I have an extra pass. I'll send someone to meet you. You know where. This is crazy. Can't believe this is happening! Looks like a flying saucer headed for the White House."

President Chang sat on a conference call with several foreign leaders. Out of the corner of his eye, he saw the saucer-like craft hovering above Pennsylvania Avenue. After a moment's pause, it gently glided across the White House lawn and set down. He watched White House security descend upon the craft. He excused himself from the call and stood at the window, as an interested spectator for a moment.

The Secret Service rushed into the room and moved Chang away from the window.

With The Secret Service and White House security occupied, the White House press corps began to make its way out to the lawn. Onlookers lined the sidewalk outside the White House fence. As the viral news spread about the craft on the White House lawn, the crowd grew inside and outside the grounds. Within minutes, military aircraft filled skies above the White House.

Maria's driver got her as close as possible. She got out and worked her way through the throngs of people standing outside the fence and to the media entrance. There she found a familiar face—Randy Matson—waiting for her.

"Hey, boss!" Randy said in a cheerful voice. "We're all going to get fired for letting you in, you know."

"I think Pete will have too much on his plate after this to worry about firing you," Maria laughed. "What the heck is going on here?"

"This craft landed on the White House lawn and now it's just sitting there. It's like The Day the Earth Stood Still or something."

They made their way to the ANN location. Cathy came up and gave Maria a big hug. "We're all going to be fired for letting you in here."

"That's what Randy said. It's so good to see you too." Maria laughed.

Maria and Michele Monroe, her replacement as White House correspondent, exchanged nods.

"It's a Vimana," said Maria.

"A what?" Monroe asked.

"A Vimana?" enthused Sebring. "Michele, a Vimana is the name given to flying craft in ancient India."

Monroe considered the information for a moment and then signaled to Randy to turn on the camera for a live report. "We are here on the White House lawn where a purported Vimana—a

small saucer-shaped craft—has landed. A massive military presence has descended upon the White House. So far, there has
been no change or movement in the craft since it touched down
some 13 minutes ago."

Monroe decided to take a risk and had the camera turned and
pointed toward Maria, as she pushed toward her with a microphone. "We are joined here by former ANN reporter, Maria
Love. Maria, weren't you testifying on Capitol Hill this morning?
How did you hear about these events?"

"Well, Michele. Senator David suspended the hearing due to
reports that something was happening over restricted airspace.
They evacuated all government. I got back to my car and hurried
over here."

"Now, you told me you believe this craft to be a Vimana.
Can you explain to the audience what that is?"

"Yes. I've been aboard these crafts. There's really nothing
mysterious about them. They're a small tender craft launched
from larger Anunnaki vessels."

"You say, Anunnaki?" What is an Anunnaki?" Monroe
asked.

"As I've been saying for weeks now, the Anunnaki are a
spacefaring race that has been intimately involved in Earth history and in genetically engineering the human race . . . "

"Wait just a moment, Maria. Something seems to be happening with the craft.

The Vimana stirred to life and a door on the craft slid open.
A long retractable ramp extended from the doorway to the
ground. A tall and aged man appeared in the doorway. He made
his way slowly down the ramp. A woman wearing a crown and
escorted by guards followed him.

"Inanna!" exclaimed Maria.

The camera continued to focus on the ship, but Monroe

questioned Maria. "Who is Inanna?"

"Inanna is the woman coming second down the ramp. She's the Crown Princess of Nibiru—the home planet of the Anunnaki. She's the one trying to help me bring disclosure to humanity."

"Who's the man?" asked Monroe.

"I don't know," replied Maria.

The security forces had set up a perimeter around the ship. Weapons were leveled and awaiting orders to fire in defense of the White House. The Secret Service agent in charge used a bullhorn to order the party to halt as soon as they reached the bottom of the ramp.

The man leading the party out of the craft spoke, "I am Lord Enki. I come in peace to undo a wrong committed long ago by my species against yours. I am here to tell you the truth of your origins and to discuss matters of mutual interest with President Chang and other world leaders."

"You are trespassing on U.S. government property," replied the lead agent. Have your men place their weapons on the ground. Place your hands behind your head and step forward to be searched."

Enki nodded to Inanna, who signaled the Anunnaki warriors to place their weapons on the ground. A SWAT team surrounded the Anunnaki delegation and searched their persons. In another situation, it might have been comical. The Anunnaki towered over the humans.

"They're clean," shouted the SWAT team leader.

"Now, may I speak to President Chang?" asked Enki.

There was silence, except for the sound of synthetic cameras clicking. No one quite knew what to do or what to say in this unprecedented situation.

Chang watched events unfold on a monitor from a secure

room in the White House basement.

"I'm going out there. I'm going to talk to them," Chang announced.

"That would be foolish, Mr. President," cautioned Jessica Cohen, his chief of staff.

"I'm the president, Jessica, and I am going out there to talk to him!"

"There's no way to secure that area, sir. It's absolutely out of the question," warned General Cortez.

"Damn it! Get out of my way, general, unless you're coming with me." Chang ordered.

Chang moved with determination toward the door. His Secret Service detail instinctively filled in around him. He arrived on the White House lawn to find the awkward standoff still in progress. He felt some trepidation as he approached the Anunnaki. Chang's eyes met Enki's from a hundred yards away and he could feel the intensity of Enki's stare.

He reached the Anunnaki with an outstretched hand, "Lord Enki, I am President Chang. On behalf of the people of the United States of America and the people of Earth, welcome."

"Thank you, Mr. President. The honor is mine."

Inanna moved around her uncle and toward Maria, who was already moving towards her. The two women embraced.

"What are you doing here, Inanna? I thought you would not intervene directly? Everything has changed, Maria. My brother, the king, has powerful new allies with a stake in preventing us from achieving our goals. Somehow, we don't know how, Uncle Enki was delivered to my ship with this information."

"The Father Creator?" asked Maria.

"We don't know. That is my belief. Enki is here to convince your leaders that we must work together. Everything is on the line, Maria—The Future Possible and even your child's life."

Suddenly, a plasma-charged vortex swirled to life 20 yards from Maria and Inanna. Three Anunnaki warriors emerged running from the vortex. As suddenly as it appeared, the tunnel sputtered and collapsed. A couple dozen U.S. Marines engaged the Anunnaki warriors in a brief gun battle. Even wounded, several men were required to subdue each one. They were taken into custody and the event was over as quickly as it had begun.

"Mr. President," Enki said, "my nephew, the King of Nibiru, has a new weapon. He intends to use it against Earth and the Anunnaki who oppose him. I believe we just saw a test of that weapon. It allows him to transport Anunnaki warriors across space and, perhaps, across time. If we allow him to perfect that technology, Earth may be doomed."

Chang stood there listening, not sure how to respond. No training or instincts could prepare any president for what had just unfolded in front of him. Finally, he said, "General Cortez, take control of the situation and peacefully disperse this crowd. Jessica, we have guests. Please prepare a conference room for a meeting."

"Yes, Mr. President."

Chang approached Maria. "You are Ms. Love, I presume."

"Yes, Mr. President . . . Maria."

"Maria, it seems you were correct all along. As our resident ambassador to the Anunnaki, I would like you in this meeting as well."

"Of course, Mr. President, anything I can do. This is Inanna. She's Enki's niece and the woman known in our mythologies by the same name."

Inanna looked deeply into Chang's eyes. "I can see you are a thoughtful man, Mr. President. Thoughtful men and women with courage and vision may be humanity's only hope."

"Hello, Inanna. Let us hope you're right. I seem to be in uncharted territory here."

* * *

De Berg felt a presence appear all around him and then The Father Creator's voice broke the silence, "You were successful in blocking one spatial vortex, Mr. De Berg, but you may not be able to block all of them."

"You've given me the power to help my friends and I'm helping them."

"You have already affected the timeline."

"In a positive way, I hope."

"You will find that what is positive and what is negative is harder to distinguish than you might imagine."

"Are you going to take the power away from me?"

"It's ALL about free will, Mr. De Berg. I won't take the power away from you, but events and your choices might."

"I'll do what I can. I refuse to allow King Ea and the Savestran to stop humanity's growth and keep it in the darkness."

"It is a big task you have taken on, but it is your path," The Father Creator mused.

The Father Creator's presence evaporated. De Berg called out, "Father Creator, will we achieve The Future Possible?"

"All futures are completely possible, my son. They always have been and they always will be."

(64)
Rewind

Maria awoke to the sound of waves gently washing ashore and a dog barking on the beach. She rolled over and found Jack lying next to her. She snuggled and smiled. Enki and Inanna worked with President Chang on a go-forward strategy. Disclosure was at hand. Jack and she were about to bring a child into The Future Possible.

Maria experienced a moment of dissonance. The happy feelings faded into a slight panic. Where was she? How did Jack get here? She didn't recall meeting him after the White House. This wasn't her bed.

Maria sat up and reached for her ComTab, searching for messages that might provide a clue. Something felt wrong. She swiped the screen. At first glance, she concluded she was in error. She wiped her eyes and looked again. The date read May 5, 2024.

"What? How can that be?" she said audibly.

Jack rolled over and massaged her arm. "What's wrong, beautiful?"

"Nothing, Jack. I'm just . . . where are we?"

"Wow, you did get too much sun yesterday, didn't you?"

"I'm serious. Where are we? How did I get here?"

"Calm down. We flew down here yesterday."

"After the White House?"

"The White House? What are you talking about? We flew here from Austin."

"No we didn't!" Maria said, growing more distraught. "I was at the White House yesterday for the landing. You and I had a fight . . . "

"Landing? Fight? Beautiful, we're in Grand Cayman. We come here every year and stay in this same condo. Are you OK?"

"Um," Maria decided to be cautious. "I'm not sure. I had a strange dream. A spacecraft landed at the White House. President Chang greeted these aliens."

"President who?"

"Chang."

"What a dream, Maria! Why you even created a fictional president."

"He's not fictional. He took over after President Paxton's assassination."

Jack looked baffled. "President Paxton? And who is he?"

"C'mon, Jack. Don't play games with me."

"I'm not playing games. I'm trying to understand this strange dream."

"Who is the president, Jack?"

"What?"

"Humor me."

"Wilson. Meredith Wilson. Remember how excited you were to vote for the first woman president?"

"They changed history," Maria said into the air.

"What do you mean changed history? Who changed it?"

"Nothing. No one. I'm fine," Maria said, leaping from the bed. "I need to splash some water in my face."

"You're sure you're OK, beautiful? Is this one of those pregnancy things?" Jack asked

"I'm still pregnant?"

"Of course you are. Babe, you're scaring me."

"Yes. I'm probably dehydrated," Maria faked a laugh.

"Before I forget," Jack yelled to Maria in the bathroom, "Your father called last night after you went to bed. Your mother is already getting into planning mode for the family reunion."

Maria stood staring into the bathroom mirror. She turned on the water and splashed her face. "C'mon, Jack. I'm not feeling well. Stop teasing me."

"What? How am I teasing you? I know you're not that excited about the reunion, but . . . "

"I don't have a father and I thought you were going to the reunion alone. Remember, we decided you would go to the reunion and I would stay in D.C.?"

"D.C.? Maria. Now you're playing with me. Hector said—"

"Hector? Who's Hector?" Maria asked.

"Your dad . . . Maria. Do you need to see a doctor? You're worrying me."

"I'm sure I'll snap out of it. Maybe, I'll call my mom."

"That's a good idea."

Maria spoke to her ComTab. "Call mom."

A male voice answered, "Hello."

"Yes, hello. May I speak with Irene?"

"Hey, sweetheart. It's dad. How was your flight to Grand Cayman?"

"Fine. Is mom there?" Maria faked. She just wanted to hear her mother's voice.

Maria's mom took the phone. "Maria. How's my favorite daughter?"

"I'm . . . I'm fine. Jack said you're concerned about the reunion. I didn't know the Loves invited you."

"You're funny, Maria. I know I made quite a scene last year, but I wouldn't miss the sixth annual Love-Gomez reunion for anything."

"Love-Gomez? Mom, I think Jack is coming alone. I'm going to stay in D.C. There are some things I need to attend to."

"Why would you go to D.C.? You need to cut down on the traveling. You're pregnant, you know."

"Yeah, mom. That's why I'm staying in D.C. I need some time at home alone."

"Are you moving to Washington D.C. and you didn't tell me?" Irene asked laughing. "Seriously, when do you arrive home in Austin?"

"Mom, are you OK?"

"I think so. Why?"

"I've lived in D.C. since college. You know, I got the big network job and abandoned you. Remember? I'm the Chief White House correspondent for ANN."

"What's ANN? Are you feeling light-headed, dear? Is everything OK with the baby?"

"Everything's fine."

"Enjoy Grand Cayman, Maria. We'll talk more when you get home. There's so much to do for the reunion."

Maria disconnected the call and said, "Twitter. Search @Ancient_Nanna."

"There is no such account," The ComTab responded.

Inanna shared Enki's warnings about the Savestran and their threats of time and alternate reality warfare. She spoke of their ability to *undo* timelines. Maria never expected to experience it firsthand. She was marooned in an alternate reality with no apparent way home.

Everything seemed perfect—a little too perfect. She had a father and a happy mother. She had a baby on the way and things appeared to be back to normal with Jack. Heck, a woman was President of the United States. Yet nothing—not one thing—was right about any of it.

What of The Future Possible? How would she expose the great lies of humanity's past? How would she find Inanna, separated by vast expanses of time, space, and dimension? Had everything been for nothing? The questions rushed through her mind, overwhelming her. Maria sat down and she wept.

Two figures covertly observed the unfolding scene. "Congratulations. You've won, My Lord."

"Victory is not yet ours, but Maria Love is."

Ray Davis is a lifelong Kansan now living in Massachusetts with his wonderful wife, They enjoy traveling, especially to their favorite spot on Earth—Hawaii. He is a writer, thinker, and speaker committed to helping people shift paradigms in ways that better their lives and better the planet.

Ray's journey in personal development began after he nearly died at 25. Seeking a better way, he studied personal development and the world's various spiritual traditions for the insight they could provide. In 2007, he founded The Affirmation Spot and was once dubbed "The Affirmation King of Twitter" by another motivational teacher. To this day, he still inspires more than 60,000 followers every day through a variety of niche Twitter accounts. In 2010, Ray released an eBook titled "The Power to Be You." The book contains 447 original daily quotes and affirmations.

Ray says, "I've tasted defeat and I've tasted victory. I believe those experiences gave me insight into how we can—individually and collectively—create a happier, more successful world. Every person on this planet deserves the opportunity to live to his or her highest potential. We're not there. Many of our current institutions work against human beings achieving that goal.

"Author Graham Hancock said, 'We are a species with amnesia.' I'm in 100% agreement with that assessment. In the absence of understanding about our origins and destiny, we have substituted dysfunctional paradigms. Until we wipe the sleep from our eyes and see the world anew, we will continue the cycle of want, war, top-down control that plagues our planet today.

"I'm writing the Anunnaki Awakening series, not because I have all the answers to these questions. I'm writing it because it is long past time for humanity to be asking these questions and having dialogue about them. Who are we really? Where did we really come from? Where are we really going? How do we fit into this vast cosmos? Who is God? The answers to these questions are deeper and more complex than our common narratives claim. And so The Awakening has begun."

Keep your eyes on the skies!

CPSIA information can be obtained
at www.ICGtesting.com
Printed in the USA
BVOW06s0858220117
474133BV00016B/756/P